LAMBENT PASS

JOHN D. MCLAUGHLIN

Lambent Pass
Paperback Edition

Wolfpack Publishing
5130 S. Fort Apache Rd. 215-380
Las Vegas, NV 89148

wolfpackpublishing.com

Paperback ISBN 978-1-64734-793-2
eBook ISBN 978-1-64734-792-5

Dedicated to

All Veterans and Scout Dogs
Who served America during the Vietnam War

With a Very Special Thanks to

Joe Darrell Lovelace, Sergeant
50th Infantry Platoon, 4th Infantry Division
and
Buck, Infantry Platoon Scout Dog

ACKNOWLEDGMENTS

I would like to express my heart-felt thanks to *Joe Darrell Lovelace*, who provided his Vietnam War experience as a Scout Dog Handler from February, 1967 through March, 1968. This invaluable experience and knowledge, which at times was uncomfortable for Sergeant Lovelace in the re-telling, provided an accurate accounting of military service and the war for the author's use as background for the main character, Jack Wetzel, in this story. Also, I extend a special thanks to Joe's wife Vicki for assisting Joe, and ultimately the author, to talk about a violent and sometimes best forgotten time in his young life.

This novel with fictional characters is not about Sergeant Lovelace, but rather a story of any of the many men and women who much like Joe served their country when they were called. And, it is a story worth telling of their stalwart, furry companions—the scout dogs.

Also, thanks to the legendary Frank Smith, real-life New Mexico Department of Game and Fish Officer from the Heart Bar Ranch for his assistance.

John D. McLaughlin

AUTHOR'S NOTE

During the Vietnam War, 2,709,918 Americans served in uniform with more than 58,000 members of the United States Armed Forces losing their lives and more than 300,000 wounded.

The U.S. military deployed about 4,300 dogs to combat zones between 1965 and 1973.

According to the military, 281 dogs died in the line of duty, but hundreds more died when the war ended and the U.S. troops departed. It has been estimated that military dogs saved about 10,000 lives in Vietnam. In those years, there were no provisions for military dogs to be adopted. Most were euthanized or left behind to uncertain fates.

DISCLAIMER

The characters in this book are fictitious, and any resemblance, living or dead is purely doggoned coincidental.

PART I

I shall be telling this with a sigh
Somewhere ages and ages hence:
Two roads diverged in a wood, and I,
I took the one less traveled by,
And that has made all the difference.

-Robert Frost, "The Road Not Taken"

CHAPTER ONE

Mimbres Valley, New Mexico
Present Day

THE OLD DOG moved slowly in the back of the truck toward the tailgate as his master exited the driver's door. Although well past middle age, the man walked lithely, his tall slender frame outpacing his companion in the bed of the '51 Chevy. As he lowered the heavy tailgate and secured each side, the dog made it to the rear of the truck; the tired eyes looked up at his master of many years. A smile formed on the dog's haggard face, his tail wagged.

"Wel-l-l now, Wally. I reckon you want me to lift you down, uh?" Jack Wetzel smiled back at the dog, gently petting the Australian Shepherd and rubbing behind his ears. Sitting beside the dog on the tailgate, the old man reached up and tipped his stained and battered Stetson back on his head with his thumb. "I know all about arthritis, boy. I reckon I got it bad, too. I had a helluva time just gettin' outta bed this mawnin'."

The dog edged closer to the man, placed his front paws and then his head in the man's lap. The old man sighed as he rubbed the dog's ears again. It was fall in New Mexico, and the Mimbres Valley had lost its summer lushness, a dreary brown replacing bright green alluding to the cold weather that would surely follow. Dusk descended over the valley as the man and dog silently watched together. The Black Range with its dark, towering mountain range accentuated the far horizon. As the shadow of the mountain drew nearer, a cool breeze rustled the mostly leafless cottonwood trees near the small adobe house that sat a quarter mile off Highway 35.

The clear sky began to bristle with stars; a lonely coyote howled out in the stillness of the night. Moments later, other coyotes responded. The old man's weather-beaten face broke into a smile again as he said softly to himself, "Thank you, God ... for another day. Me an' ol' Wally, why, we surely thank ya." The man wore a faded denim jacket over a blue and red flannel work shirt, faded jeans, and a pair of worn White's Packer boots.

They sat there, the old man and the much older dog, enjoying the quiet of the night and each other's company. The dog stirred beside his master, his ears perked. Then the old man heard the truck long before he saw the headlights. It turned off Highway 61 and then accelerated, heading north on Highway 35. As the vehicle approached, he heard the music and voices. He grimaced. *Damned loud mouths and their rock music!* He shook his head. *A man can't even enjoy the quietness of the evening.*

The big truck skidded to a stop after sliding sideways near the entrance to his graveled driveway. The headlights' beam cast a bright light well ahead of the vehicle and sliced a path through the dark night illuminating the highway. Where the road curved ahead, the huge, nearly naked cottonwood trees billowed in the breeze on the east side of the Mimbres River.

A man cursed loudly in Spanish and then English. A truck door creaked open and glass bottles shattered as they hit the pavement. The metal door creaked again and slammed shut, shattering the quiet of the night once again. The old man slipped off the tailgate, his eyes narrowed as he peered intently toward the truck parked at the entrance to his driveway. He saw a man urinating in front of the headlights and another man kicking at something near the driver's door. A high-pitched yelp. More cursing. Another yelp from a dog.

The old man walked softly to the passenger side of the '51 Chevy truck, reached through an open window to the glove box and retrieved a Model 66 Smith & Wesson revolver. This he placed in his belt at his back and under the denim jumper. He turned to his dog.

"You'd best stay here, Wally." As he started down the driveway, he said under his breath, "No need for both of us to deal with this sorry bunch, boy."

The old man pulled the Stetson down on his head as he strode toward the truck, his heavy boots crunching in the gravel. Within twenty feet of the truck, he clearly saw a young shirtless man who was kicking at an emaciated black and tan dog. The dog ducked and the drunk missed, almost falling to the ground. Multiple tattoos covered his arms, neck and back. A dirty ball cap adorned his head. "Come here, goddammit! You miserable cur." The dog disappeared around the rear of the truck; the man followed.

The old man's voice stopped him in his tracks. "Hold it, pard."

Tattoo turned, facing the old man, a beer bottle in his hand. He stared at the old man standing before him.

"What'd ya say to me?" There was insolence in the strained voice.

The old man took his time as he searched the darkness for the other man he had seen urinating earlier. The man appeared around the back of the truck and the old man turned slightly so that he could see both. The second man's hair was shaved on both sides with a tuft of hair down the center Mohawk style. The hair, what there was of it, was colored red, green and yellow.

Tattoo stepped closer. The voice rose. "I asked you a friggin' question, you ol' bastard."

"I heard you," the old man answered quietly. "What's the matter with your dog?"

Mohawk spoke, "That ain't none o' your business, *cabrón*."

Tattoo took a long drink of his beer. "What's your name, ol' man?"

"Wetzel." The old man hooked his thumbs in the front pockets of his jeans.

Tattoo snorted. "Wetzel?" The insolence returned.

"That's right. Wetzel." The old man noted Mohawk moving closer. He looked Tattoo squarely in the eyes. His eyes hardened but he kept his voice soft, "Why don't you just leave the dog?" He motioned toward it with his left hand. "He's just in your way. I'll care for him, and you boys can be on your way to the party."

Tattoo stared back into the old man's eyes, and his face twitched as he suddenly stepped back against the truck. Mohawk appeared alongside his friend and snarled, "Shut up, *viejo*!"

He advanced toward Wetzel and then stopped, a crooked smile

forming on his lips. He turned back toward the truck. "I'll show you what we do to *perros pendejos.*" A semi-automatic pistol appeared in his hand. He walked to the other side of the truck and fired four shots in quick succession. The dog yelped. Silence.

Mohawk strutted back around the vehicle. He held the pistol out with both hands as he crossed in front of the headlights. He swung his head back and forth, searching where Wetzel had stood, but couldn't find him. A devilish grin displayed on his drunken face. He laughed loudly. "Hey, *viejo.* Come here! I'll show you what we do to *viejos pendejos.*"

Wetzel spoke quietly from a new location in the darkness, "The only stupid person I see is an ugly lookin' parrot standing in front of his headlights. Drop the gun. Now!"

Silence. Mohawk's grin slowly vanished. He gripped the pistol tighter with both hands frantically searching the darkness for his prey. Two shots almost as one reverberated through the quietness followed by another quick shot. Mohawk staggered back, falling to the pavement hit twice in the chest and once in the forehead.

Wetzel spoke sharply to Tattoo, "Get your hands up! Spread your fingers."

Tattoo dropped his beer bottle as he complied, the sound of the glass breaking against the pavement startling him. "Jesus Christ! Don't shoot me." He peered into the darkness but couldn't see the old man. "I ain't armed."

"Turn around ... slowly." Tattoo turned in a circle, still unable to see the old man. Wetzel spoke from a slightly different location. "Down on the ground. *Now!*"

As Tattoo dropped to his hands and knees, he heard, "*Boca abajo. Separe los brazos, palmas arriba* (Face down. Spread your arms. Palms up.)." Tattoo lay face down with his arms out to his side, palms up as directed. Strong hands secured both his wrists within a leather belt loop tightened to secure his arms at his back. Wetzel searched him thoroughly for weapons.

The old man panted. "You move and I'll blow your damned head off. *Comprende?*"

Tattoo nodded without speaking. His eyes were wide and drool ran from his open mouth.

Gravel crunched. The old man walked over to the dead Mohawk. He quickly reloaded and placed his own revolver in the belt at his back and searched the dead man, finding no additional weapons. With a red handkerchief from the back pocket of his jeans he retrieved the semi-auto pistol lying on the ground. After making the pistol safe, he laid it on the hood and continued to the other side of the truck where the black and tan lay in a pool of blood. The old man sighed deeply. He reached down, patted the motionless dog and returned to the driver's side via the back of the truck. Tattoo lay on the ground as instructed.

Wetzel rubbed his jaw. He spoke to the Australian Shepherd as he limped slowly down the driveway, "I'm okay, Wally. You go on up to the house." He raised his arm and pointed toward the adobe house. The old dog turned and obediently started the slow journey back.

Wetzel withdrew a cell phone from his shirt pocket and dialed 9-1-1.

"Grant County Sheriff's Department." The female voice broke the stillness.

"Howdy, Stella. How ya been?"

Silence, then: "Wetzel? That you, Jack?"

"I reckon. Is Don at the office?"

"No. The sheriff rarely works late, and you shouldn't be using 9-1-1 unless you have an emergency. You know better, Jack."

Wetzel ignored the chastisement. "You'd best get a deputy out to my place. I've got a dead man and another sumbitch in custody in my driveway."

"*What*?

"You heard me. Get an officer rolling." Wetzel shifted the cell phone closer to his ear. "And get Don outta bed."

"You … all right, Jack?"

"Yeah." He started to disconnect. "Tell Don if he's interested, there's a bunch of dope in the back of these guys' truck." He closed the cell phone and walked over to the prostrate Tattoo. "You do as you're told and rest easy. You'll be all right, son."

Tattoo whimpered and began sobbing.

Wetzel sat down, and built a cigarette, taking his time. He stuck it in the corner of his mouth and lit it with a match from his shirt pocket. Drawing deeply on the cigarette, he thought about what had just transpired. It was never an easy task to take another man's life and even more difficult to live with it afterwards. *Dammit to hell!* Why hadn't he left them be to do whatever to the old hound dog? But Jeez, he had no way of knowing they were dope-runners with a propensity for violence. It just wasn't right to be mean or abusive to any animal, including man.

He sat quietly, the cigarette tucked in the corner of his mouth. It glowed brightly in the darkness and then began a slow dance from one corner of his mouth to the other. The stars winked in a dark sky with a small sliver of the moon visible. Tattoo sobbed loudly and babbled incoherently. A cow bellowed out in the night. Wetzel sighed. For no reason, he thought of his life. *Christ, can't believe I'm an old man; the years go by so damn fast.* He drew again on the cigarette as he thought of two special women in his life. *Maggie ... Lacey. I surely miss you!*

The mountain's dark shadow had lengthened to encompass the spot where the old man stood. The present slowly faded away as Wetzel smoked and reminisced about those years long ago. The cigarette continued its dance between his lips. Two mule deer crossed the gravel road behind him and Wally's short bark acknowledged their presence. Jack Wetzel's mind was elsewhere.

CHAPTER TWO

Silver City, New Mexico, 1966

The center snapped the football. Jack Wetzel sprang forward, and hit the defensive end across from him hard, and then ran an in-and-out pattern angling toward the sidelines. Sweat covered his heated face encased in the blue and silver football helmet. It ran down his neck, but he paid no mind as his cleated feet sprinted over the green turf. Turning, he looked for the football and saw it coming at him. *Too high!* Grunting, he leaped into the cold fall air; his arms stretched high, hands reaching frantically for the spiraling football that attempted to elude his grasp. He felt a Cobre High School defender slam against him as he arched high, twisting in mid-air. *Yes! I've got it.* His hands grasped the leather pigskin tightly as he fell backward. Suddenly, he was hit hard by another Cobre defender. The hit jarred his teeth and took his breath away as he catapulted in the air and landed on the frozen ground with a thud.

His vision dimmed, but he did see the referee in his black and white striped shirt and black ball cap, his arms raised, signaling a touchdown. The Silver High School Band blared out a response and the home crowd supporting the Silver High Colts football team roared its approval. As his best friend and quarterback Juan Garcia helped him to his feet, a sharp pain in his back almost doubled him over. Garcia shouted above the noise of the crowd, "We did it, Jackie, boy! We whipped 'em, by golly."

Wetzel straightened slowly, grimacing with pain. Then with effort he smiled at Garcia. "You bet, pard." He couldn't help thinking, *I've got chores to do early in the morning at the ranch, and it ain't goin' to be an easy task.*

* * *

WETZEL SAT QUIETLY on the bench in front of his opened football locker. He rubbed his hands through his sweat-dampened hair. He had removed his heavy football shoes, his jersey bearing the blue number 89 along with the shoulder pads but had failed to progress any further. A wet, soggy T-shirt clung to his slender frame.

Cleated feet approached where he sat on the bench. Wetzel looked up and saw teammate Joe Peach standing over him. A burly boy with a light complexion that appeared sickly who had beaten Wetzel out for the starting end position, Peach had challenged him for the position last year as well as this, his senior year, but failed to compete for the job. Displaying his unhappiness at his own lack of success, he periodically made smart-aleck comments behind Wetzel's back. For the most part, Wetzel ignored him, realizing it was tough to lose out on what was important in life. He had talked the situation over with his mom on several occasions, and she agreed he had taken the best course of action.

Peach glared down at him. Wetzel returned the gaze. Although tired, he tried to keep the shortness out of his voice. "What is it, Joe?"

Grinning, Peach reached down and picked up one of Wetzel's football shoes and said, "Think you're pretty hot, don't ya?" Then he threw the heavy cleated shoe down the length of the locker room into the showers. Other football players already in the showers yelled out. His thin lips curled back from scraggly, unclean teeth as he sneered, "Well. Go on. *Fetch,* hot dog."

Wetzel sighed and narrowed his eyes but said nothing. He straightened his lanky frame, wincing as he did so, walked down to the shower and retrieved the wet shoe. Walking past Peach, he placed the shoe on the bench. As he turned toward the locker, Peach reached for the other shoe.

Wetzel's voice had a metallic edge to it. "Don't do it, Joe. You've had your fun. Now, move on!"

Peach grinned broadly, scanning the room to see if others would join him in his play. He picked up the shoe and cocked his arm to throw as Wetzel hit him square in the face with the retrieved wet football shoe. Peach's front teeth shattered and blood erupted from his mouth and nose as he went down to the floor like a pole-axed bull. Wetzel jumped astride him and continued beating him in the face with the heavy cleated shoe. His eyes wide with fright, Peach attempted to ward off the blows but Wetzel was too strong for him. He screamed, first in fright and then for help, but the blood and broken teeth muffled his incoherent cries for help. He choked on the blood and debris in his mouth.

Strong arms encircled Wetzel and pulled him from the prostrate bully. "Easy, Jack. Easy now. It's me. Your buddy, Juan." Garcia continued to hold tightly to his friend's shoulders as he looked down at what had been a face and was now totally unrecognizable. "Geez, Jack," was all he could say.

Wetzel's blazing eyes filled with anger dwindled to hard, black simmering coals as he dropped the shoe with a loud clank on the cement floor of the locker room. He looked down at the frightened, bloodied, bully pointing at him. "*You* ... stay away from me," he choked, "or I'll break your damned neck." Between clenched teeth he struggled for enough air to speak. "You ignorant son-of-a-bitch."

* * *

A YOUNG GIRL sauntered down one of the many crowded hallways at Silver High School. Her bright red hair was pulled back into a pony tail and fastened with a single rubber band. The pony tail bounced from side to side as she walked, carrying an armload of books. Her pretty features were accentuated by bright green eyes and an honest face which broke easily into a warm smile. She wore a plain cotton, red blouse with a knee length full pleated blue skirt. About her shoulders, a black sweater kept the fall coolness at a distance. On her slender ankles and tiny feet, she wore white cotton socks encased in brown penny loafer shoes.

Maggie O'Brian stopped at a set of lockers lining the hallway where a tall, dark headed boy was retrieving books from his locker. Cheerfully, she hailed him, "Hi, Jack!"

He turned quickly, a smile appearing on his tanned face. "Maggie! How are ya, kid?"

She smiled back. Why in the world did this handsome guy not have a girlfriend? They had been close friends for many years as he and her boyfriend, Juan Garcia, were best pals. He was shy around most girls in school, but not with her. The three of them hung out together. She had met Jack Wetzel's mother once and immediately liked her. She was a nice, hard-working ranch lady who had her husband taken away from her way too early in life. Jack's dad had worked for the U.S. Forest Service in the Gila National Forest, and during the summer of 1955 had lost his life trying to save another crewmember on the Little Creek Fire.

Maggie sighed and shook her head. Jack worked at a part-time job helping the veterinarian in Arenas Valley, and the full-time job helping his mother work their small ranch to make ends meet. No doubt he didn't have a lot of time to date girls.

Wetzel cocked his Stetson back on his head with his thumb. He was wearing a denim shirt and jacket and faded wrangler jeans with brown Roper boots. His thick brown hair curled out from under his hat. She'd heard other girls at school refer to his hazel eyes as "bedroom eyes". She didn't know about that, for she only thought of him as a good friend, but she did know there was a kindness behind those eyes and Jack Wetzel was a good, honest person.

Maggie shifted the heavy books in her arms. Wetzel stepped forward, reaching for the books. "Here, Maggie girl. Let me hold these for you." She reluctantly agreed.

"Where's Juan?" Wetzel slammed his locker shut with his elbow.

"He said to meet me at your locker." She looked down the hallway. A smile lit up her face. "Here he comes now, Jack."

Wetzel looked at her and then smiled. "You like Juan a bunch, don't ya?"

Maggie gazed into somber, hazel eyes. She did not hesitate in answering, "I love him more than anything in the world, Jack." Eyes glowing, she watched as Juan approached them. Garcia waved and then shouted. A Hispanic, his handsome features included short curly black hair, dark complexion, broad shoulders and thick chest. He wore his high school letter jacket, blue and gray, the letter "S" on the front right breast bristling with football, basketball and track insignias.

"Hey, guys," he said as he strolled up. "How's my two favorite friends?"

"*Bien, amigo.*" Wetzel gave him a lazy grin.

Garcia slapped him on the back while he patted Maggie's shoulder affectionately. "Let's do something together tonight." He peered from Maggie to Wetzel. Before Maggie could respond, Wetzel said, "I dunno, pard. You two deserve your quiet time together." He pursed his lips. "Besides, three's a crowd as they say."

"The hell they say!" Garcia countered. Frowning, he turned to Maggie. "What about you setting Jackie boy up with your friend Juanita?"

Maggie's eyes lit up. "Sure. You betcha. I'm sure she would *love* to go out with him."

Garcia laughed a throaty laugh as he leaned toward Wetzel. "You just be careful of that Juanita. She's one of them hot-blooded Latin women looking for a husband."

Maggie' face blushed red. "*Juan!*"

"I'm just kidding ol' Jack. How 'bout going to the drive-in together? I'll take my car."

Wetzel shifted from one foot to the other. His face was flushed. "Sure, Juan, but I got to do the chores at home first."

"No sweat. I'll go with you after school and help out. I've not seen your mom for awhile." Garcia's face turned serious. "I'm sorry they kicked you off the football team for that whipping you gave Peach. Don't seem fair with him starting the ruckus an' all."

"It's all right, Juan. I had a choice to make, and I made the wrong one by hitting him. I could've left it alone, but I let my temper get the best of me." Wetzel took a deep breath and exhaled. "My mom says everyone makes choices in life and sometimes you suffer the consequences, depending on which road you take. I got no beef coming."

Maggie intervened, "How did the court appearance go with Peach's father filing aggravated assault charges against you?"

"I pled guilty to simple assault. Wasn't much use in denying it didn't take place what with all the witnesses present in the locker room. The judge says I got two choices—go to jail or join the army. Either way it leaves my mom alone to work the ranch. If I join the army, he'll suspend all jail time in lieu of service to my country and lessen the charge to a misdemeanor."

"But ... but ... Jack. There's a war going on over in Vietnam. People are being killed. You—" Maggie pleaded, her voice trailing off.

Wetzel's somber face reflected his displeasure with the idea as well. Garcia slapped him again on the shoulders, "Well, pard. If you're thinking about joining the army, you've got some serious living to do here in Silver City ... starting tonight at the Drive-In with Juanita Flores!"

CHAPTER THREE

Fort Benning, Georgia, 1967

Wetzel filed off the TWA commercial plane with the seven other men from his company. Fort Benning appeared to be a large military base. The red clay soil, pine trees and dark and muddy Chattahoochee River nearby was a nice change from Fort Ord, California, with endless sand hills where he and his company had participated in lengthy marches and drills at the Advanced Infantry Training (AIT) site. He hated Fort Ord with a passion. The instructors told them they would never see the sun shine once there and damned if it wasn't so—he never did for the entire eight weeks. On his meager time off, he traveled to Monterrey or Carmel. At least the sun always shone there.

He'd completed Basic Infantry Training at Fort Leonard Wood, Missouri. Like the rest of the draftees, his hair was shorn and he was subjected to constant yelling and screaming by drill instructors, physical training (PT)—the forty yard crawl, grenade throwing, running the mile under five minutes in full combat gear including boots, pull ups, and the bars. His attitude and athleticism from high school assisted him in excelling in PT with high scores and being awarded a weekend respite from the dreary, stressful training.

While marching one day on the drill field, he bounced along

gaining the attention of the Drill Instructor. The DI walked up alongside him and tapped him on his steel helmet with his stick. "You raised on a farm, boy?" Wetzel had answered the affirmative, and the DI grinned, "It figgers. You march like you was walking behind a damned mule and plow."

He learned to take the Korean War vintage M14 rifle apart and put in back together, know all the parts by name, and he became a fair shot. And at AIT he'd learned to use a map and compass and to shoot a .30 caliber machine gun, .45 caliber pistol, and practiced extensive bayonet training.

Once graduation was over, the "old man" or captain of their company singled out seven of the men, Wetzel included, and advised them they'd received great orders, outstanding assignments as Scout Dog Handlers. Wetzel asked what the handlers did and was told they were point men for the infantry. Somehow, he didn't feel as elated as his superior officer. It certainly didn't feel like such a great assignment to him. He felt apprehensive; however, he knew the rest of his company from AIT had orders to report immediately to Vietnam for assigned infantry duties.

The lucky seven were shown their quarters and the head trainer Sergeant First Class Miller took all twenty-six handlers for the platoon down to the kennels where the dogs were kept. Miller was a ramrod straight "lifer". Although smaller, he reminded Wetzel of his late father—what he could remember of him. The sergeant wore his baseball cap cocked slightly to the right on his closely cropped graying hair, the brim curled, the fatigue shirt with its rank proudly displayed on the shoulder, and pants pressed and creased to military correctness. The pants were tucked into highly polished black boots.

In a deep, penetrating voice, Sergeant Miller advised the men they should be proud to belong to Infantry Platoon Scout Dog (IPSD) School, and the dogs were to be used for searching out enemy snipers and ambushes, booby traps, but most importantly to save the lives of American infantry soldiers. Each of the handlers was instructed to choose one of the dogs. Wetzel moved in close to observe the dogs inside the kennel. He stood for a while and then squatted on his heels as his quick eyes spied a smaller black and tan with brown eyebrows sitting back on his haunches in the corner watching the wild melee of other dogs barking and snapping at the men advancing toward them. The German Shepherd weighed about fifty pounds. His eyes were red which intrigued Wetzel, but he was more interested in the calm way the dog acted in the midst of such chaos. A soldier approached him; he growled, bared his teeth, and laid his ears back, but he didn't lunge at the man as other dogs were doing. Nervous and most likely not accustomed to animals, the soldier backed up and turned toward another dog nearby. Wetzel retrieved the five foot choke chain and leather leash from the ground, stood and walked directly to the black and tan. The mature dog looked to be about two years old to Wetzel, who had been around stock dogs all his life. He smiled. *Those red eyes!*

Feeling no fear, Wetzel did not hesitate as he neared the dog and his eyes locked with the red as he and the animal surveyed each other for less than a second. Then Wetzel reached out with the chain and said softly, "Easy, boy. It's just ol' Wetzel." His unflinching hand touched the dog's head, and he slipped the choke chain in place. The growling and bared fangs ceased, but the ears still remained laid back. He saw a name plate titled "Smoky" riveted to the leather collar. These dogs had been owned by others outside the military and donated to the U.S. Air Force. The Air Force had kept the larger dogs and given the rest of the lot to the army.

Wetzel squatted on his heels directly in front of the dog that he now claimed as his. He reached forward and with both hands held the shaggy head firmly between them. "Well, Smoky ol' boy, I reckon you an' me ... we're a team from now on ...till death do us part," he said grimly to his new partner. The dog's eyes remained locked with his new master, and his ears stood at attention.

Sergeant First Class Miller had them line up with their prospective dogs. He looked at each of the men, many of whom were trying unsuccessfully to control their dogs. "Listen up! This dog is your companion from here on—that is till your tours in Nam are over—so get to know him. And I mean know him *well*. It might just save both your lives as well as countless other fellow soldiers. This training will last a total of three months with you and the dog bonding and learning together. During this time, you and *you alone* will take care of your dog, including feeding him each night. You will go through obedience school, teaching your dog basic commands to heel, sit, down, stay, and come. This will be accomplished by verbal means as well as hand signals. Lastly, you will train together to scout for the army."

"Gentlemen, your dog's personality will in essence over time become *yours.* As I've said many times, *feelings always run down the leash.* If you're a lazy son-of-a-bitch, your dog will become the same. However, if you have spirit, likewise he will perform well for you." Sergeant First Class Miller paused, looking again at each of the dog handlers. "Maybe he'll save your life or those of others. It's up to you. And gentlemen, *I* will be watching ... especially for the lazy sons-a-bitches."

CHAPTER FOUR

Central Highlands, South Viet Nam, May, 1967

Buck Sergeant E-5 Jack Wetzel stood motionless near his scout dog watching the sun pop out from under the thick clouds. An ivy leaf insignia and three chevrons adorned the shoulder of Wetzel's combat fatigue shirt. The dog had started alerting that morning, getting hot on something, but they couldn't find the enemy. Smoky nudged his leg, and as he looked down at the wet animal, rain dripped from his camouflaged helmet. The ace of spades on the front of the helmet signified the U.S. Army's 4th Infantry Division.

Damn monsoon! He cursed silently to himself then said out loud, "Sorry, Mom." When he'd first arrived at Jackson Hole Fire Base in the Central Highlands of Viet Nam in February, it was the latter part of the dry season, and boy was it dry—like a popcorn fart! But since April the weather had consisted of constant light shower and then the sun would emerge unexpectedly for a short while only to disappear with the unrelenting rain. He was told this monsoon wet pattern would continue day and night until October when the rain would cease and the dry season cycle began again. He shifted his weight to his right side and felt the water squish in his wool sock and canvas combat boot. Boots didn't last long as they rotted quickly during the monsoon season. About every other month, he'd swap for two new pairs of boots and acquire some new thick wool socks.

It was hard to work the dog in the rain and dangerous. The scent simply wasn't as easily detected in wet weather. Undoubtedly, the scout dogs proved to be valuable assets for the infantry. He knew from training that dogs have the ability to scent forty times better than man, had twenty times better hearing, and ten times better sight. He and Smoky had done well though for the first few months, and the "old man" liked using their team since they discovered a huge cache of weapons and rice the month prior. The "old man" was captain of B Company, Second Brigade of the 4th Infantry Division. The title "old" was an affectionate term and didn't really have true meaning to the nineteen-year-old Wetzel as he knew the captain to be twenty-six and regular army.

Wetzel's tent sat in the middle of the forward fire camp near the company commander's tent. The "old man" wanted the dog close by. The dog always slept at Wetzel's feet. Wetzel tried to find a place where he could chain Smoky to a tree or heavy bush due to all the foot traffic in camp. Smoky would growl at the soldiers passing by. Many tried to pet him, but he simply did not like it and he snapped at them. Several officers yelled at Wetzel for his dog scaring the men as they walked by at night, but the "old man" always backed him up by saying, "Dammit, you tell your men to stay the hell away from Jack's dog."

Generally, two scout dog teams from the 50th Platoon would work together in the field. There were 10-12 dog handlers or four to five scout dog teams at the Main Base Camp in Pleiku, and they were alternated back and forth for use in the field at Jackson Hole and Oasis Fire Bases. Spotter planes saw something suspicious, and the company commanders would call for the dogs to assist in searching out and ultimately finding the enemy. Occasionally, the dog teams participated in air assaults for the First Brigade of the 7th Air Cavalry Division, flying in helicopters with the combat troops.

Smoky growled, arousing Wetzel from his thoughts. He slung the adjustable stock M-16 rifle to his shoulder as he saw Weapons Platoon Sergeant Bill Merrell approach. Sergeant Merrell was a 27-year-old army regular who knew combat operations well. Wetzel admired and appreciated working with the professional soldier. Dressed ready for the field, Merrell was a stocky, well-made man; a tough hard man, but affable to those he liked, and he liked Jack Wetzel.

"Howdy, Jack." He pulled a pack of cigarettes from the pocket of his fatigue shirt. He offered the pack to Wetzel, who took one of the Lucky Strikes, lit it with his pocket lighter and lit Merrell's cigarette for him. "You an' Smoky ready to work?"

"We're ready, Bill." Wetzel looked up at the cloudy, rain-filled sky. "I hate working in this damn rain—the dog has so much trouble finding a scent." Tobacco smoke drifted from his nostrils.

Merrell nodded his sandy, short-cropped head, enjoying the smoke. Wetzel felt his blue eyes studying him. "Why don't you feed your dog, Jack. Let him rest a bit. You've been working hard all morning an' it's close to noon. I'll take my platoon out in a small circle 300 meters or so for a quick looksee. Then we'll come back in and take you and the dog with us for a better surveillance look."

"You sure? Me an' Smoky are ready to go," returned Wetzel.

"Naw. Get some rest. I'll need you later." He slapped Wetzel on the back, turned and was gone.

Twenty minutes passed. Wetzel had finished feeding Smoky and was placing his field gear into his ruck sack—eight to ten canteens of water, c-rations, dog food and the scout harness, poncho and liner. Suddenly, the stillness of the day was broken as heavy fire erupted from the direction Merrell's platoon had gone minutes before. Mortar and rocket fire exploded; thunderous, earth shattering explosions. The Nine Days in May Battle had begun.

Smoky whined as Wetzel stood, momentarily caught off guard, his heart pounding. Then he grabbed the leash and he and the dog sprinted for the company commander's tent.

From just outside the tent, he heard Sergeant Merrell on the radio calling in air strikes—something about running into a regiment-sized North Vietnamese force. A short time later, Merrell advised via radio that his platoon was cut off from returning to base. Wetzel froze from what he was doing, a deep gut wrenching feeling overcame him.

As the afternoon progressed, the situation worsened. Wetzel was assigned to help defend the perimeter with everyone else in B Company. The fire base itself was being pounded by mortar and rocket fire. In the night the North Vietnamese troops began probing and attacking the perimeter.

Wetzel positioned himself near what back in the States would be a big Cypress tree. Smoky lay near his feet. A claymore mine exploded in the distance, and then another, men screamed, followed by continuous, and then sporadic shooting. Shots whined over Wetzel's head. He returned fire where he saw muzzle flashes in the dark night from the perimeter. Mass confusion enveloped the camp. It seemed as though everyone in camp was yelling, screaming, or talking on the radios all at once. Through all the chaos, he felt truly alone without any faith that he would survive; his hands trembled as he feared for his life.

The sky lit up with a loud explosion nearby. The thunderous roar split his ear drums and the shock wave threw him violently to the ground. When he came to, it was as though he wore super ear protection; he could hear absolutely nothing. He reached frantically for his rifle, found it nearby, and had the presence of mind to remove the nearly empty magazine and insert one fully loaded from his ammo pouch. As an afterthought, he reached down, procured the bayonet from its scabbard and snapped it into place on his M-16. *Where's Smoky?* An icy chill ran up his spine as he searched. Unable to hear, he decided to yell for the dog anyway, but still could not find him. Crawling a short distance on his hands and knees, he felt something warm against his hand. Smoky! He felt the dog's body with his hands searching for wounds. His hands came away wet. He held them up to his face and smelled blood. The dog stirred against his leg. Wetzel began to sob, tears filled his eyes. *He's alive!*

Wetzel looked up just in time to use his rifle to parry a bayonet thrust from an enemy soldier directed at his chest. He came up fast from the ground and drove his own bayonet deep into the North Vietnamese soldier's torso. He slammed his right boot hard against the man's chest and jerked the bayonet free. As the soldier fell, Wetzel shot him. Swallowing hard, unable to breathe, he dropped to his knees again.

Seeing other enemy soldiers approaching, he fired three-round bursts into each silhouette racing towards him in the darkness. Rounds whizzed and zipped past him in the dark rain-filled night of terror. He slung the rifle over his shoulder, grabbed the dog as best he could and dragged him back to the large tree. His heart pounded incessantly within his chest as he gasped for breath.

Upon further inspection, he found the immense tree was hollowed out near the base with barely enough room for him to crawl into. Quickly pulling the injured Smoky in with him onto his lap, he searched for enemy combatants, the unslung rifle held tightly out in front of him. Air Force F-105s swooped in, dropping bombs, and the artillery from Jackson Hole Fire Base pounded the enemy farther up the mountainside. The ground shook, the night sky lit up intermittently, but Wetzel still couldn't hear a thing. His strained eyes ached in dry sockets from searching for the approaching enemy and attempting to determine friend from foe as he sat propped up, hugging the injured scout dog tightly to him. *Our Father who art in heaven—* Silence. *Hallowed be thy name … please help me.* Ominously, in the inky blackness of the deadly night and unbeknown to man and dog, the shadow of the mountain crept ever so slowly toward the two sitting quietly in the hollowed-out tree.

* * *

THE FOLLOWING DAY, the North Vietnamese advance was stopped and the enemy retreated into the mountains. Smoky had nonlife-threatening shrapnel wounds. The Americans found Merrell's platoon all dead—with one exception. The North Vietnamese had overrun their position, killing anyone still alive. The lone survivor told of enemy soldiers walking among the dead and dying American soldiers and shooting those still living in the head after stealing all their belongings. That soldier's survival was credited to his ability to play as though he were dead. A North Vietnamese soldier took his clothes, boots, rifle, and then while sitting on his back stole his wedding ring. Somehow, no doubt due to concentrating on the theft, he simply forgot to shoot the American in the head upon receiving orders to withdraw hurriedly from the field.

Wetzel observed the lone American survivor. The man had truly been all alone with an intensity of fear experienced beyond all limits. A lump appeared in Wetzel's throat. He felt very sad as he peered at the pale, frightened face; his fellow soldier rocking back and forth, moaning to ghosts that would never be forgotten. Would this man forever be a "basket case" due to the harrowing experience?

That was when Wetzel realized his hearing had returned.

CHAPTER FIVE

THE BATTLE OF DAK TO, SOUTH VIETNAM- NOVEMBER, 1967

IT WAS fall and the dry season had begun the previous month. Wetzel leaned over Smoky, removed the choke chain and leash to replace it with the scout harness. That meant business to Smoky. He urged the dog, "Search, boy ... search ... *hunt 'em up*!"

The point team headed directly into the thick jungle in advance of the infantry company's main body. The green mountains shimmered in the morning sun. Water from the natural, clear mountain springs reflected sunlight as the moving body of water descended from high ridgelines to the valleys below and the awaiting rice paddy fields. Wetzel, his M-16 slung over his shoulder, hung onto the scout harness strap with both hands. He was flanked by his armed bodyguard and the platoon sergeant immediately behind the dog team with compass in hand to lead the way.

It took all of Wetzel's intense concentration to watch the scout dog for any indication of danger. A missed calculation on his part could cost him and everyone in the platoon their lives. He observed the dog's nose and ears. At night, he taped white tape on the back of the dog's ears so he could see the alert movement advising of danger. The wind was blowing directly at them. *Perfect for scenting the enemy.* He hated working his dog with the wind at his flanks narrowing the scent tunnel. A man could get into trouble real quick, and he flatly refused to work the dog with the wind at his back. They moved steadily through the jungle, the platoon sergeant advising the direction of travel. Suddenly, Smoky threw his head up in the air.

"Watch, boy ... watch, boy," encouraged Wetzel, a bad feeling in the pit of his stomach.

If he stops, it'll be a trip wire. His shoulders tightened. But the scout dog didn't stop, only slowed his walk, his ears up and pointing forward, nose raised. Wetzel stopped the dog from proceeding further into the jungle. He turned to the platoon sergeant and whispered, "There's something up there, Sarge ... a sniper ... maybe ... hell, I don't know."

The sergeant nodded, spoke into his radio, and then turned to Wetzel. "The old man says to move back to the ridge behind us. Word is the 66th and 88th North Vietnamese Regiments might be in the area. He'll send in airstrikes to clear the way for us."

Wetzel sat high on the ridge with Smoky at his feet. The dog heard the planes approaching long before he did, his ears up and alert. They roared over the company's position, all F-105 jet fighters, the Air Force's best. One after the other, he watched them come in low at the position called in and drop their bombs. All morning long he watched strike after strike with fascination as the area was flattened like a pancake. As with the other bombed-out areas, he knew very few animals would survive—maybe a few monkeys if they were lucky. One of their claymore mines at the camp perimeter had killed a tiger once. Blown his belly out. Wetzel winced recalling the incident.

It was noon. The Air Force had completed their bombing runs. Time to "lock and load" and move up the mountain, find the enemy or whatever was left and destroy them. Wetzel and Smoky along with his bodyguard, a young red-headed soldier, and the first squad with the platoon sergeant were the first up to the flattened ridge top—about seven or eight of them. The rest of the men were strung out further down the slope coming up behind them. Smoky lay down to rest. The platoon's first lieutenant arrived and immediately gave orders: "You men set up a machine gun over here for covering fire." He pointed to another location along the ridge. "I want –"

Wetzel heard a "pop" much like a cap pistol. The first lieutenant silently fell to the scorched earth without a sound, a bullet hole in his forehead. *Sniper!* Caught off guard like the rest of the squad, Wetzel hesitated momentarily, and the North Vietnamese, who had been hiding in bunkers, opened fire.

Someone shouted, "Let's get the hell outta here." The American soldiers scrambled down off the hill. Wetzel's bodyguard dropped his rifle, clutched his chest and fell backward out of the dog handler's sight.

Wetzel felt Smoky at his side, warm against his leg. Raw fear ate at his belly. Bullets pinged overhead and burrowed into the ground nearby, kicking up dust and ashes from the bombing. He resisted the urge to run downhill, turned, and ran to the fallen officer. Reaching out to grab the man's fatigue shirt front, he felt someone beside him—the platoon sergeant. The sergeant's face was grim but showed no fear. He helped Wetzel hoist the dead lieutenant up onto his shoulders and then supported him as they both struggled off the hill and down the slope amidst withering enemy fire. Wetzel didn't know why he wasn't killed. He remembered a saying of his mother's: "Just meant to be ... living to do something else worthwhile in this ol' world of ours."

His legs began to falter after fifty yards; he stumbled and would have fallen if the platoon sergeant had not supported him and his heavy load. "Let me take 'im, Jack," he called out in the roar of battle. Wetzel shook his head and somehow forced his body to align with his mind that was already set to get the job done. As they made it to safety, the roar of jets low overhead filled the air. *Boom!* Loud, thunderous roars, followed by the seared earth shaking, twisting, turning. Wetzel sank to his knees and lay next to Smoky. The red eyes beneath tan eye brows did not tell him what the scout dog was thinking.

* * *

Jets bombed the surrounding area over and over again. Silence replaced the deadly roar, and once again Wetzel found himself trudging back up the same hill he had fled hours before. After attaining the summit, he searched diligently for his point bodyguard. He had to dig in the churned-up mounds of scorched earth, but he found the dead red-headed soldier who was stripped of his gear, weapons, and clothing except his fatigue trousers. Wetzel covered him with his poncho liner. Enemy soldiers lay on the ground, some halfway out of bunkers that had been hidden prior to the second wave of airstrikes. The Americans soon discovered the bunkers were connected by tunnels that encircled the entire mountain.

Wetzel stood over a dead North Vietnamese soldier. He was struck by how closely the man resembled an American Indian. The long black hair and facial features looked almost Manchurian. The soldier had a brand new uniform, a ruck sack containing a new unused razor, and an AK-47 rifle with the bayonet fixed. On his feet were sandals made of tire tread secured to his feet by straps of inner tubing.

Jack Wetzel drew air deep into his lungs and exhaled slowly. He looked out over the surrounding countryside as far as he could see, beyond the bombed-out, denuded wasteland to the green sun-lit hills and mountains in the far distance. He felt a lump forming in his throat as he thought of home, his mother, and his beloved New Mexico. It all seemed so far away.

CHAPTER SIX

SYDNEY, AUSTRALIA- CHRISTMAS, 1967

WETZEL EXHALED a huge sigh of relief. Two weeks R&R! Rest and relaxation, courtesy of the U.S. Army. He stepped out onto the veranda of the White Haven Hotel located on Kings Cross Highway, Sydney, Australia. The wide, blue ocean had no end to it; the yachts, the larger boats carrying goods, the ferries carting people in the harbor was almost as pleasing to his eyes as the blue, sunny skies overhead reminding him of New Mexico and home. He had forgotten about a world worth living in. Ten long, grueling months of war, only two lousy months left, and then home. He adjusted his new suit and tightened the neck tie, all courtesy of the U.S. Army. *Damn, I feel good!*

The telephone rang in the room. He stepped back inside and saw his R&R buddy, Jim Lane, pulling on his trousers near the bed. Lane hailed from Houston, Texas and was assigned to the First Air Cavalry. Wetzel answered the phone. It was Mrs. Dorothy Higgins, their "adopted" mother, who had graciously assisted them during their short stay in Sydney on behalf of the Australian government. Mrs. Higgins was a wonderful sweet lady of sixty years. She reminded Wetzel of Aunt Bea on the "Andy Griffith Show".

"Good-dayee, Jack. How are ye an' Jimmy this fine day?" Mrs. Higgins' voice crackled over the phone line.

"Fine, Mrs. Higgins. Thank you for all you've done for us." Wetzel cradled the heavy phone on his shoulder as he straightened his tie once more while looking in the mirror.

"You Yanks ... don't party so bloody hard that ya don't make the yacht race in the harbor tomorrow morning, ya hear?"

"Yes, ma'am. The sailboat race. What time is that again?'

"Ten o'clock sharp. I'll send a limo over for ya."

"We'll be bright-eyed and bushy tailed, ma'am." Wetzel hung up the phone. He looked to his partner, who had finished dressing and was straightening his tie. Grinning from ear to ear, he said, "Shall we?"

Lane bowed, sweeping his arm toward the door of the hotel room. "After you. I must say, ol' chap, it's a *cracker* o' a day."

"Too right, mate. A bloody good 'un." Wetzel chuckled at their sad attempts to sound like true Australians.

* * *

It was late. How late Wetzel had no idea, and furthermore he couldn't care less what time it was. They had taken the cab from the hotel to the nearest pub and immediately asked for two large mugs of beer, which they quickly downed. Wetzel reached in his back pocket for his billfold to pay for the beers and found it wasn't there. He panicked, cold chills running up and down his spine and couldn't think what to do next. Calming down, he remembered the name of the cab company and that the cab was #19. He called and asked the same cab to return to the pub. Luckily, the cab hadn't picked up any other passengers, and Wetzel found the billfold on the floor of the cab next to the door. His airline tickets, shot records, and $300 cash were still inside. He breathed a huge sigh of relief.

Hours passed, beer flowed. A large, raw-boned man entered the pub with two women in tow. They stood for a moment just inside the crowded, noisy establishment looking for a place to sit. The man spied Wetzel and Lane at a table with empty chairs nearby. The trio sauntered over, stopping in front of the two soldiers.

"Good-dayee, mates." The man's round face produced a big smile. "I wonder ... if you would be so kind as to allow us to sit at your table." He looked furtively around the crowded room. "Bloody crowded, ain't it?"

Wetzel stood, although unsteadily. "Sure. No problem, have a seat."

The man guffawed, turned to the two women. "Bloody Yanks 'es what we go 'ere." Both women smiled and sat next to the soldiers. The man continued to stand. "Me name is Mike, mates, an' these two sheilas are Betty … me sister, and 'er friend …" Confusion showed on his rotund face.

The woman sitting next to Lane answered sweetly, "Cora." She licked her red lips as she held out her hand to Jim Lane. "Me name is Cora." She was not quick to remove her hand from his grasp. Mike sat down in an empty chair and ordered a round of beer for everyone.

An hour and several large beers later, Wetzel noticed Mike had disappeared. His sister, Betty, was snuggled up next to him. She placed her arm around his shoulder, the other hand on his knee. "Sooo … Jack," she whispered in his ear, "found any pretty Australian women to run with?" She nuzzled his ear, her hand firm on his leg.

For the first time during the evening, he noticed her as a woman and appreciated her closeness, her warmth and femininity. He said with a thick tongue, "No, ma'am."

Betty grinned mischievously, and then as an afterthought, she quipped, "Ahh … an' a polite one, too. You Yanks could teach our Australian men a thing or two."

Wetzel reached over held her by the shoulders and kissed her softly. For the first time in almost a year, he felt a stirring in his loins.

CHAPTER SEVEN

Jackson Hole Fire Base, Central Highlands
South Vietnam, February, 1968

The monsoon season was still a few months away. Wetzel shrugged. *Not till April, thank you, God. I only have a week left to go on my tour of duty, and then adios, amigos.* He'd be the hell outta Nam and on to sunny New Mexico. When he returned from R & R in Australia, it hadn't been the same. His hands shook when out in the field, and he didn't volunteer anymore for others' combat duties. He'd tasted and seen there was *real* life out there in the world, and he wanted more than anything to be a part of it now. Lately, he'd been assigned "palace guard", patrolling the perimeter of the fire base with Smoky.

His mother wrote many months ago that things were hard but fine at the ranch. Neighbors were helping her and for him not to worry. She also said his friends Juan Garcia and Maggie O'Brian married right out of high school and were expecting a child. A more recent letter from his mother contained bad news. Juan Garçia had been drafted into the army and was most likely headed for Vietnam.

Wetzel walked to the company commander's headquarters in the center of the fire base. Numerous tents covered the sprawling base, with bristling artillery pieces on the south end. He straightened his baseball cap before entering. Passing several clerks busily working on their typewriters, he was allowed to enter the "the old man's" office.

Captain Mossman answered his salute, "What can I do for you today, Jack?" He eyed the mound of paperwork cluttering his desk and in-box.

"Well, sir. It's about Smoky."

Eyebrows raised and genuine concern showed on the officer's face. "Oh, is he hurt or sick?"

"No sir. He's fine." Wetzel bit his lower lip. "I ... uh ... I'd like to take him home with me when I go."

Captain Mossman sighed, leaned back in his chair, and looked directly at the young scout dog handler standing before him. "We've been over this before. The dog belongs to the U.S. Army. They say *no.*" He leaned forward in his chair, elbows on the desk. "And I echo their answer, *No, goddammit!*"

"But, sir. He's a one-man dog—answers only to me; has for some time now. He'll kill a replacement handler he doesn't know ... or seriously hurt him."

The captain stood. "It's not up to me." He scratched his head as he made direct eye contact with Wetzel. "I don't want to hear any more about this, Jack. This is the end of it. Do you understand?"

"Yessir." Wetzel dropped his gaze.

"There's another matter." The captain walked around his desk. "I need you and Walters to escort the payroll back from Saigon."

"Sir?"

"You heard me. I want your two dog teams ready to go in the morning."

"But ... I've only got a week left, sir. Can't someone else—"

"No. I want you to go. I can depend on *you* to get the job done."

Wetzel hesitated, his heart in his throat.

"That'll be all, soldier."

"Yes, sir." Wetzel saluted and then left headquarters.

He kicked at the ground outside. *Shit!* A low level helicopter flight 350 miles to Saigon *and back.* Even if they weren't shot down, the awesome responsibility for the company's payroll of ... say seven to nine *million* dollars! *Shit!*

* * *

THEY MADE it to Saigon without any problems. No one even shot at them. The two dog teams sat guarding the payroll all night before they started the return trip. The dogs were muzzled. The dark morning sky suggested rain. Wetzel grinned. *Halfway to getting back home.* Light rain drops bounced off the helicopter as they left Saigon. Then it began to rain hard, and they were in the middle of a severe thunderstorm. The pilot hollered at a flight crewman to get the dog handler to close his damned door. The crewman tapped Wetzel on the shoulder and pointed at the door.

Wetzel saw the door latch wasn't properly closed on his side of the aircraft. He attempted to secure the door and lost his grip on the wet, slippery handle. The door flew wide open and the storm tore it from its hinges. It was there one moment and then gone the next, blown completely clear of the helicopter. Heavy rain poured in on all of them, drenching them to the bone. The pilot yelled something and began to turn the ship around in a fairly tight circle searching for the door.

Within minutes they flew low to the ground almost touching the tall bamboo trees and passed over the mangled door lying on the jungle floor beneath them. The pilot turned to Wetzel and said into the microphone, "Son, take a good *long* look down there. You just cost the U.S. Army $1,500." Nothing else was said to him for the rest of the flight back to base. Everyone was thoroughly drenched and cold. And mad as hell at him. Wetzel swallowed hard. *Shit!*

BAGS WERE PACKED and ready to go. Jack Wetzel wore his dress uniform for his return trip to the United States and home. They would be shipped back via the northern route through Tokyo to Alaska, and on to Fort Lewis, Washington, home to the 4th Infantry Division. His tour of duty in Vietnam was over and service to his country almost complete. He should have been elated. So happy that he'd jump high in the air and kick his heels together. Hell, he should've been laughing out loud, but he wasn't. He was crying like a damn love sick fool. Quietly, he sobbed as his heart ached deep within his breast.

He squatted on his heels as he had done in the beginning, as he had done for months in the field, holding this great friend of his … this wonderful animal who had saved his life countless times. Tears rolled down his cheeks as he held Smoky tight to him not wanting to let him go. *Ever!* He breathed in the very essence of his friend and companion so he would never, ever forget him.

A loud voice sounded off behind him. "Goddamn it, Wetzel. Hurry it up! Let's get the hell outta this damn war zone."

Wetzel released his grip and leaned back still squatting on his heels. Sad hazel eyes locked with red. He saw the deep understanding of true friendship and unrelenting love in those red eyes just as he had when he'd first met him.

"I'll be seein' ya one day, pal."

CHAPTER EIGHT

NEAR THE GILA NATIONAL FOREST BOUNDARY, NEW MEXICO, 1973

ROGER O'BRIAN STOOD on the front porch of his old ranch house. His old stock dog had alerted him to the arrival of unlikely guests. He tipped his battered, sweat-stained hat back from his forehead as he watched the green Forest Service truck bounce its way toward him on the rough unmaintained road leading to the ranch house and outbuildings. The dog barked loudly, reminding him that the animal didn't take to strangers. In fact, he'd bitten the last visitor. O'Brian laughed softly to himself. Tore the seat right out of his green breeches, by God. The Forest Service son-of-a-bitch deserved it. *Tryin' to reduce the cattle on my allotment!* And him a green behind-the-ears college boy who knew nothin' 'bout ranchin' in the first place.

His Irish temper flared, his cheeks flushed. O'Brian was a big hulk of a man, over six feet tall, barrel-chested, and in his mid-sixties. His old faded Wrangler jeans hung from his narrow bony hips and bowed legs. Outdoor living and the incessant New Mexico sun had burned his face a dark brown and baked deep creases in the leathery skin. *What the hell does the Forest Service want now? The sons-a-bitches never show up unless they want something.* He withdrew a red handkerchief from his back pocket, blew his nose, and then tucked it in the back pocket with a frayed hole at the bottom.

The green truck bearing U.S. Forest Service insignia on both door panels came to a halt. The metal door creaked as it opened and a tall young man stepped out. He wore the Forest Service uniform, the tan shirt complete with insignia patch on the right shoulder and an official badge pinned to his shirt front. The slender man moved easily in the faded Wrangler jeans and well-used White's Packer boots. The old man sensed that he knew this man, this intruder who worked for his hated enemy. Leaning forward, he squinted his eyes so as to clearly see the face, but he could only make out a deep shadow beneath the wide-brimmed straw hat.

As the man neared the porch, the stock dog ceased barking and moved stealthily toward him low to the ground. The man turned his attention to the dog. It wasn't a hurried, fearful move, but he kept the dog from flanking him as he changed course and walked directly at the old dog saying, "What's the matter ol' boy? Don't remember me?"

O'Brian frowned. *That voice? I know it. Who the hell—*

The man stood over the now uncertain dog. His voice was firm but not harsh. *"Sit!"* The dog hesitated and then obeyed as he looked up at the stranger. Reaching out a firm hand, the stranger patted the dog on his head. The old dog's tail wagged and, upon seeing that, the man huffed a soft laugh and squatted down on his heels in front of the old dog. Tilting the straw hat back on his head with this thumb, he turned his gaze to the dazed rancher standing on the porch. "I think ol' Pepper remembers me, Mr. O'Brian."

The old rancher's mouth flew open. *A spittin' image of Tom Wetzel ... only taller.* He tried to speak, swallowed and finally found the words, "Jack? Jack Wetzel?" He took a tentative step off the porch.

Jack Wetzel stood and stepped forward to shake hands heartily with the old rancher. "I reckon it is, Mr. O'Brian."

Pleased with the firm handshake, O'Brian surveyed him from head to toe, and smiled. "I'll be damned." He shook his head. "You look just like your daddy, boy. Jest set a mite higher up from the ground is all."

Jack Wetzel's flushed face showed his appreciation for the compliment.

"Tom Wetzel was a good friend, boy. Why, back in them days the Forest Service didn't have nothin' but old time Rangers who done it all in the field. Men like your daddy, Jack. They was all goodun's."

"Thank ya, Mr. O'Brian." Wetzel hooked his thumbs in his jeans pockets.

"How's your mama, son?" queried the old man.

"Fine, sir. Still working hard and enjoying it."

"Good." O'Brian knew Helen Wetzel for the salt of the earth. They didn't come any better. Then he remembered his long-forgotten hospitality. "Would ya like to come in? Set a spell?"

"Porch steps okay?"

"Shore is." The old man moved down a step and sat down heavily as the young man sat next to him. O'Brian reached in his shirt pocket, procured tobacco and paper and started to build a smoke. His knarled, arthritic fingers fumbled with the makings. Tobacco spilled from the curled paper and onto the unpainted porch steps.

Wetzel offered him a store-bought Lucky Strike. O'Brian set his makings on the porch step, accepted the cigarette, and broke off the filter tip. He lit it, drew the smoke deep into his lungs and then exhaled slowly. "What brings you out here?" He gazed into the young man's hazel eyes.

Ignoring the question, Wetzel asked one of his own, "How's Maggie, sir?"

The gray eyes softened. "She's doing all right, I reckon ... considerin' everything that's happened. She don't make it out here too much anymore. It's too hard a trip for the boy an' gas costs so damned much now-a-days."

Wetzel said nothing. He stuck a cigarette in the corner of his mouth and lit it.

"That goddammed Messican knocked her up then took off for Vietnam. Left her to fend for herself, by God." O'Brian spat the words.

Wetzel's voice had an edge to it. "Juan Garcia is my friend just as Maggie is, sir." He tossed his cigarette to the ground and stood, eyes blazing.

"The hell ya say!" The old man was caught off guard. *The boy's got some guts to 'im.*

"Juan loves your daughter—"

"He's dead an' you know it, boy."

"Missing in action ... and he was drafted," corrected Wetzel.

"That was over *two years* ago." He motioned for Wetzel to sit again. "Jest calm down. Maybe I was a mite rough on the boy."

Wetzel hesitated and then sat.

"Maggie always thought highly of you, Jack." He sighed as he gazed at the silhouette of Granny Mountain in the distant horizon deep within the Gila Wilderness. Pepper found a place to sit next to Wetzel.

The young man broke the awkward silence. "The District Ranger wants to cut your allotment numbers in half."

"I know it. Pepper run the Range Con off a few days ago when he come with the good news."

"What are you going to do, Mr. O'Brian?"

"I can't make it if they do that to me. I'm already on a shoe string with cattle prices gone to hell, drier'n all get out, an' no rain in sight."

Wetzel stood and lit another cigarette with his pocket lighter. "Split the difference."

"What?" O'Brian's mouth fell open.

"The Forest Service wants to cut half; you want status quo." Wetzel rubbed his tanned jaw as smoke drifted from his nose and mouth. "Range is hurtin', Mr. O'Brian. Country won't sustain your full numbers—not now. Offer to cut a quarter in numbers. Compromise. Then promise to rotate those cattle however often the Forest Service wants."

The old man shook his head slowly, chewed on his lower lip; he started laughing. "Hell, the sons-a-bitches might just buy off on it." The furrow between his bushy, gray eyebrows deepened. "My fences ain't up in a lot o' places for rotating them cows."

"I'll help you. You just give me a holler when you're ready. Don't have a phone myself, but you can leave a message with the Forest Service office at the Cliff Dwellings." Wetzel started for his truck. "I got to be going, sir."

O'Brian stood and walked with him. "You're a growed man now, Jack. You call me Roger, uh? I don't take much to that mister stuff anyhow." He stopped near the hood of the hated green Forest Service truck.

Wetzel opened the driver's door. "Please say hi to Maggie for me."

The old man's quick eyes saw no wedding ring. "Why don't ya … drop by and tell her yourself, Jack. She'll be glad to see you. Been staying with a *viejita*—a nice little Mexican lady in an apartment over across from the Catholic Church. Her and the boy that is."

Wetzel got in and slammed the door shut. He leaned out the

window. "I'll do that, Mr. —er, Roger. See ya." The engine roared to life.

O'Brian walked around to the driver's side as Wetzel put the truck in reverse. "You tell that district ranger, I won't deal with anyone but you. They come out here again ... I'll sic Pepper on 'em." For the first time in months, he was smiling from ear to ear as he turned and walked toward the house.

CHAPTER NINE

EX-TENNESSEE WILDLIFE RESOURCES OFFICER ROBERT MCMURTRY guided his twenty-six foot U-haul truck along in the right lane on Interstate 10 a few miles west of Las Cruces, New Mexico. He had taken it slow and easy all the way from Maryville, Tennessee, as he was pulling his old '67 Chevy truck behind the U-haul. Everything he owned was in the trailer. It wasn't much by most folk's standards, but then he wasn't most people. He was Bob McMurtry, an old farm boy from the Smoky Mountains. A backwoods boy who sure as hell didn't figger owning material things was very damned important in a man's life.

He hadn't ever gotten along with his old supervisor at Tennessee Wildlife Resources or TWR. Bobby Tate was *the* dumbest sumbitch he'd ever met in his entire life of thirty-five years, and there'd been a passel of fellers he'd knowed and worked with who weren't exactly the sharpest axes in the tool shed. Tate didn't have the ability to catch a poacher out in the woods if his own life depended on it. But he sure liked to ride rough-shod over his subordinates once he had become the boss.

McMurtry laughed out loud. *But then again there ain't nobody who kin catch poachers like me—the master, by God!* He'd had enough and when a game warden job opened up in New Mexico, he'd jumped at the chance. He was to start his job with the New Mexico Game and

Fish Department in one week. The Heart Bar Ranch would be his new home and work station. It was located about 80 miles north of Silver City, New Mexico deep within the Gila National Forest according the map McMurtry had studied.

McMurtry turned off I-10 at Deming, New Mexico onto Highway 180 and headed north toward Silver City. *This dadjimmed country's flatter'n a pancake.* Then he noticed a high mountain peak jutting against the blue sky lined with light, wispy white clouds. He took a quick look at his map lying in the seat beside him. *Cook's Peak. Huh.* At least they've got some mountains in this here dry, desolate, hot country. He removed his well-worn ball cap with "Tennessee Vols" insignia on the front and ran his coarse stubby fingers through his unruly sandy hair. Replacing the cap, cocking it slightly to the right side, he rubbed his bearded jaw and yawned.

McMurtry stood five feet eleven inches tall with stocky legs supporting a stout wide torso that was beginning to show a small paunch near his belt line. He wore a faded denim shirt and worn, patched brown overalls with the suspender straps tight against his broad shoulders. Unkempt brown hair covered his head, peeking out from under the cap and a brown beard displaying some gray adorned his square face. Bright blue eyes studied the road ahead.

Reaching over to the dash, he picked up the opened cigarette packet, shook one out and stuck it in the corner of his mouth. After lighting it, he rolled the window down about halfway. The cool spring air felt good on his face. He thought he'd like this dadjimmed weather.

He turned off Highway 180 onto 61 and glanced at the Mimbres River running adjacent to the highway. *Members River, huh?* There was no visible water in the dry riverbed. The typical desert vegetation had given way to flat grasslands. He saw a sign indicating the turnoff for City of Rocks State Park. Stopping at the junction of Highway 61 and 35, he saw where Highway 152 headed east to the small village of San Lorenzo and then on through the Black Range, a huge mountain range in the Gila National Forest. He looked briefly at the map and saw Hillsboro Peak was 10,011 feet in elevation. *I'll be dogged. These New Mexico Mountains make the Smoky Mountains look like dadjimmed ant hills.*

McMurtry enjoyed the drive with the highway traversing along the Mimbres River. He felt more at home in the tall pine trees, and when he spotted the sawmill operation on the east side of Highway

35, he grinned. Continuing on north from where the highway veered west away from the river and the U.S. Forest Service Mimbres Ranger Station, the country rose in elevation and its scenery became even more enticing to the old country boy.

Easing the U-haul truck and its extra load around a curve in the road, he spied a beautiful little lake into which fed Sapillo Creek. Lake Roberts the sign advised. He pulled the U-haul truck and towed pickup into the gravel parking lot of a store. The small store was built of stained rough wood and sported a board sidewalk in front of a tall storefront with upstairs windows overlooking the parking lot. His belly growled. For a man who always ate more often and a lot more than he should've, he'd forgotten to eat.

Locking up the truck, he stretched his stocky frame, hitched up his overalls, and walked up the wooden steps and into the country store. A bell jingled merrily as the door opened and closed. An elderly couple stood in the trinkets area, but the remainder of the store appeared empty. McMurtry sauntered over to the counter, his soft-bottomed lace-up hunting boots making little noise. He wondered where the clerk was when he saw a woman bent over behind the counter retrieving a box from a storage cabinet. The woman wore faded jeans that fit snuggly around her shapely hips and a red and white, checkered cotton blouse tucked into the jeans. Enjoying the view from behind more than he should have, McMurtry blushed and looked off at the elderly couple when the woman straightened from behind the counter.

"Valgamé," she gasped and covered her mouth with a hand. McMurtry could see that she was tall for a woman, maybe five feet seven inches. *Tall and shapely.* Again his face blushed. Her shoulder length black, hair hung loosely about her oval brown face. Then his attention was riveted to her smiling, pretty brown eyes that glowed.

"Lo siento mucho, señor. I deedn't hear you come up." She placed her small hands on the counter. Discretely, he checked to see she didn't wear a wedding ring. "How may I help you, *señor*?"

He rubbed his scruffy beard with his left hand. "I've got me a powerful hunger, ma'am. What ya got fer vittles?"

The pretty eyebrows knitted. "Veetles?"

He laughed. "You know, ma'am, food. I've not et fer a spell."

She stood and peered at him, apparently taking him all in—the clothes, scruffy appearance, and the dialect.

McMurtry tried to break the awkward silence. "If ya don't mind my asking, ma'am. Jest what exactly are you anyways ... an Injun?"

The woman's brown eyes gazed into his. She smiled and said, "I'm Hispanic, *señor.*" She saw the blank look on his face. "Mexican descent."

His face lit up. "Oh ... yeah. I plumb forgot where I was, I reckon."

"And you, *señor*? Exactly, what are you?" The brown eyes were laughing.

"Lil' ol' me?" He removed the ball cap and scratched his unruly hair that stuck out in too many places. "Why, I reckon I'm jest a good ol' country boy from the mountains o' Tennessee." He perched the ball cap back on his thick head, cocking it to the right side.

"We don't get too many ... like you ... around thees here parts," she teased.

Laughing at himself, he said, "I reckon not, ma'am." He gathered the courage to ask, "What's your name, ma'am? If'n you don't mind my askin'?"

"I don't mind, *señor. Me llamo, Juanita. ¿Y usted?"*

McMurtry's face frowned. "I'm sorry, ma'am. I don't understand Mexican talk."

"Call me *Juanita*. What ees your name?"

Tucking his hands in his patched overalls, he replied, "Robert McMurtry. All my friends call me Mac, and if ya don't mind, just leave off that signor title."

The smile returned to the eyes and mouth. The woman seemed to be enjoying the conversation. "Of course. But I think I weel call you ... *Roberto*. Do you mind?"

"If you kin get me some hot vittles shortly so's I can et, you can call me jest 'bout anything that pleases ya, ma'am."

She laughed a pleasant throaty sound. If everyone was a nice and friendly as this lady, he was going to like this country. He looked into those pretty brown eyes once more and felt the warmth of genuine friendship. He pursed his lips. "Thank ya, *Juanita." She's smilin' at me agin. Wel-l-l now.*

"You're welcome, *Roberto*."

McMurtry had no idea of the meal that awaited him. He ate heartily of the *huevos rancheros* and them green thangs Juanita said were green chilis from Hatch, New Mexico. The very *best* chile in the world, she told him as she offered him a second helping, and then a third. As he finished eating his new-found meal with several extra helpings of chile, he thought *I'm beginnin' to like this dadjimmed New Mexico.*

Having made a new friend and with his belly full, McMurtry turned onto the Clinton P. Anderson Highway toward the Gila Cliff Dwellings and the Heart Bar Ranch. He drove several miles on the winding road that ran adjacent to Copperas Creek. His belly made deep rumbling sounds. As he saw the header canyon come down off Copperas Peak to his left, he felt a sharp twang in his gut. He wheeled into the parking area called Copperas Vista and barely had enough time to grab the toilet paper from the glove box, jump over the rock vista wall and scramble down the slope into the cover of a piñon pine tree.

You ol' gal, Juanita. He grinned, his blue eyes smiling. *You knowed that there chili was goin' to fix ol' Mac, now didn't ya?*

CHAPTER TEN

Wetzel parked his 1951 Chevy truck in the parking lot behind the Gila Cliff Dwellings Visitor Center. He slammed the door as he exited and said softly, "Stay, Montie," to the young Border collie leaning over the side, wagging his tail. The summer day was warming, and he needed to get on the trail soon. His horse was saddled and ready, and his packed gear and food for ten days was waiting for him at the Forest Service barn just down the hill from the Visitor Center. But first, he needed to speak with the district ranger, his boss.

The Gila Cliff Dwellings administrative site was located deep within the Gila National Forest about 80 miles north of Silver City, New Mexico. The highway and associated administrative buildings, residences, fire helispot and crew quarters had all been completed in 1968. The Gila Wilderness, established as such in 1924, was the very first designated wilderness in the United States. Folks were right proud of the fact and even more proud that Senator Clinton P. Anderson had arranged for federal funding to provide adequate year around access into the area as well as funding for building the administrative site.

The U.S. Forest Service and the National Park Service shared joint responsibility for administering the site with a park superintendent who oversaw the pre-historic Cliff Dwellings and the Visitor Center. A district ranger was responsible for managing the forest wilderness area itself. It wasn't a difficult task for the wilderness district ranger as there were no timber operations allowed within the wilderness. This reduced the stress and workload, but recreation, range, and of course fire suppression duties kept the new ranger more than busy.

Wetzel removed his Stetson as he entered the back office complex behind the Visitor Center. He wore the tan uniform shirt with the badge over his left pocket and the shoulder emblem designating he worked for the U.S. Forest Service, Department of Agriculture. Over the larger emblem patch was displayed a smaller half-moon emblem, "Gila National Forest". He passed several fire helitack crewmen gathered near the coffee pot in the break room.

One of the men called out to him, "Hey, *guero.* Why don't you come with us to Millie's tonight?" Fernando Cortez grinned broadly displaying even, white teeth beneath his trimmed black mustache. A short, stocky Hispanic in his early twenties, he, too, had served time in Vietnam. Cortez worked directly for Wetzel and was in charge of the helitack crew consisting of thirty-eight seasonal firefighters stationed in quarters at Gila Center. These men were flown by helicopter deep into the wilderness to suppress wildfires caused by lightning and misbehaving humans. Cortez removed his fire hard hat and placed it next to his coffee cup; he filled the worn cup with hot, scalding coffee.

"Naw. I reckon not, Fernando." Wetzel's face broke into a grin. "I'm headed for White Creek today. Besides it's too much money for them ol' ladies."

Cortez's face registered a change from solemn smirk to one of surprise. "*¿Codo duro?*"

Wetzel laughed out loud. "You still want to keep my dog, Montie, for a few days? And I'm not being cheap, just honest!"

"*Sí,* Jack." Cortez slurped the hot coffee.

As Wetzel continued down the hall to District Ranger Bill Hood's office, he said over his shoulder, "He's out back in the truck. Best take him now; if he gets down to the corrals, he'll want to go with me."

Wetzel shook his head as he thought of Millie's brothel located on Hudson Street in Silver City. Millie had been established there for as long as he could remember. Word was the town fathers had suddenly gotten religion or maybe a conscience. They were finally going to throw her out and shut the lucrative business down. Cortez had referenced in Spanish that Wetzel was too cheap to spend his money there, knowing fully well Jack Wetzel had never been inside the establishment.

He stopped at the entrance to Hood's office. Bill Hood looked up over thick glasses set low on his large, bulbous red nose. His close-cut crew haircut made his large head seem even larger, the ears small in comparison. He quickly looked down and shuffled papers on his desk, but did not speak or indicate for Wetzel to enter the inner sanctum of his small, cramped office. Wetzel stepped into the office uninvited, hat in hand.

"Bill, I need to speak with you, if you have a moment."

District Ranger Hood snorted and threw his glasses on the desk in disgust. He leaned back in his plush chair. "What d'you want, Jack? Can't you see I'm busy? I thought you were headed for White Creek. A bit late, aren't you?"

"Yessir. But my two mules are missing. D'you know where they are?"

Hood leaned forward in his chair, his elbows on the desk, eyebrows arched. "D'you think I don't know? I'm stupid?" He didn't wait for an answer. "Of course I know where they are; I traded them to the Beaverhead District."

Wetzel clutched his hat tightly, careful not to raise his voice. "What on earth for, sir?"

"The new mules will be cheaper to feed and care for ... that's why." Hood spoke emphatically.

"But ... sir. There are two small burros down there in the corral. They're not mules. Hell, they're even little for burros. I can't—"

District Ranger Hood stood suddenly. "Don't you sass me, Wetzel! I'm in charge here, and I made a great trade deal with those *mules*." He turned away toward the window which was directly behind the desk. With his hands on his hips he blurted out, "You don't like it, get yourself another job."

Wetzel's eyes narrowed. He took a deep breath. "They'll be fine, sir." He turned to go.

"Good. I'm glad we understand each other." Hood turned from the window. "You ought to know how to take orders without question." His voice was slightly conciliatory. "They tell me you're a frigging war hero—bronze Star and all that rot."

Wetzel said nothing.

District Ranger Hood placed his hands behind his back, his belly protruding over his belt. "I hired you as general district assistant because you were a ten-point vet." Hood snorted. "And I've *never* supported that war."

Wetzel bit the inside of his cheek. He would not be provoked.

Apparently sensing an upper hand, District Ranger Hood grinned broadly. "You take good care of my new *mules*. Ya hear, Jack?"

Placing his Stetson on his head, Wetzel said, "Yes sir." He strode out of the office.

Back in the parking lot he slammed his truck door closed. He was reminded of the alleged story of his predecessor. Supposedly, when this man had worked for Hood a mere few months ago, he had needed assistance in filling out a fire report. He went to District Ranger Hood and asked for help, to which he was told angrily, "Hell, I haven't time for you. Go look it up in the goddamned manual." Of course, Hood was referring to the huge assortment of manuals the U.S. Forest Service kept for reference on a plethora of management topics from fire to range and recreation issues, just to name a few.

Anyhow, the man somehow figured out how to complete the report, no thanks to his boss. Several months later, he and District Ranger Hood were saddling up at the barn below the Visitor Center and Hood, being a novice rider at best, had mounted a black gelding appropriately called Midnight. Midnight, overly anxious for a field outing, had swung around swiftly as Hood swung on board upright, and he damned near fell off the other side of the big horse. Well, sensing a poor rider and no doubt feeling his oats, Midnight tossed his bit into the air and took off down the West Fork of the Gila River with District Ranger Hood hanging on as if his life depended on it—which it did.

He shouted to the then general district assistant, "What do I do, Roy? *Help!*" As his glasses fell from his large bulbous nose, he screamed again, "*What do I do*?"

Well, ol' Roy, having had his fill of District Ranger Hood, just stood there watching his boss disappear behind a thick clump of rabbit brush along the riverbed. He shook his head slowly then said quietly, "If'n I was you, Bill, I reckon I'd go look it up in the goddamned manual." Then Roy walked up to the office and turned in his time.

* * *

Jack Wetzel rubbed his square jaw as he stood inside the corral. He held a nylon halter with a long lead rope attached. As he gazed at the small jenny burro, who stood in the enclosure gazing back at him, all the pent-up anger left him. Short and pot-bellied, her tail and long wooly ears swished at flies. Her dark, large eyes were soft, eyelids fluttering as she stood casually surveying him. As he walked directly toward her, she abruptly turned away, trotted to the furthest corner of the corral and lithely turned her butt toward him, ready to kick when approached. He laughed out loud, paused and quickly stepped to the side toward her shoulder while tossing the long lead rope over the top of her neck. Tricked into believing that she was roped, she immediately ceased all defensive activity. He moved in close to her neck and secured the halter.

"My God, lil' gal ... you're not any bigger'n a pound o' soap, are ya?"

She looked up at her captor with those sad, soft eyes. The eyelids fluttered. He grinned, "I think I'm gonna like you. I'll call you ... lemme see ... Rosita." He tied her to the corral post. *Maybe I can leave some of the gear? I don't think you can handle even a hundred pounds, kid.* He felt something tug at his back, and turning, he saw the other burro standing close to him.

The jack burro was a few pounds heavier than Rosita, but not by much. His hair coat was a light gray with a white underbelly; a dark hair line ran down the center of his back from the withers and two lateral dark lines proceeded halfway down his shoulders. The burro raised his head, pulled his lips back away from his teeth and brayed loudly. Wetzel couldn't help being amused at the sight. His brow furrowed as he slipped a halter on, thinking of an adequate name for the second burro. He led him over and tied him adjacent to the jenny, Rosita.

Then it came to him. *Chochi*! Spanish for Georgie would be perfect for this little character.

As he placed blankets, sawbuck pack saddles, and panniers on the two burros, he was reminded of his father's tales of old Ben Lilly. The legendary mountain man had hunted lion and bear in and around the headwaters of the Gila River for many years. Claiming to have killed

426 mountain lions and 210 bears from 1914 to 1925, he lived in the wilderness with his hunting dogs … and his burros. Heck, if ol' Ben Lilly had used burros, Wetzel reckoned he could do the same and be damned proud to at that.

CHAPTER ELEVEN

WETZEL TOUCHED HIS SPURS LIGHTLY TO THE BAY GELDING AS HE RODE along the West Fork of the Gila River and passed the trail junction for Little Creek and Little Turkey Park to the west of Brushy Mountain. The alligator juniper and piñon pine trees provided some shade from the heat of the mid-day sun. No clouds were visible in a blue sky. The two fully loaded burros followed passively along behind the bay; Chochi in the lead with Rosita in tow, trotting hard to keep up. A small dust cloud followed their movement along the beaten and weathered Forest Service trail.

Jack's father, Tom Wetzel, had been district ranger for the Mimbres Ranger District in the 1950s. In 1955, he'd been assisting to suppress a large project fire, the Little Creek Fire when he was killed. He left a designated safety zone to go back into the raging wildfire to find a missing firefighter. Jack had never really gotten to know his father as well as he would've liked. He was barely eight years old when his father perished in the fire along with the firefighter he was trying to pack out on his back.

Continuing up the West Fork for another five miles, the heavily loaded burros pulled back, and he had to dally the lead rope around his saddle horn so he could keep moving forward at a decent pace. He still had a long way to go to White Creek Cabin. A rattlesnake buzzed at him nearby from beneath a rock a ways from the running water. The horse's metal shoes clanged against rocks as the horse and burros splashed through the water at one of hundreds of crossings in the trail up the West Fork from Gila Center. Large rock pinnacles spiraled up into the air, towering over them on either side of the tall canyon walls. Ponderosa pines provided respite from the sun as Wetzel zigzagged around the numerous deadfalls in the trail. *The trail crews got their work cut out for them this year.*

He came to where the West Fork turned back sharply south. The trio was almost to the confluence of White Rocks Canyon and the West Fork. He smelled wood smoke in the air. Suddenly, a man in camouflage appeared on his right, spooking the burros. They bolted behind him and his bay reared, almost unseating him. Wetzel whirled his mount to the right and regained control of his horse and the pack stock. He looked again for the sudden intruder and found him leaning against a large Ponderosa pine, his arms folded across his chest. Dressed fully in camouflage shirt and pants, the stocky man grinned as he shouted, "Howdy there, neighbor!"

He dropped his arms to his sides and strode toward Wetzel, who noted the leather shoulder holster underneath his left armpit encasing a .357 revolver, the lace-up hunting boots, the hatless scruffy brown hair and beard. Wetzel gazed into wide, bright blue eyes set on a square face of a solid-built man in his mid-thirties.

"Mister, you damned near caused me a wreck with these pack animals," Wetzel barked.

The man stopped near the bay's shoulder. He appraised both burros carefully, taking his time. "You kin handle these lil' 'uns well 'nough." He guffawed loudly. "Hell, they ain't any bigger'n a minute, are they? Why, back in Tennessee, we'd toss these lil''uns back in."

"They're more'n big enough to get the job done all right," Wetzel spat out.

The hunter took a step back, looked thoughtfully up at Wetzel. "Don't get all dadjimmed white-eyed on me, son." He pursed his lips while trying to suppress a smile on his face. The blue eyes were already smiling.

Wetzel's eyes narrowed. "Don't get ... *what?*"

"Why, you know—all lathered up—hot under the collar."

"I'm not," insisted Wetzel with a somewhat more conciliatory tone of voice.

"We-l-l-l ... I'm sure proud you ain't. I was fixin' to introduce myself."

Wetzel said nothing as the hunter extended his hand. "The name's Bob McMurtry. My friends call me Mac." They shook hands. "I'm the new wildlife officer stationed at the Heart Bar."

"Mr. McMurty—"

"I'd take it as a personal favor if you'd call me Mac."

Wetzel grinned, flicking the reins in his hand. "Pleased to meet ya ... Mac. I'm Wetzel."

The hunter scratched his scruffy brown beard then his thick, unruly hair. "You Jack Wetzel, the ranger that works outta Gila Center?"

"I am. Though my title's not ranger."

"You look like a sure 'nough ranger to me, Jack." McMurtry pointed toward the badge and uniform. Wetzel didn't argue. Mac placed his hands in his pants' pockets.

"You got any law enforcement authority, Ranger Wetzel?"

Wetzel's brow furrowed. "Yeah. Why?"

McMurtry turned on his heel and headed down the trail. "Come on, I'll show you."

* * *

As he trailed along behind the stocky man with the burros in tow, Wetzel saw four individuals. Two played in the water and the others lay or sat along the bank of the West Fork on the north side across from White Rocks Canyon. Several tents were erected, displaying blue and red colors in contrast to the green river bank. Everyone stared at the approaching wildlife officer and the ranger on horseback. They were all naked and appeared to Wetzel to be in their early twenties: two men and two women and none appeared embarrassed to be caught in their natural state of being.

McMurtry walked up to the nearest man standing in the creek. Waving his arm to the others, he hollered, "All you dadjimmed hippies ... gather round here. We need to talk to y'all."

As Wetzel rode up alongside the skinny naked man standing in the creek, he saw the angry expression on the man's bearded face. Stifling his laugh by dropping his head and letting his hat brim shade his eyes, he said quickly, "Mac, I'll handle this—"

But it was too late, the man exploded in a high pitched screech directed at McMurtry. "You ... *you Gestapo!*" He moved in close to McMurtry, body parts flopping about. "How *dare* you order us around?"

McMurtry looked hurt. "Well now, don't go gettin' all white-eyed on me. Y'all look like hippees. You've sure 'nough got long hair." He motioned toward the others. "And all o' ya are standing here on public property all necked an' sech."

"Mac!" Wetzel interjected. "I said I'll handle it."

"Why sure, Jack. You bet." His eyebrows arched, the face feigning apologies but only hiding the jest of the whole incident. "I'll ... uh ... jist round up these here other hippies so's you kin talk to 'em all at once."

The skinny man standing in the river flung his long wet, stringy hair back from his bearded face and screamed, "*Nooo!*" His pale face transitioned to red, his eyes blazed anger. "You goddamned Smoky Pig *sons-a-bitches!*"

He ran around behind Wetzel to get on the south side, screaming profanities as he went. He slipped on the wet rocks in the riverbed, almost fell headlong into the water but recovered as he stood directly behind Rosita. Her head turned and she peered back at him as though he should've known better than to be at that location and range. Her long wooly ears twitched, the soft eyelids fluttered, and she kicked straight out behind with both back feet. A sharp, hard kick, legs fully extended, landed between the man's legs. He let out a blood curdling scream as he fell back, splashing water high in the air. Both burros spooked. It took all Wetzel could do to regain control of them and pull them with him over to the north side away from flailing skinny man.

McMurtry approached the injured "hippee" as the man stood unsteadily on his legs, the cold water rushing past his pale, white body. "Y'all all right?" he drawled.

The man grasped his private parts tightly with both hands. He swayed forward then back as he stood hunched over moaning loudly. McMurtry leaned in to take a closer look, resting his hands on his knees. Shaking his head, he frowned. "Took the hide ... plumb off, I'd say." He whistled low as he took another look and spit to the side. "Best git y'all o'er on the bank yonder and lay down. Come morning you're goin' to be in a world of hurt there, feller."

Wetzel tied his horse and burros a short distance from the group, who were all gathered around the injured man offering suggestions. The man refused to allow any first aid to his damaged parts. Wetzel succeeded in getting the others to clothe themselves after advising them that family groups with children routinely traveled along the main trail of the West Fork. Then he observed a small plastic bag of marijuana hanging partially out of one of the men's pants pocket. He confiscated the marijuana, obtained identification from the man and wrote him a citation for possession of less than an ounce of marijuana. Wetzel asked a final time if he could assist the injured man and was blatantly refused.

As he walked back to his horse and placed the citation booklet in the saddle bags, he could not help but hear the swearing and cursing from the group intended for his ears. He was reminded of a similar incident when he first returned from Vietnam. In dress uniform at the bus stop in El Paso, he was approached by several individuals with long hair. They called him "baby killer" among other things, spat on him, and chanted anti-war slogans in his face. Remembering his past negative experiences when he had resorted to violence, he hadn't hit any of them even though he'd wanted to in the worst way. *Most likely ignorant and misinformed. Hell, he didn't ask to go over to Nam in the first place.*

McMurtry appeared as Wetzel mounted the bay and trotted the horse over to where the burros were tied. As Wetzel secured the lead rope for Chochi, McMurtry said, "I'm sure proud you had the opportunity to meet me, Jack Wetzel." He smiled broadly. Bright blue eyes smiled.

"Likewise ... Mac." Wetzel tucked a store-bought Lucky Strike cigarette in the corner of his mouth and lit it with his silver lighter. The swearing and cursing continued unabated. He offered McMurtry a cigarette.

The wildlife officer shook his head and shouted, "Y'all, *shut the hell up*! If I hafta come o'er yonder, I'll throw the whole dadjimmed lot o' ya in jail." The afternoon quiet returned to the West Fork.

"I heerd you was a good tracker, Jack."

Wetzel returned the lighter to his shirt pocket and reached for the lead rope around the saddle horn. "Fair to middlin', I reckon." Smoke drifted lazily from his nose and mouth.

"I ain't too shabby myself. Maybe we'll track together sometime."

Wetzel grinned at McMurtry. "Maybeso." He swung the horse around and headed upstream toward White Creek. He was beginning to like this straight-forward man from Tennessee.

CHAPTER TWELVE

SEVERAL MILES FURTHER UPSTREAM, WETZEL AND HIS BURROS PASSED NAT Straw Canyon at the confluence of the West Fork of the Gila River. He was reminded of the Gila Mountain man, Robert Nelson "Nat" Straw, who arrived in the Gila Mountains in the 1880s and lived the rest of his life trapping grizzly bears, lions, and wolves in the wild country. Unlike Ben Lily, Straw didn't use hounds to hunt them, only the dangerous, heavy forty-two pound steel traps. By the 1930s, the grizzlies and wolves had vanished from New Mexico and "Nat" Straw had retired to a small farm near Cliff, New Mexico, to spin tales about his adventurous life in a unique wilderness he had come to love.

Old mountain men and grizzly bears filled Wetzel's mind as he traversed the steep, rocky trail above a deep pool of water just a mile or so down the West Fork from White Creek Cabin. The golden sun had set the sky on fire and cool air had begun to flow down into the canyon bottom as Wetzel rode up to the barn and corrals at White Creek. As he rode by, he saw the horse and pack mules belonging to Jim Hawkins, one of his wilderness patrolmen, standing in the corral, their tails swishing at flies. Wetzel rode up to the green exterior door of the cabin leading directly to the kitchen. He ground-tied his bay horse near the door, tied the lead rope for his burros to the saddle horn with a slip knot, and untied the diamond hitch on Chochi's pack. After removing the aluminum food panniers from the sawbuck pack saddle, he carried them inside to the kitchen. Hawkins hollered hello at him from upstairs as Wetzel started outside to get his bedroll and clothes bag.

The White Creek Ranger Station had been built for the U.S. Forest Service by the Civilian Conservation Corps (CCC) in the 1930s. The well-built log house or ranger quarters was nestled in the northwest end of Pine Flat at the confluence of White Creek and the West Fork of the Gila River. Unseen from the cabin site because of its location down in the river bottom, the Jerky Mountains with its dominant peak, Lily Mountain, were due north of the cabin about four miles as the crow flies, with Mogollon Baldy towering due west at 10, 788 feet in elevation about nine air miles away.

The two-story White Creek cabin included a kitchen complete with a large wood cook stove and pantry, a living room with a stone fireplace, and strong wooden stairs leading upstairs to several bedrooms. A handmade wooden rocking chair painted an ugly yellow sat in the living room near the fireplace. A single metal bed had been placed in the dining room near the window that faced south toward the barn and corrals. Wetzel tossed his bedroll and canvas bag containing his clothes and toiletries on the bed. He'd sleep downstairs this time around. Military-style metal bunk beds were arranged in the master and upstairs bedrooms with mattresses rolled atop the metal bed springs.

The sturdy log barn and corrals were located on the south end of Pine Flat about one hundred yards across a broad meadow from the residence. Wetzel walked the distance leading his bay horse and the two burros. The evening shadows were reaching out tentatively to the meadow from the canyon walls. The sun had already set to the west high on the ridge overlooking the ranger cabin. A slight breeze teased the fringes on Wetzel's riding chaps as he walked along, his spurs clinking occasionally on rocks as he strode near a beaver pond. He tipped back his Stetson with his thumb. *God, I love this country. I'm so blessed to work here.* Without warning, Chochi brayed loudly behind him with Rosita following suit. Startled, Wetzel turned quickly to look behind him. Then he laughed out loud, a throaty laugh that could be heard clear across the meadow. Startled by Choci's warning, a white-tailed deer readying to feed on the lush green grass of Pine Flat hesitated behind the cover of thick conifer growth.

Wetzel unsaddled the horse and burros, placing the saddles, pack gear, grain and pellets inside the barn. He took time to walk each animal over to the West Fork, allowed them to quench their thirst in the cold running water, and then turned them into the corral adjacent to Hawkins' animals. After they had rolled and shook to their satisfaction, he placed canvas *morals* or feed bags containing pellets and grain on each animal. He watched them toss the bags and eat hungrily as ominous canyon walls loomed above dark and craggy.

Later, as he and Hawkins ate supper, a full moon lit up the landscape outside the log cabin. The other man slid his chair back from the table and patted his belly. "That sure was a fine supper, Jack. Them biscuits you made was an extra treat."

Wetzel yawned. "Not too shabby at that, huh?"

Hawkins leaned forward, a serious look on his face. "A damned bear broke into the kitchen some time back. The door was busted and ajar when I arrived yesterday."

"Really?"

"Yep. Hope he don't come back soon expecting more goodies like he raided from the pantry."

Wetzel stood. "Not too likely, Jim." He yawned again as he took the dishes over to the sink to wash them.

"I'll do the dishes." Hawkins stood. "You cooked supper. By the way, you'd best move that damned kindling bucket near your bunk bed to the living room before you trip over it tonight in the dark."

Wetzel didn't respond but stood looking down at his feet. He had removed his heavy Packer boots earlier and noticed both his big toes were protruding from his socks.

Hawkins looked at his feet and chuckled. "Jeez, Jack, you need to get married and have them holey socks repaired."

Wetzel grinned. "Maybeso."

It was late when Wetzel awakened in the night. The moonlight poured into the living room through the dust-covered panes of the window near the bed. He sat up, listened intently as he heard the horses and burros milling about in the corrals below the house. The horses nickered loudly and the burros brayed out into the still night. *What the hell?* He knew from past experience not to ignore what his animals told him. A good horse always knew way before a man had any idea if something was amiss. He sighed deeply as he thought of his old scout dog Smoky. That dog *always* knew when all hell was ready to break loose. He'd been infallible during the war.

Wetzel stood near the metal cot, listened to the night sounds, but couldn't discern anything that seemed out of order. He wriggled his toes protruding through the holes in his socks and straightened his frame. His white, long-handled underwear made him feel like a ghost in the darkened interior of the cabin. Yawning, he scratched his buttocks near the buttoned trap door in the back. He sauntered over to the opened window, careful to walk around the kindling bucket in the floor and leaned out the window peering at the corrals a hundred yards distant to the south. The cool night air brushed against his cheek and rustled his thick, disheveled brown hair. The horses, burros, and mules were running back and forth in the corrals, whinnying and braying. *Wish ol' Montie was here.* Wetzel's mind cleared somewhat from sleep as he placed his hands on the windowsill to take a better look outside at the commotion.

Suddenly, his view was obscured. He felt a searing, hot breath directly in his face, and then a loud roar bellowed out in the night instantly breaking the still silence and deafening his ear drums. He saw the huge, shaggy face, the gaping mouth with large, menacing teeth inches from his face!

Wetzel had thought many times over the years of what he would do if a bear attacked him, but he just stood there, his mouth open his feet frozen to the floor. The roar, again, this time much louder. His ears rang; the hair on the back of his neck stood up, and he had a bad feeling in the pit of his stomach. Raw fear!

Spittle flew into his face, and Wetzel broke and ran from the window. He heard the bear come through the window behind him as he turned to run, its heavy weight hit the floor. He slipped in his loose stocking feet losing traction and tripped over the kindling bucket directly in his path. As he went down, he felt the bear swipe at him, clawing his back side with one of its paws.

The buttons on the trap door of his long johns in the back burst and Wetzel cringed, clenching his teeth as he felt the sharp claws cut into his buttocks. He literally dove under the metal bed with the bear right behind him.

Unable to get under the bed, the bear roared as he stood on his back feet in the moonlit room. He landed heavily on the metal bed as Wetzel curled into a tight ball beneath it. Wetzel felt the bear reach around and under the side of the bed with one of its paws, as if searching for its prey. The weight of the bed and bear on top of him made it difficult for Wetzel to breathe. His heart pounded in his ears; another loud frustrated roar from the bear. All Wetzel could think of was why in the hell the damned Forest Service didn't allow them to carry firearms in the wilderness.

A loud BOOM! Then the bear's weight was no longer on the bed and Wetzel was again able to breathe. Another boom, its sound reverberating in the small confines of the cabin, and he knew it was a firearm that had been discharged at close range. He could hear the bear's clawed feet scrambling on the floor, and then the sound of the large body going through the window.

"Son-of-a-bitch!" exclaimed Jim Hawkins.

The breathless Wetzel gingerly crawled out from beneath the metal bunk bed. Hawkins lit the lantern. As the room was enveloped in light from the Coleman lantern, Wetzel felt himself to ensure all body parts were intact. His eyes quickly assessed the room, the upturned kindling box, the rumpled bedroll and mattress, the blood on the floor and windowsill. He turned to Hawkins, who stood staring at him, eyes wide with a heavy revolver grasped tightly in his right hand.

"Son-of-a-bitch," he said again with much conviction.

Wetzel walked gingerly to the window, his toes still protruding from his socks, and looked over his shoulder, "You already said that, Jimmy."

"You reckon he's gone?" Hawkins rasped.

"Maybeso," was all Wetzel managed to say. He wiped his trembling, sweating hands on the front of his long johns and turned to Hawkins standing behind him. "Thanks for ... running him off," he stammered.

A quirk began at the corners of Hawkins' mouth. "That damned bear put a scald on your butt, Jack. Your trap door is hanging open—helluva sight for sore eyes, I'd say."

Wetzel quickly reached down and pulled the trap door closed. "Well, I don't recall anybody askin' you to say one way or the other, Jim Hawkins."

Hawkins laughed, grinning broadly. "Wait'll *this* story gets around the Forest."

Wetzel did not smile. "Maybe the story of *you* having a firearm on duty against Forest Service policy would make an even better story, uh?"

A sobering new expression appeared on the wilderness patrolman's face. "Maybe we can come to a gentlemen's agreement an' keep tonight's happenings between the two of us?"

It was Wetzel's turn to smile. "Maybeso, Jim. Thanks for giving me a leg up tonight. And you were right about the kindling box." He walked into the kitchen holding the trap door in his left hand, opened the cabin door, and stepped out into the night. The air felt cold to his clammy skin. The horses, mules and burros had begun to settle down in the corrals. He breathed in deep then released all the air in his lungs. *Hell of a time not to bring my dog along.*

Hawkins stood framed in the doorway, holding the revolver at his side. "Son ... of ... a bitch!" he murmured.

CHAPTER THIRTEEN

ROGER O'BRIAN PULLED HIS BATTERED SOMBRERO LOW OVER HIS TANNED, weathered face as an early autumn wind began to pick up. *Damn these old, brittle bones o' mine.* He touched the spurs to his dun gelding as they climbed to the top of Goose Lake Ridge. The horse struggled through the rocks and steep grade. AS O'Brian topped out on the ridge, he was glad that he had worn his brown canvas ranch jacket. The cold air stung his cheeks. *Fall's comin', I reckon.*

From atop the long, flat ridge, he looked out over the country as his horse recovered from the steep climb. The Gila River cut a wide swath below him directly to the north, its steep rocky banks appearing much closer than they were in reality. He could clearly see where the river made a sharp bend at the confluence with Sapillo Creek to the east then he scanned westward to the dark crevasse of Turkey Creek and its confluence with the Gila River. Granny Mountain to the north-east beckoned to him as he sat horseback reflecting on the day.

Brushy Mountain was located just north and on the other side of Granny. O'Brian recalled the story of James "Bear" Moore, a mountain man who emerged at the head waters of the Gila River in the latter part of the nineteenth century. Moore, unlike his counterparts Ben Lily and "Nat" Straw, did not care for notoriety, and in fact, much preferred to stay in the wilderness and away from other people. He had been attacked and severely wounded by a she bear. His face was left mangled and twisted to one side for the rest of his life and hence the name "Bear" by the locals. Ol' "Bear" Moore had lived in the wilderness until the time of his death in 1924. His body was found frozen in the snow about six miles from Alum Camp on the west side of Brushy Mountain overlooking Little Creek; they had buried him there. O'Brian glanced at the mountain. *Not so far from here as the crow flies.*

O'Brian had worked cattle most of his adolescent life and all of his adult life in the Gila country. He had wanted nothing more. He felt he could relate to the old mountain men of yesteryear who had come to love this wilderness. He'd had a wonderful life with his wife of forty years until she'd become sick and died of the cancer. His whole world had turned upside down. In addition, the drought and the damn Forest Service were not making life easy for him. *Jeez, it's gittin' hard to just make a livin' nowadays.*

He had missed around ten head of his cows for some time and searched relentlessly for them to no avail. Seeing several cow tracks and fresh manure along the ridge top, he smiled. Following the tracks for a ways on the ridge, he saw where the tracks traversed down off the ridge along Pack Saddle Canyon and toward the river. *More'n likely drinkin' at the river.* Dismounting, he stretched his chap-covered legs, and then checked and tightened the cinch on his horse.

As he rode down to the river taking his time, he thought about his daughter, Maggie, and wished with all his heart she would come out to the ranch and live with him. But she had refused him thus far by citing the remoteness and lack of a school close by as the reasons for her declining the invitation. She married Juan Garcia right out of high school against her father's wishes, and they'd had a son, Robbie, soon after. He was a good lookin' kid, too. O'Brian laughed out loud. His grandson took after his ol' Grandpa.

He was not happy with Maggie working as a waitress in Dottie's Café or her living with that *viejita,* Doña Consuelo Vasquez. The old lady was pleasant enough, but there was something about her—a coldness behind those dark eyes. He couldn't put his finger on what bothered him about her, and it kept nagging at him from time to time. One thing was for sure—he didn't like all that *cuandera* healing crap that she was known for doing around town. Witchcraft is what it was as far as he was concerned. Supposedly, she practiced the ancient art of *cuaranderismo,* treating folks with physical, emotional, and dysfunctions of their soul or curses. He admitted to himself he didn't know all that much, only that the Mexican folk-healing had originated for treatment as far back as the Aztec days before the Spanish conquistadores arrived. Ah, to hell with the ol' witch anyhow.

He got to thinking of maybe selling his ranch and cattle and buying a little place in Silver City to finish out his aging years. Then maybe Maggie and the boy would come and live with him. Damned lonely life he led … that was for damned sure. He knew Maggie prayed everyday for the Garcia boy to return home safe from Vietnam, but O'Brian figgered he was dead. Hell, it'd been two years since he was listed MIA. He admired his daughter for her belief in her husband and her turning to God for guidance. Hell, he hadn't set foot in a church after his wife had been taken from him and him being Irish and a staunch Catholic all his life. Maybe he'd have more time to attend church one of these days.

O'Brian's eyes searched the riverbank for sign of his cattle as he noticed the water level was relatively low, the muddy brown water coursing along lazily to the west and eventually into Arizona where it merged with the San Francisco River. Then on to the San Carlos Reservoir and by the time it reached the Phoenix area it became a dry wash nine times out of ten. He decided to ride eastward along the riverbed toward Sapillo Creek. The cottonwood leaves had transitioned from green to yellow gold as had the sycamores with the occasional hackberries a bright red. In the midst of all the color contrasts along the river, he spotted something ahead that seemed out of place with its surroundings. *What the hell?*

He put his horse into an easy lope and covered the quarter mile quickly. His mouth dropped open as he rode up to the carcass hanging from a large limb of a sycamore tree. *Someone butchered one of my cows!* Whoever it was had used a block and tackle to hoist the carcass high up in the air to butcher it. Rustling had not been a problem in these parts for many years, but O'Brian knew it still continued with a few cows being loaded into a trailer in the middle of the night occasionally. But this—

Riding slowly around the carcass, he observed the imprints of at least one man's boot; the soles appeared to be some type of hiking boot. The man, whoever he was, had traveled up and down the river numerous times from the carcass location. O'Brian reined his dun east, following the tracks at a trot.

He had traveled about a mile when he smelled wood smoke in the air. Pulling the horse up, he turned in the saddle to look behind him, his brow furrowed as he inherently felt something was wrong. Had he missed a side camp trail or someone hidden in the vegetation?

O'Brian thought he heard a soft shushing sound to his left, and as he started to turn back, something impacted his rib cage on the left side. A sharp, burning pain began in his chest and continued to the other side. Something was terribly wrong he just couldn't determine what it was. Then he looked down at his right side. The jacket had been shoved sideways. Blood was spurting out of the hole in his shirt at his rib cage. He followed the life blood exiting his body toward the sycamore tree immediately to his right. A bloodied arrow was deeply embedded in the tree. *What the ... hell?* Blood continued to flow from his body and pain wracked his upper torso. A wave of nausea overcame him as he recognized both his lungs and possibly his heart had been nicked by the arrow.

It was all he could do to muster enough strength to look to his left. His eyes widened in horror as he saw the camouflaged figure, another arrow being fitted into the bow. *Jesus, Mary, mother of God!*

O'Brian slipped from his horse, dead before he hit the ground.

CHAPTER FOURTEEN

ROBERT MCMURTRY SCRATCHED HIS BELLY AS HE STRODE PAST THE BARN to begin feeding the twenty hound dogs chained at various locations adjacent to the barn at the Heart Bar Ranch. The hounds were a mix of black and tans, walkers, and red bones. All were used by the wildlife officer in tracking mountain lion in the Gila Wilderness. Weekend or not, he had to feed the dogs, horses and mules that belonged to the New Mexico Department of Game and Fish. He didn't kill the mountain lions he caught, only tranquilized and tagged them for future study.

He was thoroughly enjoying his new duty assignment in this dadjimmed New Mexico country. The Heart Bar Ranch headquarters sat just off Highway 15 near the bridge where the converged West and Middle Forks of the Gila River coursed under the two-lane highway that dead-ended a short distance later at Gila Center. Gila Center was home to a visitor center, government residences, a large helispot and fire crew quarters. McMurtry also enjoyed being a part of the small community of folks living in the isolated area. Doc Campbell's General Store was located several miles down the river and claimed to be the meetin' place for government and other local folks living in the Gila Center area. Campbell had arrived in the Gila country many years prior and established himself as an outfitter and guide, National Park Service caretaker of the Gila Cliff Dwellings, and then as proprietor of the general store. His two sons and two daughters assisted him in running the store and a lucrative outfitting business.

The Heart Bar Ranch had been a working cattle ranch in the old days with a U.S. Forest Service grazing permit for 1,500 cows within the established wilderness boundary. The New Mexico Game and Fish Department had attempted to re-establish elk in the forest for many years with the Forest Service objecting due to existing large cattle permits and the fact that cattle and elk competed for the same forage. In the 1940s, the Game and Fish Department decided to up and buy the Heart Bar Ranch—lock, stock, and barrel—including the Forest Service permit for 1,500 cattle grazing in the Gila Wilderness thereby eventually giving them the opportunity to re-introduce elk in the headwaters of the Gila in 1954.

A blue 1970 Pontiac four-door sedan turned off the highway and into the driveway. McMurtry quickly finished feeding the animals and sauntered over toward the old ranch house. He broke into a grin as he saw Juanita Flores exit the driver's door, wave at him and open the rear passenger door allowing two young boys to jump out and run at him.

"Mac!" the boys yelled in unison.

"Wel-l-l now, boys." He rumpled their close-cropped dark hair with his big coarse hand. "How the hell are ya anyhow?" Then McMurty saw another woman get out of the Pontiac from the front passenger side.

The oldest boy hugged McMurtry, looked affectionately up at him and said solemnly, "Mother doesn't let us swear, Mac." The other boy grabbed his leg, pulling hard on it.

McMurtry knelt on one knee, eying the boy who had just spoken. "Wasn't planning on lettin' her in on the conversation, Jose. This here swearin's a man's business." His blue eyes twinkled as he peered into the boy's dark brown eyes. "Ya'll know what I mean—just between you, ol' Elfigo here, an' me—our little secret." He winked at Elfigo after placing an arm around Jose.

"I'm sure proud you boys could come an' see me." McMurtry stood peering again closely in the direction of the newly arrived car. "Who's the woman your mom brought with her this time, fellers?"

Elfigo spoke this time, placing his little hands on his hips. "That's mom's cousin, Mac."

Jose was not to be outdone in the passing of state secrets to his friend. "Yeah, her name's Norma."

McMurtry patted the boys on their heads. He smiled as he adjusted his battered ball cap, cocking it slightly to the right side. "You boys gonna help me distract her just like we did with the last one your momma brought with her?"

Jose's face was pensive, his brown eyes serious in the morning light as he pursed his lips. "Mac, me an' Elfigo's been thinking. You got to offer us more'n a soda pop at Doc Campbell's store like last time."

Elfigo stood beside his brother and placed his arm over his brother's shoulder. He nodded his head with furrowed brow.

McMurtry rubbed his bearded chin, turned and spat behind him. Clearing his throat loudly, he said, "I reckon you boys got me in a pickle barrel beings that I sure 'nough need your help." He rubbed the back of his neck with his left hand. "Tell ya what, fellers ... you help me out with this here matter involving your momma, an' I'll take you both down to Campbell's store in my Game and Fish truck and buy each of ya a soda *and* a candy bar."

Jose nodded his head, licking his lips, but Elfigo the youngest demurred. It was his turn to rub his chin thoughtfully then the back of his neck. "I dunno, Mac. Mom was pretty mad at us last time—"

McMurtry knelt in front of both boys. "Now come on fellers! Hep your ol' *compadre* just a little now." He placed a soft hand on each of the boy's shoulders. "Tell ya what, boys." He hesitated, again stroking his scruffy beard. "I'll run the si-reen on my truck as we drive over to the store! Is it a deal?"

Both boys grinned from ear to ear as they nodded the affirmative. The conspirators shook hands as a soft voice floated over to them from the car, "Roberto, are you coming?"

"Yes, ma'am, Juanita. Me an' the boys are headed your way." A huge grin appeared on his square, rough face and the blue eyes were smiling.

* * *

JUANITA FLORES STOOD inside the large screened back porch of the Heart Bar Ranch main house, her *prima* or cousin Norma beside her. The tin-roofed old ranch house was truly a *hacienda* to her with its odd

"U" shape and two small front porches, each leading to a bedroom on either side of a grand living room with a large rock fireplace. Each bedroom had a fireplace of its own to warm its occupants in the cold of winter. A bunkhouse stood near the main house on the river side with the small, old original log bunkhouse to the east, which was no longer in use.

They had finished a bountiful supper of *enchiladas* with a fried egg on top, *frijoles,* rice and salad. She heard her sons playing behind the bunkhouse near the river. The setting sun provided an orange glow to the west as she enjoyed the quiet, the peacefulness of the moment. *Thank you, God, for a wonderful day.*

Elfigo laughed aloud, and Juanita saw him standing near the bunkhouse. He waved at them and yelled, "Come on Norma! Come to the river with me and Jose. *Andelé!*"

Norma waved back and stepped from the porch. The boy ran up to her, grabbed her hand and pulled her with him out of sight behind the bunkhouse and on down to the river where his brother Jose was squealing and splashing in the river.

Juanita smiled as she started toward the screen door that had banged shut just moments before. A voice stopped her in her tracks. "Juanita?"

She turned and saw him step out onto the porch. The wildlife officer tucked his big coarse hands into his overalls. *"Sí, Roberto."*

His bright blue eyes peered at her then looked down at the porch. He started to reply, mumbled something, then said, "Meal sure was fine, Juanita. A man can really enjoy your home cookin'."

She laughed. "Why, *gracias, Roberto."*

"Thing is ... I'd ... uh, I'd like to ... talk to ya." He bit his lower lip and shuffled his hunting boots. "That is if ya don't mind bein' alone with me for awhile."

Her brow furrowed. *"Roberto,* I told you before. It eesn't proper."

"An' I told you, Juanita." Blue eyes met hers directly and held the gaze. "I would never harm you or your reputation. I just want *to talk* without one o' your relatives listening in on every dadjimmed thang I say."

She sighed deeply, placed her small brown hands in the back pockets of her faded Levi jeans. *"Bueño, Roberto.* Let's talk, *mi amigo.* What ees on your mind?"

His gaze dropped. He couldn't find the words. Hesitantly, he licked dry lips.

She stamped her foot. *"Well?"*

He rubbed the back of his neck with his left hand, stuck his hands in and out of the pockets of his overalls several times. "The thang is ... well, I've come to ... to like you ... a whole bunch, Juanita," he blurted out.

She smiled, and then her pretty mouth followed suit. "I like you, too, *Roberto.*"

McMurtry's bearded, coarse face broke into a grin, eyes wide. "An' I like them dadjimmed boys o' yours, too. A whole bunch."

She said nothing, allowing him time to fidget with his cap, first tipping the old ball cap with the "Tennessee Vols" insignia back, and then cocking it slightly to the right.

"Thing is ... I'd like to ... marry you, Juanita."

Still, she said nothing as her heart pounded in her breast.

The wildlife officer turned away, his head down. "I ain't much to look at ... I know that more'n anybody. An' I ain't got much in the way o' material things."

She started to speak, but he held up his hand stopping her. "Lemme git it all out, Juanita. Now that I'm all warmed up and blabbing like a dadjimmed fool."

Walking to the other end of the porch, he stood there looking out over the country near the river as a red-tailed hawk circled above. Then he turned. "I'd be a good husband to ya, an' a good daddy to them boys."

Juanita walked over to him, stood on her tiptoes and kissed him on the cheek. Placing her hands on her hips, her solemn dark brown eyes held his blue. "After my divorce—*que horror*! I thought I would *never* marry *otra vez, pero ...* you are a good man *y creo que te amo.*"

Puzzled, he blurted out, "I don't reckon I understand all that Mexican talk, Juanita."

She threw back her head and laughed out loud. "Well ... ees about *dadjimmed* time you learned, *Roberto*!"

He took off his cap, grasping it tightly in both hands. "Y'all marry an ol' country boy like me?" His hunting boots shuffled on the cement floor of the porch.

She looked at him longingly, understanding fully the true goodness in this coarse rough man, knowing without question that he would always take care of her and her boys. "*Gracias*, for thinking of me and the boys, *Roberto*. I theenk veery much of you, but I need time."

His blue eyes softened. "Well-l-l, you've not said no."

Juanita smiled. "No, *Roberto*. I haf not said, no."

"Wel-l-l, I'll be dadjimmed." It was his turn to smile, and then he kissed her gently on her lips.

CHAPTER FIFTEEN

A cool fall breeze blew in the open driver's window of Wetzel's old truck, rustling the collar of his flannel shirt as he descended the high country of Pinos Altos to Silver City. He thought Pinos Altos probably looked pretty much like it did nearly 150 years ago when gold was first found in the area by the Spanish and Mexican miners. The Anglos had rediscovered the gold in 1859 and for a while it was called Birchville after the first man to find gold there. The fierce-some Apache warriors chased most of the miners clear of the area for several years, but it was re-established in 1866 as Pinos Altos and this time the Spanish name stuck as its official handle.

Simon and Garfunkel were singing, *Mrs. Robinson*, on the radio. He turned the channel knob to the Arenas Valley country western station. Tammy Wynette crooned *D-I-V-O-R-C-*E over the airway. The headlights cut through the inky darkness as the heavy growth of Ponderosa pine trees gave way to much smaller piñon pine and alligator juniper, and then to the cleared residential areas lining Highway 15. The sky, clear and bright with stars and a full moon, made the evening drive enjoyable.

He geared down at the first stoplight, turned right onto Highway 180 or Silver Heights Boulevard and drove south toward downtown Silver City. Several children were playing along the street. A pretty little Hispanic girl with black hair and rosy cheeks looked at him and smiled as he drove by. He returned the smile and waved to her. A slender black man sporting a black fedora on his head and wearing a long black overcoat with a white scarf around his neck strode hurriedly past the little girl, seemingly going nowhere and everywhere at the same time. *Johnny Banks!*

Wetzel shouted, "Howdy, Johnny!" out the truck window. The man smiled and waved as he continued on down the street. A man who many said just wasn't all there mentally. Wetzel grinned. *Maybe we're the ones who aren't all there, come to think of it.* Banks lived with his mother and grandmother, and as far as Wetzel knew, he didn't bother anyone in town. Just made his daily rounds all over town and to the University where everyone had welcomed him as the perpetual student for the past 20 years.

Silver City, New Mexico, had sprung up overnight during the summer of 1870 with the discovery of silver and the ensuing onslaught of miners trying to get rich quickly. They were, of course, followed by the merchants, who had decided early on to build a town that would last. They created the townsite by laying out the streets running north, south, east, and west just like the cities back east. In 1895 and again in 1903, flash floods gouged out a huge ditch in what was then Main Street. Wetzel noted only one original brick building along Main Street still remained. The rest of Main Street had simply been turned backwards, with business continuing through the back door.

Turning onto Bullard Street, Wetzel progressed through the quiet downtown area illuminated by street lights. A cute blonde lady wearing a short skirt walked along the sidewalk holding a poodle in tow. The young woman waved at him seductively. Wetzel couldn't help but look first at the pretty woman, and then the dog. The poodle was dressed up in a little hat with ribbons hanging down, a strap under its chin with a big rose attached on top. Most everyone in town knew it was Madam Millie's way of announcing that a new girl was now in residence, ready for business. Wetzel grinned broadly at the woman and waved at the little dressed up dog. *What had some of the guys on the fire crew said the dog's name was? Lulu?* He chuckled.

As he exited Bullard onto Market Street, he saw the bright neon lights of the Buffalo Bar just down the street; the parked cars and motorcycles signified an active, busy night. The bar's name came from an old buffalo head inside the establishment behind the bar with red light bulbs for eyes that could be switched on and off at the proprietor's discretion.

Proceeding west on Market Street and passing Saint Vincent de Paul Catholic Church, Wetzel paused at the stop sign, looking both ways, then crossed the street and parked behind a dark green Dodge sedan on the north side. The small single-story, flat-roofed apartment duplex stood out in the moonlight. Each apartment was designated by a door and accompanying porch light. Wetzel tipped his hat back on his head, tucked in his new shirt, and polished his Roper boots against his Wrangler jeans. Taking a deep breath, he walked up to the apartment on the right and knocked.

Moments passed. No one came to the door; he reached to knock on the screen door again. The porch light came on, the interior door opened slightly; the security chain was still attached inside. A female voice crackled in the stillness of the night, "*¿Que quieres?*"

"I'm looking for Maggie O'Brian, ma'am." Wetzel hooked his thumbs in his jeans pockets.

Silence. A man laughed loudly from the adjacent apartment and a woman giggled annoyingly.

"*¿Quien es?*" The hard voice carried authority.

"I'm Jack Wetzel, ma'am." He shuffled his boots on the doorstep. "*¿Doña Consuelo Vasquez?*"

The security chain was removed, the interior door opened to display a tall dark slender woman. She did not reach to unlatch the screen door. The dark deep-set eyes were hard and unsmiling, the mouth's thin lips set cruelly in a shallow face that was wrinkled by a lifetime of incessant wind and sun. Shoulder-length gray and white hair was pulled back from her gaunt face. Adjusting a dark, blue sweater to better cover herself, she said sharply, "*Sí.* I am *Doña Consuelo.*"

Wetzel removed his Stetson and smiled. He regarded the simmering dark brown eyes of the older lady. They stood there, surveying one another, and Wetzel felt as though her piercing eyes were peering deep into his soul. "I'm an old friend of Maggie's, ma'am. I'd sure like to see her tonight if it's not too much trouble."

A quirk pulled at the corner of the older lady's mouth. The eyes softened but remained unsmiling as they surveyed him from head to toe. "Maggie's not here, Jack Wetzel." She pointed toward the church. "You'll find her praying ... over there." The door slammed shut, and he heard first the dead bolt, and then the chain lock being replaced.

He just stood there, hat in hand, not sure exactly what to do. Then he remembered his mother's recent words. "You go see Maggie, son. If she needs help ... why, you give it to her, and the boy, too."

Wetzel turned and walked slowly back to the street past his parked truck and crossed the street to the church. He stood silently in front of Saint Vincent de Paul Catholic Church. The church stood out like a medieval castle in the darkened night. The structure's high domes topped with crosses stood as tall sentinels guarding the sacred premises. He was plagued with a feeling of uncertainty, and doubt crept into his head as if he was doing something wrong. He turned to go, thought better of it, and slowly climbed the numerous narrow concrete steps. A soft voice murmured to him as he labored up endless steps to reach the very top. *It's all right, Jack.*

He found the main door open and slightly ajar. After taking off his hat, he stood there in the quiet of the night. The evening breeze toyed at his thick hair and brushed against his cheek. There was no sound inside the church. He took a deep breath of fresh air, exhaled, and stepped into the church. Hearing his heart pound inside his chest, he moved forward toward the many rows of wooden pews. They, in turn, directed him from both sides toward the ornate, white altar at the back of the church. The Stations of the Cross were aligned on both walls reminding Wetzel of Christ's brutal march to his fatal crucifixion that saved all mankind. He saw Maggie kneeling at the altar, her scarf-covered head bowed in prayer in front of the massive statue of the Sacred Heart of Jesus.

Pausing momentarily halfway to the altar, Wetzel felt as if he were imposing on something very private; he lost his courage and turned to leave. Then something caught his eye. The lit candles on either side of the altar wavered and flickered. Then both flickered noticeably again, seemingly beckoning him forward. His brow furrowed, he bit nervously at his lower lip. The candles flickered yet again. He hadn't imagined it; somehow it *was* real. Or was it?

He gained enough courage to step forward again to within a few feet of the kneeling woman. He licked his dry lips and grasped his hat tightly with both hands as he heard her sob silently. Wanting to console his friend, he said softly, "Maggie, it's Jack Wetzel."

She turned quickly, eyes wide and mouth open. As she saw him standing there, she covered her mouth and stifled the sound. Her red shoulder-length hair was pulled back from her face into a pony tail and covered by a bright blue scarf. The slender figure that Wetzel recalled from high school days was filled out, displaying a pleasant transition into womanhood. Maggie wore faded Levis and a white blouse covered by a denim jacket.

Her face brightened and smiled at him. The pretty green eyes were smiling too, as she wiped at her tear-streaked face. "Jack! Is it *you*?"

Wetzel grinned as he peered at his friend. "I reckon so, Maggie." There was character in the set of her mouth and chin and grace in the outlines of her body.

She ran at him, almost knocking him off balance, and hugged him tightly. He held her close, feeling her warmth. "Oh ... Jack—" And she started crying again. Looking up, Wetzel saw the lit candles at the altar were no longer wavering. He felt her body against his, smelled her hair as he pulled her even tighter to him. Then he was ashamed of his thoughts toward another man's wife—his best friend's wife—and he stood back away from her, hands awkwardly at his sides.

They sat outside the church on the top step. The stars twinkled in the sky; the lights of downtown illuminated the skyline. Answering Maggie's many questions Wetzel told her that after his stint in the Army, he had attended New Mexico State University on the GI bill. He'd finished in four years with a degree in range management. After graduation, he had applied with the U.S. Forest Service and received an offer for a job, not as a range conservationist as he'd wanted, but a job nonetheless. And, yes, he liked his job at Gila Center. His mother was doing just fine. And, yes, he'd been glad to help her dad out with the fence repair work on the Forest Service allotment.

"And you, Maggie? What have you been up to since high school?"

"Juan and I married right after you left for Viet Nam." She pursed her lips then spoke, "He got a job out at Tyrone—a good job at the mine. I was pregnant and life was going so well for us, Jack." The brightened eyes dulled, showing her sadness. He felt a lump in his throat as he saw her struggle to speak, but he said nothing.

She sighed looking out into the night. "Then he ... he was drafted and left for Vietnam." She bit her lip, the green eyes closed. "He ... never came back ... didn't even get to see our son." Dropping her head to her knees, she cried out loudly in the night.

Wetzel swallowed hard and softly rubbed her back. The crying stopped. Silence. Still he knew to say nothing.

"If only they'd told me he was dead, Jack. I know it sounds terrible, but at least there would be some sort of ... closure or something. You know, time to move on in life as hard as that would be. But he's been missing in action for some time. I don't know if he's dead *or* alive!"

"I'm so sorry, Maggie," murmured Wetzel.

Green eyes met his. "You're a good friend, Jack. You were always there for me and Juan." She reached out and held his hands in hers. "I pray every day that Juan will return to me and Robbie. I just *have* to believe that he's still alive."

Wetzel put his arms around Maggie's shoulders. Softly, he said, "Maggie, I haven't been to church since I don't know when, but if you help me, I'll pray with you for Juan's return to us."

The breeze gently picked up out of the south at their feet beckoning them back into the small church that sat atop one of the many wind-swept hillsides in Silver City; a beautiful church built centuries ago to serve those in need just as it now served a modern population with strikingly similar needs.

Wetzel stood. "Come on, kid. Let's say our prayers then I'll walk you home."

CHAPTER SIXTEEN

WETZEL DREW DEEPLY ON THE LUCKY STRIKE CIGARETTE AND THEN tucked it into the corner of his mouth, the smoke drifting from his nose. He enjoyed the coolness of the early fall morning. Vehicles passed along Highway 180 behind his parked Forest Service truck. He figured they were headed either into Silver City or the other direction toward Arenas Valley, Bayard, and maybe even south to Deming.

Dottie's Cafe stood along the south side of Highway 180 just north of the turn-off to Hudson Street. It was an excellent place to have a hearty breakfast and served equally well as an ideal meeting place. Wetzel didn't frequent the cafe often, but it had been selected by Deputy Sheriff Don Ramirez for the two of them and New Mexico State Police Sergeant Steve Hunt to discuss business.

He pulled his Stetson lower on his face, shading his face beneath the hat. Dressed in his Forest Service uniform and green jacket with the shoulder insignia, he placed his foot, protected by a dusty Packer boot, on the back bumper of the truck. He watched the uniform-clad deputy step out of his patrol car in the parking lot some twenty feet distant. Don Ramirez had played football with Wetzel in high school and they knew each other fairly well. A tackle on the team's offensive line, Ramirez was as stoutly built as Wetzel was slender. His arms bulged under his uniform shirt and his thick, sturdy legs carried the heavy-set torso well. As the young deputy approached, Wetzel extended his hand. "Howdy, Don. *¿Como estas?"*

Ramirez grinned as he shook hands. "*Bien,* Wetzel. How you been, partner?"

Wetzel liked the firm handshake and the smiling brown eyes that met his own directly.

"Good." Wetzel's cigarette bobbed along his lips from one corner of his mouth to the other. "What's this meetin' all about, Don?"

"Our department needs your help, Jack."

"Oh—?"

A black State Police car pulled into the parking lot, and a short, stocky officer stepped out. He placed his black dress cap on his head over close-cropped sandy hair. Looking very official in his black uniform complete with badge, black leather shoulder strap, belt and holster, black creased trousers with a stripe down each side, and polished black dress boots, Sergeant Steve Hunt made quite an impressive sight that fall September day.

The three men filed into the restaurant, and the bell on the entry door jingled cheerfully as they made their way to an open booth in the corner, Wetzel trailing the others.

A leering voice called out loudly, "Hey ... *war hero*! Been saving anybody lately?" The bitterness and hatred exuded from each spoken word.

Wetzel saw Joe Peach seated at a booth on the far side of the café. He was dressed in a uniform as well, but it was unkempt, the middle shirt button popped loose from the pressure of a huge belly that protruded over his Sam Brown duty belt. One of a handful of officers working for the City Police Department in Silver City, New Mexico, Peach was seated with three young men. Wetzel recognized them as trouble-makers for the most part. Two had long hair down to their shoulders. A bearded man wore camouflaged pants, the others bell-bottom jeans. Wetzel had heard through the grapevine that Peach bullied the prostitutes at Millies and had even attempted extortion on the madam herself.

Wetzel didn't respond but continued toward the booth where Ramirez and Hunt were seating themselves.

"HEY! I'm talking to you." Peach's voice carried across the room.

Wetzel turned and spoke softly. "I can hear you, Joe. I'm just surprised you can talk so well with those dentures you wear these days."

Peach looked at the two officers with Wetzel and then glared at him, eyes blazing with hatred, but he said nothing as Wetzel continued over to the booth where the other officers waited. Ramirez frowned. "What was *that* all about?"

"Nothing … just a little past history is all." Wetzel sat and picked up a menu.

"Oh, yeah. I remember now. You knocked out all his teeth in high school."

The State Police Officer couldn't resist the question, "You *what*?"

Wetzel didn't answer.

Ramirez said, "I'll tell you the story one day when you have lots of time, Steve."

Hunt peered intently at Wetzel. "*Are* you a war hero?"

Wetzel exhaled turning a coffee cup right side up. "Nope."

Ramirez frowned. "Why would you say that, Jack?"

Wetzel thought of Weapons Platoon Sergeant Merrell. He sighed. "Because I was there. I fought with real heroes, and I'm here to tell you I'm not one of 'em."

A startled loud gasp interrupted, followed by the sound of dishes breaking loudly as they came in contact with the hard, concrete floor. Wetzel saw the busboy had fallen, the ceramic dishes he had been carrying shattered into many pieces and scattered in various directions. A boy, whom Wetzel had seen in the restaurant on several previous occasions and had appeared mentally challenged, now lay sprawled on the floor his eyes wide with fright. He could clearly see the boy didn't know what to do. Confusion, fear, embarrassment, and anger totally incapacitated him for the moment.

Laughter came from the booth next to the boy where Peach and his friends sat. The man in camouflaged pants laughed the loudest. "You *stupid* idiot! You better watch where you're going, boy."

Wetzel eased from his seat and walked to the boy. As he knelt on one knee beside him, Wetzel placed his hand on the shaking shoulders and saw tears trickling down the scared pale face.

Arrogantly, Peach said to Wetzel, "What the hell d'you think you're doing?"

Ignoring the question, he spoke to the boy, "I'm Wetzel. What's your name?"

"Will ... ie." The boy sobbed.

"Well, Willie. What say, let's you and me clean up this mess, uh?" Wetzel knelt down on both knees and began picking up pieces of plates.

A belligerent voice bellowed out, "What the *hell*'s going on here? Willie, you—" The proprietor had arrived from the kitchen.

Wetzel spoke sharply, "No harm done." He glared at the man.

Camouflaged pants snorted. "The stupid, clumsy oaf can't keep his feet."

Willie turned toward his boss and shouted while pointing, "*He* tripped me!"

"Why you lying little—"

"I need some help over here, Willie," said Wetzel.

The boy looked at Wetzel busily picking up the larger ceramic pieces and placing them on an adjacent table. He wiped his tears away, grinned and began emulating his benefactor. "You betcha, Wetzel."

As Wetzel continued working, he spoke to the proprietor. "Me and Willie ... we sure could use a broom, dust pan, and a trash can."

The man grunted, turned abruptly, and disappeared into the back of the restaurant.

Hearing soft footsteps, Wetzel looked up into pretty green eyes set in a freckled face, surrounded by a full head of shoulder-length red hair. Maggie O'Brian's furrowed brow and narrowed eyes studied him carefully with new found respect.

"Hi, Jack."

"Maggie! How are you?" He stood holding pieces of ceramic in his hands. He set them on the table, took the coffee pot from her, and handed it to a startled Deputy Ramirez who was now standing beside him. Then he hugged her tightly. Holding her close, she felt so good to him. Deputy Ramirez stood holding the coffee pot a surprised expression on his face. He said nothing.

Peach's cronies stood and headed toward the door. Snide comments and laughter drifted over their shoulders. Camouflage pants kicked several pieces of ceramic as he exited with the others to the front of the restaurant. Peach stood briefly next to Maggie and nodded his thick head toward Wetzel. "What's *he* got that I haven't?"

Seemingly puzzled, she stood without responding and then said softly, "Me, Joe." She swallowed hard as she peered into Wetzel's eyes. "He's got me."

Deputy Ramirez grinned. Officer Peach snorted as he turned to leave. "Screw the both of you!"

The proprietor returned with a broom, dust pan, and trash can. They all pitched in to clean the mess on the floor. Maggie told Wetzel she had been working at the cafe for several months. Ramirez asked after Robbie. Maggie responded her son was doing well, four years old going on five.

"Any news on Juan?" Wetzel asked and regretted it immediately.

The smile faded from her radiant face and eyes. "No, nothing."

A loud voice shouted from the kitchen, "Hey, Maggie. Get to work! If you wanna stand around and talk, do it somewhere else on your own dime."

She retrieved the coffee pot filled their cups. All the orders placed, she turned to Wetzel. "Will you have some time to talk tonight?"

"Not tonight, Maggie. We've got plans for him," interjected Deputy Ramirez. "That is if he'll help us find where your father is hiding out. We need a good tracker."

A concerned look on her face, she said, "The lady who cleans his house weekly reported he wasn't there when she arrived to clean, and it looked as though he'd been gone for at least a day." Her pretty brow furrowed as she looked over her shoulder at the kitchen as if expecting to get yelled at again. "He might've been thrown or something, Jack."

"He'll turn up, Maggie. I'm sure he's okay." Wetzel looked at the two officers and grinned. "He's a tough ol' bird, and he knows the country better'n all of us put together."

Maggie asked they keep her informed and returned to the kitchen. State Police Officer Hunt leaned forward on his elbows across the table from Wetzel. "I was thinking of getting a couple of posse search teams together and a helicopter."

Wetzel thought a minute. "Why don't you hold off on calling 'em out just yet? Go ahead and put 'em on standby if you want, but I don't want people out at the ranch wallering around any sign Mr. O'Brian may have left. I'll head out to the ranch tonight and be ready to check for sign and begin tracking at first light tomorrow."

Officer Hunt rubbed his square jaw. "And the helicopter?"

"You goin' to use one from the Forest Service helitack base?"

"Yep. Already got permission from the supervisor's office to use it in the wilderness."

Wetzel drank heartily of the hot coffee. It never failed to taste good to him in the mornings. "That's great, Steve. It'll only be a few minutes flight time over Brushy Mountain to where I think we'll find him. Can you spare me one of your portable radios?"

"Done. What other resources do you need?"

Placing the coffee mug on the table, Wetzel peered at Deputy Ramirez. "I'd like Don to go with me if he's got the time."

Deputy Ramirez nodded his head. Officer Hunt frowned and asked, "That's *all* you'll need?"

"I reckon so. If I need additional help, I can call you on your handy-dandy walkie talkie."

Officer Hunt grinned broadly as he saw Maggie approaching with his plate full of huevos rancheros bathed in red chile sauce, hot fried potatoes, and flour tortillas. "I think I'm going to like working with you, Wetzel."

Wetzel thought of where the old rancher might have gone and fervently hoped no one had obliterated any fresh tracks. According to the latest weather forecast, the weather ought to cooperate with him while he was tracking the old man. His thoughts were interrupted as Maggie brushed against him placing his bacon and scrambled eggs with green chiles on the table. He smiled a quick assurance into the worried green eyes.

CHAPTER SEVENTEEN

DAWN COULDN'T COME SOON ENOUGH FOR WETZEL. HE'D ARRIVED AT THE O'Brian ranch the previous night with Deputy Sheriff Don Ramirez. His heart sank when they found the rancher's horse standing near the corral, reins broken and missing from the bridle. Then they saw blood on the saddle. It had been a sleepless, worrisome night for both lawmen, but they knew better than to try and track at night.

Wetzel placed a second water bottle in his backpack, secured the top flap and then tied his rolled denim jacket on top. The fall air had a chill to it, and he shivered slightly without his jacket on. But he knew it would be foolish to wear it while hiking uphill. Dark skies turning pink ushered in the dawn as he peered at Ramirez, who swung his backpack up and onto his large shoulders. "We'd best be getting' to it, Don. You set to go?"

The deputy hooked his thumbs in the pockets of his jeans. His worried face showed deep concern. "Yep." Walking over to his patrol car, he reached inside and brought out a 1911 .45 caliber pistol and a Ruger Mini-14 rifle. Returning, he handed the pistol to Wetzel. "Best take it, Jack. We don't know what we're up against out there."

"I never had much use for a pistol in the war, Don. The officers were always trying to get me to carry one on point ... I never did." He sighed. "I've done enough killin' to last me a lifetime. I want no more of it."

"They're reliable enough." Ramirez ignored Jack's latest comment as he closed the door to the sedan. "Just don't forget to take the safety off if you have to shoot the damn thing." He placed his hand on the .357 revolver he carried in a leather holster at his side.

Wetzel hesitated. Then he placed the pistol inside his pack and swung it over his shoulders. He whistled softly and tapped his left hand against his right shoulder. O'Brian's old stock dog appeared, tail wagging, and sat beside him. Wetzel bent down and rubbed the graying head. "Come on, Pepper, let's go find Mr. O'Brian."

Wetzel circled the ranch buildings looking for sign, and easily determined the only route the rancher had followed. They followed the obvious horse tracks leading up to Goose Lake Ridge to the north, laboring up the steep grade toward the ridge top. When they stopped to catch their breath from time to time, the old dog raced past them only to find a shady spot to rest a short distance from the trackers.

On one such break Ramirez removed his pack, took a drink from his water bottle and wiped his mouth with the back of his hand. "You ought to get a *real* job, Wetzel. Come to work for the sheriff's office with me. You'd move up fast in the organization." He pulled his straw hat down to better shade his face. "Me ... I plan to be sheriff of Grant County someday."

Wetzel grinned at his friend. "Naw, I reckon not, Don. I kinda like working for the Forest Service. Thanks just the same."

The deputy shrugged. "Suit yourself. Nobody likes the damn Forest Service."

"Oh, there's a few that do." Wetzel grinned and stood stretching his tall, slender frame. "Not many, now that I think about it, but a few."

"How the hell did you get that job anyhow?"

"I sent in a job interest card to the Civil Service in Albuquerque and a few months later they hired me."

"Seems easy enough."

"It was. Not like the old timers in the early 1900s from what my dad told me." Wetzel shook his head.

"How's that?"

"My father said the old rangers had to take a written exam starting in 1906, and they didn't have multiple choice questions back in the day. Questions requiring written answers like: How many men does it take to run a 10,000-board-foot sawmill? How do you fight wildfires? Surveying and mining questions, too. Then the applicants had to saddle a horse and demonstrate how to ride and pack."

Ramirez grunted as he lifted his pack to his shoulders. "You won't have to do all that shit to become a deputy, Jack."

Wetzel laughed without replying. He turned and trudged uphill his eyes glued to the sign ahead on the hillside.

The sun was high in the sky overhead when they topped out on Goose Lake Ridge and started down toward the Gila River descending Packsaddle Canyon on the north side of the ridge. So far Wetzel had observed two sets of horse tracks: one horse going and returning via the same route. What the hell happened to the ol' man? Had he been thrown and hurt badly and, if so, why the blood on his saddle? The more he thought about the possibilities, the more it made no sense to him at all. He knew the old man well, and it was difficult to believe he had met with an accident, as proficient as he was in the wilderness and horseback.

The descent to the Gila River was extremely steep and rocky, and Wetzel had to pay close attention to any rolling rocks that Deputy Ramirez sent his way inadvertently. Ramirez would yell, "Rock!" and Wetzel scrambled out of the way, the rocks bouncing high in the air down into the steep canyon. It seemed as though it took longer in the descent from the ridge than the ascent, but finally they heard running water in the river bottom amongst the thick vegetation.

Wetzel sat on his heels surveying sign along the sand bar leading to the east along the Gila River toward the confluence with Sapillo Creek. He removed his Stetson and scratched his head. He looked up at Deputy Ramirez. "I don't get it, Don. There's no sign of the horse going up or down the river from here. In fact, there's no sign of any wildlife along this stretch of the river either."

He stood, replacing his hat squarely on his head. Motioning with his hand, he pointed in the direction of Turkey Creek. "Why don't you check for sign a ways down river? I'll head the other way, and maybe between the two of us, we'll find something."

Ramirez nodded. "Okay, Jack." He slung the rifle over his shoulder and turned to look at Wetzel. "You be careful. I can't read sign like you do, but I'd say someone brushed out all the tracks."

"Maybeso."

It didn't take long to find overturned river rocks and other sign left by the horse's shod hooves. Wetzel pressed his lips into a hard line as he strode along the riverbank following the disturbed sign. He progressed about a mile and stood observing an area where he would've ridden had he been horseback. It was obvious someone had used cut vegetation in an attempt to sweep out the horse's tracks. Whoever it was had gotten sloppy or tired of covering the numerous tracks as they had progressed up river.

Withdrawing a Lucky Strike from his shirt pocket, Wetzel watched several band-tailed pigeons fly past him as he lit it with his lighter from the same pocket. O'Brian's old dog Pepper trotted up and lay down beside him. Squatting on his heels, he drew deeply on the cigarette, listening intently, his eyes seeing everything. There was a bad feeling deep in his gut increasing his anxiety. *What the hell's goin' on here, anyhow?* He hadn't felt raw fear like this in his stomach since Nam. *Why would someone want to hurt the ol' man? Hell, he was cantankerous as all get out, but harmless.* The cigarette bobbed back and forth between his lips from one side to the other as he sat quietly smoking and thinking about what the hell he'd gotten himself into.

He observed several blood spots on an upturned river rock that someone had attempted to remove and then ground disturbance of an apparently panicked horse. A shudder ran through Wetzel's body. Still, he sat smoking, listening, not moving. The old dog moved closer, his head up, ears tipped forward facing north. A low growl began in his throat; it ceased as Wetzel placed a hand on his neck.

The faint smell of smoke and burning hide filled Wetzel's nostrils as a breeze picked up from the north and then dissipated as the wind changed direction. Wetzel ground the cigarette out on the sole of his Packer boot, stood, adjusted his backpack on his shoulders, and walked approximately thirty yards to the north side of the riverbank. There he clearly saw the remnants of a vibram boot print beside a cottonwood tree. Only the toe portion of one print remained, the rest had been brushed out. He stood behind the partial print careful not to disturb it and gazed back from where he'd come.

He took his time canvassing the area south of his position, his brow furrowed. *What am I missing?* It was apparent to him that something tragic had occurred at that location, but what? Did the old man fall off his horse and hit his head? Was he pulled off? So intense was his thought, Wetzel only faintly heard Deputy Ramirez calling his name from downriver. He didn't respond. The skin prickled on the back of his neck as his horrified gaze centered on a large cottonwood tree across from him and the broken end of a bloody, impaled arrow shaft.

CHAPTER EIGHTEEN

Officer Joe Peach grinned as he pulled the collar of his blue Silver City Police uniform jacket up around his bulging neck. The stupid son-of-a-bitch had actually agreed to meet at his choice of locations. He maneuvered the police sedan south on Bullard Avenue, and crossed the railroad tracks. Then he turned onto Mill Street under the recently built re-routed Highway 90 and drove easterly past the old train station that had been closed for several years. He continued down the graveled road where there were no street lights. Several huge metal storage buildings stood out eerily in the moonlit night.

Painstakingly, he ensured there were no other vehicles in the vicinity by driving up to Bard Street and then returning to check if any were parked with occupants near any of the metal storage buildings. Convinced there were none, he switched off his headlights and backed his patrol sedan behind the metal building closest to Mill Street out of sight.

He waited ten minutes in the shadows before he heard the sound of an engine traveling his direction. As the vehicle approached his position, he stepped from behind the building and quickly directed it to where his sedan was parked. The unmarked police car came to rest adjacent to his marked rig. A tall, muscular man sporting a crew haircut and wearing a white long-sleeved dress shirt and cotton slacks stepped out of the car and strode to where Peach stood.

"How the hell are ya, Lieutenant?" Peach didn't attempt to keep the sneer out of his voice.

The man peered at him. "I'm fine, Joe." He looked all around where they were parked and placed his hands in his pants pockets. "Why meet here?"

"Why not?"

A frown formed on the good-looking man's face replaced by a hardening of the eyes. "I don't have time for games, Peach. Get to the point."

Peach's large bulbous head leaned forward in the moonlight. "Oh, I will Lieutenant Harding. Rest assured, I will get to the point."

Placing his right hand on the revolver at his side, he said, "My sources tell me you've been investigating me, Charlie. That so?"

"As Internal Affairs Officer, it's my responsibility to ensure that none of our officers are working outside the law."

"I didn't ask you for a job description," snarled Peach.

Hardings' voice was sharp. "You watch your mouth." His hands balled up into fists at his side.

"Hell, I don't mean nothin', Lieutenant; just tryin' to find out if mah job is in jeopardy. That's all." Peach placed both hands in his coat pockets.

Lieutenant Harding folded his arms against his chest. "Look Peach, I can't guarantee anything except that if you cooperate in the investigation, I'll make sure the prosecutor is aware of your help."

Peach said nothing. As if sensing compliance, Harding continued, "Tell me who your contacts are, where the marijuana fields are located, Joe."

"I dunno, Lieutenant." Peach withdrew his left hand from the jacket pocket and scratched his chin thoughtfully. "What I really need is for you to tell me who's been rattin' *me* out."

"Even if that were so, you know I couldn't tell you, Joe."

"Sure ya can, Charlie." "You give me the information I want, an' I share some of the profits with you." Peach grinned at his astonished superior. "What's the matter? Conscience botherin' ya?"

Lieutenant Harding's eyes were on fire. "You arrogant, rotten bastard!" He turned to leave.

"Oh, Lieutenant—"

Harding turned and found himself uncomfortably close to the larger patrolman. So close he could smell body odor emanating from the man. He attempted to step back and away as Peach moved in close, his right hand in his pocket. Lieutenant Harding felt the muzzle of a revolver against his stomach through the officer's coat pocket. The roar of the .38 revolver muffled his response. A hot burning sensation pierced his body followed by an agonizing pain in his abdomen and then his back. Staggering backward, he stumbled and fell to the ground as his legs melted out from under him.

Peach knelt close to the shocked, moaning officer and calmly searched him for weapons. Finding a .38 in an ankle holster, he retrieved it and placed it in his back pocket. Chuckling, he leaned in close to a gasping Lieutenant Harding. "Now ... *you* listen to me, you piece of shit," he whispered contemptuously. You'll tell me everything I need to know or die a slow, horrible death before I'm done with you."

Gritting his teeth, Harding hissed, "Go to hell!"

Peach laughed aloud. "Charlie, Charlie. You mucky mucks never cease to amaze me." Sighing, he pulled the previously discharged .38 from his jacket pocket and shoved it into Harding's groin. Cocking the hammer, he rasped, "Now start talkin' or I'll make you suffer *big* time before you die!"

Lieutenant Harding gazed into the hate-filled eyes of his subordinate. Summoning all his strength, he spat directly at those eyes as he braced himself. The gunshot reverberated out into the still moonlit night followed by subsequent screams of a man in agony.

CHAPTER NINETEEN

WETZEL AND DEPUTY SHERIFF RAMIREZ STOOD OVER THE STILL-SMOKING fire pit. Although the fire had died down considerably, the stench of burning hide staunchly remained and the men stood on the windward side of the fire. Following sign they had hiked up a side canyon heading north from the river toward Granny Mountain. Approximately a half mile in, where the canyon forked, they found the camp. It appeared to Wetzel that one man had been living there for several months evidenced by one particular track found everywhere in and around the campsite—a vibram soled boot, size 10. There were other infrequent tracks of additional men as well at the site.

Finding a stick, Wetzel poked at the near dead fire and bones. A cloud of ashes rose in the air as the wind momentarily changed direction. He directed his comments at Ramirez, his eyes on the fire pit. "Better let Mac at the Heart Bar know of this poaching, Don." Burnt deer hooves lay to the outside of the fire perimeter, and many large bones remained unconsumed by the huge fire.

Ramirez moved out of the smoke as it changed direction in the swirling wind. "Why in the hell would a man burn up game he's poached, Jack?" He slung the Mini-14 rifle on his shoulder. He didn't wait for an answer. "You reckon whoever was here hightailed it out?"

Wetzel said nothing as he continued poking and spreading the pile of bones from within the fire ring. He turned over several large bones that appeared to be from legs and sifted through the pile, shifting ashes and bones out from the center. His stick struck something metallic. He dug more aggressively at the object with the stick. Ramirez moved in closer, leaning forward as he gained renewed interest in the activities of his partner.

Within minutes Wetzel had the object separated and pushed out away from the pile of bones and ashes. Retrieving his canteen, he poured water over it and watched it hiss and emit steam.

"Son-of-a-bitch!" Ramirez scratched the back of his neck with his left hand, holding the rifle sling tight in the other hand. "Why ... it looks like a belt buckle."

Wetzel'a stomach churned as he read, "Silver City Bull Riding Champ, 1951." He cleared his throat. "Mr. O'Brian was wearing that belt buckle the last time I saw him."

"Jeez—" Ramirez swallowed hard. "They burned the body with the deer carcass?"

Tipping his hat back with his thumb, Wetzel released all the air from his lungs. "Don, you need to get Sergeant Hunt and his state police forensics folks in here as soon as possible. Several of these unburned bones are bound to be human." He thought for a moment, his eyes narrowed. "I'll follow the sign on up the canyon. The killer's only an hour, if that, ahead of me."

"I dunno, Jack." Deputy Ramirez's brow furrowed into a frown.

"Don't have much of a choice, Don. Somebody's got to stay at the scene and protect the evidence till help arrives. That's within your purview, amigo. Not mine."

Wetzel tapped his shoulder and the dog, Pepper, appeared and sat near his dusty boots. "Besides trackin's what I do best." He held up a hand to stop the deputy from interrupting. "I'll take the portable radio after you call in. When I figger out where he's headed, you can move whoever you want in for the arrest."

Wetzel removed the .45 pistol from his pack. Ramirez watched him check the magazine, insert it, charge the weapon, and place the safety on, as he called in their position and what they had found to Steve Hunt with the New Mexico State Police. He tucked the pistol in the belt at his back. Shouldering his backpack, he reached in his shirt pocket and withdrew a Lucky Strike from the pack. Lighting it, he drew smoke deep into his lungs and then exhaled. *My God, Maggie's goin' to take this hard.* He heard Ramirez finishing his radio conversation with the State Police as he looked up in the direction of Granny Mountain and the steep, difficult hike ahead.

Handing him the radio, Ramirez said, "You be careful, Jack, and keep us informed."

Wetzel nodded. "There's a spring on up the canyon. They call it Rock Spring. I'd say someone has marijuana planted up there. Most likely they've been taking it out along the river and Sapillo Creek to Highway 25. You might have a deputy check for sign."

"It's a bit late in the year for harvesting."

"Maybeso. But our killer's here an' he's still tending something worth killing for."

"Yeah, you've got a point." Ramirez shook his head.

Wetzel tossed his cigarette into the pile of smoking ashes and turned to stride up the canyon with the old dog at his heels.

The canyon proved steep and rocky as it ascended toward Brushy Mountain, but it was easy to follow and indicated at least some travel in the past. For the most part, the killer kept to the numerous rocks when traversing the canyon, not leaving many tracks, but there were several along the way with other telling sign for the determined Wetzel to follow and to know he was still following the size 10 vibram soled boots.

It was past mid-afternoon when Wetzel found what he was looking for—black irrigation pipes under the vegetation adjacent to the trail. Upon closer inspection, he saw the smaller feeder pipes leading to where marijuana plants had been harvested. He squatted on his heels behind a gambel oak tree, fear knotting his stomach. Clutching the cocked .45 pistol with the safety off in his right fist, he moved slowly forward to where he remembered the spring was located, the old dog in front of him. He closely monitored the dog's ears and overall demeanor to alert him of possible ambush. Knowing he was dealing with someone with bush skills similar to his own or even better, maybe a hunter or ex-military, he couldn't be too careful.

Wetzel found the spring without incident and slowly canvassed the entire area feeling more and more secure that the killer had left the area. He found an extensive network of plastic pipe coming from the spring and fanning out under the local vegetation to alleviate any possibility of sight from the air. He estimated possibly a thousand plants or more that had been harvested from the site.

He heard the helicopter long before he saw it, flying low over the river to the east headed to rendezvous with Deputy Ramirez. The killer would know something was up. What would he do? What the hell was he up here for anyhow? It appeared all the marijuana plants had been harvested and hauled out. He called Ramirez on the portable radio and advised of his findings and that the killer had continued north, turned onto the Forest Service trail coming up from the river near the top of Granny Mountain, and was headed westerly along the ridge top. Wetzel memorized the boot print he followed in the dusty, maintained trail.

Large alligator juniper trees near the trail marked with the Forest Service heel and sole blaze provided unnecessary shade on a cool September day. Wetzel's woodsman stride carried him quickly along the old Forest Service Trail as he followed the easy sign. Grama grasses swayed in the breezes atop Granny Mountain as the piñon pine, gambel oak, and occasional Ponderosa Pine stood steady in the wind. Intermittent mountain mahogany bushes rustled in the occasional wind gusts. Then suddenly there were no more visible tracks in the trail.

Craggy Granite Peak and the Forest Service Lookout tower stood tall against a cloudless blue sky to the northwest. Brushy Mountain, where an old, tired "Bear" Moore had died many years ago on its snow covered slopes, lay to the north. Wetzel knew the trail junction about a half-mile distant led either to Granite Peak itself or down into Turkey Creek in a westerly direction. He'd surmised the killer was headed for Turkey Creek and then south to another marijuana field. The lack of sign in that direction baffled him and made him suspicious of ambush again.

Pistol in hand with the old dog close, he circled for sign where the tracks ended and easily found where the killer had abruptly dropped off the ridge on the northwest side of Granny Mountain headed straight down into the steep and treacherous Sycamore Canyon. Why in the hell would he do that? It made no sense at all, but the sign did not lie. It was hard as hell for a man to hide his sign while descending into steep territory. Would the killer take the canyon down to the river? If that had been his intent, he could've headed back to the river following the Forest Service trail from atop Granny Mountain.

As Wetzel tucked the pistol back in the belt against his back, he contemplated on what to do. He had only a few hours of daylight left and had no intention of tracking at night. Squatting on his heels,

Wetzel rubbed Pepper's head; the old dog's eye lids closed momentarily, his tongue protruded as he gently panted enjoying his new master's attention.

"Wel-l-l ... Pepper ol' buddy, there's only one way to find out where this guy is headed." The old dog turned his gray head toward him and waited for instructions. Wetzel narrowed his eyes as he peered down into the steep canyon. He murmured, "He's good, boy, an' I'm bettin' he knows we're after him."

The old dog stood slowly, carefully stretched his gaunt frame, shook himself, and trotted down into the canyon with a surprised Wetzel scrambling to his feet to follow him down the steep incline.

It took the better part of an hour to traverse the steep canyon. Intent on following the tracks, Jack barely noticed the sun setting. They stepped onto and around boulders and rocks to ascend the other side of Sycamore Canyon following obvious sign left for pursuers to follow. Wetzel kept the dog near him as he scanned the steep hillside they were ascending. As he labored up the incline, perspiration ran down his face and neck. Breathing hard, he stopped just beyond where the brush began and there were no large boulders or rocks to navigate around.

Peering intently up the hillside where the sign led, his sharp eyes saw nothing. No movement. No discernment of colors or shapes that seemed out of place in the landscape. He breathed a sigh of relief as he removed the pack from his sweaty back and lowered it to the ground beside him. It was then he noticed the old dog. Pepper leaned into the wind; his ears pointed up at attention, a low growl escaped his mouth. *Shit!* Wetzel forced his frozen body to react. As he dove to the ground reaching for the pistol, an arrow hissed overhead where his chest had been a second before.

Frantically, he gripped the pistol, pointing it uphill and pulled the trigger. Nothing happened. *Dammit!* He'd forgotten to release the safety. He did so quickly, re-positioning to fire. Pepper yipped loudly, and then whined shrilly as Wetzel saw he was impaled with an arrow that had entered his left side.

A flitting movement of camouflage appeared in the trees. He fired two rounds from the .45 at the hillside above him as he grabbed the old dog and dragged him behind a nearby gambel oak tree. Chill ran through him. The arrow shaft resembled the one left in the cottonwood tree at the murder scene. It had not exited completely as it had struck a rock on the far side. After several attempts to break the shaft, he finally did so, and then swiftly withdrew the bloody arrow from the old dog's torso.

Wetzel's mind clouded. To his horror, images that had been shut out from his memory for a long time suddenly appeared. Loud explosions, dying and disfigured soldiers, screams, the blood—so much blood. Then fear overwhelmed him. He struggled to erase the images, to send those skeletons back into the closet where he knew they belonged. *Not now, for God's sake.*

Trembling from the adrenalin rush, he tried to stop the blood gushing from the dog's side. Pepper was hit behind his shoulder where the jagged wound indicated a lung and possibly heart pierced by the arrow. The old dog emitted a low whine, his tired eyes locked on his new-found friend's face. The eyes fluttered, the lids finally closed in death.

Wetzel lay there cradling his savior in his arms behind the oak tree. *Oh, my God. Pepper, I'm so sorry, boy.* Tears ran down his cheeks. His teeth clenched, eyes hardened as he held the old dog even closer. The large, dark shadow of Brushy Mountain loomed overhead and extended its tentacles down the rock-strewn slopes into the recesses of Sycamore Canyon. Night fell on the two friends.

CHAPTER TWENTY

McMurtry maneuvered his Game and Fish truck south along Silver Heights Boulevard and turned onto College Avenue headed west. Western New Mexico University beckoned to him from atop a high knoll further west. He slowed down as he neared the Gila National Forest supervisor's office and parked the truck along the street in front of an old, white two-story house located across from the green government office complex.

Scratching his scruffy beard, he pondered if he should go inside. He wasn't afraid. It wasn't that atall. He was just wary of the dadjimmed hippy place. Ah, hell, he might just as well get it over with. Shrugging his massive shoulders, he stepped out of the truck and adjusted the old ball cap on his head, canting it just slightly to the right. Then placing his hands inside his worn, patched coveralls, he strode up the worn, cracked concrete sidewalk to a house that appeared extremely narrow in proportion to its height.

There he hesitated momentarily as he read the sign near the ornate glass door to the establishment, "Massages — A Far out Experience". Rolling his eyes, he shook his head as he stepped up on the stoop porch and to the front door. He rang the door bell and waited impatiently for someone to come. The thought ran through his mind to leave, and he turned to step off the porch.

But he didn't have long to wait. Soft footsteps sounded nearby, a shadowy figure appeared on the other side of the glass door; it opened, creaking on rusty hinges. A smiling woman with lots of teeth answered the door. "May I help you? Mister—?"

McMurtry took his cap off hurriedly, grasping it in his big hands. "Well, ah … McMurtry's mah name, ma'am."

A grin widened and her big, brown eyes smiled. Her long, dark hair was pulled tightly back on her head and trailed down her back to well beyond her thin waist. A fresh flower was tucked into her hair on the right side above her ear. She was wearing a white cotton blouse. Numerous beads of various bright colors adorned her neck and flat bosom. A beige, cotton skirt flowed down from her waist to her ankles. The toenails of her bare feet, painted red and green, protruded from under the skirt.

"Won't you come in, Mr. McMurtry?" She opened the door to its full width and stepped back to allow entry.

McMurtry shuffled his boots before answering, "Thank ya kindly, ma'am. Believe I will." He stepped into the interior of the house, grasping his cap. He scanned the tiny parlor with wooden floors; a mattress lay on the floor in one corner, the only furniture in sight. Directly in front of him, a steep, wooden stairway wound its way up to the second floor of the house.

As his eyes darted quickly around the room, he was unable to ascertain from where he stood if there were any other rooms adjacent to the parlor. Licking his lips, he said, "I … uh … understand y'all do … uh—"

The woman's teeth were displayed again as she looked him over. "Massages?"

The sweet smell of incense quickly filled his nostrils. He thought maybe sweet for some but sickening pungent for one so used to the fresh smells of the clean air outdoors.

McMurtry crushed his cap tightly with both hands. The insignia "Tennessee Vols" on the cap cried out for him to cease. "Yes, ma'am," he replied thickly.

Her soft brown eyes searched his. "For … yourself, Mr. McMurtry?"

He stepped backward instinctively from those piercing inquisitive brown eyes, and damn near fell down as he tripped over his own feet.

"No!" His short laugh had a quiver in it; he shook his burly head. "Not for *me*, ma'am. I ain't into them dadjimmed massages or sech goin's on."

The woman waited for him to continue; the smile was gone.

McMurtry looked furtively around the room. "What I mean to say, ma'am, is mah girlfriend—well, Juanita told me she'd like one o' them m*a*ssages that y'all hippies do." He couldn't decide if he wanted to put his cap in a back pocket or hold it.

"*So* ... you would like to set an appointment for your girlfriend to have one ... *o' them dadjimmed massages*. Is that the short of it, Mr. McMurtry?" The brown eyes smiled.

He stood unsteadily on his feet, glanced at the circling staircase, the mattress on the floor in the corner, and again for any possible adjoining room on the first floor. Finding none, he retorted, "Yep. I reckon that's about it, ma'am." Turning slightly to his left, he saw what he had been looking for—a small doorway behind the staircase. It was covered with long strings of several sized beads of various designs reaching to the floor.

The woman stated she needed to jot the necessary information down and would return in a moment. As she disappeared through the doorway of dangling beads clinking gently together, McMurtry noticed again the faint scent of incense and other unfamiliar scents from things he imagined hippies most likely concocted.

She returned, scheduled the appointment and accepted payment from him. Thanking him for the business, she opened the door. A half-grin pulled at the corner of her mouth. "You're not from around here, are you, Mr. McMurtry?"

It was his turn to grin as he stepped onto the concrete porch stoop, placing his ball cap on his head. "Somehow, I've heerd that before, ma'am." They both laughed loudly. "My friends call me, Mac."

"Well, Mac, my name's Naomi. And it's been a *real* pleasure meeting you."

* * *

McMurtry reached his parked truck, feeling mighty proud of himself for completing what he considered to be a daunting task. Breathing in the fresh fall air, he opened the door and began to climb in when he heard a scream. Frowning, he listened intently. Another more muffled scream came from behind an abandoned house farther down the street. A dog barked. He jumped in and drove his truck down the street, sliding to a stop in front of the old dilapidated house.

Running through the tall weeds and grass and around to the rear of the house, McMurtry observed a tall, good-looking blonde woman in a mini-skirt backed up against the side of the house and a large, powerful-looking man grasping her by the throat. The man wore a Silver City Police uniform and carried a sidearm. *What the hell?*

Still grasping her by the throat, the man pulled her toward him and then slammed her head hard against the wall. "You'll do as I say, damn you!"

McMurtry shouted, "Hey!" and lurched forward, still unsure what to do as it involved a police officer. It was then he noticed the little dog —a poodle—all dressed up with a cute hat on its head secured with a ribbon. The dog snapped at the officer, growled, then bit him directly on the leg. The enraged officer shouted profanities at the little dog, who kept dodging kicks aimed in its direction without losing the tiny hat perched on its head.

The young woman pulled free from the grip on her throat and shouted, "Stop it! Joe, you stop … right now." The policeman hit her square in the face, knocking her to the ground, turned on the dog, and swung his leg back to kick it. His red face with bulging eyes turned toward McMurtry, who now stood beside him. He hit the policeman hard in the face, knocking him to the ground. Reaching down, he retrieved the revolver from the officer's duty belt and placed it in a front pocket of the coveralls. He blurted out, "Just … what the hell's goin'on here?"

The dazed officer struggled to get up. He weighed more than McMurtry but wasn't as strong. He spat. "You stay the hell outta this, you goddamned country hick!"

Looking at the officer's name plate on his uniform shirt, McMurtry said dryly, "Well now, Officer Peach, that there is the *wrong* answer," and he hit him again this time on the point of the chin knocking him senseless. Quickly, he turned the stunned officer on his stomach and handcuffed him behind his back with cuffs from the policeman's duty belt. He didn't bother to secure a key to double-lock them.

The woman had retrieved the little poodle and leaned heavily against the building.

"You all right, ma'am?" rasped McMurtry as he searched for additional weapons, finding a .38 caliber revolver in an ankle holster. This he placed in a back pocket as he stood, breathing hard.

Her eyes wide with fright, she wiped blood from her mouth and nose with her trembling left hand while holding the poodle with her right. Looking at McMurtry, she nodded.

He said, "I'm a Wildlife Officer with New Mexico Game and Fish Department, ma'am. Why did that officer hit ya?"

"I'd rather not discuss it, if you don't … mind," she stammered.

McMurtry stepped closer. "I reckon ah *do* mind." He waved his hand sharply toward the handcuffed officer on the ground then in her direction and shouted, "I just beat the hell outta 'nother peace officer and arrested 'im after I watched *him* assault *you!*" He took a deep breath and lowered his voice. "Now, you're goin' to tell me why that is."

"He'll kill me if I talk."

"He ain't gonna kill nothin'. He's goin' to jail—now talk!"

Her pale blue eyes looked at him momentarily and then down at the ground before she spoke. "I work for Millie." She looked up to see if he understood. "You know … at the … house over on Hudson Street —," "an' Joe's been taking money from Millie for some time now. A lot of money; that an' takin' *me* for free whenever it pleases him."

McMurtry said nothing and made no judgments.

She licked bloodied lips and wiped at a bloody nose. "I told him today I wanted nothing more to do with him—"

He completed the sentence, "An' he didn't cotton to that, did he?"

"No."

McMurtry pointed to the still unconscious police officer lying on the ground. "I'm goin' to the truck, ma'am, to get my notepad, and call for transport assistance from Grant County Sheriff's Office on the radio." His clenched his teeth, "If'n I ain't back an' he tries to git up, why, you turn that lil' ornery dog loose on 'im and holler at me, you heah?"

The woman nodded as she cradled the little poodle closer in her arms.

As he strode away, McMurtry muttered, "It ain't right, dadjimmit. Hittin' a woman. I don't care if'n he is a peace officer. The low-down, yeller sumbitch."

He was still muttering as he reached in his truck for the Game and

Fish radio microphone. "Why, there's no call for it. None atall, an' fixin' to hurt that lil' dog, too!"

CHAPTER TWENTY-ONE

Wetzel clutched the .45 caliber pistol in his blood-stained hand. He carefully snaked his way up Brushy Mountain following sign left by the assassin. It was a hot day for September, and he sweated profusely as he crawled amongst the dense shrubs and trees. However painstakingly slow, he had determined not to fall into a death trap again. His clothes had been drenched in the dog's blood. At first light he'd attempted to contact law enforcement authorities but was unable to get out on the portable radio.

A mourning dove cooed high on the mountain. Wetzel recognized a ladder-backed woodpecker, an uncommon resident in the Gila wilderness, as it hammered away high on a dead limb of a gambel oak tree. He reckoned it was mid-morning due to the position of the sun in a blue, cloudless sky. The hot sun blazed down on him as he worked his way up the south slope of Brushy Mountain. The dense vegetation provided excellent cover for the killer and slowed Wetzel's movements considerably.

Upslope winds increased in velocity. Wetzel shoved his stained Stetson farther down on his head to keep from losing it. The more he questioned why the killer had chosen to travel to Brushy Mountain, the more it made no sense at all. To be sure there were Forest Service trails that traversed the north side of the mountain and led to the river as well as to Little Creek, and even Turkey Creek, the destination he had initially envisioned the killer using. But as the saying went, it was the long way around the barn. Again, it made no sense to him.

Two things happened simultaneously. He heard Don Ramirez calling him on the portable radio, and he smelled smoke.

Scrambling mid-slope, he secured the radio from his pack and called the deputy sheriff. He heard Ramirez answer him, asking if he was all right.

"I'm okay, Don, but the dog's dead."

"What the hell happened?" Ramirez asked.

"He took an arrow meant for me." Wetzel reached to further secure his hat in the wind.

Ramirez quickly responded, "We need to get you out of there, Jack. Is there a helispot up on Brushy Mountain somewhere we can use?"

"There is ... but I'm not sure where the killer is." Wetzel heard a helicopter approaching. Peering down slope from his position, he observed heavy smoke and flames below him. *What the hell?*

Ramirez's strained voice broke his train of thought. "Where *are* you, Jack?"

"Maybe half-way up South Brushy from the river." He concentrated his gaze solely on the growing dense smoke and flames directly below his position.

The helicopter circled below him, disappearing momentarily from time to time in the thick, dense smoke. The deputy sheriff's radio transmission came across garbled and unreadable. Then, "... setting fire below ..."

Before Wetzel could respond, he heard the gunshots cracking out in the morning air. *A high powered rifle!* More rifle shots rang out. Wetzel could see the helicopter now. It was trying to gain elevation quickly.

"Jack! Some son-of-a-bitch is shooting at us! Break."

Again, shots rang out.

Ramirez's excited voice, "We're hit!" Then: "The pilot's been hit! We're headed back to Gila Center if we can make it. Jack, get the hell outta there. *Now!*"

Wetzel murmured "10-4," but his mind was elsewhere. A chill ran up his back. *Did the killer circle around below me during the night while I slept*? Could he have done that? If so, Wetzel had a new-found respect for his dangerous adversary. And where did he get the rifle? Did he have it with him and the bow as well ... or was there more than one assailant? His mind reverted back to the sign he'd been following. No, there had been only the one set of tracks. He was sure of it.

The small fire below him was gaining in size with several huge smoke columns billowing up into the sky, which was now rapidly turning gray. The fire, fueled by the strong winds, was taking advantage of the steep slope and continuous fuels. Wetzel shouldered his pack and quickly assessed there was no close safety zone to run for. The raging fire began a strong run straight up the drainage where he stood; he was unsure of where to go for safety. An inner voice screamed at him to to make a run for it.

Turning his back to the fire below him, Wetzel jogged to the east hoping to get out of the chute and the serious danger it posed to him. After fifteen minutes or so, he paused in his flight. The fire had hooked well around his right flank and it was now running hard up the entire slope of South Brushy. He had nowhere to go to escape the raging inferno below him. *Run, Jack ... run like hell.* But he simply stood there, eyes wide, watching Hell a thousand times over coming straight for him.

It was then, in total despair as he knew he couldn't escape the inferno and death, he heard the voice. At first, he thought he imagined it. Then again, the soft voice spoke, "Jackie. It's me, son."

A chill ran up Wetzel's spine. He peered through the smoke and haze to where the voice had come. *Yes!* A hundred yards or so upslope from where he had stopped jogging, a man stood motionless, standing easy. He wore a battered, dull red fire helmet, the old style from the 1950s, a khaki long-sleeved shirt, and faded blue jeans. Who could it be? Keeping his eye on the man, Wetzel ran toward the tall figure. He stumbled over dead fall and rocks as he kept the man in sight.

Somewhat closer he recognized the bronzed face under the old fire helmet. *His father!* No, it wasn't possible. He stopped in stride and swallowed hard, his chest heaving from the exertion of running up the steep slope. No. *No!* It couldn't be ... his father had been dead since ... how long ago? Burned to death saving another firefighter on the Little Creek Fire in 1955.

The figure turned uphill, waving his arm. "This way, Jack. Hurry, son."

Wetzel stood, frozen in his tracks. "Dad?" he whispered.

The man turned and smiled. "We haven't much time, boy." The

smile faded and a hard look replaced it. "You follow me, and you run hard!"

Wetzel ran past Murdock's Hole and sprinted straight uphill on Upper South Brushy, the pack bouncing on his back. He fell, got up and fell again, but somehow managed to keep on running, his father just ahead of him. Smoke completely filled the air, burning his lungs and his eyes. The intense heat from the billowing flames licked at his back. The searing heat burned his overworked, struggling lungs.

Tripping over a large deadfall, he fell headlong; the .45 pistol in his belt gouged his back. He struggled to his knees. The air was intensely hot. He couldn't breathe. Flames encompassed whole trees and a constant roar deafened his ears. *Dad! Please don't leave me.*

He stood, looking for his father, not knowing which way to run. A calm voice said, "Over here, Jack." Then through the dense smoke and searing flames, he saw his father again. A tall, good man, looking out for others just as Wetzel remembered him as a boy.

"I'm coming, Dad. *I'm coming!*" Wetzel willed himself to run. Made his failing lungs work, his rubbery, wasted legs perform when there was seemingly nothing left to give.

A large snag fell on his left as the conflagration raged all around him. Trees erupted in flames as he sprinted past, all the while behind his father on up through the South Brushy slopes to the summit of Brushy Mountain itself.

He lost sight of his father's broad back in the thick smoke but caught sight of him again. The whole world was as though in slow motion. Wetzel felt he was a spectator watching what was going on rather than being in the middle of an unforgiving inferno; an inferno that sapped his strength and every ounce of air from his failing lungs.

Still, somehow he ran. Much more slowly, but he followed his father to the crest and beyond. Then he fell heavily, rolled and came to rest against a large boulder that lay about fifty yards from the summit. Wetzel crawled behind the boulder. He dug down to mineral soil with his hands and placed his face next to the cool soil. Smoke permeated the air, but the heat was not as intense as it had been moments earlier. Gasping for air, he called out weakly for his father.

The fire continued to rage on the south side of Brushy Mountain but had spent itself at the summit of the ridge. Wetzel called out again for his father. Nothing. Visibility was much better now, but he saw nothing of his dad. He lay back on his stomach sucking in fresh air close to the ground. His lungs ached, his chest heaved. Fire talk crackled on the radio in his pack with Forest Service wild land fire personnel coordinating an attack on the demon that had been unleashed on an unusually hot, windy September morning.

Wetzel sat against the boulder still breathing heavily. With stinging eyes, he looked from the north side of Brushy Mountain where he lay toward the large cut in the landscape which he knew to be Little Creek far below him. Then he scanned the vast, black, charred terrain to the west—thousands of acres that had been utterly consumed by the Little Creek Fire of 1955. And he did something he hadn't done for many years; he broke down and cried.

CHAPTER TWENTY-TWO

Ellen Wetzel was thoroughly enjoying the picture-perfect fall day at her small place nestled in the Mimbres Valley. Barely past forty-five years of living, she still could command a man's attention in her faded jeans, boots and a worn pull-over sweater. She placed a steaming, hot cup of coffee in front of her son. "Tell me what happened up on the mountain, Jack."

He quickly recounted what had transpired on Brushy Mountain. That the killer had escaped after the fire was set and hadn't been caught; the wildfire had been suppressed after the area was secured. Further, he spoke of his father appearing, calling to him and saving his life. As he spoke, his hazel eyes brightened, his young, strong face beamed with admiration he felt for his dad. Ellen said nothing, but she smiled at her son.

Jack hesitated. "Why? What is it, Mom?"

She sighed as she turned to pour herself a cup of coffee. "He … called you … Jackie?"

"Yes, he did," Wetzel said emphatically.

Sipping at the hot cup, she finally set it on the kitchen table and sat. "Well, I'm not surprised. He always called you that when you were a little button."

The room was still with neither mother nor son saying anything. The sunlight from a clear New Mexico fall day passed through the kitchen window, warming them as they sat quietly enjoying each other's company. Jack looked into her eyes, his hazel eyes locked with hers. "He *was* there, Mom." He looked out the window. "And he saved my life."

"I believe he did at that, son." She reached over and patted his hand. "You see … I had a dream that day … the day of the fire, and I heard him call to you." The smile returned to the pretty face. "And he *did* call you Jackie."

"*What*? How could he do that?" His brow furrowed, and he licked at dry lips. "How could he appear to me *and* to you at the same time, Mom?"

She said nothing for several moments, placing her elbows on the kitchen table and leaning forward. "Does it really matter *how*, Jackie?"

He sighed heavily. "No, I reckon not. What's important is that he was there for me, and I'll never forget it as long as I live."

"That's my boy!"

She blinked back tears. How she missed her husband and best friend. How many times over the past eighteen years had she struggled, desperately living without him there at her side? Not a day went by that she did not grieve for his untimely death. In the aftermath of his death, she had asked why? Why had he felt compelled to go back into the fire after the missing firefighter? Even now, sometimes in a state of desperation, she asked, "*Why*?"

And the answer stared her square in the face. Because he was a good man who truly cared about others and felt it was his responsibility to help. She knew without a doubt that he couldn't have remained the man he was had he not tried to save another man's life that day so many years ago. But losing him had been so difficult for her, and at times, she lost her faith, felt sorry for herself and had even cursed God for her misfortune. She had many suitors interested over the years since her husband's death, but she found none the equivalent of her Tom. Even in the loneliness and desperation she had chosen to remain single.

Today, Ellen Wetzel blamed no one as she silently thanked God for allowing her son to escape the raging wildfire and live another day. A tear trickled down her cheek as she peered out the large kitchen window. Then she smiled. *"And thank you, Tom Wetzel, for being there for our son! One day … I'll be seein' you."*

Jack stood, walked to his mother and encircled her with his arms.

He hugged her and said softly, "I came home from Nam to find peace and quiet in these mountains. As of late, things have kinda gone to heck for me."

"I know, Jackie." She sighed. "I know."

CHAPTER TWENTY-THREE

Sergeant Steve Hunt slammed his fist down hard on the desk. His face was livid as he stood facing the seated Silver City Police Chief, Pete Thompson. "What the hell's going on, Pete?"

Thompson said nothing. His impassive poker face was impossible to read.

Hunt calmed his voice. "I've got a murdered rancher whose body, by the way, was burned after he was killed by some crazy son-of-a-bitch with a bow and arrows." He shook his head and sighed deeply. "If that wasn't enough, the goddamned son-of-a-bitch tries to shoot down a Forest Service contracted helicopter with a sheriff's deputy inside. Then he sets a fire on Brushy Mountain and attempts to murder my tracker, Jack Wetzel!"

Chief Thompson stirred in his chair. "Sometimes life's a real bitch, Steve."

"Thanks, Pete," said Hunt facetiously.

Thompson leaned forward in his chair, elbows resting on the desk piled high with papers. "Just what do you want from me, Steve?"

"For starters, I want to know who your Internal Affairs Officer was investigating when *he* was murdered." Before Thompson could respond, Hunt continued, "*And* … I want to know why one of your officers felt it was his unfettered duty to assault a woman right here in Silver City—in public no less, and in broad daylight!"

"You mean Millie's whore?"

"I don't give a good goddamn what she is, Pete. She didn't deserve that, and you damned well know it!"

Thompson picked at his teeth with a forefinger then looked out the dirty office window. "I'm gonna close that whorehouse down one o' these days."

Hunt leaned forward placing his hands on the desk. "I've got way too many corpses to investigate lately to worry about Millie's place, Pete." He glared at Thompson. "Hell, Millie doesn't cause any problems; never has that I know of. Now, what can you tell me of your Internal Affairs investigation?"

"Officers were allegedly looking the other way, not arresting suspects in drug busts," said Thompson quietly out of the corner of his mouth, "and being paid to keep quiet on locations of marijuana grow sites and sellers around town."

Hunt sat down heavily in the chair. "Which officers?" When the Chief did not respond, he shouted, *"Who, goddammit?"*

Thompson's eyes flared momentarily at him and then averted his gaze toward the floor. "The lieutenant was murdered before he confided in me who was responsible."

Sighing heavily, Hunt rubbed his heated face with both hands. He spoke with obvious control to his voice. "The file, Pete. Where's the IA file with all the information I need?"

Chief Thompson rose without responding and stood gazing out the dirty paned window again.

"Well?" Hunt breathed loudly through an open mouth.

Thompson did not turn to answer. "Gone ... disappeared from the file drawer."

"You're shitting me."

Thompson turned. "No. Someone pried the locked drawer open and stole everything." He placed one hand on the other with his outside fingers drumming incessantly on the inside hand. Looking through the window again, he said almost absently, "There was a confidential informant the lieutenant worked with ..."

Hunt stood abruptly. "Now, we're getting somewhere. Where's this informant?"

Silence, then: "Unfortunately ... he's dead, too. He was murdered the same night as the lieutenant."

"*What?*" rasped Hunt.

The silence in the room was almost deafening. Thompson returned to his seat behind the desk. "You heard me."

Placing the palms of both hands on the desk, Hunt leaned forward. "Jeez, Pete. What the hell kind of officers do you have working for you?"

"Don't you get testy with me, Steve!"

"All right, dammit. Hell, you only have a handful of officers. Who's most likely … say, in your opinion, to be involved in all this shit?"

"I'd say most likely, Joe Peach, but I don't have anything to back up my accusation."

Hunt was interested. "The officer who assaulted Millie's whore?"

"Yep. But he's on administrative leave pending trial."

"Give me his home address, Pete." *Finally, a lead.* Receiving the written address, he headed toward the closed office door. Opening the door, he turned. "If Peach calls or comes by, you keep him here and call me, right away."

CHAPTER TWENTY-FOUR

IT WAS A DARK NIGHT; ONLY A SMALL SLIVER OF A MOON TO ILLUMINATE the star-studded night sky. Market Street in Silver City was unusually quiet, traffic non-existent. The man stirred in the shadows of a large Chinese Elm. Dressed in black with a black ski mask covering his face, he was indiscernible to any possible passersby. His gaze focused on one of the small, faded blue, single-story, flat-roofed apartments located just west of St. Vincent de Paul Catholic Church. His right hand moved inadvertently in toward his darkened torso, the thumb and forefinger touching as if cupping a cigarette in the hand with the little finger nervously flicking at the ashes on the end of a cigarette that did not exist.

Another thirty minutes passed; the door opened on the apartment closest to the church. The dark figure melted back further into the shadows of the tree. A female voice resounded into the quiet night. "Robbie, stop playing with your toys and lock the door behind me." A slender, red-haired woman appeared at the door of the apartment wearing a denim jacket and carrying a purse. She hesitated before closing the door, repeated the order to the child and closed it securely.

The man watched closely as the young woman stepped lithely down the two steps onto the sidewalk leading to the church across the street. She ascended the numerous steep steps to the church and entered. Instantly, he secured a pistol that was tucked in his back pocket and a silencer he now held in his left hand. Walking covertly as he crossed Market Street to the apartment, he attached the silencer into the muzzle of the semi-automatic pistol. Reaching the door of the apartment, he placed his black gloved hand on the door knob and turned it counter-clockwise. Beneath the ski mask he grinned in the darkened night as the knob turned easily in his hand.

Opening the door, he slipped into the room noiselessly. A small boy about four years old lay on the floor playing with cowboy and Indian figures. As the man entered, the startled boy looked up at the intruding figure, but said nothing, his mouth open. Hearing the sound of dishes being handled in the kitchen, the man in black passed the boy with his finger against his lips and moved toward the kitchen. His right hand, which held the pistol, was now out in front of him supported by his left as he entered the small kitchen.

An elderly, slender woman turned from the kitchen sink holding a plate in one hand and a dish towel in the other. Gray shoulder-length hair fell into two braids, one over each shoulder. The dark, deep-set eyes widened as she saw him, the thin lips and mouth tightened in a shallow, wrinkled face, but she didn't drop the plate.

The man stood staring at the woman, the pistol lowered near his leg. He hardened his gaze under the ski mask. *"Yo la recuerdo, Doña Consuelo Vasquez,"* he said softly. "I remember you, *Doña Consuelo Vasquez."*

The woman placed the plate carefully in the kitchen sink as she stared calmly at the intruder.

"You killed my brother with your … *veneno …su pinche* poison, *y brujería …*your damned witchcraft."

She said nothing. Her eyes hardened but showed no fear as she saw the pistol again come to bear on her. Placing both hands at her sides, she stood straight and tall in the small dimly-light room. Her voice was calm. "You're afraid of *me*? Of what *I* do?" She laughed. "I tried to protect your brother … and *you* … from the *brujo* you work for, Tomás. *He* … his powers are what you should be afraid of … not me."

The eyes of the man in black blazed at the old woman through the ski mask. *"Mentirosa.* Liar. He's *not* a witch! He's been like a father to me … taught me everything I know."

The old woman's eyes narrowed. "And he's taught you *well,*

Tomás. How to be a thief and a killer!" Her voice exuded contempt and disgust.

"*Vete a la chingada, bruja,*" he murmured as he shot her twice in the head, "Go to hell, you damned witch."

She slipped to the floor without a sound. He bent and swiftly retrieved the empty shell casings, removed the silencer, placing the pistol in one back pocket and the silencer in the other. He turned to the living room. He could see the child had not witnessed the murder from his position on the floor. As he stood over him, the boy asked softly, "Who are you, mister?"

"A friend," the man said as he pondered what to do.

The boy stood. Soft, fine, brown hair covered his small head; two small brown eyes beneath long dark lashes peered at this stranger who had entered his home unexpectedly. The man detected no fear in the child's eyes, only bewilderment at the ski-masked intruder. The boy wore a flannel shirt, and blue jeans covered the tops of worn tennis shoes. "I don't know you," Robbie said emphatically. "Why do you have a mask?"

"Practicing for Halloween." The man studied the boy.

The man made his decision. He motioned toward the door. "You need to come with me, Robbie. We haven't much time."

The child backed up, clutching his cowboy and Indian toys in his fists. "My momma told me to *never* go with strangers." His brow arched. "How do you know my name?"

"I told you. I'm a friend." The man shrugged. "Besides, your momma told you to lock the door after her, too, didn't she?"

The boy hesitated as if feeling guilty. "How did you know that, mister?"

The man smiled. "I know everything, Robbie. Your momma won't like that you didn't do what she asked, will she?"

The boy was quiet, contemplating what the man had said.

"You come with me." He shrugged again. "Maybe I can get you off the hook. What do you say?"

Pursing his lips, the little boy put his hands on his hips. "I *meant* to lock it, mister. Honest Injun, I did."

The man grinned under the ski mask. "I know that, Robbie. Come on. You an' me'll square it with her. Okay?"

He took the boy's jacket from a hook near the door. "Put this on, boy; Hurry!"

Hustling Robbie out in front of him and closing the door, he peered both ways on the street to ensure there were no vehicles. He took the boy by the arm; they crossed Market Street and walked quickly around the corner where a pickup truck was parked. He placed Robbie in the passenger seat, seat-belted him in, and locked the door. Returning to the driver's side, he got in and started the engine. He thought the stolen truck would serve him well tonight.

The little boy looked over at him. "Are you *really* my friend, mister?"

The man glanced at him as they drove away. His gaze softened slightly then hardened again under the ski mask. He didn't answer. Free from the steering wheel, the right hand cupped with the thumb and forefinger touching and the little finger flicking at the ashes of an invisible cigarette.

CHAPTER TWENTY-FIVE

DRESSED IN HIS OFFICIAL FOREST SERVICE UNIFORM, WETZEL WALKED UP the well-beaten path behind the Gila Visitor Center toward the helispot and living quarters. It was a beautiful fall day, the weather picture perfect. He rubbed his jaw and remembered he had forgotten to shave. He laughed at himself and adjusted the day pack more comfortably to his back. If forgetting to shave was the worst thing he did today, he'd be all right he reckoned.

Topping out on a small mesa above the visitor center, he saw the black New Mexico State Police helicopter sitting at the helispot, rotor blades spinning, and he had an instant flashback to Vietnam; he and his scout dog Smoky on their epic journey to Saigon. He thought of his old friend. *I sure hope you're at peace now, Smoky. I reckon I'm not quite there myself.* He sighed deeply, expelling the air from his lungs. *Maybe someday?*

Steve Hunt waved at him from the front of the helicopter. There were two other New Mexico state policemen standing nearby. They were all dressed in camouflage clothing and heavily armed. As Wetzel walked toward them, someone in a green Forest Service truck intercepted him near the housing area. District Ranger Bill Hood poked his large head out the window. His eyes squinted in the bright sunlight beneath heavy brown horn-rimmed glasses.

"I need a moment to visit with you."

Wetzel stepped up to the driver window. "Yes sir?"

District Ranger Hood used his right forefinger to push the heavy glasses back up on the bridge of his large bulbous nose. Then he tilted his pointed chin down, peering over the newly adjusted lenses. In the bright morning light, his short crew cut made him look almost bald. "I don't want you carrying a gun today. You hear me?" Before Wetzel could answer, he added, "Forest Service policy, son. Forest Service policy mustn't be violated."

Wetzel's eyes betrayed nothing. "Yessir."

District Ranger Hood picked at his teeth with his tongue. "I heard you might've had a gun the day of the fire on Granny Mountain." He cleared his throat. "Won't do, son; won't do ... can't—"

"—violate Forest Service policy," retorted Wetzel, "I understand, sir."

"Very well. Very well. I'm glad you understand. I'll fire any man who does so." He cleared his throat again. "Got to have rules, you know." He peered over his glasses. "Are we clear on that?"

Wetzel licked his dry lips and then let the air out of his lungs. "Yessir; very clear, sir."

District Ranger Hood straightened in the truck seat, attempted to put the truck in gear, and stripped the gears in doing so. He looked straight ahead. "I've work to do, Wetzel. Carry on with my orders." He drove away, the truck lurching in the wrong gear.

As Wetzel walked up to Steve Hunt, the New Mexico State Policeman swung his head toward the retreating Forest Service truck. "What the hell did *he* want?"

Wetzel grinned as he removed his day pack. "Nothin' much, Steve."

Hunt watched as Wetzel unzipped the pack and withdrew a Colt .45, Model 1911 pistol and stuck it in his belt behind his back. "Something about Forest Service employees not being authorized to carry firearms or some such thing."

"I see. Well, we wouldn't want you to violate policy and say ... *get killed*, now would we?"

Wetzel said nothing, closed the pack and slung it on his right shoulder.

They walked back to the other officers, and over the whine of the helicopter engine, Hunt said, "Let's go to Haystack Mountain and catch some dopers, boys." He nodded at Wetzel, "You ride up front with the pilot and lead us in."

* * *

WETZEL ADJUSTED his headset for the intercom system over his green Forest Service baseball cap. The helicopter pretty much followed along the West Fork of the Gila River, passing White Creek Cabin to the north. Off to Wetzel's right, prominent Mogollon Baldy stood majestic at 10,778 feet. He pressed the intercom button as he pointed ahead. "Steve, the drainage directly in front of us running perpendicular to our route of travel is the West Fork of Mogollon Creek. The next smaller canyon is Rain Creek, and Haystack Mountain is that high point up on the ridge just west of Rain Creek."

Hunt's voice crackled over the intercom. "Where can we land this thing?"

Wetzel pointed for the pilot's benefit as he spoke. "There's an old helispot near the top. See?"

The pilot nodded, heading for the landing zone.

Wetzel spoke over the intercom for everyone's benefit. "Haystack Spring is due south about a half mile from Haystack Mountain. There's another spring another half mile or so down that header into Rain Creek."

He pictured the terrain in his mind. "Foster Spring is due west of Haystack Mountain—about a half mile as well. If you get turned around as to where you are later on, just follow the drainage you're in down to Rain Creek and the forest boundary or from Foster Spring down Cherry or Minton Canyons to the boundary."

Hunt replied, "You and I'll go south, Jack. The other officers west," and then he spoke to the pilot, "Keep this bird flying for recon and commo, but keep it up high where the sons-a-bitches can't shoot at you."

"10-4," replied the pilot over the intercom.

The pilot landed without incident at the old helispot, the officers jumped out with their packs and weapons then moved to a safe distance out in front of the helicopter. With every man accounted for, Hunt gave the pilot a thumb up sign and off it went to higher elevation and safety.

Weapons and packs secured, Hunt nodded to the other two New Mexico state policemen, and they headed down off the ridge toward their pre-arranged destination, Foster Spring. Wetzel moved south toward Haystack Spring and looking over his shoulder he saw Hunt, cradling the shotgun in his arm, following suit.

Wetzel waited till he figured he was close to the spring, pulled the pistol from his belt and flipped the safety off, his finger outside the trigger guard. He moved much more slowly and deliberately, using any cover and concealment available. The latest ambush attempt on his life was still vivid in his mind. According to reliable informants, there were several marijuana grow sites in and around both springs, all fed by plastic pipe and smaller feeder lines. The Grant County Sheriff's Office had officers stationed below them near the Forest boundary. Wetzel's friend, Deputy Don Ramirez, was in charge of the deputies waiting at the boundary. They had driven in part way, stashed their vehicles and hiked in via an old jeep trail the night before, the same route the drug smugglers allegedly used. The added bonus, according to the state police informant, was the Silver City Police contact with the dopers would be on site.

Wetzel scowled. *Yeah, right. Everyone is most likely running like hell down to the forest boundary after hearing the helicopter land up on the mountain.*

Just as he thought, Haystack Spring had adequate water and sure enough a black pipe extended from the spring downhill. As he descended warily through the thick brush with Hunt a few paces behind, he observed the smaller feeder lines leading to marijuana grow locations beneath numerous trees. From sign on the ground, Wetzel saw the illegal plants had been harvested recently. There were several footprints in the dry, sandy soil, but none appearing of the size or style of the man who had attempted to kill him previously.

Wetzel dropped over to the other header canyon that fed into Rain Creek and waited for Hunt to catch up. He pointed at recent sign on the well-beaten path. "We could have company up ahead, Steve." Taking his pack off, he withdrew his plastic water bottle and drank deeply.

Hunt did the same and then whispered, "How much farther to the second spring?"

Wetzel shrugged. "Maybe a hundred yards ... maybe more."

They continued down the header drainage making little sound.

Wetzel saw the camouflaged man first. He was kneeling beneath a large juniper tree near a bundle of marijuana plants that had been neatly tied together for easy transport. Hunt leveled the shotgun at him while striding quickly toward him. "Throw your hands up!" he commanded, "or I'll shoot!"

The man stood, turned slowly toward the advancing State Policeman. He raised his hands to shoulder height. Wetzel recognized him. Joe Peach! Wetzel raised his cocked pistol as his pulse intensified.

Peach grinned broadly, his large, ugly face creased into a smile. "Why, howdy there, Steve!" He peered up at the blue sky overhead. "That your helo up there?"

"Shut up!"

"I'm sure glad you showed up. I've been lookin' for this marijuana site for awhile now." His hands began to lower.

Hunt stood directly in front of him, the shotgun leveled chest high. "I said shut the hell up, Peach. You're under arrest."

"Sure, Steve. Whatever ya say, man," Peach murmured, "but ... uh, what about them boys down yonder?" He nodded his large head down the drainage.

Hunt took his eye from Peach for just a second, and the Silver City policeman grabbed the shotgun barrel with both hands. The shotgun discharged, echoing up the canyon. Wetzel looked in horror as the two officers struggled. He scrambled toward them, his pistol raised.

As Hunt and Peach wrestled for control of the shogun now held high, Wetzel saw Peach reach into his camouflage jacket pocket with his left hand. Then he pressed the pocket next to Hunt's torso while he held onto the shotgun with his right hand. The report of a handgun startled Wetzel. He saw Hunt stagger back holding his stomach, losing control of the shotgun to Peach. As Peach turned toward him, Wetzel slid to a kneeling position and aimed at his old high school classmate. He yelled at the top of his lungs, "Drop it, Joe!

Peach grinned as he racked a round in the shotgun. "Come on, war hero! Come an' get some o' this, boy." He swung the shotgun up to his shoulder and fired.

Wetzel dove to his left as he fired the Colt .45. He felt buckshot hit the ground near where he had knelt moments earlier. Continuing his roll to better cover behind an oak tree, he peered out from behind the tree with his pistol extended. Peach was gone, mostly likely running with the others toward the forest boundary.

Wetzel rose quickly and ran to the downed New Mexico state policeman. As he ran, he heard shooting below them.

CHAPTER TWENTY-SIX

POLICE CHIEF PETE THOMPSON AWOKE FROM A HEAVY SLUMBER. HE heard a noise outside his house he was not familiar with. He looked at the alarm clock on his dresser. It was 2:30 a.m. *What the hell?* He heard it again; a scratching noise from the direction of his back porch. Fully alert, he slipped out from under the sheets without waking his wife who was enjoying a deep sleep. Reaching in the top dresser drawer, he pulled on soft leather gloves, withdrew a .38 caliber Smith & Wesson Model 60 two-inch revolver, and padded barefoot to the darkened living room dressed in his pajamas. Pausing briefly before continuing to the kitchen toward the back door, he could hear his heart pounding in his chest. The absence of a moon made it impossible to see outside through the kitchen window.

Thompson took a deep breath, opened the door slightly and slipped out into the darkened night, his revolver extended. He moved to his right and stopped, allowing his eyes to adjust even further. Still he couldn't discern any shapes or forms that did not belong in his back yard. The huge cottonwood tree stood out even in the darkened night. The noise again! But where? Then he heard a low moan. *From where, dammit?*

Cautiously, Thompson made his way out slowly from the cement porch. He stopped in his tracks as he saw a form lying on the ground near the old cottonwood tree. As he aimed his revolver, his finger tightened on the trigger. "Who *are* you? And what the hell are you doing in my backyard?"

The form stirred, a large bald head appeared out of the darkness. With difficulty, a man responded, "It's me, Pete. Joe Peach." And arm extended from the torso and the man moaned loudly. "I'm hurt badly, Pete." Another gasp as the form moved on the ground.

"What *the hell* happened to you?" Thompson asked. He knelt beside the camouflaged officer and saw blood covered the entire left shoulder and most of the policeman's chest.

The police chief repeated his question this time more sharply. *"What happened?"* He assisted the officer up to a sitting position against the tree.

"The state police raided the marijuana sites below Haystack Mountain. I had to ... kill ... that state policeman ... Hunt." Peach groaned holding his injured shoulder. "Wetzel guided them in—the son-of-a-bitch!"

"*You* killed Steve Hunt?" asked Thompson incredulously.

"I ... I ... think so. Shot him in the belly ... then tried for Wetzel ... missed. He got me with a lucky shot." "It hurts like hell, Pete!" Peach cried out in the night.

"You've ... *got* to help me". The wounded officer grabbed his superior and Thompson smelled Peach's blood. "I'm most bled out ... can't walk ... anymore." His voice trailed off in the still star-studded night.

"Who knows you're here, Joe?"

Peach swallowed hard. "No one ... everyone else ... is ... dead."

"Everyone?"

"At Haystack." Peach struggled to speak. "Sheriff's deputies ... were ... waiting for us."

Thompson looked back at his quiet, darkened house. That his wife was still sleeping soundly he had no doubt. "We've got to get you some help, Joe." He patted Peach lightly on his right shoulder. "Are you armed?"

"Revolver ... in ..." Peach gasped as he swallowed with difficulty, "jacket ... pocket."

Thompson retrieved the weapon from Peach's pocket. He changed position near the officer, faced the house and fired two quick shots, both from the kneeling position that hit in the yard near his residence.

Peach struggled to sit up higher against the tree. *"What ...?"*

Thompson now faced him in the darkened night, and he heard the report of yet another firearm and the accompanying muzzle flash close in the stillness of the dark night. The burning pain began instantly, now in the center of his chest, emanating out. He struggled to speak as his large widened eyes displayed unimaginable fright and his sweating face total bewilderment.

He sank back against the cottonwood tree, tried to speak but could not as blood trickled from his mouth.

Thompson leaned in close almost touching the officer's face and whispered in an almost conciliatory tone of voice, "You're a liability for me now, Joe. Can't have you shooting off your mouth, now can I?" He straightened as he saw the light come on in the house. His wife called out to him as he reached out and felt for a carotid pulse on the mortally wounded officer. Finding no pulse, he placed Peach's discharged revolver in the officer's still right hand and stood, walking back toward the house, stopping briefly to tell his wife to call police dispatch. He himself moved to dispose of the gloves in the trash can.

CHAPTER TWENTY-SEVEN

It was approaching midnight when the man dressed in black turned the stolen truck off Highway 15 onto the road leading to the Gila Cliff Dwellings. His teeth gleamed in the confines of the truck cab. The black stocking mask still covered his face. No traffic; just as he had ascertained. He peered at the boy asleep in the passenger seat next to him. The man laughed under his breath. He knew they'd come after him now with the boy kidnapped from a murder scene. He passed Woody's Corral and slowed the truck as he neared the parking lot.

Maybe they'd send the same tracker as before? Í*Como chingan! How they f… with me!* He'd welcome the challenge, but his confidence told him no one, not even that guy could equal his skills in the woods and especially his ability as an assassin. He laughed again under his breath.

Leaving the keys in the stolen truck, he got out. He slammed the metal door hard, walked around the truck, and retrieved his backpack from the bed. He slipped it over his shoulders, adjusted the straps then opened the passenger door. The boy sat upright, only half awake.

"Get out!" the man barked in the still, cool night air. It was a full moonlit night with twinkling stars in the sky.

The boy hesitated. The man grabbed him by the shirt front and dragged him out of the cab and onto the asphalt parking lot. "Damn you. When I tell you to do something, by God, you do it!"

Fully awake and frightened, the boy looked up at the man. His dark brown eyes under furrowed brows and long lashes widened in disbelief. He spoke with childlike softness to his voice, "Why are you treating me so rough, mister? I haven't done anything to you."

The man did not respond, but withdrew a pistol from his belt, checked if it was loaded, and holstered it. He withdraw a large bow and arrows in a quiver from the back of the truck. These he placed over his shoulder.

The boy persisted. He stood and spoke with emphasis. "I don't like you, mister." His little lips pursed as his big brown eyes began to well up. "You're a *bad* man. My momma wouldn't want me to go with you." His lips trembled.

The man peered intently at the little boy from under the dark mask. The boy stood with his small hands on his hips. "You got guts, Robbie. I'll say that for you."

The little boy took a step back.

The man knelt and looked directly into the boy's eyes. "Here's the deal, boy. I don't give a damn what your mother wants. She doesn't mean shit to me." He pointed a forefinger at the boy. "You either come with me ... or ... I'll kill you where you stand." He waited for the words to sink in. "*¿Comprende?* You understand me?"

The man in black stood watching the boy's face turn from bewilderment to outright fright. He waved for the four-year old to walk in front of him. "Now *move*, and don't stop till I tell you to."

With tears silently wetting his cheeks, the little boy walked down the trail in his little tennis shoes toward the West Fork of the Gila River.

Once in the West Fork, the man made him stay in the riparian area and the water as they passed the trail junctions to Little Bear Canyon and after another couple of miles, Woodland Park. The boy nearly stepped on a rattlesnake out hunting near the trail adjacent to the riverbed. He cried out loud and then sobbed as he stumbled his way into the darkened night, his wet tennis shoes squishing as he walked. The shadows of the huge Sycamore and cottonwood trees displayed intricate bizarre designs on the trail ahead as the light from a full moon filtered its way through the heavy tree canopies. A Great

Horned owl hooted in the night. The man watched the boy jump in his tracks and yet not a peep out of him.

The gruff voice resounded in the quiet night, "Keep moving, boy."

Robbie grudgingly complied with the order and mumbled, "You're *real mean,* mister. I'm going to tell my momma on you."

They crossed the West Fork on several occasions following the trail. The boy had difficulty maintaining his balance on the smooth river rock. His tennis shoes and pants legs were water-logged, and he shivered in the cool, fall air. Still, the man in black pushed and prodded him on into the dark night.

CHAPTER TWENTY-EIGHT

WETZEL AROSE EARLY, GRABBED A CUP OF COFFEE TO TAKE WITH HIM AND drove his truck down to the Forest Service barn to feed the horses and burros in the corral. They were waiting for him. Rosita sauntered up to the gate with Chochi close behind as Wetzel brought part of a bale of alfalfa hay out to the adjacent corral. Rosita stuck her nose through the opening in the corral. As she brayed in the cool morning air, her long eye lashes fluttered at the master she had come to know.

"All right, girl. Here ya go." Wetzel laughed as he threw a flake of hay to her and one to Chochi. His saddle horse, a buckskin gelding, trotted up to chase the burros away from their morning breakfast. Throwing another flake to the gelding, Wetzel ensured all the animals were spaced far enough from each other so all could eat without interruption.

He heard a vehicle drive down the road toward the barn. A door slammed as he pulled himself up on the top rail of the corral and sat watching the animals feed noisily. Footsteps sounded on the barn's concrete floor, and then Don Ramirez appeared. In the full uniform of a Grant County deputy sheriff with a .357 revolver strapped to his hip, Ramirez walked to where Wetzel sat on the corral.

"Howdy, Jack."

"Howdy yourself, Don." Wetzel's brow furrowed, "What you doin' up here at this hour of the morning, *amigo*?"

Ramirez leaned on the top rail, placing a booted foot on the bottom. At first he said nothing. "It's turning out to be a busy day for me."

"Oh?" Wetzel turned his full attention to the deputy.

Sighing, Ramirez said, "A stolen truck was left in the Cliff Dwellings' parking lot last night."

Wetzel said nothing.

Ramirez tipped his straw hat back from his forehead. "We think it's the same truck that was used in the kidnapping of a young boy from Silver City."

Behind the barn the sunrise appeared in the east, casting an orange glow to the clear sky void of any clouds.

Wetzel leaned forward on the top rail of the pole corral. "Why in the hell would someone kidnap a boy and bring 'im all the way up here from town?"

Ramirez pulled his hat back down on his head shading his face from the sun. "Can't make any sense of it. I thought you might help us figger it out." He grinned. "That is if you're not too busy with the Forest Service an' all."

Wetzel rubbed his jaw with his right hand. "Me busy?" He laughed aloud and shook his head. "I'm suspended from duty for carrying a firearm in violation of Forest Service policy. The district ranger wants to fire me." He jumped off his perch to the ground. "And I don't have any idea when my hearing will be scheduled."

Ramirez's dark eyes softened. "I heard about that. I'm sorry." He looked down at the ground and then directly at Wetzel. "You'll help me?"

It was Wetzel's turn to grin. "Bein's I got lots o' time, I reckon you got my undivided attention, *amigo*."

***

DURING THE SHORT trip from the barn to the trailhead, Wetzel was silent, thinking of all the possibilities why someone would bring a kidnapped boy up to the forest. He could not think of one logical reason.

He stepped out of the sheriff's car and walked up to the truck parked at the trailhead. Seeing nothing in the bed, he looked in the cab and saw a key in the ignition. Shaking his head, he peered at the trail just beyond the asphalt edge of the parking lot. A small tennis shoe imprint was clearly legible in the sandy soil. His interest piqued; his trained gaze continued up the trail and saw what he was looking for—a larger boot print also clearly legible. Leaning forward, he looked more closely at the boot print. The skin prickled at the back of his neck, sending a shiver through his body. Instantly, he was absolutely certain the vibram print belonged to the killer he had tracked previously; the same killer who had nearly ended his life not so long ago.

Wetzel turned to Deputy Ramirez, who now stood at his side. "The boy?"

"An old woman was murdered," Ramirez hooked his thumbs into his jeans pockets, "and the boy was taken."

"Judging from the tracks, I'd say the boy's not much older than four or five years." Wetzel looked up the trail, thoughts racing ahead from his memory of what lay beyond on the trail and possible destinations. Still, nothing made any sense to him.

Ramirez cleared his throat. "I ... ah ... the boy ... he's Maggie and Juan Garcia's boy, Jack"

A chill snaked up his spine. "*What*?"

"The son-of-a-bitch took Robbie. And we have no idea why."

"*Jeez.* Maggie knows about all this?"

"Only that the boy was taken."

"Better he's taken than murdered outright, Don."

A Game and Fish Department truck drove up and parked alongside the sheriff's car. A truck door opened and slammed shut. Officer McMurtry was out of uniform; as usual, his battered ball cap tilted slightly to the right. His large frame ambled up to the other officers. He tucked his hands into the pockets of his brown coveralls, "Howdy, boys." He grinned broadly and breathed deeply of the cool air. "Fine mornin' ain't it?"

Wetzel grinned back. "How ya been, Mac?"

"Couldn't be any better, boys." He nodded to Ramirez. "How you fellers doin'?"

Turning from the edge of the asphalt parking lot and trailhead, Wetzel said, "We've got a killer who murdered a woman and kidnapped a boy." He shrugged and shook his head. "Then for whatever reason that same killer brought the boy out here last night and headed up the West Fork."

McMurtry's eyes brightened as he knelt at the trailhead, peering intently at the obvious sign left in the sandy soil. He spoke without looking up at Wetzel. "Size ten boot, I'd say. That feller walks mostly on the outside edge of his heels an' his left leg drags jest a mite." He scratched at his beard, "Maybe a war injury or some sech thang, boys."

Wetzel snorted. "I suppose you'll tell us how much change he has in his pockets, uh?"

Not hesitating, McMurtry stood. "A dollar an' a nickel. Four quarters and a nickel to be exact."

Ramirez chuckled. "Damn you're good, Mac."

"Damn good bullshitter, I'd say." Wetzel smirked.

McMurtry tucked his hands in his coveralls and spread his feet to a more comfortable stance. "I'm the master, Jack. Ain't nobody as good as me in trackin', son."

Ramirez' face became serious. "I asked both of you here to see if you two would track this killer and get the boy back."

Both men were silent for a moment. Ramirez squared his shoulders. "I've got a call to make at the Roberts Ranch—suspicious persons. I can be back by mid-afternoon to go with you guys."

Wetzel said, "The news this morning says it's supposed to rain by tonight."

McMurtry nodded. "It'd be best if Jack and I got on this within the hour. If it does rain, we'll have a helluva time tryin' to find any sign."

Ramirez looked at both men. "So you'll work it together?"

Both men nodded. The deputy sheriff breathed a sigh of relief.

"*Bueno*. You'll need a radio." He tossed a handheld at Wetzel.

Wetzel looked at the radio. "Unless he climbs out of the West Fork, we might not be able to contact you by radio."

"Whenever you can, Jack. That's all I ask."

McMurtry started for his truck. "Best quit lollygaggin' and git to work, boys."

Wetzel winked at Ramirez. "The *master* calls, Don. We'll be see'n ya."

CHAPTER TWENTY-NINE

THE CRUMPLED LETTER GRASPED TIGHTLY IN HER TREMBLING HAND, Maggie Garcia sat on the edge of the bed. Her head bowed as tears flowed from her reddened eyes down her cheeks. She cried out, "My God, what's to become of me?" Her pursed lips trembled uncontrollably.

She knew she was feeling sorry for herself and she shouldn't do so, but somehow she just couldn't help herself. Coming home after praying at church, she'd found Doña Consuelo murdered, lying in a pool of blood in the kitchen and her son kidnapped. *Kidnapped!* The murder scene horrified her beyond belief, but the fact that her son had been taken brought unimaginable horror and grief to her.

Drying her tears on the back of her hands, she straightened the letter and peered at its contents once again. It was a letter from her husband, Juan Garcia, posted May 14, 1970:

Dearest Maggie,

I thought about not sending this letter to you as I know you do not comprehend what it is like here in Nam. Honestly, I'm not sure that I do. So many of my friends have died—so many that I have literally quit making friends any more.

I'm sitting alone in my tent. I feel lonely and afraid. Not so much for myself anymore, but for the others. The killing just goes on …and on. I can't wait till my year is up, and I get the hell out of here like my friend Wetzel did.

I live in a horrid world of death and violence with no escape. One of my friends was killed yesterday when we were on patrol. He hit a trip wire and a land mine bounced up at groin height, exploded, and blew his stomach, private parts, and legs apart. He didn't die right away, and I can still hear his screams ringing in my ears.

I have always done my duty and volunteered where others wouldn't or couldn't do their duty, but my dreams are fading and my outlook on life is so different now. I may live through this war, but I'll never be the same person who asked you to marry me in a time that seems so long ago. I just have to go on ...like Coach used to tell us when football games were tough.

Will there be an ending to all this? If there is, I'm ready for it, whatever that entails.

I love you so much, Maggie, and lil' Robbie, too. I know you are taking good care of him. I look forward to seeing both of you soon.

Your loving husband,

Juan

"I lost you several years ago, Juan, and now ... I've failed to take good care of Robbie. I've *failed* you, Juan." Maggie's body shook uncontrollably and she cried out. When the tears stopped she stood still trembling, leaving the letter on the bed, walked aimlessly into the empty living room and started out the front door of the apartment. The phone rang. She hesitated in the doorway. The phone continued to ring several times. Finally picking it up, she said nothing.

"Maggie?" The voice on the other end of the line was urgent.

She couldn't answer.

"Maggie, it's me, Don Ramirez."

Still she could not speak.

"Maggie, Jack Wetzel and the wildlife officer from the Heart Bar are tracking your son in the Gila Wilderness."

Maggie's heartbeat quickened; she choked but still couldn't respond.

"Answer me, Maggie." Ramirez paused. "Jack said he'd find him—for you not to worry."

"Don ... I ... thank God for you and Jack." She had to get to the church and pray for those helping to find her son, her Robbie.

"I'll keep you informed, Maggie. You need anything, you call me. Everything will be all right."

Hearing nothing but sobbing on the other end of the line, Ramirez closed his eyes for a moment and hung up the phone.

CHAPTER THIRTY

ROBBIE SHIVERED, WAKING UP. HIS JACKET WAS TOO LIGHT FOR THE FALL night air. His teeth chattered. He heard the water running into the river, and suddenly the urge to pee overwhelmed him. Afraid to move, he held his groin tightly with his hands as his eyes searched for the man in black. The man slept close by. The boy very slowly and quietly rose to his knees and then to his feet. The man did not stir. *Momma, I don't know what to do. I'm so scared—of that man, the dark, and the scary woods.*

He heard his heart thumping loudly in his little chest. His ears roared as he backed ever so carefully, away from where the man in black lay. In the water, the shadow of a dog appeared to him a short distance away. The little boy frowned, his eyes strained to see more clearly in the early morning light. The dog waited for him and then turned, splashed up the river, turned and again waited patiently for the boy to come. As the boy neared the water, a voice whispered to him, *stay in the water, Robbie. It'll be harder for the bad man to find you if you stay in the water.*

"Daddy? Is that you?" the boy whispered in the stillness of the night. Silence.

He looked back from where he had come; he could no longer see the man lying on the ground. He turned and walked into the water, heading upstream toward the strange dog that waited patiently for him. He didn't know which direction he was headed—only away from the man he was so afraid of. He slipped on the rocks and fell headlong in the river, but he did not cry out. Getting up and keeping his balance, although with difficulty, he continued on in the cold water. Thoroughly soaked, the little boy shook uncontrollably, his teeth chattered continuously as he plodded on his hurried course away from the man in black. He had to get away from the bad man and not allow the man to catch him. And he had to find momma.

He cried as he walked, crying and sobbing intermittently. *Momma, where are you? What do I do, now? Oh, I'm so afraid. That man is so mean, Momma. I've got to get away from him and not let him find me.*

An owl hooted and he nearly fell again in the river. Frightened, he stood motionless in the running water that swirled around his legs, and his full bladder rid itself of its contents by its own volition. The scared little boy just stood there, cold and shivering, and wet his pants.

He thought he heard something behind him and turned to see nothing in the blackness. He walked hurriedly again always staying in the water and always away from the man in black. The dog disappeared from his sight.

CHAPTER THIRTY-ONE

WETZEL TOOK THE NORTH SIDE OF THE WEST FORK AND MCMURTRY THE south side as they searched diligently for any sign to indicate the man and boy they now hunted had left the river. It was slow work, but Wetzel was pleasantly surprised at how well the wilflife officer worked. For a big man, he moved quickly and obviously was a skilled tracker.

Wetzel watched him work the shoreline slowly and methodically, missing nothing before moving on up stream. McMurtry was dressed in camouflage except for his old ball cap and a leather shoulder holster containing a .357 Ruger revolver. Like Wetzel he carried a light pack on his back for water, food, some extra clothes and a jacket.

Wetzel wore faded blue jeans, his White's boots, a denim work shirt, and his Stetson hat. The .45 Colt pistol Deputy Ramirez had given him was in the bottom of his pack; he carried a .30-.30 Winchester rifle that had belonged to his father slung over his shoulder.

Working in tandem, they reached the confluence of White Rocks Canyon and the West Fork, the same location where he and McMurtry had encountered the hippies months before. They rested briefly near the river and ate the lunch McMurtry brought for both of them.

His mouth full, McMurtry said, "That Juanita ... she can make a heck of a boo-ree-toe, caint she?"

"You bet, Mac. She's a good woman." Wetzel swallowed a bite of his burrito with water from his canteen. "When are you' all getting married anyhow?"

"Juanita's … thinking on it."

"Maybe you ought to get her boys to help in the decision process."

McMurtry smiled broadly. "Them boys are dandies, now ain't they?"

Wetzel took another bite out of his burrito, tasting the green chilis. "It's a shame we don't have time to make coffee."

McMurtry nodded, resting now on his elbows watching the river coursing by.

Wetzel felt talkative. "My dad told me when he was a young, recently-hired ranger with the Forest Service, he met with his boss at a campsite near Lily Park one night. His boss was one of the old-timers who'd been hired as a ranger in the early 1900s during the infancy of the Forest Service. Anyhow, my dad was camped and his boss rides into camp about dark and says, 'You got any coffee?'"

"Well, my dad's all embarrassed 'cause he don't have any. The old ranger swings down from his horse and just looks at Dad like he's not hearing right. My dad had been working in the wilderness for a couple of weeks and was plumb out. Anyhow, he tells his boss he's outta coffee, but that he has some beef stew and he's welcome to a hot meal."

Wetzel grinned at McMurtry. "My dad said that old man didn't say a damn word; no sir, he just mounted his horse and rode off into the night." Laughing, Wetzel continued, "He never did come back to the camp."

McMurtry sat up, his interest piqued. "The hell ya say. Did he fire your old man?"

"Naw, he and Dad became good friends over the years."

"I'd be willin' to bet your old man had plenty o' coffee for him the next time."

Wetzel laughed again. "He sure did, Mac."

A tassel-eared squirrel darted up the trunk of a large Ponderosa pine tree as a Cooper's hawk circled overhead. The sky had become inundated with clouds, a sign both men knew to indicate possible rain within hours.

Wetzel stood, stretched his lanky frame, placed his backpack over his shoulders and reached for the rifle. "This guy's a real bad one,

Mac. He's very good in the woods, and he'll kill you without blinking an eye."

"Uh-huh."

"I should've had him the last time. If I had, he wouldn't have the boy now."

"Caint blame yourself, son. He's a slippery one fer sure. Most likely has some military background or some sech thang." McMurtry shrugged on his pack and headed upstream; Wetzel followed but on the opposite bank.

Working tirelessly, they were careful to watch for an ambush and to not miss sign showing that either the boy or man they were pursuing had left the West Fork. Then without warning, Wetzel found their quarry's camp from the previous night. After whistling low at the wildlife officer, he unslung his rifle and knelt near where the man and boy had slept. McMurtry came splashing through the water to his location.

They both reviewed the sign, and it was McMurtry who whistled low. "I'll be dadjimmed, that lil' boy plumb scooted outta here while that bad *hombre* slept." He laughed as he walked out around the foot sign, following both sets of tracks to the river. Wetzel's heart pounded in his chest. He saw McMurtry check for any sign at the mouth of White Rocks Canyon.

"Think he'll kill the boy when he catches him, Mac?"

McMurtry thought carefully before he spoke. "Maybe he ain't caught him yet, Jack." They looked at each other and quickly began their search along both sides of the river.

It was Wetzel who caught the subtle sign left by the man with the size ten vibram-soled boots leading off from the West Fork on the north side into a steep side canyon. He whistled at the wildlife officer as he stood looking up at the steep rocky terrain that jutted out of the riverbed. Why leave the river here? There were canyons ahead that were a lot less steep and rugged, some with trails. The man would make obvious sign as he worked hard at climbing out. Wetzel searched intently for the boy's tracks and found nothing.

McMurtry now stood beside him, the rushing water of the West Fork thrashing at his wet camouflage pants. He, too, looked for the boy's sign and then up into the rugged canyon to the north. He almost whispered, "Where in the hell is he headed anyhow?"

Wetzel tipped his hat back on his head. "It's hard to say, but most likely Woodland Park." He was silent for a moment, "Maybe to set an ambush farther up, Mac."

McMurtry grinned, his blue eyes bright, "You an' me, why, we're thinkin' the same, son."

Frowning, Wetzel peered upstream. "You thinking the boy got away?"

"Yup." The wildlife officer waved a hand upstream. "Still goin' thataway, I'd say."

Wetzel's hazel eyes locked with the blue eyes of the big man from Tennessee. "You find the boy, Mac, and I'll catch the kidnapper." As he started toward the canyon, he felt a strong hand on his shoulder. The .30-.30 Winchester was removed from Wetzel's shoulder.

"I reckon not, Jack." McMurtry grinned again and scratched his beard, his blue eyes twinkled. "Bein's I'm the *master* at trackin', this here sumbitch belongs to me. I've not tracked anybody as good as him in a spell." As he peered up the canyon he squinted and the lines around his eyes wrinkled, displaying crow's feet. He slung the rifle over his shoulder. The clouds overhead darkened the sky and thunder rolled in the far distance.

"You go find thet boy, Jack, an' take him home to his momma." McMurtry's voice had a metallic ring to it, "An' I'll find this here killer sumbitch." With that he was gone, the big man moving lightly up the steep canyon and was soon lost in the thick vegetation.

CHAPTER THIRTY-TWO

Wetzel hurried as much as he dared; he was running out of time. Darkness would overcome him soon and the black skies were rumbling ever louder by the minute. The canyon walls were steep, almost straight up. He didn't think the boy would be able to climb out, but he didn't want to bypass him hiding somewhere near the river. Robbie had to be frightened beyond belief, alone, wet and cold.

An hour had elapsed since he and McMurtry had parted ways. If he didn't find the boy soon, he'd have to stop for the night. He had difficulty reading sign as the ambient light diminished. *Please, God. Help me find Robbie. Please!* A tremor shot through his body. On the south side of the river, he observed a flat rock that was maybe two feet from the river. Was it wet or his imagination? No, it *was* wet and others as well.

The wet tracks led to a large Sycamore tree then disappeared. A willow thicket was located nearby. The boy had to be close. *What should I do? Call out?*

Wetzel stood under the giant Sycamore tree and pondered his options. It was almost dark. No rain, but it was coming and he knew it. He made his decision. Taking his pack off, he quickly found dry kindling and wood and built a fire under the sweeping branches of the big tree. Kneeling down, he gently blew into the fire; it came to life with bright yellow flames and crackling sounds. He added larger wood, a little at a time, and soon had a roaring blaze going among the rocks. Next he tied one end of his poncho to the tree and secured the other end with two stakes he made and drove into the ground. *I reckon the tree canopy and the poncho ought to keep us dry.*

He warmed his hands next to the fire as he squatted on his heels facing the willow thicket. Talking in a low voice but loud enough to be heard several feet away, he said, "My name's Wetzel, Robbie. I'm a *friend*. I'm not here to hurt ya."

He saw no movement within the thicket. His heart pounded in his chest. He wanted badly to charge the thicket, find the boy, and bring him next to the fire. But he knew better. *Patience, Jack …patience, dammit.* Not moving, he said louder, "I'm here to *help* you, Robbie—to take you back to your momma."

Still no movement.

Wetzel reached slowly in his pack and withdrew an extra shirt then a box of fire C-rations. "I have some fruit cake and a can of beans, son. Why don't you come over to the fire … warm up … then eat some food, uh?"

No movement in the willow thicket.

Nightfall had overtaken the canyon bottom of the West Fork. Lightning flashed across the sky followed within seconds with booming thunder.

Wetzel detected slight movement within the thicket. A boy's voice was barely audible over the thunder. "Mister … Wetzel … you're not … friends with that bad man, are you?"

Wetzel's grinned as he squatted before the fire, trying not to move and scare the boy away. "No, Robbie. I'm one of the good guys, and a friend of your momma."

No response. He waited several moments. "Come to the fire, Robbie. Let's get you warm and dry before the storm hits."

Nothing.

Wetzel sighed deeply. Lightning flashed and the thunder rolled almost simultaneously. He heard a whimper and then the little boy cried out, "I don't … know … *what* to do, mister!" Jack heard the desperate sobs, and his heart went out to him.

Not moving, Wetzel waited a moment. "I can't decide for you, Robbie. You think with your heart, boy. Do what your momma would want you to do."

Robbie appeared tentatively at the edge of the willow thicket. He was shaking and shivering from the cold and wet. Soaked from head to toe, he just stood there looking at Wetzel unsure of what to do.

"Might just as well come on over and warm up—get something to eat."

"There's a ... *bad* man out there ... try ... ing to hurt me."

Wetzel stood slowly. "I know all about it, Robbie. Your momma sent me to find you and take you home."

"But ... the bad man—?"

"I won't let him hurt you." Wetzel gestured with his hand. "Come to the fire, son."

"He ... shouldn't be so *mean*, Mister Wetzel."

"No. I reckon not, Robbie."

"My momma ... she ... wouldn't like him," the boy said emphatically. He hesitated then moved slowly, stumbling toward the fire.

Wetzel recognized hypothermia had already set in. When the boy stood across the fire from him, Wetzel was cautious not to approach him too quickly. "You cold?"

"Yes ... sir." Robbie shook badly. It was pitch black; the wind began to blow, whistling as it pulled hard at the Sycamore tree canopy and Wetzel's Stetson. A flash of lightning lit up the sky and thunder reverberated in the canyon. Wetzel smelled the aroma of moisture in the fresh mountain air.

Wetzel tossed his flannel shirt over to him. "You take off those wet clothes and put that shirt on. I'll warm up these beans and see if we can dry your clothes before the rain comes, uh?"

A rifle shot sounded high up near the rim of the canyon. Wetzel stood, unconsciously touching the .45 Colt pistol in his belt at his back. His hazel eyes met with the little boy's dark brown eyes across the flickering camp fire.

CHAPTER THIRTY-THREE

McMurtry stood behind an oak tree on the downhill side of the steep slope, his hands on his knees, breathing deeply, his chest heaving. *Dadjimmed country's steep! Have to keep going … it'll be dark soon … an' rain like hell.* He gazed through the foliage of the tree as he rested. The obvious tracks lead straight up out of the canyon bottom. The sumbitch wasn't trying to hide anything. Of course it would be difficult at best due to the steepness of the terrain not to leave sign, but—McMurtry was suspicious by nature, and somewhere in his gut he knew the man he pursued would attempt an ambush. Somewhere near the top?

Peering again through the foliage, he figured he was maybe halfway out of the canyon bottom. He placed his hands on his knees again. His thoughts raced back to the past, a time when as a young wildlife officer in eastern Tennessee he had attempted to arrest a poacher hunting bear out of season. He'd not waited long enough behind the huge white oak tree before confronting the violator. He shook his head. *I was way too antsy in them younger years.*

The man had seen him from forty yards distance, turned and ran. McMurtry pursued him, but the distance was just too great with the poacher fleet of foot. The wildlife officer lost sight of his quarry and then he would catch a glance of him through the trees just ahead. For quite some time the two men raced through the hardwood forest.

Finally, McMurtry tired, his heart beat furiously in his chest, and his lungs burned for air. He stopped about mid-slope then as he had now, his hands on his knees, breathing deeply. Eventually, after regaining his wind, he looked upslope for his quarry and was surprised to find him resting on his own knees just above him about the same distance as they were from each other at the initial encounter.

McMurtry stood upright that day and hollered, "You 'bout rested up, son?" He saw the man's surprised face and bewildered look; then a smile appeared, and the poacher replied, "Whenever you're ready." They began the chase again, but time got the best of the wildlife officer. Darkness overcame him, and he had to terminate the chase.

Just like today, dajimmit! Darkness would be on him soon. He looked up at the sky overhead. Dark billowing clouds added to his concerns of rainfall that would obliterate the tracks and sign he needed to pursue this ... killer ... this kidnapper sumbitch.

Sighing deeply, he formulated his plan quickly in his mind, drank water from his canteen and then began a lateral movement from his rest location. He felt like a dadjimmed billy goat, stepping from rock to rock, and hanging onto trees, shrubs and rocks to assist in standing upright and making little or no sound. Then there was the concern of losing his footing and falling.

He came to a granite rock shelf, skirted around it and started up hill only to be startled by a buzzing, coiled rattlesnake a few yards away in the shelter of the rock outcropping. Moving stealthily along, using whatever cover he could find, he progressed slowly up the steep hillside.

The Ponderosa pine trees were more numerous near the canyon rim. Despite the cool breezes brought on by the storm, McMurtry wiped at perspiration running down his face, the salt burning his eyes. After removing the old ball cap and stuffing it inside his shirt, he crawled on his belly for about a hundred yards. It seemed like a damn mile. Periodically, he stopped and listened intently. The clouds were mostly black overhead, lightning lit up the darkened sky and thunder rolled in the distance.

Cautiously, he inched forward on his belly in his camouflage gear. He grinned. *Been quiet as one o' them church mice, now ain't I?* Pulling himself up and over the rim, he rolled over on his belly onto a bed of soft pine needles beneath two large pine trees. He lay still for several minutes, peering to the west of his location, knowing the sign of his quarry led to that portion of the canyon rim.

He saw nothing. No movement.

The lightning and thunder had increased in the evening sky. McMurtry knew about where he would set up an ambush if he were the one being pursued, but he saw nothing out of the ordinary. He lay still, knowing his adversary had skills equal to or better than his own. *Don't doubt yourself, Mac. You're the master, son.*

Night began to fall on the canyon rim, but the wildlife officer did not move from his location. His strained eyes began to ache from his meticulous searching for a quarry who had eluded him and all his efforts thus far.

A large bolt of lightning flashed across the blackened sky and within a half second thunder boomed loudly. The closeness of the strike startled McMurtry and his widened eyes discerned subtle movement from behind one of the large pine trees approximately a hundred yards west of his position. *What the ...?* Then nothing. He focused his full gaze on the site that was etched in his mind. His heart pounded in his chest; the adrenalin rush pulsated through his body as he lay still on the carpet of pine needles covering the forest floor.

Minutes passed that seemed like an eternity to him. Still, he saw no further movement. Maybe he'd imagined it? Should he move toward where he thought he had seen something? It would be nightfall shortly. He didn't have much time left in the day. But something in his gut told him to stay put and to not move.

Another flash of lightning, and he saw what he had been searching for—a man dressed in black clothes standing upright behind the largest Ponderosa pine. McMurtry eased his rifle slowly along the ground out in front of him. The man in black shouldered his bow and turned to leave.

Now! Hoping Wetzel's rifle shot straight, McMurtry shouldered the rifle and peered through the open sights; he cocked the hammer back and his finger tightened on the trigger. The man in black hesitated briefly, seemingly unsure of what to do, turned and looked down into the vicinity of the West Fork.

The rifle discharged reverberating throughout the darkened night and within the steep canyon walls. *I outfoxed ya! Ya sumbitch!* Then thunder boomed loudly, roaring its displeasure in the black skies. McMurtry levered another shell into the chamber and knelt behind the tree. Lightning flashed, and his eyes focused again on where his quarry had been just moments before. Nothing. No movement. No sound. No shapes discerned to be out of place in the natural setting.

McMurtry felt strongly he had hit his target, but had he? It was almost dark. Time had run out for him. He took a deep breath and stepped out from behind the tree, crouching as he did so. Suddenly, something thudded into the tree near his head. Dropping instantly to the ground, he heard two more distinct impacts into the tree within seconds of each other. He rolled to his right and behind another large tree. His heart pounded furiously again in his chest.

Lightning flashed and lit up the sky once again. McMurtry looked at the pine tree to his left and to his horror; he saw three arrows imbedded in the tree, one below the other about a foot apart. *Jeez!* He swallowed hard not sure of what to do next. It was pitch black now and he could see absolutely nothing as he lay clutching the rifle. It began to rain and then it poured, raining hard and steady.

CHAPTER THIRTY-FOUR

It rained steadily during the night with the sky occasionally opening up and the rain pounding McMurtry who lay huddled under a large pine tree. Darkness faded to the gray of dawn and cloudy skies persisted with no precipitation. Still he lay quietly, listening for any sound to alert him of the presence of his quarry, who now may have turned hunter.

Not until McMurtry felt satisfied that the man in black had gone did he sit up and lean against the tree. Only then did he release the cocked hammer on the lever-action rifle, leaving a round loaded in the chamber. The day showed full light in the dark, overcast skies.

He stood, rifle at the ready, and slowly approached the location a hundred yards distant where his quarry had been the previous night. As McMurtry figured, the man in black was not there. *Most likely hauled butt and made use of the rain all night to cover his tracks.* It was what McMurtry would have done himself had the roles been reversed.

He searched to no avail for any sign that he had actually hit the man the previous night when he shot at him. No sign of blood or any other indication the man was hurt or injured. Removing his pack, McMurtry retrieved a Forest Service map and determined he was west of Grave Canyon. If he continued north a couple of miles, he should reach the Middle Fork of the Gila River and could take it down to Gila Center. That was if he didn't find the killer up here somewhere first. *I sure hope Wetzel found that kid.* He thought of his friend Juanita and her two boys.

Realizing he needed to concentrate on the dangerous task at hand, he shook off thoughts of the kids and headed north, walking softly on the pine-needled forest floor. Traveling about a half mile, he saw an old grave site marked by a pile of rocks and a dilapidated wooden cross near the head of Grave Canyon. Just beyond, he crossed a well-maintained Forest Service Trail that headed east and west. It was here on the north side of the trail he knew his quarry was alive and well. The sign was subtle, almost invisible, but his trained eye saw where someone used a branch to brush out tracks near the trail after crossing headed north. *I've got you now, you sumbitch.* He felt elated, almost giddy.

From that point on, he followed marginal sign or merely guessed as to where his adversary might travel. He came to another Forest Service trail and stopped short in his tracks. Clearly, in front of him on the trail were muddied tracks of a size ten vibram-soled boot. The tracks led down the trail a short ways to a trail junction where an official sign indicated one could either continue westerly to Prior Cabin or drop off the ridge into the Middle Fork of the Gila River to the Meadows.

The man in black had chosen the Meadows. As McMurtry followed suit, it began to rain steadily again. Lightning crackled in the dark skies and thunder resonated in the distance.

The trail down into the Meadows soon displayed numerous switchbacks and steep downhill grade. The grade was considerably more than the Forest Service standard of six percent. If a man rode horse back down this trail, he'd best tighten his cinch before descending into the canyon or he'd be hanging onto the horse's ears by the time he reached the bottom. The rain continued a steady down pour as McMurtry worked hard at staying on his feet in the mud and steep terrain. By the time he donned his green army poncho, he was completely soaked and didn't have a dry stitch of clothing.

He lost all sign of his quarry as he descended. Water cascaded down portions of the steep trail, running over and around logs or wooden water bars that had been placed in the trail by the Forest Service to contain erosion.

Finally, he saw he was less than a quarter mile from the canyon bottom; muddied water flowed in the Middle Fork of the Gila River.

The area immediately below him contained a short meadow full of tall green grasses bent over from the intense rainfall. McMurtry squatted down on his heels in the trail and surveyed the Meadows area thoroughly from east to west. He rested his eyes for a few moments and then surveyed it all over again, this time more thoroughly. Nothing out of place. No movement of anything or anyone.

Cautiously, he descended the remainder of the Forest Service trail to the Meadows. He skirted around the edge of the entire meadow, his rifle cocked and at the ready, but he saw nothing—no one, not even an animal stirred as he strode through the vegetation surrounding the meadow. When he was completely satisfied it was safe, he walked to a large cottonwood tree near the Middle Fork and stepped under it. The huge canopy created an "umbrella" for some protection from the incessant rain. Chilled to the bone, his hands shook as he found some dry kindling under the massive tree and with some difficulty built a fire.

If McMurtry intended to pursue the killer and beat him when he did catch up to him, he would need rest and dry clothing. Breaking dead branches from the tree beneath its canopy, he was able to increase the size of his fire to where it warmed him and somewhat dried his clothes as he ate jerky from his pack. The afternoon became evening. The rain began again, pounded mercilessly down on the tree he had chosen for shelter. Darkness came and the rain ceased, but McMurtry did not realize it. He was fast asleep under the massive cottonwood tree where many a weary traveler, Indian and Anglo alike, had slept over hundreds of years. Even in his slumber, he clutched the rifle tightly in his hands.

A majestic bull elk with a large rack atop his head appeared tentatively on the eastern edge of the Meadows. He stopped momentarily as he stared in the direction of the old cottonwood tree, but he was upwind from the wildlife officer and proceeded gracefully out into the lush grasses of the meadow and began to eat hungrily.

CHAPTER THIRTY-FIVE

THE NEXT MORNING WETZEL HIKED OUT OF THE WEST FORK DRAINAGE AT White Rocks Canyon via the Forest Service trail to a high point so he could talk and be heard on the Grant County Sheriff's portable radio. There he advised dispatch he had found Robbie Garcia and the boy was unharmed. He apprised them of the rifle shot he'd heard from the previous evening, knowing McMurtry pursued the killer. Further, he had no other information in regard to the incident involving the wildlife officer.

The little boy stayed constantly at Wetzel's side and insisted on hiking the steep trail out to call on the radio when Wetzel suggested he remain in the West Fork drainage under the shelter of a large tree. The sheriff's office advised they would contact the boy's mother and transport her out to the Gila Cliff Dwellings parking lot.

Wetzel and Robbie returned to the West Fork. The rain continued steadily, and they crouched under the protection of a sycamore tree to allow the storm to subside. Sitting next to Wetzel, the boy stared off into space. Eventually, he scooted closer, resting his head on the Ranger's shoulder.

Procuring a Lucky Strike from the pack in his shirt pocket, Wetzel stuck it in the corner of his mouth and lit it with his silver lighter. Drawing the smoke deeply into his lungs he exhaled, the gray smoke exiting his mouth and nostrils to drift in the cool breeze that had picked up as they sat quietly near the river bank.

The boy who spoke first. "Mr. Wetzel ..."

"Call me Jack, Robbie. Please."

"Yessir. Do you think ... I mean, well, will my momma be mad at me?"

The question caught Wetzel off guard. The cigarette glowed as he drew on it, pondering; it danced along his lips from one side to the other and then hesitated in the middle dangling there precariously. "No, Robbie. I reckon not."

The little boy stood, his small feet soaking wet in his tennis shoes. He looked like a little drowned mouse to Wetzel. His round face, red from being out in the elements, displayed seriousness. Robbie placed both hands on his hips and looked squarely at Wetzel. Frowning, he said emphatically, "I reckon you're wrong, Jack. She'll be plumb hopping mad, I'd say."

Wetzel returned the gaze, grinned as he took the cigarette from his lips with his left hand and flicked at the ashes with his little finger. He looked at the cigarette and flicked again, removing the remaining ashes from the end. "Naw, she won't, son. She's goin' to be tickled to have you back safe with her again."

The boy peered intently at him, his brows knitted. "That bad man ... he flicked his hand ... like you just did, Jack. But he didn't have a cigarette."

Wetzel was all ears. Kneeling close to the boy, he asked, "Did he smoke, Robbie?"

"No sir."

"But, I thought—?"

The boy appeared to think more about what had been said. "No, he never smoked—just acted like he really *did* have a cigarette in his hand and was wiggling his little finger like yours."

"Uh-huh."

"I don't want to talk about him anymore, okay, Jack?"

"Just one more question, Robbie." Wetzel saw the rain was lessening as they talked. "Tell me, when you ran away from the bad man that night, how did you know which way to go?"

The little boy put his hands on his hips. His face became serious again as he concentrated on his thoughts. "There was a dog." His little round face smiled, the breeze pulled at his disheveled soft brown hair. "The dog … he showed me the way."

Wetzel stood and dropped his unfinished cigarette to the ground. "What did this dog look like, Robbie?"

"Oh, he was black … mostly, and … brown," Robbie bit at his lower lip as he touched his own eyebrows, "and he had brown eye brows, Jack."

Kneeling before the boy, Wetzel felt his pulse quickening. "This dog, did he run off?"

Robbie laughed. "Oh, no, he was only in my dreams; I think he wasn't *real*."

Wetzel sat back on his heels. His face clearly showed the shock of the revelation before him. "I knew a dog like that once."

The little boy's face became pensive. "Did he show you the way, Jack?"

"Yes. He surely did that, Robbie." Wetzel sighed deeply, "On numerous occasions, son. And just like he did with you, he saved my life, too."

"He was a *good* friend, huh, Jack?"

Wetzel's eyes moistened; a lump rose in his throat; he forced it back. "He was the *best* friend a man could ever have." He stood and patted the boy on his head. "Come on, son. Let's get you back to your momma."

"Okay, Jack. I still think she'll be madder'n all get out."

"You just remember you did nothing wrong, Robbie. It was the bad man who was wrong, not you."

"Yes sir."

"Good boy. Now, let's move out. We've got some miles to hike."

As they started down the West Fork trail, the little boy reached up and took Wetzel's hand. He looked down at the boy, who was intent on hiking as fast as he could and smiled. *If I had a son, I'd want him to be like Robbie. What a fine little fella you got here, Maggie.*

They hiked along for a time, the boy and man each in their own thoughts and neither one spoke. It was enough to enjoy the wilderness in each other's company. The rain ceased and the sun peeked through the least threatening clouds, appeared for awhile before it disappeared, and then reappeared moments later. Reaching the trail junction to Woodland Park, Wetzel sat on a rock, took off his pack and placed his jacket inside after procuring his canteen. He offered the canteen to Robbie as the boy scrambled up on the rock next to him.

Robbie drank thirstily, water running down his chin and onto his already wet shirt. Wetzel laughed as the boy handed the canteen back to him. "We're 'bout a mile out from the Cliff Dwellings; might just as well rest a tad before we head in."

"I went to the Cliff Dwellings once with my mom."

"Oh?"

The boy's face became pensive again. "I don't know how in the heck those Indians hauled water up to their houses so high up from the river."

Wetzel thought about what the boy said. From what he remembered about the cliff dwellers, they had built approximately forty rooms inside the natural caves and alcoves high above the canyon floor most likely for protection. They were a part of the Mogollon culture and lived only a short time at the dwellings. Building their structures with mortar, rock, and timbers from trees cut between 1276 and 1287 A.D., these pre-historic Indians forged a suitable subsistence on the abundant game and crops of corn, beans and squash from the rich, fertile soil of the Gila River valley until about 1300 A.D.

Wetzel cocked his hat back on his head with his thumb. He said nothing, sensing the boy had more to say.

"Anyhow, I would worry about stepping on a snake and breaking the water jug on the way up." He shook his head and pursed his lips as he looked at the older man sitting next to him. "I wouldn't make a very good Injun, would I, Jack?"

Wetzel almost laughed but then saw the sincerity on the little boy's face. He said solemnly, "If I was an Indian living at the dwellings, I can't think of anybody in the whole world I'd want with me more than you, Robbie."

The little boy's eyes brightened. "You wouldn't spoof me now, would ya, Jack?"

"I reckon not." Wetzel laughed as he pulled his hat down on his head and helped the boy down off the rock. They started down the trail and the boy took Wetzel's hand again. He looked up at the older man and smiled. "Jack Wetzel, I'm *glad* you're my friend."

CHAPTER THIRTY-SIX

McMurtry was up before first light, ate the rest of his jerky, and swallowed it down with water from his canteen. Slinging the rifle over his shoulder, he headed down the Middle Fork of the Gila River. He had lost all sign of the killer in the heavy rainfall and figured he'd just as likely headed that direction as any other.

Two hours passed as the wildlife officer hiked steadily down the Forest Service trail that lay adjacent to the river. Heading eastward, he passed through very steep portions of the canyon that were heavily wooded. Large towering Ponderosa pine trees stood watch over the yellow and red-leaved cottonwood, sycamore, hackberry, and box elder trees; thick willows and emory oak added to the beauty of the riparian area. Rock spires standing alone extended up toward the sky that was clearing with patches of blue appearing periodically.

He emerged from the tall timber into a small meadow on the north side of the river and walked through a thick stand of brilliantly yellow sunflowers, towering above his head. Enjoying his hike and the country, he nearly missed the trail junction sign advising him to turn south via Little Bear Canyon enroute to the Cliff Dwellings some three miles distant.

Pulling on the pack straps, he adjusted the pack higher on his wet, tired back. As he turned to proceed up Little Bear Canyon, he hesitated. There in the trail, he plainly saw a partial vibram boot print in the sandy soil. He stepped close, squatting on his heels as he unslung the rifle from his shoulder. There was no mistaking the imprint of a vibram toe from a hiking boot. Quickly, he looked for other prints, but could not find any legible vibram-soled prints. *Is it the killer's track?* It was difficult to make that call with a partial print, but McMurtry decided to take no chances.

Cocking the hammer on the rifle, he moved stealthily along, observing occasional fresh sign headed north up out of the river bottom toward Jordan Mesa. No sole prints, but broken branches, disturbed vegetation. It was difficult climbing out of the canyon, and he was breathing hard when he topped out. He knelt down behind a piñon pine; the mesa was covered in thick stands of alligator juniper and piñon pine with a sprinkling of oak trees.

McMurtry smelled the faint odor of smoke in the air, determined the direction of the wind and walked cautiously in that direction. After traveling about a quarter of a mile, he saw a tent through the thick vegetation. His heart pounding, he held the rifle at the ready as he approached the camp hidden deep on top of the mesa.

He dropped to his knee with the rifle butt against his shoulder. A man was resting in a hammock slung between two juniper trees. A rifle leaned against the tree where his head lay. The man was dressed in camouflage. A small campfire smoldered nearby. McMurtry watched the tent for several minutes to see if there were other occupants. Seeing none, he moved to better cover behind a juniper tree about fifty yards from the sleeping man in the hammock; he could still see the tent clearly if anyone should exit.

His voice rang out in the stillness of the wilderness, "*You,* in the hammock! Throw your hands up!"

The man jerked upright, looking around frantically to see where the voice was coming from and he reached for the weapon.

McMurtry leveled the rifle at his chest. "Touch that dadjimmed rifle, an' I'll kill ya, son."

The man's hand hesitated near his rifle.

"I'm a wildlife officer. You're under suspicion for kidnapping and murder. Put them hands in the air. *Now!* Damn you."

The man complied as he stood. McMurtry moved from cover and quickly walked up to within ten yards of the man in camouflage, covering him with the rifle. The man was dirty, unshaven with several days of beard stubble on his face and hair to his shoulders. His swarthy complexion was accentuated by his small black eyes set close together.

He spoke with a Spanish accent, "What's this all about?"

McMurtry motioned him to the ground with the rifle. "Shut up, on your belly; git on the ground."

The man started to speak again, "What—?

McMurtry stepped in swiftly and knocked the man to the ground with the rifle butt. He rolled the man in camouflage over and placed handcuffs on his wrists behind his back and double locked them. Roughly, he grabbed the prisoner by his hair and belt and jerked him to his feet. Pushing him toward the tent, he asked, "Who's in the tent?"

The man mumbled, "Nobody."

McMurtry shoved him to the ground and aimed the rifle at the tent. Cautiously, he opened the flap. No one; the inside was littered with camp gear, clothes, a sleeping bag, and standing in one corner was a hunting bow.

McMurtry thought of the kidnapped boy. "Where's them black clothes you been wearin'?"

The man frowned, "What black clothes?"

"Don't lie to me, you—" McMurtry slapped him hard in the face.

Struggling to speak, the man coughed, spat blood. "I ain't got no black clothes. I ... I just got outta the army ... back from Nam. I ain't bothering nobody up here."

"The hell ya say." McMurtry shoved him back to the ground, looking at the man's feet judging the size and then peered at the vibram-soled hunting boots next to the hammock.

"Like I was sayin', you're under arrest. You so much as twitch or cause a problem for me takin' you outta here, I'll bust you wide open." He grasped the man tightly by the shirt front and hauled him up to within inches of his own face. With clenched teeth, he rasped, "We *clear* on that, son?"

The man in camouflage said nothing, his small black, hate-filled eyes burned holes into the wildlife officer's; he nodded his shaggy head.

CHAPTER THIRTY-SEVEN

WETZEL SWUNG HIS OLD TRUCK INTO THE SILVER CITY POLICE STATION parking lot off Hudson Street. Sitting close to him was the little boy, Robbie Garcia. His mother rode shotgun near the passenger door. He parked and shut off the ignition. It was Wetzel's favorite time of the year—late fall with cool weather and for the most part clear, blue skies.

As usual, Robbie spoke first. "I'm kinda scared, Jack."

Wetzel looked across the seat at Maggie Garcia sitting next to the passenger window. Her pretty green eyes showed concern, but she said nothing. She was the most beautiful woman he'd ever seen.

She said, "Jack, I appreciate all you've done for my son. I ... *we* can't thank you enough."

Pretty and really nice. He took a deep breath.

He smiled at her then twisted in his seat turning his gaze to the little boy, sitting between them. "Nothin' to it, Robbie. I'll be right there with you and your momma. Like I told you, the police will have some men in another room. All you have to do is look at 'em and point out the man who kidnapped you, if you can."

"I don't want to be near that ... bad man again, Jack."

Wetzel took the boy gently by the shoulders. "He can't hurt you anymore, Robbie. He's behind bars." He continued softly, "If you can identify him in the lineup, they'll lock him away for good. Okay?"

The little boy pursed his lips. "Okay, Jack." He looked up at Wetzel and smiled. "We're burning daylight out here, huh?"

Wetzel laughed. "I reckon so, son."

The three entered the crowded police station. New Mexico State Police Sergeant Steve Hunt greeted them and he stepped forward with outstretched hand to Wetzel. He grinned. "My belly still smarts a bit, Jack, but I'm back at work."

Wetzel noticed no heavy gun belt around his waist. "I'm glad you're doing well, Steve. Is the lineup all set for Robbie? He's a tad nervous 'bout this whole affair."

Hunt turned to the little boy and knelt gingerly in front of him. "No need to be nervous, son. We just want to know if any of the men in the next room is the same man who kidnapped you. You'll be looking through a one-way window at several men, and they won't be able to see you." He stood and ushered all three of them into an adjacent small room then closed the door.

A large, heavy-set man in a Silver City Police uniform sat at a table. His voice was deep and gruff when he spoke. "Bring the boy up here by me, Steve."

Beyond the window in another room, two police officers lined four men up against a wall. Robbie walked up to the window with Sergeant Hunt; he looked intently at the four men, a frown on his face. The gruff policeman said, "I'm Chief Thompson. I want you to look very closely at all these men and tell me if any of them is the man who kidnapped you, okay?"

"Yes sir." The boy peered through the window as he tentatively placed his small hands on the windowsill.

"Remember, Robbie, they can't see you," said Hunt.

Wetzel saw all four men were dressed in camouflage clothing. All appeared scruffy with unkempt hair and unshaven faces.

The boy turned to Chief Thompson. "I … I don't know. The man was wearing black clothes and a black mask."

The police officers had the men turn first to one side then a full 180 degrees back to facing the boy. An intercom was turned on and each was asked to repeat the phrase, "Get into the truck!" When that was accomplished, Chief Thompson asked impatiently, "Well, did you recognize the kidnapper's voice?"

Robbie looked at the men again for several minutes while the chief drummed his fingers on the desk. "No," he answered, "but the bad man's voice sounded kinda like the man on the end." He pointed to his left.

Thompson stood from his chair, pointed at the man. "That one? The Mexican?"

"Yes sir, but I'm not sure that's him."

"What the hell do ya mean, you don't know? You were with him for some time," growled Thompson.

"If he says he doesn't know, he doesn't know, Pete." Wetzel took a step toward Thompson. "Lay off him."

Thompson turned to Wetzel. "Who the hell pulled your chain?"

Hunt stepped between the two men. "Now, hold on here. There's no need to get at each other's throats." He paused before speaking, "Robbie, are you saying you don't recognize the kidnapper in that room?"

The little boy started to cry. "It was so dark ... he had a mask."

"It's all right, son." Hunt motioned for Wetzel to take the boy out into the main foyer.

* * *

AFTER WETZEL the boy and his mother had left, Sergeant Hunt closed the door and turned to Chief Thompson. "What the hell was *that* all about?"

"*Well*? He pretty much pointed to the Mexican didn't he?"

"He said the man *sounded* like him, but he couldn't identify him as the *one*."

"Good enough for me. Besides he's the one McMurtry arrested with the bow."

"True enough, but I'm not sure how circumstantial evidence alone will hold up in court."

"We've made plenty of cases on circumstantial evidence over the years."

It was Hunt's turn to drum the fingers of his left hand on his right arm. "The suspect says he didn't kidnap or murder anybody, and McMurtry didn't find any black clothing or arrows for the bow."

Thompson grunted. "Hell, they all say they're innocent. He most likely burned the clothes and buried the arrows."

"Maybeso, Pete." The state policeman turned and peered out the dirty window. He spoke over his shoulder. "You ever hear of a man who goes by the name of *Tomás*?"

The police chief's fingers drummed nervously on the desk for several moments. His eyes flicked toward the state policeman's back then to the floor. "No … can't say that I have." He cleared his throat. "Why, what's this … uh, Tomás got to do with anything?"

Hunt turned to face Thompson. "Maybe nothing … maybe everything." Searching the police chief's eyes, he continued, "My buddy with the DEA in El Paso says an informant of his talks of a man by the name of Tomás, who comes and goes as he pleases from Mexico." Thompson's eyelids shuttered briefly.

"Word is that such a man, if he even exists, might be operating here in New Mexico working for one of the drug bosses down in Mexico."

Thompson's eyelids fluttered again. "Sounds like a ghost story to me, Steve." He chose to look at his fingers drumming on the desktop and not at the state policeman.

"My DEA friend says this … ghost … is ex-Mexican Marine Special Forces." Hunt's voice had a metallic ring to it. "If such a man were operating here in Silver City, I find it hard to believe *you* wouldn't be aware of it."

Thompson slammed his fist on the desk, his eyes blazed. "You believe whatever the hell you want. I don't give a damn."

Hunt placed his palms on the desk; his eyes locked with the police chief's. "You'd better give a damn. In case you haven't noticed, we've got dead bodies stacked up here like cord wood—a rancher murdered in the forest, an old woman murdered right here in town along with your Internal Affairs officer for Christ's sake! Then there's the assault on my tracker and Sheriff's deputies, a little boy kidnapped, your shootout with one of your *own* officers! *Jeez,* Pete, what the hell does it take to light a fire under you, anyhow?"

Thompson sighed. "You've got your man, Steve. He's sitting in jail at the courthouse."

Hunt's shook his head as he strode to the door. "Maybeso."

"You … uh, keep me informed of any new developments. Huh, Steve?"

The door closed with Hunt's exit. Chief Thompson sat at the desk deep into his own thoughts, his fingers continued to drum nervously on the desktop.

CHAPTER THIRTY-EIGHT

WETZEL SAT QUIETLY WATCHING DISTRICT RANGER HOOD SHUFFLE PAPERS in his lap at the Gila National Forest Supervisor's Office located east of the VFW hall in Silver City, New Mexico. He shared the room with Hood, a human resources employee for the U.S. Forest Service, and the forest supervisor himself, Warren Carter.

Carter was a self-made man who had worked his way up in the Forest Service ranks over many years, most of his service in the Southwest. He was a solid-built man with a barrel chest, and thinning, short gray hair that had been thick and dark in his younger years. Proud to be in the ranks of the U.S. Forest Service, he always wore his tan uniform shirt, green jeans and a pair of cowboy boots with pride. Carter was well respected by the Gila National Forest staff and within the Silver City community as a fair man who was quite knowledgeable as a natural resource manager and leader.

Wetzel sat with his Stetson in hand and listened as his boss, District Ranger Hood, articulated how he, Wetzel, had violated Forest Service policy on several occasions after he had been clearly advised not to ever again carry a firearm while performing his duties as the general district assistant for the Wilderness District.

District Ranger Hood's thick dark-rimmed glasses slid down the bridge of his large red bulbous nose where they skidded to a halt. His high-pitched voice droned on about how this employee had been insubordinate in the regard of carrying a firearm on duty. He stated that he could not allow any employee under his supervision to violate policy.

Wetzel thought the man's short crew hair cut looked especially official this morning. But Hood was about to lose a lower button on his uniform shirt where his protruding belly attempted to escape confinement above his belt buckle.

As Hood finished with his assessment of the facts in the case, Carter leaned back in his chair and rubbed his tanned jaw without speaking. Eventually, he turned his gaze to Wetzel. A quick, easy smile appeared and then was gone. "Well, well, Jack. How the hell are you?"

Wetzel stirred in his chair gripping his Stetson. "Fine, sir."

"How's your mom?"

"She's doing well, Mr. Carter. Still ranching and enjoying it."

"Great woman—Helen Wetzel." He paused. Ranger Hood's face turn redder as Carter discussed matters other than the hearing itself. "I knew your dad quite well, Jack. He was a good man and an exemplary Forest Ranger."

Embarrassed, Wetzel pulled at his hat brim. "Well, thank you, sir."

The forest supervisor continued, "I worked for him when I first started my career with the government. Did you know that?"

District Ranger Hood squirmed in his chair. "Sir, with all due respect—"

Carter locked eyes with Hood until the latter dropped his gaze. "Hood, you've had time to tell your side of this. Now it's time to let others talk and for you to keep your mouth shut."

"Yes sir," District Ranger Hood mumbled.

Carter leaned forward with his elbows on the desk. "Now then … this matter of the firearms; what do you have to say, Jack?" His brown eyes beneath shaggy gray brows searched Wetzel's eyes. The old ranger's eyes displayed openness, an interest in hearing another side of the events that had transpired.

Wetzel took a deep breath and exhaled. "Don Ramirez asked—"

Carter stood suddenly. "Let's see if I understand the facts, son." Turning, he peered out the large window in his office as he spoke over his shoulder, "You were asked by the New Mexico State Police to help find a missing rancher, and after *voluntarily* agreeing to do so, the very man who murdered the rancher came very close to killing you." He turned back to face Wetzel. "Hood, here," he motioned toward

Wetzel's supervisor, "alleges you had a firearm with you when tracking this criminal."

Wetzel started to speak, but Carter raised a hand to silence him. "I spoke with the deputy, who accompanied you on the search, and he stated when he offered a firearm to you for protection, you told him you had enough killing in Viet Nam." Carter sat in the desk chair his dark blue eyes blazed at Wetzel. "Is that accounting correct so far, son?"

"Well, yes … but—"

"Yes or no?"

Wetzel exhaled. "Yes."

Carter turned to District Ranger Hood. "And, since we have no other corroborating eye witness stating to the contrary, I find the allegation for the first violation of forest rules in regard to possessing a firearm unsubstantiated and therefore dismissed."

Hood's face reddened, but he said nothing.

Leaning back in his office chair, Carter continued, "As to the second allegation, I understand you took a pistol with you when assisting the New Mexico State Police in their raid on the marijuana garden below Haystack Mountain." He grinned. "No real point in attempting to deny that as one of the bullets found in Officer Peach came from your pistol and, after all, you were there, on forest property."

Wetzel started to reply; Carter again held up his hand. "Lastly, the third allegation when you assisted the Grant County Sheriff's Office to search for the Garcia boy who was kidnapped. Hood says you took a pistol *and* a rifle with you." He interlaced his fingers as his elbows rested on the desk. "I spoke with Wildlife Officer Bob McMurtry yesterday in regard to this third allegation, and he very succinctly told me that if I was so … *dadjimmed* interested in what my Forest Service employees took with them when they *voluntarily* tracked dangerous criminals, I ought to have been there myself."

Carter chuckled. "Then he proceeded to tell me he didn't recollect what the hell you had with you or what you were wearing during the search incident. He obviously had more important considerations."

Carter slapped his desk with his hands. "So, that leaves us with one out of three, now doesn't it, Jack?"

Wetzel said nothing.

Motioning toward District Ranger Hood, Carter said quietly, "He wants your head on a platter, boy." Pausing, he scratched the back of his head. "Fired; terminated for insubordination."

Wetzel sighed, but again knew better than to speak.

"We have forest policy in regard to prohibiting the possession of firearms while performing official duties for a couple of reasons: the most obvious is liability for the agency and secondarily to keep our employees out of harm's way. The problem today is that we actually put our employees smack dab in harm's way by sending them into dangerous situations without proper training or equipment, such as firearms, when raiding a marijuana field."

Carter stood again and turned to peer out the window. "We're going to rectify that situation very soon by having Forest Service Law Enforcement Officers on the districts. These officers will be properly trained and armed for that type duty. It may take awhile, but by God, we'll make it happen. The Special Agents assigned in the regional offices just aren't available for the work load we have in the forests." His brow furrowed. "I'd think a man with your skills and temperament would make an excellent Law Enforcement Officer for us, Jack."

Hood attempted to speak. "Warren, I hardly think—"

Turning abruptly, Carter said, "I haven't finished," as he pointed a finger first at Hood then at Wetzel. "That being said, Jack, you had *no* right to take a firearm with you on duty when your supervisor advised you not to do so against Forest Service policy." Carter strode to the other side of the room and then back.

He stood in front of Wetzel with his hands in his pants pockets. "It's for that reason that I've decided to suspend you for fifteen days, son. Since I figger the Forest Service caused half the problem, we'll split the thirty days I would normally suspend you." He nodded at the human resource specialist. "That's *without* pay, the suspension to take place forthwith." He gazed individually at each person in the room. "Do I make myself clear?"

No one dared speak. "Good! I consider this matter closed. Show yourselves out; I've got work to do."

CHAPTER THIRTY-NINE

NOVEMBER, 1973

McMurtry eased his Game and Fish truck in parallel with Little Walnut Road next to an older one-story house. The night was cold; Thanksgiving was just around the corner and the hint of snow was in the air. As he exited the vehicle, he pulled his brown canvas jacket out and put it on over his coveralls.

Juanita had invited him to a party at her *tia's* home, and although he welcomed the opportunity to see her and the boys again, he wasn't too sure about the family event or the aunt. Striding to the door, he heard Mexican music playing and loud voices of folks having a good time. He stepped up on the porch and knocked on the door. No one answered. Knocking several times more loudly with no one coming to the door, he proceeded on around the house to the rear following a faint trail.

He found everyone in the back yard enjoying the music, visiting, and eating; food—lots of it—sat on two long tables. As he entered the lighted area, someone shouted, "It's Mac!" and a little boy ran toward him, tackling his leg.

Grinning, McMurtry reached down and tousled the boy's hair. "How ya been, Elfigo?"

The little boy looked up at him. "You wannna put me in the

gazookus hold, Mac?" He referred to a wrestler's hold that McMurtry had placed many times on both boys while playing with them.

McMurtry laughed. "No, I reckon not right now, son. I've got me a powerful hunger. How's them vittles?"

Elfigo's brother appeared next to them. Jose smiled. "Them veetles is good, Mac," he said, trying to emulate the wildlife officer's speech.

"Wel-l-l now," McMurtry knelt in front of both boys, "I'm sure proud you boys are gettin' to see me tonight."

A voice behind him said, "Are you proud to see me, *Roberto*?"

He stood, and turning, saw Juanita. She was the prettiest woman he could ever recollect seeing in his entire life. Her dark hair hung to her shoulders. She wore a light beige jacket over a blue sweater and Levi jeans with comfortable black shoes. Her brown eyes smiled.

"You bet I am."

She took his arm, directing him toward the food and folks partying. McMurtry's stomach growled; he hadn't eaten since breakfast. An older Hispanic woman walked over to them as they headed for the food table. With her gray hair pulled back into a tight roll at the nape of her neck, the woman wore wire-rimmed glasses, and appeared tall and strong for a woman of her age. She wore black cotton slacks with a warm-looking white sweater. As they stood there the older Hispanic woman casually surveyed him from head to toe with piercing black eyes. She broke the silence, "So you're *Roberto*—?"

"That's the rumor, ma'am." He smiled at her.

She did not return the smile, and finished the question, "—the *gringo* who has been seeing my niece?"

Juanita intervened. "*Sí, Tia. Este es Roberto* McMurtry, *mi novio.*" She turned to McMurtry. "Thees ees *mi Tia Josie.*"

McMurtry extended his hand, "Proud to make your acquaintance, ma'am."

The elderly woman did not shake his hand nor address him. Instead, she turned to Juanita and spoke in rapid fire Spanish. "Why do you like these *gringos*? Do you not see that you should marry your own kind?"

Juanita's eyes blazed as she heatedly replied to the woman in Spanish. Then she abruptly took McMurtry by the arm and steered him toward the food once more. He did not understand what had transpired in the conversation but knew it had not been cordial.

Watching as she literally threw food on his plate, he said softly, "Easy, Juanita. I got to eat that once you've throwed it all over my plate."

She stopped filling the plate, closed her eyes, and exhaled slowly. "I'm so sorry, *Roberto*."

"No need to be." He placed his hands on her shoulders. "Not everybody's goin' to take a likin' to me." He shrugged. "That's just the way it is in this ol' world. Come on, let's eat and enjoy the party."

Later, he met all the other family members who were very kind and respectful to him. McMurtry especially enjoyed visiting with Juanita's father, Pedro Flores. Flores had worked at the copper mine in Santa Rita for thirty-five years as an electrician. Señor Flores was not a tall man, but he did not appear short either. Dark eyes and complexion with deep creases in his leathery face weathered by the outdoors and incessant sunshine, distinguished white hair, and a quiet easy way about him made Pedro Flores a favorite to McMurtry immediately.

Juanita's mother was shy, and although she did not converse at length with him, he felt comfortable and at home around her. The uncles were loud and boisterous, and of course full of *cerveza*. Tio Beto approached him with *flan* for dessert as he finished his second helping of tamales, rice, and re-fried beans.

Beto was the youngest brother of Pedro Flores, and unlike his older brother, Beto had never worked much at anything for very long during his lifetime. However, according to him, he was an expert on everything. Sporting a big belly that extended over his belt, he slapped McMurtry on the back. "*¿Qué pasa, guero?* What's happening, gringo?"

"Not much, Beto. Just fixin' to head back up to the Cliff Dwellings."

Beto laughed. "Haf a beer man, enjoy the party."

"No thanks on the beer. I got to drive the state truck."

"Suit yourself, man. I'm gonna haf another." Beto snorted and turned toward the ice chest.

McMurtry looked for Juanita as he tossed his paper plate in the trash and readied to leave. He thought he heard her voice inside the house so he moved in that direction. As he stepped inside from the back porch, he heard a man's voice. The man shouted loudly in Spanish then English. Stocky of build, he wore a straw cowboy hat, western shirt, Wrangler jeans and boots. A black pencil mustache made his head appear thinner than it actually was. His face was dark as was his close-cropped hair. McMurtry saw the man had directed his comments to Juanita and her father.

Moving in closer to hear what was being said, he stopped just short of standing adjacent to *Señor Flores.*

Juanita's eyes blazed as she stood toe to toe with the man and exchanged heated comments. The man switched to English. "I'll discipline my sons however I want, and neither you nor your two-bit father will tell me otherwise."

"Don' speek about *mi papa* that way."

The man sneered. "Shut up, you ... trashy—" and he shoved her back from him. A surprised McMurtry leapt forward and hit him hard below his left ear. Staggering backward, the man attempted to stand upright and as he turned, looking for his adversary, McMurtry swung his right with all his weight behind a punch that landed on the man's jaw. The man's head snapped back and he dropped to the floor.

Quiet blanketed the room full of stunned people who now peered down at the prostrate man lying still on the floor. Those same sets of eyes turned up toward McMurtry; total silence. Tio Beto burped and farted loudly.

McMurtry cleared his throat and addressed Juanita's father. "Say ... Pay-dro Floor-eez, just who in the hell *is* that feller yonder on the floor?"

"He ees my daughter Juanita's ex-*esposo, Roberto,*" the elderly gentleman said softly with amusement in his dark eyes.

"Ez-pozo?" queried a cautious McMurtry as he leaned in close to the older man. "Jest exactly what is one o' them ez-posos anyhow?"

Juanita answered. "He wass *mi* ... husband, *Roberto.* You know, before the divorce."

"Wel-l-l ... I'll be dadjimmed." McMurty tucked his big, coarse hands inside the front of his coveralls. He winked at Juanita Flores, nodded politely to her father and headed for his truck.

CHAPTER FORTY

WETZEL SAT ON THE PORCH OF THE RENTED APARTMENT ACROSS FROM THE Catholic Church. His new-found friend Robbie sat next to him in the quiet evening. Sunset arrived; the clouds in the west were accentuated by an orange glow of a tired sun about to call it a day. He pulled the collar up on his jacket as he felt the chill of the fall night creep slowly into his bones.

"Robbie, why don't you go inside where it's warm, uh?"

The little boy looked up at him, his big brown eyes smiling under long lashes. "Okay, Jack. Let's you and me play a game of checkers!"

Wetzel laughed as he stood. "You wanna get beaten *again*?"

Robbie's face took on a solemn look. "I'll get you this time. I know it."

Patting the boy's shoulders Wetzel opened the door to the apartment. "All right, but I've got to find your momma at the church first, okay?"

The little boy entered the apartment. "Okay, Jack."

"You close and lock the door, son." He motioned toward his border collie lying on a rug in the living room. "Stay with Montie. I'll be right back."

Only when he heard the door close and the dead bolt click did Wetzel step down off the porch and walk across the street toward the church.

* * *

THE BOY PLAYED with the dog for several minutes, throwing the stuffed toy across the room with Montie chasing to retrieve the toy and returning it to his friend. Robbie laughed hard at the dog running about, flipping the throw rug up and losing traction on the slick linoleum floor.

The dog stopped suddenly and ceased all activity. He cocked his head to one side, both ears perked at full attention. Then a slow, low growl began deep in his throat, he bared his fangs and barked loudly.

Robbie started for the door as he admonished the dog for being so loud, but the dog wouldn't let the boy past him. The boy tried again in vain as the growling dog kept him away from the door.

The little boy's brow furrowed as his lips pouted and he placed his hands on his hips. "*Montie, come here!*" he said with all the authority he could muster in his best command voice, but the dog remained in front of him always and would not let him pass.

It was the boy's turn to cock his head sideways. Listening intently, he could not hear anything outside, but the longer he listened, he thought he heard someone try the door then soft footsteps outside the apartment. Images of the bad man dressed in black filled his head, the skin on his neck prickled and a severe shudder went through his little body followed by a fear greater than any he had ever known filled his whole being. He sobbed as he ran for the bedroom and hid under his bed. The growling dog followed, nestling against him.

CHAPTER FORTY-ONE

MAGGIE GARCIA FINISHED HER PRAYERS AND LIT A CANDLE FOR HER missing husband. As usual each evening, she had prayed not only for her Juan but also for her deceased father and now *Doña Consuelo Vasquez.* The church was quiet and dark with only limited lighting to minimally illuminate the interior for those few, like herself, who visited at such a late hour. The church was never locked.

The large wooden door in the rear of the church creaked and she looked up to see her friend Wetzel appear, hat in hand. She smiled. He was the most polite man she had ever met. Walking quickly, she met him at the rear door.

His tanned face showed a worried expression. "I didn't interrupt you, did I, Maggie?"

She smiled at him. "No. Not at all, Jack. I was just leaving."

He followed her out of the church. The dusk had been swept away by the darkness of the night. Two cats screeched at each other as they fought down the street. They walked slowly down the steps in front of the church breathing in the clear, fresh air.

Wetzel spoke first. "Feels like snow."

"Maybeso. Thanksgiving's just around the bend."

"Do you mind sitting a spell on the steps?"

She looked quickly at him, unable to read his face in the dark of the evening. "Sure … okay. How's right here?" She pointed at the bottom step near Market Street. He nodded and sat next to her. Reaching into his shirt pocket, he withdrew a Lucky Strike cigarette, stuck it in the corner of his mouth, and lit it with his silver lighter.

He smoked in silence for some time and Maggie knew to say nothing. He would talk when it was time. They had come to know each other well of late. A bright red Dodge Charger cruised past, momentarily illuminating them in the headlights and then disappeared down Yankee Street. Wetzel tipped his Stetson back on his head with his thumb. He finished his cigarette and stubbed it out at the bottom of the step. Shifting uneasily on the concrete step, he said, "Maggie, what's to become of us?"

She turned to face him, brows knitted. "What do you mean, Jack?"

"I mean *us*, you and me."

Hesitating before answering, she replied, "I'm sorry, did I do something to make you angry?"

"No, nothing like that. Maggie, I mean no disrespect for Juan, but I ... don't think he's coming back."

She gasped. "Oh—"

"It's been too long ... and ... God help me, I love you!"

Clasping her hands tightly in her lap, Maggie peered through the darkness of the evening at the young man sitting next to her. She saw he had dropped his hat and was distinctly reminded he had never done so in her presence before. The evening breeze toyed at her red hair and chilled her as she sat on the cold concrete steps saying nothing.

He finally spoke. "I'm sorry, Maggie."

She reached out and gently touched his hands with hers. "Don't be, Jack. I'm ... I'm greatly honored you have an interest in me. That you love me is beyond my comprehension tonight."

Wetzel started to reply, but she placed her finger on his lips. "I love you, too, my friend."

"But—?"

"I'm married."

A great sigh escaped his lips, and he took her in his arms and hugged her tight to his breast. "Oh, Maggie, I know ... I know." He held her at arm's length and said softly to the heavens above, "Dear God, I mean no disrespect, only love for this woman, who I want to be my wife."

"Jack!" she cried out.

They sat awkwardly on the concrete steps, holding each other tightly not wanting to let each other go. A vehicle drove west on Market Street illuminating the couple as they sat in front of the church steps. The bright blue car passed them, moving very slowly, then stopped and backed up to where they sat. A young man leaned across the passenger side of the 1962 Chevy Impala and spoke through the window. "Hi there. I'm looking for a Maggie Garcia. Do you have any idea where she lives?"

Still holding each other, they said nothing. The young man gazed at one then the other, shrugged and started to drive away.

"I'm Maggie Garcia!" she shouted.

The brakes were applied firmly, and the young man backed the car to his original location in front of the church. "Good," he replied with a smile, "You'll make my job easier tonight if you sign for this." He produced a brown envelope, holding it out to her from within the car.

"What is it?" she asked.

He paused. "Oh, I'm sorry. I work for Western Union." He pushed the envelope closer to her outstretched hand without getting out of the car. "It's a telegram from the U.S. Army, ma'am. And it's addressed to you."

CHAPTER FORTY-TWO

Police Chief Pete Thompson yawned loudly and stretched his arms above his head. He stood from his desk and looked at the clock on the wall. It was ten o'clock. He'd stayed later at work than he intended and it was definitely time to go home. His wife had called him twice, advising him that his supper was cold.

He'd done enough police work today for the citizens of Silver City. Yawning again he reached for his jacket hanging on the office wall peg. He put the jacket on, closed the open file on his desk and placed it in the metal file cabinet near the window. Taking a key from his heavy key chain on his duty belt, he securely locked it.

Walking down the small hallway, he opened the door to dispatch and stuck his head in. It was a weekday and only one dispatcher was working the night shift. The woman quickly placed a novel she had been reading down on the desk at her work station.

Thompson laughed to himself. *Hell, I don't give a damn if she reads her book when it's slow. Only that she answer the goddamned radio when officers call in.*

"How's it going tonight, Amanda?"

"Slow, sir; very slow."

The old chief grinned as he chuckled. "That's the way I like it, quiet and peaceful."

"Yes sir."

"You have a good evening. I'm going home." He closed the door and proceeded down the hallway to the back door. Opening the door, he stepped out in the clear, cold night. *Damn near forgot. Hell, it's Thanksgiving tomorrow. I can make up for all the suppers I've missed.* The stars literally danced in the sky overhead as a partial moon illuminated the parking lot behind the police station and showed him the way to his old truck he used to commute to work each day.

Yawning again, he fumbled with his keys, trying to find the one for his truck door and ignition. He sensed something first then he thought he heard a very subtle sound behind him close by. He shrugged it off to the wind that had begun to pick up. *I need to start wearing my heavier jacket. Damn, it's cold out here.*

He found the key and opened the door, the old metal door creaking in the quiet night. As he started to get into his truck, he heard the subtle noise again and turning nonchalantly toward the sound, he gasped. *"You!"*

His officer awareness attempted to move from ground zero in the white zone all the way to red. It never made the transition.

A soft popping sound broke the stillness of the night, an impact and then another a second from the first. The first bullet tore through his chest, destroying his heart, and the second bullet entered his head between his eyes, blowing out the back part of his head. Chief Thompson dropped to the ground dead.

The assailant quickly picked up the shell casings, unscrewed the heavy silencer from the barrel of the semi-automatic pistol and slipped them into each jacket pocket. He turned and walked down Hudson Street for a block and disappeared into a side street. Standing there momentarily, he listened for any sound of alarm or pursuit. Hearing none, he smiled as he removed the black ski mask.

His right hand inadvertently moved in toward his torso, the thumb and forefinger touching as if cupping a cigarette in the hand with the little finger nervously flicking at the ashes on the end of a cigarette that did not exist.

* * *

IT WAS THANKSGIVING DAY; the warm New Mexico sunshine on a clear, cloudless day morning reassuring to the old retired priest as he shuffled his tired feet up the steps and entered the mission church at San

Lorenzo. The small village and church sat to the west and below the Black Range Mountains.

As dusk approached, the priest grunted as he genuflected in front of the altar in the little empty church. After making the sign of the cross, he prayed, *"Padre nuestro, que estás en el cielo ...Our Father, who art in heaven ...*

He prayed tonight for resolution and an end to the Vietnam War, for peace in the world, for the poor parishioners who frequented the small church and struggled daily to make ends meet. And lastly, he prayed for the souls of those who had been slain in the Silver City area —a rancher, police officers, an old woman, and alas, the police chief. The old priest sighed; so much violence and death for such a small community. There was talk of drugs being the basis for the killings; drugs, the devil's tools.

Outside, the shadow of the mountain slowly crept over the dwellings in the small village then the little church itself. Closing his eyes, he continued, *"...y líbranos del mal ...Amen. ...and deliver us from evil ... Amen."*

PART II

I walk down the valley of silence
Down the dim, treeless valley alone.
And I hear not the fall of a footstep
Around me, save God's and my own
And the hush of my heart is as holy
As heaven where angels have flown.

-May Kittrell McLaughlin

CHAPTER FORTY-THREE

Juarez, Mexico, Spring 1974

The man walked briskly across the Bridge of the Americas to Mexico. Beyond El Paso to the west the sky appeared as if someone had taken a large stick and stirred up the heavens to create a mosaic of red, yellow, white, and blue. Dressed in black with a dark backpack hung over his right shoulder, the man's obvious athletic build and movement gave him an aura of strength and agility as he moved. Black military-style boots cushioned his average sized feet. He wore no hat or cap only dark sunglasses that shielded dark brown penetrating eyes. Coal black hair cut short on his handsome head failed to disguise the semblance of curls. His gait was easy, seemingly without effort or strain, but there was something about the man—unquestionable confidence and hardness exuding from him—that distinguished him from the hundreds of other men crossing from El Paso, Texas into Juarez, Mexico.

Midway across the bridge, he hesitated; his right hand inadvertently moved toward his torso, the thumb and forefinger touching as if cupping a cigarette from the wind with the little finger flicking at ashes of a cigarette that did not exist. His gaze took in the numerous shanties and shacks on the Mexican side of the border. These makeshift structures were strewn up and down the steep hillsides, some near the Rio Grande River, the permanent border between the United States and Mexico. *Pobres Mexicanos. Poor and a helluva lot of them with no way in hell to ever better themselves.* He sighed as he moved on over the bridge. Each time he crossed over into Mexico, he was reminded how fortunate he was and when he returned to the United States, he never stopped or looked back.

Ciudad Juarez was a very important city in Mexico and economically more important for the State of Chihuahua. The 1970 census showed the population at 400,000 and the city had grown by leaps and bounds each year. Economically, the state had been traditionally one of agriculture and ranching. However, since 1964 and the introduction of the *Maquiladora* Program of border industrialization, the city had become a major manufacturing hub.

The man strode past the American Customs officers, who were busily checking folks coming into the United States and passed through heavy metal revolving doors into Mexico. As he passed two Mexican Customs officers standing on the sidewalk surveying the returning pedestrians, one of the officers, a short, squatty man with a large belly, eyed him suspiciously and then stepped directly in front of him with his hand on his sidearm. "*Su mochila ... demela!*"

The man in black did not hand him the backpack, but instead ignored him as he turned toward the other officer and said in Spanish, "How are you, Michael? Your family?"

The second officer immediately recognized the man in black; his eyes widened, fear exuding from them. "*Hola,* Tomás!"

Hitching the heavy gun belt higher up around his hips, he said quickly to his fellow officer, "I know this man. We served in the Marines together." He cleared his throat as he took the man in black by the shoulder and directed him away from the other officer and down the street toward a waiting black limousine.

"We're fine, Tomás, thanks to God."

They reached the limousine parked along the bustling street. Men jostled others aside on the crowded sidewalk, cars and trucks sped past, some honking their horns in impatience at the crawling pace.

The man in black said, "*Que bueno, amigo,*" and transferred several large bills into the palm of the customs officer's hand as they shook hands. The officer smiled as he pocketed the bribe. "*Muchas gracias! Hasta luego.*"

"De nada, amigo."

A slender dark man stepped out of the back of the limousine and held the door. A carefully trimmed mustache outlined his handsome face; in contrast to blue jeans, tennis shoes and cheap clothing of the majority of pedestrians, his expensive, immaculate suit and tie, and highly polished shoes accentuated his stature. Long dark hair was pulled back tight on his head into a ponytail. He smiled at the man in black.

"Welcome home, Tomás."

The man in black said nothing as he climbed into the car.

The Mexican Customs officer stood at the curb as the driver of the limousine directed the car into busy traffic and sped away. He reached into his pocket with his right hand to feel the wad of bills. His wife would be very happy tonight. Maybe she would make him equally as contented? *¿Como no?* He grinned as he returned to his post; his lips parted displaying yellow teeth, a front tooth missing.

* * *

IN THE DARKNESS, the limousine followed the winding narrow road up the hill to a large villa sitting atop the crest overlooking Juarez. In stark contrast to the shanties and shacks of the very poor, the villa and other expensive homes were owned by the *muy ricos* and powerful; men who controlled everything of any significance in Juarez, the State of Chihuahua, and beyond. The man in black stepped out of the car, pulling his backpack with him. He quickly unzipped a side compartment and then slung it over his left shoulder.

He walked up to the entrance as the heavy, mahogany door opened for him. A solid, muscular man with short-cropped hair and a large scar running from his right eye down his cheek to his throat stood in the foyer. Holding a fully automatic rifle; he nodded curtly at the newest guest. He slung the rifle over his shoulder and patted him down. "He awaits you in the study, Tomás." The deep, gritty voice continued in Spanish, "You're late; leave the backpack with me."

Tomás studied him warily. His voice was sharp, "He's been like a father to me, Carlos. As for you ... *vete a la chingada,* go to hell!" He turned, his backpack remaining on his left shoulder, and bounded effortlessly up the winding, marble staircase to the second floor and then down a long hallway to where it abruptly ended with an open doorway leading into a large master bedroom on the left and a closed door to the right. Standing briefly in front of the intricately carved wooden door, he rapped on the door with his knuckles. "*¿Papá?*"

A deep commanding voice called out, "*Entrale, mi'jo!*"

An older man sat behind an ornate desk littered with papers. He was tall and heavy set. Wearing an expensive, tailored blue suit and a power-toned red tie, he stood as the man in black entered the study, and then he walked around the desk to greet him. His thin, graying hair transitioned to white at his temples and sideburns accentuating his dark, swarthy complexion. Pearly white teeth displayed a full smile, but the deep set black eyes were hard and showed no emotion. Crow's feet appeared in the brown, leathery skin at the corner of his eyes. His powerful arms encircled the slender man in black as they embraced. Pablo Enrique was a very powerful man, who had become the head of one of the largest and most dangerous drug cartels in Mexico. He had achieved that distinction by being unusually cunning and cruel. He was used to having his way, and it showed in his body language and dialogue.

"Have a seat, *mi'jo*," he said in a conciliatory tone which was uncharacteristic of him; he motioned to a chair as he continued back to his chair behind the large desk and sat down heavily. Human skulls lined an entire shelf. Several large glass jars sat on wooden shelves directly behind the desk. They were filled with formaldehyde; an assortment of hands, feet, and sexual organs of men and animals were preserved in full view of any visitors who might be intimidated. Reptiles hissed and rattled at his presence from glass containers on the floor. The room smelled of substance that the man in black could not discern. Was it a drug that he was unaware of?

Tomás sat in the soft chair, his dark brown eyes searching those of the older man. He chose to say nothing. Enrique's dark eyes displayed a glowing red tint.

Pablo asked, "Do you know why you are here, Tomás?"

"No."

"No?" Pablo leaned forward resting his arms on the desk. "You have *not* been following my directions, *mi'jo*." The eyes became pointed and his voice had an edge to it. "*Why*? Why is this so? I am … confused." A large tongue licked at dry lips.

Tomás peered again into Pablo's eyes and read nothing there. He settled back in his chair still maintaining eye contact. "I *have* been following your directions ... for many years now, *Papa.*"

The older man slammed his heavy ring-laden hand on the top of the desk. "The hell you have!" Eyes blazed, the tongue licked at lips again. "I told you to kill anyone who could identify you ... to kill the boy!"

Tomás sighed and breathed in a swallow of fresh air but said nothing.

"Well?"

"I've killed just about anything that walked or crawled for you since I was a young boy. All you had to do was give the order."

"*Sí,* as it should be. I *raised you,* you ungrateful little *cabrón,* bastard. And you have always obeyed me as I taught you. *¿Verdad?"*

The man in black said nothing.

A heavy fist slammed on the desk, again sending papers flying. "Answer me, damn you! I've had men killed for less."

"The boy doesn't know me. He can't identify me."

"And *I said* ... it is better with no loose ends. I want nothing to interfere with my future plans. Since they found the gold there, it is an opportunity to fill *our* coffers with it."

Pablo pursed his lips, and then took a deep breath as he smoothed out his gray mustache. "*No one* disobeys my orders; no one, not even *you.*" He retrieved a cigar from a box on his desk, bit the end off, and lit it. Puffing lightly, he blew smoke up into the air above him. It had a calming effect on him.

Removing the cigar from between his teeth, he reached into a drawer with his right hand and withdrew a powdery substance from a tin canister then blew it from the palm of his hand into the room. Almost immediately, Tomás felt dizzy; his right hand slid inadvertently into the unzipped pocket of the backpack. His hand gripped the semi-automatic pistol as he stood unsteadily.

"Sit down, *mi'jo.*" The soothing voice continued, "*Por favor.*"

Lightheaded, *Tomás* hesitated, and then sat down heavily in the soft chair. The room began to spin around him, skulls began to take on facial expressions of men he had killed and the rattlesnakes' incessant buzzing increased to a crescendo that obliterated all other sound in the room.

The older man leaned forward on his elbows. "You will return and set up operations again. The gold—the money is there for the taking, and *I* want it! The area is prime for drugs, prostitution, and extortion. And you *will* kill the boy as ordered." He hesitated for emphasis. "I will not tolerate your failure to obey me again. You fail me, and I will have you executed." He waved toward the shelves behind him, "Your *cojones* will be added to one of these jars! Is that understood?"

Tomás could not keep his eyes open. He murmured, *"Sí, Papá."*

Pablo smiled broadly. "You have been like a son to me. I raised you and your brother. I sent you to school and to the Navy Marine training. I have given you *everything,* and all I ask in return is for your undying loyalty to me." His voice softened. "Is that too much to ask, *mi'jo*?"

The man in black lay back in the chair and closed his eyes. The room spun round and round, each time picking up in intensity. He could not keep his eyes open. He heard someone say, "Take him to his room and bring the *gringa* for his amusement."

CHAPTER FORTY-FOUR

JACK WETZEL LIGHTLY TOUCHED HIS SPURS TO THE BAY GELDING, "COME on, boy. We're almost home." The woven cotton lead rope for the trailing pack animals was dallied around a rubber-covered saddle horn as he grasped the rope near the end against his leather covered thigh. Working hard to keep up with the long-legged bay, two tired burros followed him trotting along the dry, dusty trail a mile from the trailhead, the entrance into the Gila Wilderness near the Gila Cliff Dwellings. Rosita in the lead carried the aluminum box panniers with his camp gear and the meager remains of his food supply after ten days. Wetzel's sheepherder tent and sleeping bag were covered with a tarp and lashed down tightly atop the panniers and sawbuck pack saddle with a secure diamond hitch. Chochi trailed along behind his female counterpart, his lead rope attached to a pigging string from Rosita's pack saddle. He carried a light load of trash in both canvas panniers on his back neatly tied down with a squaw hitch.

Wetzel wore a tan, long sleeved shirt with a shoulder patch signifying his employer as the U.S. Forest Service, Department of Agriculture. An official badge was pinned to his shirt front over the left pocket. Like the burros he was tired after working ten days in the Gila Wilderness and looked forward to a hot shower, clean clothes, and for some reason today a hankering for milk chocolate. As he descended from the high country, he could see Gila Center in the distance through the tree line. The administrative site consisted of a variety of government buildings: a helitack fire base complete with a helibase for landing multiple helicopters; house trailers for offices and seasonal residences for a large helitack crew; tan frame, stucco homes for full-time Forest Service employees. The Visitor Center and main Forest Service/National Park Service offices were located just downhill from the helitack fire base. The Forest Service fire cache, barn and corrals lay adjacent to the West Fork of the Gila River.

Wetzel pulled the bay up to allow the smaller burros an opportunity to rest. The bay pranced sideways, impatient to get to the barn. Wetzel gently brought the horse under control and said softly, "Easy, ol' boy. We'll get there soon enough, I reckon." Wetzel's dog Montie, an attentive border collie, took the opportunity to lay in the shade of a large alligator juniper tree, its rough, raised bark similar in appearance to that of the reptile it had been named for.

Rosita peered up at him, grateful for the short rest, and batted her long eye lashes at him. She swished her tail at Chochi, standing directly behind her and brayed loudly. Not satisfied, she took in air and brayed more loudly. The sound reverberated down into the canyon below. Wetzel's dark face broke into a smile. He thought he hadn't much to smile about lately. A startled Pinyon Jay flitted from one of the many alligator juniper trees nearby to a much larger gambel oak tree further from the trail. The sun had not yet set in the blue spring sky. The day had been windy as most spring days were in New Mexico, gusting up to 30 and 40 M.P.H. from a recent cold front passing through.

The incessant wind and sun burned Wetzel's face. A stained, gray Stetson hat covered a head of short-cropped brown hair. He peered from beneath the bent brim as his tall, slender figure sat easily in the saddle. Faded wrangler jeans and worn fringed leather chaps encased his long legs. Dust-covered White's boots with small-roweled spurs at the heels completed his foot attire. His heavy brown leather belt bore an encased portable radio on the left side and a worn brown leather holster on the right side with a .357 Smith & Wesson revolver snapped tightly inside.

Wetzel's tired brow furrowed as he recalled the nightmares from the previous night; vivid images from the war: the night sky lit up, thunderous explosions from rocket and mortar fire splitting his ear drums and shock waves throwing him to the ground. Coming to and frantically searching for his scout dog Smoky. Parrying a bayonet thrust from a North Vietnamese soldier, driving his own bayonet deep in the soldier's chest and crawling into a hollowed out tree with his injured scout dog; the F-105 jets swooping in, dropping bombs almost on top of the nearly overrun fire base. He swallowed hard as he inadvertently kept the bay's head up and away from the grama grass within easy reach of the trail.

And Maggie ... God, he loved her so! But she would never be his; she was another man's wife. Hell, she was married to his best friend from high school for Chrissake. Juan Garcia had been missing in action for almost two years, but then one day a telegram arrived stating that he was alive and coming home. He had been held captive and lost a leg to gangrene from injuries that had been untreated by the enemy. Wetzel's face flushed with shame for his thoughts in coveting another man's wife. It was difficult, if not impossible, for him to go to their house and visit them as he was afraid he might show his true feelings for his friend's wife. He honestly hadn't intended for things to turn out that way. He had truly believed that Juan was dead and would never return. And now he had fallen in love with Maggie.

The Forest Service portable radio at his waist crackled. "207 ... helitack dispatch." The bay's head jerked to attention; he pranced sideways, pawed at the ground.

Wetzel retrieved the portable radio after shifting the reins to his right hand. "207 ... go ahead."

"10-20? Grant County SO needs you pronto regarding a law enforcement matter."

Wetzel frowned. "I'm about thirty minutes from the barn. What do they need me for?"

"Robbery at the Lake Roberts store; suspects fled on a motorcycle then ditched it and are now hoofing it in the forest. Wildlife Officer McMurtry says he won't track 'em without you."

Wetzel sighed deeply as he touched his spurs to the bay and the horse and burros trotted down the trail. "10-4. Headed in. Have an agency truck at the barn for me, will you?" Montie, already ahead of him, disappeared from sight beyond the next switchback down the trail.

He smiled broadly as he thought about his friend, Bob McMurtry. McMurtry had transferred from the Tennessee Wildlife Resources Department to the New Mexico Game and Fish Department, and was stationed at the Heart Bar Ranch, a Game and Fish administrative site near Gila Center. The man fancied himself a master tracker. Wetzel snickered and then his face sobered. McMurtry had done an excellent job in helping him track and find Maggie's boy who had been kidnapped and taken into the wilderness. He had proven that he was indeed a master tracker, but Wetzel wasn't going to give him the satisfaction of letting him know his feelings about it, one way or the other.

Prior to the search for the boy, Wetzel had no official training to perform full-time law enforcement duties for the U.S. Forest Service. Forest Supervisor Warren Carter had recommended him to attend the newly established Federal Law Enforcement Training Center (FLETC) located near Glynco, Georgia, on an old naval base that had been renovated. The training center served as the law enforcement academy for all federal agencies with the exception of the FBI and DEA. Wetzel had just returned a couple of months ago, a duly commissioned Law Enforcement Officer (LEO) for the Forest Service, one of just a few within the organization. At police school, he'd received training in firearms, defensive tactics, criminal law, constitutional law, defensive and pursuit driving, crime scene investigation, report writing, and other pertinent topics.

When he reported back to his duty station, his supervisor, District Ranger Bill Hood, told him he really didn't feel that LEOs carrying guns were necessary in the Forest Service, but if the Forest Supervisor wished it so, he would not interfere. Hood had pushed his heavy brown horn-rimmed glasses back on his bulbous nose and spoke with disgust. "I guess you won't be getting into trouble with me for carrying firearms on duty anymore." He stood from behind his desk, his belly protruding over his belt, buttons on his uniform shirt straining to remain attached. "You stay in line, Wetzel, or I'll be all over you like … like … flies on *caca* … you hear me?"

Recalling the encounter, Wetzel shook his head sadly as he touched his spurs to his horse. The bay did not need any encouragement; he was already headed for the barn and much needed rest and hay. The burros trotted along behind. The wind gusted and surged through the trees, swaying the branches; a dust devil swirled below them on the trail, ascended into the sky and disappeared.

CHAPTER FORTY-FIVE

WETZEL STRETCHED HIS TIRED SHOULDERS AND THROBBING BACK AS HE SAT behind the wheel of the green Forest Service truck guiding it south along Highway 15. He grinned at his dog, Montie, sitting in the seat next to him, "Well, 'ol fella, they're going to make us earn our pay today, huh?"

Traversing Copperas Peak and Vista, he watched the Gila River meander silently far below on the valley floor as the brisk spring winds whistled, pushing and pulling at the heavy truck. The cottonwood trees and willows were beginning to take on their leaves and green up the riparian area along the wide river. It would be sunset in a couple of hours, and he was concerned about any success in tracking fugitives very far this late in the day.

At Sapillo Creek, Wetzel turned onto Highway 35; a tall, thin Grant County deputy waved him past the roadblock. Within minutes, he arrived at Lake Roberts Store. The store was located just north of a pretty little lake. The gravel parking lot was full of sheriff's office vehicles and a New Mexico State Police cruiser. Made of roughhewn lumber, the little store and eatery stood back from the highway; a board sidewalk provided an entry to the store and a porch for the local elders to gather in rocking chairs and discuss or cuss local and national politics, depending on their attitude on any given day. Today, yellow police tape surrounded an empty porch. Wetzel parked his forest rig in the gravel parking lot, and told Montie, "Stay." As he walked toward a heavy-set deputy, who was talking to several older men, he passed a young, tall, Hispanic deputy wearing dark sunglasses he didn't recognize. The deputy glanced briefly at him and nodded as he headed for his parked patrol car. Wetzel hesitated in his stride for a moment thinking there was something about the man he recognized, but then shook his head and continued over to the heavy-set deputy. Don Ramirez was a high school friend of Wetzel's and they had played football together.

"Howdy, Don! Is Mac around?"

"Howdy yourself, Jack." The deputy turned to the men he had been talking to, "Excuse me, fellers. I need a minute with this officer." As Ramirez turned back, Wetzel saw the name tag on his uniform shirt. He tipped his hat back on his head with his thumb and whistled loudly. "*Chief* Deputy D. Ramirez?"

Ramirez shook hands and grinned. The wind gusted and played with his thick, short-cropped black hair to no avail. Ramirez displayed an honest face, dark complexion, a short stout neck, large torso, and massive chest and arms that filled his uniform shirt to an almost bursting point. "The sheriff likes my work, I guess." He shrugged. "You gonna help Mac?"

"According to dispatch, I don't have much choice in the matter." Wetzel's face turned serious. "Is Juanita okay?" Juanita Flores worked at the store, was an old friend of his and McMurtry's girlfriend, at least as far as Wetzel knew she still was.

"She's a little shook up, but she played it smart, complied with their orders, gave them the money and didn't get hurt physically."

"They?" queried Wetzel.

Ramirez scratched the back of his head. "Yeah. Two men armed with handguns. The mean one is a small, skinny white *guero,* scraggly beard, greasy brown hair, walks with a limp. He was wearing blue jeans and a camouflage shirt and dirty black ball cap." Ramirez tucked his thumbs into the front pockets of his tan jeans. "The other suspect was Hispanic, medium build, long hair down to his shoulders wearing a denim jacket and green bell bottom trousers."

Wetzel sighed, "I reckon they headed south?"

"Yep. Made it to just before Thunderbird Camp and damn near ran into a state policeman who decided it would be a nice day to patrol up here in the cool pines." He hesitated then ran his fingers through his short hai. "They shot Bill Monroe ... filled him and his patrol car full and holes, ditched the motorcycle and ran into the woods onto your turf, *amigo*."

"My God," whispered Wetzel. His gaze met Ramirez's brown eyes. "And Bill—?"

"I'm sorry, Jack. He's dead."

"Jeez! We didn't have this kind of violence here in Silver City when we were growing up, Don. What the hell's going on?"

It was Ramirez's turn to sigh. "The sheriff told me just the other day that he used to know literally everyone in town till the gold and silver strike a year ago. Hell, now he doesn't know hardly anyone he sees on the street on any given day."

Wetzel had seen the ominous changes—first the gold strike in Pinos Altos and overnight the town of Silver City had ballooned to three times its population. At first everyone thought it was the greatest thing since sliced bread, an abundance of jobs and a real boom for the local economy. No more dependence on the on-again, off-again copper industry. The politicians salivated at the increased tax base. New jobs and plenty of them! Everyone was smiling from ear to ear. Then the drifters looking for a quick buck, the hard cases, the criminals, and the brothels arrived and the associated drug use, crimes and violence increased exponentially. Silver City wasn't a quiet, rural town any longer. Its tiny police force, and Grant County's small sheriff's department were not prepared for the onslaught of crimes and did not have adequate funding available to immediately hire additional officers. The construction industry had taken off overnight building new houses, apartments, and offices for new businesses. The desolate eight miles that had separated the old mining town of Pinos Altos from Silver City had disappeared with a plethora of buildings massed along Highway 25 end to end.

Wetzel shook his head. "One day your boss will have his fill and retire." He winked at Ramirez, "Then you can get your wish and become the sheriff, *amigo*."

A voice crackled over Ramirez's radio. McMurtry's voice was tinted with a southeastern accent. "Don, git thet lollygaggin' Wetzel on over heah. Time's a wastin fer trackin'."

Wetzel shook his head and headed for his truck. "Tell 'im I'm on my way." He paused, turning back to Ramirez. "By the way, Don, when did you pick up the new deputy I passed a few minutes ago?"

"Ramon? We picked him up out of El Paso about six months ago. Why?"

"Nothin', thought I might have known him. Guess not. Thanks, Don."

"No problem, Jack. You be careful out there."

Wetzel waved over his shoulder and climbed in his truck.

It took Wetzel ten minutes to arrive on scene. Parking the truck, he gathered his day pack and said, "Come, Montie." The black and white Border collie trailed behind him as he walked past the bullet-riddled State Police cruiser in the northbound lane to where a man dressed in camouflage stood waiting impatiently.

"Dadjimmit, Jack. I declare; you lollygag more'n anybody I know." Robert McMurtry grinned at Wetzel. He reached out and shook the younger man's hand. The wildlife officer average in height with a solid build; unkempt brown hair peeked out from under his well-worn ball cap with "Tennessee Vols" insignia on the front; a brown beard displaying some gray adorned his rough face. He wore woodland camos with a leather shoulder holster sheathing a .357 Smith & Wesson revolver. He removed the ball cap and ran his hand through his unruly hair, replaced the cap on top of his head cocking it slightly to the right and then scratched at his beard.

Wetzel returned the grin. "What in the hell have you got us into this time, Mac?"

The wildlife officer's blue eyes twinkled, crows' feet displayed on either side of the weather beaten face. "Ahhh ... nothin' much, ah reckon. You wouldn't want me to go it alone would ya?"

"Naw, I reckon not, Mac." Wetzel looked away from the highway for sign of the two fugitives.

McMurtry slapped him on the shoulder. "I done figgered out the sign. The sumbitches headed out on the run after killin' Bill." He pointed to the marked Forest Service trail toward Reeds Peak.

"Right up the trail?" Wetzel's brow furrowed.

"Yup, fer aways anyhow. I tracked 'em about a half-mile while I was waitin' on you a lollygaggin." He spit tobacco out the corner of his mouth. "One 'ol boy's wearing a size ten smooth sole huntin' boot, wore down on the right heel. T'other's wearin' a nine n' a half tennis shoe. I'd say one o' them canvas kind we played high school basketball in—Converse, ain't they called?"

"I played football, Mac."

"Wel-l-l, I'd figgered a slender feller like you fer more'n one sport, Jack."

"Too busy working, I guess." Wetzel pushed his Stetson hat back on his head with his thumb. "You think we can catch 'em before dark?"

"The sheriff wants 'em caught; too dangerous to leave be."

Wetzel sighed as he peered at the western sky, "We'd best get at it then. Only about two hours till sundown."

McMurtry nodded, picked up his day pack and placed the shoulder straps around his heavy shoulders. He waved at a deputy who was holding a Mini-14 rifle to come along and headed down the trail, bearing to the left of the trail itself. Wetzel fell in next to McMurtry but to the right of the trail. He hissed at Montie and pointed; the dog fell in directly behind him.

Wetzel said, "Howdy, Jim," over his shoulder to the deputy, who had stationed himself about ten feet behind the trackers. They had worked as a team before and each knew what to do. The trackers would concentrate on the sign and the ground in front of them, the deputy would look for any danger ahead and behind them, in the event someone doubled back. The trick was to have the trackers looking down and the security man looking ahead, tasks not always easily accomplished.

The wind had picked up again, gusting hard and tugging at Wetzel's hat. He pulled it down squarely on his head as he heard the deputy say, "Thanks for helping us out, Jack."

"You bet."

As they left the highway, Wetzel observed the men's distinct tracks in the Forest Service trail just as McMurtry had described them. They were hurried tracks, of individuals running and then walking rapidly, disturbing the sandy soil and vegetation as the men attempted to distance themselves from their heinous act. The meadow quickly gave way to juniper-strewn hills with numerous canyons weaving in and out through rocky hills and bluffs. Rock pedestals stood alone, weathered and formed by wind, water, and eons of time; Wetzel noted that several appeared in the likeness of a man, a sentinel, he thought, guarding the forest and its treasures within. As he walked along scanning the ground ahead of him, he felt something deep in his gut; a fear of the unknown maybe or of failing to do the right thing in an ensuing confrontation with the fugitives when they found them? He knew from his experiences during the war that he could, will himself to react even when he had been so scared that he was trembling. These men had murdered a fellow officer, a friend of his, and he would do what he could to assist in apprehending them.

The tracks remained easily identifiable on the designated trail as the pursuers pushed on with renewed urgency to catch the criminals before dark. Soon the juniper trees disappeared and the tracking party found themselves in Ponderosa pine open woodland terrain. They traveled quickly, easily following obvious tracks in a marked trail.

McMurtry slowed and then stopped suddenly as did Wetzel. The tracks of the fugitives had intermingled in the vicinity of the trail. Then both sets headed at a ninety degree angle cross-country. The trackers knelt where they were. Wetzel's dog lay down next to him, looking at his pack leader for what to do next. Wetzel reached out and ruffled his hair.

McMurtry grinned broadly. "I'll be damned; maybe they're not as stupid as I thought, Jack. They've finally figgered out they're not helping themselves by staying on the trail, huh?"

Wetzel looked over the sign before answering, taking it all in, and said to the deputy, who was waiting patiently behind them, "You see any movement in the canyon to the left, Jim?"

The deputy hesitated as he scanned the terrain ahead. "No, but I don't like these rocky bluffs with us down here in the bottom."

"As fast as we've traveled, boys, I'd say we're damned close to 'em." McMurtry turned to Wetzel, "'Pears to me, they lost their fright 'n flight way o' thinkin' heah and did some palaverin' on what next."

Wetzel nodded. "I reckon you're right, Mac. We've come about two miles east of the highway." Remaining squatted near the trail, he rubbed Montie's ears. "So are they headed back toward the highway to hijack a vehicle or watching their back trail looking to ambush us?"

Both trackers stood, surveying the terrain where the fugitives had fled. After several moments, McMurtry drew his revolver from the shoulder holster. "Let's go find out, boys." Wetzel drew his revolver and held it near his right leg.

They moved slowly, following the tracks in the sandy soil; Montie, again following his master. Approaching a thick stand of Ponderosa pine, Wetzel observed the two sets of tracks suddenly diverged: one set continued ahead while the other set of hurried tracks turned abruptly up a steep, rocky slope. McMurtry snorted and then scratched behind his neck with the barrel of his revolver considering what course of action to take.

"Dammit, Mac. I wish to hell you wouldn't do that," said Wetzel, "you'll blow your damn head off."

"Naw. Finger's out 'o the trigger guard, Jack." He turned toward the deputy behind, who was scanning the rocky butte as he held his rifle at the ready.

Shots rang out; bullets thudded into the ground and pinged through the thin mountain air.

CHAPTER FORTY-SIX

Montie ran beside Wetzel as he zigzagged toward the nearest cover which was a large gambel oak to their right. Montie didn't understand why they were running or of the impending danger, only that he wanted to stay with his friend, his master who he had known now for four years. He and Wetzel had been pack for all those years, and the dog had always been taken care of by his friend, and he, in turn, was vigilant to do the same for his leader. They were inseparable, and as such, slept together, ate together, and now they were running together; he knew no other pack leader, only Wetzel. His heart pounded with pride.

He lay panting next to the man, who was everything to him. And he smelled a different scent coming from his leader—fear. He had smelled a similar scent from other men in his life who had tried to harm him or Wetzel; men he snarled at, even attacked and bitten to protect his leader or himself. The bark on the tree splintered, showering the two of them. The thing in Wetzel's hand answered, BOOM! The sound echoed in the canyon. Wetzel reached down and touched the dog between the ears. He hissed, "Follow, Montie!"

The dog obediently followed his master as Wetzel sprinted hard to the right flank of where he thought the shots had come from; the deputy's mini-14 rifle cracked several rounds in the distance, echoing in the deep canyon. Wetzel took cover behind a large pine tree, his chest heaving, perspiration running down his face and neck. Montie knew his master was not his normal self and feared something and it caused Montie to be on high alert.

They were off running again, up the steep slope through the trees; on and on they ran. It felt good to run with his pack leader. Protect Alpha. Guard.

Reaching the crest of the hill, they entered a rock outcropping and stopped momentarily behind a large boulder. Montie smelled another man; he distinctly heard him moving as he was close. His hearing intensified; his ears pricked up, eyes searching for the enemy. Then his master was up and running again, this time the thing in his hand made noise once more. They ran together. Together they were pack. Montie ranged ahead of Wetzel. Protect and defend.

Suddenly, Wetzel went down and grunted, "Get'm, Montie."

Alpha hurt. Montie's anxiety turned to rage. The enemy's scent of fear reached his nostrils. Protect and defend. He charged the man now in front of him, leaping high in the air going for the throat. *Kill!*

An arm flung out in front of the throat, and Montie bit hard into it, sinking his fangs deep into bone and muscle and simultaneously slammed into the man knocking him to the ground. Alpha hurt. Kill enemy.

Montie bit viciously again, deeper this time into the arm tasting blood. The man screamed, tried to pull away. The fear smell was strong and the smell of blood further enraged him. He shook the arm while clinching hard with his jaws, ripping and tearing. The enemy—the prey—attempted to escape. Montie released his bloody grip. The enemy got up to run, but Montie charged and sank his fangs into the prey's leg just below his buttocks, dropping him to the ground. He bit again and again, tearing fabric, muscle. Prey ceased to move. Montie released his grip and stood back growling and snarling, blood dripping from his muzzle. It was only then that he heard his master calling to him.

CHAPTER FORTY-SEVEN

Wetzel limped forward, his revolver at the ready. He rasped, "Montie … come, boy." The dog turned toward him. The emblazoned red eyes locked with his and slowly the dog's eyes transformed from unbridled rage to those of obedience to his pack leader, affection and then devotion for his master; the rage dissipated and the dog trotted toward him.

The suspect was wrapped up into a tight ball, shaking with fear and moaning with pain. Wetzel observed injuries to back of the man's leg. He positioned him on his back and saw severe bite wounds to his left arm that were bleeding profusely. Nevertheless, he handcuffed the man in front for his own safety and methodically searched him, removing a pocket knife from his dirty jeans pocket, a plastic packet of what appeared to be marijuana, and his billfold. The man's pistol lay several yards away on the ground close to his black baseball cap; Wetzel kicked it sending it several feet further from them. A camouflage shirt covered a thin, gaunt frame.

"*Help me!* For God's sake, help me before I bleed to death, dammit!" The man's craggy pinched face was covered with a scraggly, dirty-brown beard splattered with blood.

Wetzel knelt down, opened his pocket knife and cut the man's shirt from his torso. *You want help?* Wetzel gritted his teeth thinking of the dead state policeman—his wife and little boy left behind with no one to care for them because of trash like this. *You murdering son-of-a-bitch!*

The whimpering stopped momentarily. "What ... what are ... you *doing* to me?"

"Shut up." Wetzel pulled on the cut fabric and tore it free from the rest of the shirt. He wrapped it tightly around the man's arm and tied it off. He opened the billfold and found a folded piece of paper next to some twenty dollar bills, "What's this?"

The man stammered, "It's my ... pay slip."

"*Pay slip*? Why the hell are you robbing a store if you have a job?"

The whimpering began again with no answer.

Wetzel opened the pay stub. The Silver Cell Mine had paid Jake Farnsley wages for 80 hours of pay, substantial bi-weekly wages, certainly more than Wetzel made in his government job. Why would a man making that kind of money want to rob a store?

"You work at the Silver Cell north of Pinos Altos? I didn't know it was operational."

No answer.

"How long you been working there?"

Whimpering, no answer.

Wetzel slapped his face.

"A month now! God, I hurt something awful. Your dog 'bout killed me."

"Who do you work for at the Silver Cell?"

No answer.

Wetzel's voice had a metallic edge to it. "I won't ask you again."

"Tomás."

"Tomás *what*?"

Jake Farnsley whimpered again, moaned, his pinched face drawn tight with pain. "I ... don't know ... his last name. I only seen him onct."

Wetzel placed the billfold in the front pocket of his shirt and using his handkerchief he picked up Farnsley's handgun so as to not disturb or create any prints and tucked it under his belt near the small of his back. He reached down and jerked Farnsley to his feet.

"I ... I can't walk, man. Can't ya see, I'm hurt real bad."

"Walk, crawl, or drag yourself. I don't give a damn, but you're moving." Wetzel looked down at his own pant leg; a bullet hole near the calf and blood-encrusted green jeans. He carefully pulled up the pant leg and saw that a bullet had dug a furrow on the inside of his calf muscle. The bleeding had almost stopped, but he noticed for the first time that it hurt like hell.

He shoved Farnsley. "Move, damn you!"

Montie growled deep in his throat and began "herding" the man downhill. The Border collie breeding and experience dictated it.

The sun had set and dusky skies now prevailed. The harsh wind had quieted somewhat, but continued to pull at Wetzel's hat and clothes.

They stumbled down off the rocky hillside and met McMurtry at mid-slope. The baseball cap with the "Tennesee Vols" emblem was pulled down on his shaggy head. The faded camouflage shirt and pants were covered in dirt and sweat. Wetzel had never seen him in an actual uniform and wondered if he even had one. He thought the man would most likely appear out of sorts in uniform. The thought made him want to laugh even in the midst of all that had occurred.

McMurtry surveyed the scene, taking in the injured, handcuffed prisoner and Wetzel's bloodied pant leg. He returned his revolver to the shoulder holster. "You all right, son?"

Farnsley stammered, "I'm hurt real bad, mister. This officer ... his dog—"

McMurtry's temper flared, *"Shut up!* I ain't talkin' to you." His blue eyes bored into Wetzel's face, showing his worry, deep concern for his friend.

"I'm fine, Mac, just a nick in my leg."

The solemn face transformed to a grin. "Wel-l-l, I'll be dadjimmed if you wasn't lollygaggin' after all. I figgered as much."

Wetzel grinned. "What about the other one?"

McMurtry scratched his chin whiskers and drawled, "Don't reckon he'll be needin' medical help, Jack. 'Ol Jim plugged him dead center with thet mini-14 once he opened up on us. Law, he's deadern' a mackerel, son."

Wetzel looked at the darkening sky. "We'd best get moving. It'll be dark soon."

McMurtry agreed. "I figger if we cut due south to the highway, marking our trail as we go with some flagging, won't take jest a shake to git there. Jim done called in and the sheriff'll have one 'o them ATVs come in and pick up the body."

Farnsley stumbled and complained of his injuries.

McMurtry grabbed him by the shoulders. "Now you listen, son, and listen *real* good, cause I ain't one to repeat myself. You keep yore mouth shut whilst yore around me an' we'll get along jus' fine; I ain't interested in any whimpering an' sniveling on yore part. You keep it up, an' I'll sic thet dog on ya."

Wide eyed, Farnsley swallowed hard and nodded that he understood.

Wetzel thought about the long day and how tired he was as he took orange flagging out of his pack. He was so tired he felt a little light-headed. Reaching in the pack again, he withdrew his water bottle and drank several swallows. He turned and saw McMurtry peering at him.

"You all right, Jack?"

Wetzel nodded as he replaced the plastic water bottle in his pack and secured the straps.

"You go on ahead and flag our trail, Jack. I'll keep an eye on our quiet friend heah."

The trio walked southward toward the highway; the wind whistled in among the pines, pulling and twisting limbs and branches; a darkening sky slowly enveloped the men and the terrain as though a giant curtain had been pulled to. Wetzel tried not to stumble as he stepped softly on pine needles and litter.

CHAPTER FORTY-EIGHT

LATE SPRING, 1974

THE STRANGER WALKED along an old rutted, mountain road, pausing occasionally to take in all the beauty surrounding him. Relieving the weight from the pack on his back, he leaned forward on his makeshift cedar walking stick he had found along the way. As he peered up at a red-tailed hawk circling above in the bright, blue New Mexico sky, a Mexican jay darted among the foliage of the nearest Ponderosa pine tree. He took a long breath, drawing the fresh, piney, mountain air deep into his lungs, and then breathed out slowly, savoring the smell. The hawk continued in its floating, circular pattern above him, head darting left then right as it searched patiently for a field mouse or gopher.

The man's tailored clothes were strangely out of place in the mountain wilderness; the long-sleeved cotton dress shirt and beige slacks showed recent signs of being pressed, the dusty shoes recently polished. His well-kept beard and hair were tinged gray and white; bright green eyes that beamed with intelligence peered out beneath bushy white brows. The stranger squared his shoulders. He stood at somewhat less than six feet tall, a height he'd held for many years until age had intervened, but he carried himself with the confidence of a man who has done great things in life … and yet, there was sadness about him.

The stranger sighed, and then began his trek again; he stopped, listening intently with his head cocked to one side. His ear had caught the distinct metallic ring of a horse's hoof against rock further up the canyon. He stepped to one side of the narrow road and waited.

A horse and rider appeared suddenly before him. The rider, a young woman, sat tall in the saddle, as the sorrel mare trotted along with a grace that mesmerized the old man. The rider and horse were as one, and he marveled at the horsemanship of the woman and the beauty of the animal. They stopped alongside of him where he leaned against the cedar walking stick.

"Howdy."

"How do you do, ma'am."

The woman shifted forward in the saddle, and then swung her right leg over the horn and pommel of the saddle. She observed him closely, taking her own good time of it, lastly gazing into his eyes.

"I take it; you ain't from around these here parts, mister—?"

A smile worked at the corner of his mouth, as he appraised the woman. Her head was covered with a battered straw hat, sweat-stained and dusty. The hat protected a pretty head of dark brown hair secured in a ponytail near the nape of her neck and trailed down her back. She wore a blue denim work shirt, tucked into faded work jeans patched at the knee, which in turn, were tucked into the tops of worn, dusty riding boots.

He countered her question. "No, I am from the world of cities … Miss—?"

The woman grinned, a wide, hearty grin. "I figgered that much straight away, and I ain't the smartest gal there is, mister." Her brown eyes locked with his.

The stranger saw the goodness, the honesty, and the wholesomeness of her in those moments and liked her for it. "My name is Daniel Reagan." He bowed elegantly, "and it is indeed my pleasure to meet you, ma'am."

She threw back her head and throaty laugh rang down the canyon.

He grinned at her feeling somewhat unsettled. "I fear I am lost, young lady."

"Lost?" She looked at him incredulously then pointed to the peak behind him. "That there is Black Mountain. T'other side of that is

Pinos Altos Mountain. You most likely passed it gittin' heah." She pushed her hat back on her head and slipped her leg that had been draped over the saddle horn down and her foot into the stirrup.

"This heah is Whiskey Creek, Mister Reagan, and yonder nawth is Sapillo Crick and the Gila Wilderness. There's a passle of wilderness country up heah in these parts."

Daniel Reagan nodded. "I thank you, ma'am, for that information. I'm looking for the proprietor of the Whippit Ranch."

The woman looked at him without speaking for a moment. "Pro-*pri*-a-tor, you say?"

"Yes ... the ... owner, so that I may speak with him."

She straightened in the saddle, a puzzled look on her face, "We-l-l-l, ah reckon that'd be me, Mister Reagan; me or my two brothers."

Taken aback, his mouth dropped open. Recovering, he said hesitantly, "And ... what might your name be, ma'am?"

"Lacey Whippit. An' mah brothers is Larrimore and Lattimer Whippit."

Reagan's mouth opened wide again, and then his mind was flooded with the childhood recollection of his mother telling him as a young boy to close his mouth before the flies flew in; his mouth twitched but did not break into a smile or laugh; he respectfully closed it.

He stood up straight. "I am inquiring about a job at the Whippit Ranch. I read in the advertisement section of the local paper that you're in need of someone to take care of your sheep."

Her eyes softened, but she did not laugh nor did her mouth twitch as his had done. With furrowed brow, she looked him up and down once again, pursed and licked her dry lips. "*You* want to work our sheep, Mister?"

"Yes, ma'am, I do."

"You ever work with sheep 'afore?"

"No, ma'am," he said quickly, "but I can learn to do anything."

"Uh huh."

She swung down from the horse, dropping the reins. "You got any *work* clothes, Mister?"

Reagan saw that she was tall for a woman, shapely, and good looking even in her dirty clothes. "I have some hiking boots in my pack."

"Uh huh."

Silence.

"And where might *you* be from, ma'am?" he asked trying to break the discomfort silence can exude.

She exhaled and rubbed the back of her neck, keeping her current thoughts to herself. "Me? Oh, I'm from Nawth Carolina. My pa, me and mah brothers come out heah five years ago. Staked the mining claim up yonder," she waved back up the canyon, "and Pa, he was killed in a cave-in 'bout two years ago."

"I am sorry, ma'am."

Without acknowledging him, she said, "I always took care of the sheep, but with Pa gone now, I don't have time to help the boys with the mine and tend to them sheep, too."

It was his turn to lick dry lips. "I would be most grateful if you would accept me for employment, ma'am."

"Uh huh."

Silence, again.

She kicked at the dusty road. "I might could take ya on; I was kinda hoping for a Mexican feller who knowed something 'bout sheep and sech."

Reagan started to speak, but she cut him off. "Course I can't pay much, and you'd have to live in the old line shack a ways up the canyon from our place." She looked him over again: the new, expensive clothing and shoes. "To be honest Mr. Reagan, it ain't much to offer."

He smiled. "Whatever is commensurate for the position, ma'am. I'd be grateful for the job."

She peered at him quizzically with those dark brown eyes, a frown appearing on her tanned face. "Uh huh."

"What I mean, ma'am, is any pay or quarters you deem appropriate, is fine with me."

"You running from the law, Mister Reagan?"

He looked her straight in the eye. "No … not from the law."

"Uh huh."

Brown eyes locked with his eyes once again. She broke her gaze with him, turned and mounted her horse in one fluid motion.

"Aw'ight then." She motioned back up the canyon. "You'll find our place 'bout a mile on up Whiskey Crick. Name's on the mailbox. Go on in, make yorese'f ta home. I have some business to attend to, and I'll be along directly. I'll rustle ya up some grub when I git there. Boys won't be in till dark." She started the horse down the canyon.

"Thank you, ma'am."

She pulled the reins in, halting the sorrel. "And another thing—, I go by, Lacey. Nothin' in front of it or behind it ... no ma'ams neither."

A smile pulled at the corner of Reagan's mouth. "Thank you, *Lacey*."

Her dark brown eyes were smiling as she looked at him. "Aw'ight then."

CHAPTER FORTY-NINE

THE SERGEANT TURNED TO HIM, GRINNING. HE SPAT TOBACCO JUICE. "Garcia, get your ass up here on point, you god damned spick. Move it!"

Juan Garcia shifted the M-16 rifle from his shoulder to port arms as he stepped forward. A light rain had begun wetting the men in the platoon, a minor respite from the humidity and heat that was so prevalent in Vietnam. As he passed, the sergeant kicked him in the buttocks. Garcia seethed with anger. You son-of-a-bitch! *Sergeant Wilkerson was a true Tejano who hated Hispanics and had made him the target of his racism on numerous occasions since Garcia had arrived in the war zone. Sometimes, he wondered just who the hell the enemy truly was. He was sick of it all—the war, the violence, the hatred—all of it. He just wanted to go home to his Maggie and their son, Robbie, whom he had never met — home to New Mexico where the sun shone almost every damned day; none of this rain, rain, rain … or the killing.*

They entered a small village looking for Charlie, methodically searching each hut, and found nothing but civilians hiding wherever the poor souls could find a likely place. Garcia entered a large hut, his M16 tucked into his shoulder covering the interior. Two women cowered in the far corner arms over their heads; an old man did likewise in another corner of the room. They all spoke simultaneously, fear exuding from their speech, their eyes. Garcia drew in a sharp breath. Jesus, they're more scared than me.

"Shut up!" he shouted, pointing the rifle at them. "Shut up, I said."

They intensified their chatter as he searched the room for hidden weapons caches. Then Sergeant Wilkerson appeared in the hut. As the sergeant waved his rifle at the Vietnamese civilians, he yelled, "Get these dammed gooks to shut up, Garcia! What the hell's the matter with you? Can't you do a simple, frigging task? You stupid, god damned spick. Do it, DO IT!"

Agitated, Wilkerson turned toward the Vietnamese. "I'll show you how, you stupid bastard!" And he fired point blank at the scared women. Blood splattered the walls. The old man screamed and then was silenced as rounds laced his body.

"Nooo!" Garcia turned on the sergeant, eyes blazing as he pulled the trigger on his M16 in full automatic mode. He stitched the sergeant's body from crotch to head with .223 rounds, the head disappeared from the body as he continued firing. Blood splattered his own face. He screamed as he continued shooting. When he ran out of ammo, he reversed the magazine and fired an additional twenty rounds into whatever was left of the sergeant's body.

Then he sprinted outside, shouting, "Oh, my God ... my God!"

Juan Garcia jerked upright in bed; suddenly he was wide awake as the horrifying images of war and violence rocked his stunned brain. *No! No ... God, no more! Not again.* He swallowed hard, clenching his teeth, wet with perspiration.

He felt sick and dizzy. His heart pounded in his chest. He slid off the bed, scooted on his buttocks to the bathroom; his missing left leg prevented him from walking. Leaning over he vomited in the commode. He retched again and finally took a deep breath. His hands shook uncontrollably and the dizziness increased. He thought he would pass out, but eventually the light-headedness lessened, and he sat on the floor peering down at what they had left of his leg—a stump on which to secure a prosthesis. A goddamn stump! He was a cripple. A worthless, pathetic cripple and nobody gave a tinker's damn. No one cared or gave a damn ... except his wife and son. Thank God for Maggie and Robbie or he would have blown his brains out long ago. He wept bitterly as he sat there on the floor bathed in perspiration, a little at first then full out not caring what anyone would think of him for doing so. Then he heard his wife.

"Juan? Honey, you okay?"

She was beside him, kneeling, reaching out to him. "Oh, sweetie, not the horrible images again?"

He nodded, swallowing hard. He could not speak. His nose ran and tears streamed down his cheeks.

She enveloped him in her arms, hugging him tight against her. "It's all right, Juan. Let it all out. I'm here for you." Tears appeared on her pretty face.

That damned war! Oh, my God, can you ever forgive me for all the terrible things I've done? He sobbed outright, his body convulsing. *Please God … please forgive me.*

CHAPTER FIFTY

WETZEL TURNED THE GREEN FOREST SERVICE TRUCK OFF HIGHWAY 15 north of Pinos Altos onto the forest road. Montie rode in the back enjoying the afternoon breeze. Wetzel turned his gaze to the man sitting next to him. Steve Hunt was immaculately dressed as always in his New Mexico State Police uniform: the black cap with polished bill, starched black shirt with leather strap running down from the shoulder, polished shiny badge, polished black duty belt and holster, creased black pants and highly polished black boots.

Wetzel took a pack of Lucky Strikes from his shirt pocket, shook out a cigarette, placed it in the corner of his mouth, and then replaced the pack. He flipped open his lighter, lit the cigarette and drew deeply thinking of what he had to do today. Primarily, he was to assist the state police in interviewing the manager of the Silver Cell Mine in connection with the murder of a state policeman.

"It's not too far up the canyon from here, Steve." The truck bounced on the rough road. Wetzel's cigarette rolled slowly between his lips from one side to the other until he removed it. "We'll pass the Arrastra Mine and then it's only a few miles to the Silver Cell Mine."

Hunt grimaced as they bounced along the rutted road. "How long has the Silver Cell been active?"

"Don't rightly know, Steve. I didn't realize that it was up and running."

"Does the Forest Service oversee the mining operations up here?"

"No. Miners have to file for claims with the Bureau of Land Management and they handle the administration of dealing with plans of operation and the like." He grunted. "Thank God, I don't have to deal with these guys much. Some of 'em can be a handful."

Hunt peered at him. "What do you mean by that?

Wetzel took a long draw from his cigarette and blew smoke out the corner of his mouth. "Well, most of these miners haven't been bothered much in years past. The old 1872 Mining Law pretty much lets them get away with whatever they want. Not much enforcement on reclamation and no teeth in enforcement on anything else as far as I can tell."

"Criminals?"

"No. I wouldn't go that far; just eccentric and stubborn and they don't want anyone, least of all, the government, to tell them what they can or can't do out here."

"Hmmm." Hunt reflected and then changed the subject. "I heard Juan Garcia's home from the war. How's he and Maggie and the boy doing?"

"I wouldn't know," said Wetzel icily.

Hunt's brow furrowed. "I heard you guys were buddies in high school." He bit at his lower lip. "I thought you might've kept in touch ... you know like you did when the boy was kidnapped."

Wetzel sighed. "Yeah. Well, Juan's back now, and I don't see 'em much." He tried to shake the image of Maggie from his mind.

"That boy thought the world of you, Jack."

"Yeah, I reckon." *I've lost her ... lost everything.*

They rode along in silence. Wetzel finished his cigarette as they passed the Arrastra Mine. The road narrowed and got rougher. Wetzel shifted to a lower gear, slowing down to keep from bouncing his head on the cab roof. Dust sifted into the interior of the truck and onto the immaculate, black state police uniform of Sergeant Steve Hunt.

Hunt slapped at the dust for a moment but after realizing the futility of it, he shrugged. "Jeez, Jack. Is this a typical day for you?"

Wetzel grinned, "No. Not typical but a good day. I'm usually riding horse back or hiking in the wilderness. I need to check on a sheep allotment further up Whisky Creek after we stop in at the mine." He glanced over at this friend. "That is if you don't mind?" It was a beautiful day in New Mexico; the cloudless blue sky, sun shining brightly, the sweet smell of pine trees and ground litter, and even the summer temperature was agreeable. *A helluva fine day except for the dust and getting banged around in the truck.*

Hunt peered out the window, cleared his throat, and mumbled, "Sure, no problem."

They crossed Whiskey Creek for the tenth time, maneuvered around a large boulder in the creek bottom and the Silver Cell Mine operation lay before them. An antiquated, deteriorated plywood sign was posted at the entrance "Silver Cell Mine, Trespassers Keep Out" and underneath the letters were scrawled, "Violators will be shot."

Wetzel drove past the signs and onto the property.

Hunt grunted. "Not very friendly, are they?"

"Nope." Wetzel steered the Forest Service truck past remnants of old, late eighteenth century buildings toward a more modern tin-covered building set back in a grove of Ponderosa pines. The building had few windows with closed beige curtains covering all of them.

Hunt rubbed his smooth-shaven jaw. "What's story behind this place, Jack?" He gazed around. "Looks like most of these buildings haven't been used for many years."

Wetzel geared down. "The story is that in the 1890s three Dimmick brothers ran a dairy down here on Whiskey Creek and sold milk in town. One day two of the brothers, who were looking for some of their cows, spotted an odd-looking piece of rock about the size of a man's fist lying on the ground. After picking it up and noticing that it looked like iron ore, one of them bit into it as he had no pocket knife on him to scrape it. Surprisingly, they saw a distinct set of teeth prints in the piece as if he'd bitten into a cake of beeswax."

"No kidding?"

"No kidding. Story is they went back and found the main silver vein, sank a shaft down 65 feet; in those days no small feat, and took out $15,000 worth of malleable native silver almost immediately; *mucho dinero* back in the day."

"Wow, and the present owners are mining gold, not silver?"

"Maybeso. That's what their Mining Plan of Operations says."

They pulled up next to several vehicles parked in front of what looked to be an administration building, a recently constructed single story framed building. Behind it and to the north a larger two-story frame building that appeared to Wetzel to be living quarters. A large tin-covered warehouse structure sitting adjacent and behind the administration building had been recently renovated and added onto from an older existing structure. Three of the vehicles were vans, all painted white, with the remaining vehicles being pickup trucks of various colors and wear. Wetzel figured they were personally owned by staff who worked at the mine.

As the Forest Service truck came to a stop, two men came out of the administration building and before Wetzel and Hunt could get out of their vehicle, one of the men shouted at them, "Can't you read, dammit?" The man's stocky build was accentuated by a tight black T-shirt, and he carried a revolver in his belt that held up faded bell bottom jeans. His dusty, work boots crunched on the gravel lot as he stomped toward Wetzel. "Get the hell outta here. This here's private property." Montie growled from the back of the truck.

Both law enforcement officers slipped quickly out of the truck, using their respective doors for cover. "Hold it right there!" Wetzel placed his hand on his revolver and pointed with his other hand at the man confronting him. The man hesitated in mid-stride.

"We have law enforcement business here, and let's get a couple of things straight."

The man protested, "You have no right—"

"We have *every* right to be here. Now, shut up and listen." Wetzel's voice had a metallic ring to it. "First of all, we're investigating the murder of a law enforcement officer by one of your employees, and *we'll* ask the questions. Secondly, for the record this isn't private property. It's *public* land owned by the tax payers of the United States, and since you filed your claim after 1959, you don't have the right to order *anyone* to leave as long as they're not interfering with the mining operation." He drew his revolver and pointed it at the man. "Now ... slowly, use your left hand, thumb and forefinger to remove that gun at your waist, drop it to the ground and step back away from it."

Hunt told the other man to comply as well. Both men hesitated.

"NOW! Damn you," shouted the state policeman.

The men complied. Wetzel moved forward and gathered up the men's firearms from the ground. Hunt obtained their identifications. He looked at each driver's license and then handed them to Wetzel. "Run 10-28s, 10-29s for me, will you?"

Wetzel returned to his truck and called Grant County Sheriff's dispatch. Both licenses came back valid, no wants or warrants; however, the other man, a Hispanic with a thin mustache wearing a dirty, white T-shirt and woodland camouflage pants had a record of being arrested in Silver City recently for possession of marijuana. Wetzel advised Hunt of his findings. Hunt had just asked the men if the manager, Tomás, was on the premises.

The bearded man, James Oldman, stated their boss wasn't there, that he traveled a lot, and in fact, was rarely at the mine.

Hunt asked, "Really? Who runs things around here then? You?"

Oldman grinned. "No, not me. I'm just a worker bee."

"Who then?"

"Señor Francisco Cordova."

"This Cordova ... is he here today?"

The Hispanic man answered, "No. He ees not here."

Hunt looked at him, remembering his identification. "Ricardo Martinez, you know a Jake Farnsley?"

"Sí, Señor. I know heem. Hees not here anymore."

"Hell, I know that. We put him in jail for robbing a store and murdering a state policeman." He looked hard at Martinez, "Now, why would he rob anyone? He had a good job working here at the mine, right?"

Wetzel heard the vehicle coming before he saw it and glanced at Hunt. "Incoming."

A brand new Ford pickup bounced up the road toward them, turned in and drove up behind the Forest Service truck. A tall, Hispanic man stepped out. His long, dark hair was pulled back into a pony tail that hung down to his shoulders; a thin black mustache and goatee covered his brown face; he was dressed in a light beige polyester suit and dress shirt.

His face broke into a wide smile as he walked up to Wetzel. The dark eyes were not smiling. "How may I help you officers today?"

Wetzel studied the man with his hand on his revolver. Hunt covered the other two men.

"I assure you, officer—?"

"Jack Wetzel, Forest Service LEO, and my partner is Steve Hunt with New Mexico State Police."

The man carefully lifted his jacket and turned sideways to show he carried no weapon. "I assure you Officer Wetzel that I mean you no harm." He bowed graciously and another wide smile. "Señor Francisco Cordova ... *para servirle,* at your service." Dark unsmiling eyes viewed both officers.

Wetzel removed his hand from his revolver and pointed at the two men. "These two don't seem to have the same attitude toward law enforcement, Señor Cordova."

"Please! Call me Francisco," he said softly and then turned, the eyes hard, piercing, and shouted, "*Pendejos! Babosos!*" He pointed to the large warehouse, "*Vayanse, cabrónes! Fuera del alcance de mí vista.* Idiots! Go! Get out of my sight."

Obviously frightened, both men turned and walked toward the warehouse.

Cordova clasped his hands together. "My men sometimes lack proper manners, gentlemen; I apologize for them. How may I assist you?"

Steve Hunt stepped closer. "You the head honcho around here? It was our understanding that a ... Tomás is the boss."

Cordova's eyes narrowed for a moment. "And where did you get that name, Officer Hunt?"

"From a scum bag by the name of Jake Farnsley; you know him?"

"Ahhh ... Farnsley. Unfortunately, I do know him. He worked here for a very short time; unreliable, lazy sort." Cordova clasped and unclasped his hands and then clasped them again tightly.

Hunt's eyes met Cordova's. "He robbed a store and murdered a New Mexico State Policeman. If he had a good job here at the mine, why would he do that, Cordova?"

"I assure you, Officer Hunt, I have no idea."

"And this ... Tomás, who is he and how do I get in touch with him?"

Cordova placed his hands in his pockets. "I run the mine; I hire and fire and run all operations. You're speaking to the right man. I know of no such person."

"Okay. I understand Farnsley resided here on-site. That right?"

"Why, yes, he did."

"I'd like your permission to search his living quarters."

A wide smile. "Of course, Officer Hunt." Cordova motioned toward the apartments. "Please, come this way. I'll escort you myself."

Wetzel said, "I'll wait here, Steve. I've got to call in on the radio before they send in the cavalry."

Hunt nodded and followed Cordova toward the two-story building.

Wetzel called in and advised their status. Grant County dispatch acknowledged. "10-4, please have Sergeant Hunt call the sheriff ASAP. His prisoner Farnsley was out in the exercise yard moments ago and someone with a rifle shot him in the head. He's dead!"

CHAPTER FIFTY-ONE

MIDNIGHT APPROACHED; A FULL MOON BRIGHTENED THE DARK DESERT landscape, casting eerie shadows on the lee side of trees and shrubs. A cow bellowed in the distance and her calf answered. The black pickup truck was parked under cover of a large alligator juniper tree a short distance from Highway 90 and off a dirt Forest Service Road called Gold Gulch Road. Two men sat in the cab; the driver, who was wearing a silk black shirt as well as expensive black dress slacks and shoes, nervously tapped his fingers on the steering wheel. The truck was idling silently with all lights blacked out. He turned to the passenger, "Do you think they will come, Tomás?"

The other man screwed the silencer on the automatic pistol. Dressed in black military fatigues and boots, he sat ramrod straight in the seat as he carefully laid the pistol on the dash. A smile tugged at the corner of his mouth. "*Sí*, Lalo, they will come." His left hand rubbed his square dark jaw; his right hand settled in his lap cupped with the forefinger and thumb touching, the little finger flicking at the ashes of a non-existent cigarette.

His face hardened and his eyes narrowed. "I have only *good* informants, Lalo." He shrugged, "If they are not … they are of no further use to me, *que no*?"

Lalo swallowed hard. "*Verdad*, Tomás."

The handheld radio crackled between them startling the driver.

The man in black reached for it with steady hands. He spoke quietly and succinctly in Spanisha and then placed the radio on the floorboard, picked up the pistol, and said, "*Listo*?"

The driver nodded that he was ready. Tomás peered at him for a moment. "You'll do fine, Lalo. We cannot allow these people to come in and take over our territory." He patted the driver on his shoulder with his left hand. "Remember, you must force him off the road before he can pick up speed. Force him off and let me do the rest. You stay in the truck."

Headlights suddenly appeared from the south and a green Volkswagen van sped past. Lalo jammed the gas petal to the floor, spinning the heavy tires in the sandy soil, accelerated onto the dirt road and then Highway 90. The black truck roared in pursuit out without running lights. Lalo pulled alongside and then swung the wheel sharply to the right, slammed into the van forcing it off the road into the desert; the Volkswagen van bounced high in the air, crashed through the right-of-way fence and stopped right side up fifty yards from the highway. The driver attempted to move the vehicle to no avail; the tires spun deep into the sandy, loose soil. Panicked, he forced the door open, pistol in hand, and stepped out. A soft, popping sound resounded in the quiet night; the back of the man's head exploded and he fell where he had stood.

The man in black methodically checked the cab for other passengers and finding none, he stepped to the side door and carefully opened it. The interior of the van was filled with packages wrapped in burlap bags tied with baling twine. A smile pulled at the corner of his mouth.

Ahh ... just as I was told it would be. He carried a load of marijuana to the waiting black truck on the highway. It took several trips, but no more than fifteen minutes. He returned to the van and picked up the single shell casing. Returning to the loaded truck, he saw headlights appear, heading south from Silver City. He swore to himself as he stood by the truck with his pistol hidden behind his leg.

The vehicle, a late 1960's Dodge Dart, slowed and pulled over next to the black truck and stopped. The driver, an unshaven young man with long hair down to his shoulders, leaned out the driver window. "Was there an accident?"

The man in black looked into the interior for other passengers, and finding none, he said, "Yeah, seems like someone lost control and drove off the road."

"Anyone hurt?"

"Yeah."

"Need any help?" The young man looked toward the van. He swung his head back and saw the deadly end of a black silencer aimed at him inches away. Surprise led to fright; his eyes widened as he was shot through the right eye; he slumped forward onto the steering wheel.

The man in black bent down, picked up the spent shell casing, and climbed quickly into the truck. It roared north toward the Tyrone Mine, turning off the highway onto a dirt road that ran through mine property to Highway 180.

The light from a full moon danced off the two lonely vehicles as they sat in the desert; a slight breeze increased to a gust and picked at the churned-up soil near the Volkswagon van. A section of the *El Paso Times* newspaper fell from the van; the wind toyed with it, picked it up, and carried it hesitantly toward the highway. The newspaper sat precariously perched atop a clump of rabbit brush alongside the road momentarily and then floated gently across the road past an interpretive roadside sign detailing the site as where the McComas family had been murdered by Apaches almost a century before.

CHAPTER FIFTY-TWO

JACK WETZEL SAT IMMERSED IN THOUGHT AS HIS GREEN FOREST SERVICE truck bounced along up Whiskey Creek; the rutted, rocky narrow road hadn't improved since his last trip to the Silver Cell Mine. Due to exigent circumstances, he'd returned to Silver City with State Policeman Steve Hunt to investigate the murder of the prisoner being held in the county jail.

Wetzel had received a "chewing out" from his boss, District Ranger Bill Hood, for his failure to complete the assigned task of checking on the sheep allotment at the upper end of Whiskey Creek. Hood had been waiting for him when he had returned late last night to Gila Center. Hood stood in the middle of the private road leading to the residences, with bandy legs spread wide, hands on hips, belly hanging over his belt. His head, protruding forward from his shoulders, sported a brand-new crew cut making him appear bald in the bright moonlight. Heavy, horn-rimmed glasses hung low on his large nose. Glaring at Wetzel over the top of his glasses, Hood was not interested in hearing about any law enforcement incidents that took precedence over more important duties, those that had been assigned by a supervisor.

Wetzel drove past the Silver Cell Mine. The illegal signing "No Trespassing, Violators will be shot" was still in place. Shaking his head, he breathed in the fresh mountain air through the open driver's side window. The sun shone on the tree tops above in the canyon, but had not yet settled to the canyon floor; it was still early in the day. Thin cirrus clouds floated by in a lazy, blue southwestern sky.

Wetzel thought of his friends Juan Garcia, Maggie, and Robbie. Word from his law enforcement cohorts was that Juan had been hanging out with a bad crowd, drinking a lot and maybe was into drugs. That worried him, not only for Juan's sake but also for family. Jack had been hesitant to visit them as he was still in love with Maggie and didn't know if he could keep his secret from his friend Juan when he saw her again. He sighed deeply. The truck bounced in the air, and he grabbed for a better grip on the steering wheel. He made up his mind to go by and see them on his way home tonight.

The Whippit place appeared suddenly near the head of the canyon. Horses grazed in an open meadow of lush, green grass and a small dirt tank was filled to its capacity. An old log barn stood back in the trees to the south of the creek; a newer log corral adjacent to the barn branched out from it toward the creek. In one section of the corral, a Jersey milk cow munched on a flake of hay. Several pigs lay in the mud in the other section that had been re-enforced with woven wire to keep them in. A larger pen stood empty.

The ranch house, located about a hundred yards from the barn in a thick stand of Ponderosa pines, was constructed of river rock. A large picture window in front would provide a clear view of anyone approaching from the road. Smoke spiraled into the sky from the chimney, indicating the absence of any inversion in the atmosphere. A saddled sorrel horse, tied to a log hitch rack in front of the house, cocked his head sideways as Wetzel approached.

He parked his truck some distance from the horse, got out and reached in the back to pet his dog. "Stay, Montie." He walked up past the saddle horse to the porch. A young woman appeared. "Bring thet dog on in heah, if'n ya want. We ain't too particular 'bout animals in the house." Smiling, she held the screen door open, "We was expectin' ya yesterdee, Mister Wetzel."

Ascending the rock steps to the porch, he shook hands. "Miss Whippit?"

She giggled, a small girl giggle. "Naw, I jest go by Lacey, nothin' else."

He felt a firm handshake as he looked at an honest face; pretty, tanned with dark brown hair tied back in a ponytail. Dark brown eyes met his gaze evenly. She wore worn and patched denim work clothes. Dusty, worn Nocona work boots covered her small feet. Tall and slender, she exuded athleticism and strength.

Wetzel swallowed and cleared his throat. "Well … Lacey … I wouldn't want my dog to cause any problem. You know, tie into your dog—?"

She laughed. "Don't you worry 'bout thet, Mr. Wetzel. I ain't got no dog noways. Jest a big 'ol tom cat."

Wetzel turned and tapped his right shoulder; Montie hopped deftly out of the bed of the truck and trotted up to the porch. It was Wetzel's turn to smile. "Thank you, Lacey. Please call me Jack."

"Uh huh."

She took him all in without any hurry; hazel eyes set in a tanned face, curly brown locks peeking out beneath a stained gray Stetson hat, the lithe, slender frame dressed in a Forest Service uniform wearing a gun belt and White's packer boots. Then she held her hand down, palm away near the dog. Montie sniffed at it, and she petted him lightly on the head. "Y'all come on in the house an' I'll tell ya 'bout mah cat."

Wetzel entered the rock structure. An old sofa faced a rock fireplace in the living room, two arm chairs on either side of the sofa. His boots resounded on the rough wooden floors as he followed her toward the kitchen and small dining room. Two bedrooms led off from the small living room, one on either side. She motioned toward the table. "Have a seat there, Jack. I'll get us some coffee." Montie sat at his feet, placing his face between his paws.

She poured coffee and placed a steaming cup in front of him, got her own cup, and sat opposite of him. As he held the hot coffee cupped in both hands, she glanced briefly at them. The brown eyes smiled. "Oh, heck, Jack. I plumb forgot to ask. You want some cream or sugar?"

"No thanks, Lacey." He sipped at the hot coffee. "Reckon we can count sheep this morning?"

She smiled broadly. "Not to worry, Jack. My hired hand is bringin' 'em down from the mountain; should be here any minute. We'll put 'em in the corral yonder an' you can count 'em fer as long as ya want." She sipped her coffee, set the cup on the table, and leaned forward on her forearms, her small tanned hands clasped. Her brow furrowed; the dark brown eyes displayed a serious concern for matters at hand.

"You see, Jack. As I told ya, I have a big 'ol tom cat. Name's Reggie. Helluva cat! Big boy, Reggie is ... ain't here right now. I reckon he's out trolling fer them females or some sech thing." She took a drink of coffee.

"My neighbors down the road at the Silver Cell Mine had a big 'ol pit bull dog. Meaner'n a damn badger he was. Well, they brought him over one day, them an' thet mean pit bull dog, three 'o 'em snickerin' an' laughin', carryin' on. They'd seen Reggie around and planned to sic thet dog on pore 'ol Reg." Lacey shook her pretty head and smiled.

Wetzel's eyes narrowed, his jaw set. "Was Reggie here at the house?"

"Yessir, he surely was here thet day, an' I told them they'd best take thet dog outta here 'afore somebody got hurt," she said emphatically.

"But they had no intention of going anywhere, did they?"

Lacey shook her head, the ponytail bouncing. "Nope. They was lookin' fer trouble an' thet mean dog, too." She sipped her coffee, set the cup down. "Anyhow, when we was standing there lollygagging, 'ol Reg, he jest saunters around the corner of the house, stops, looks over at them thugs and their thug dog. The dog ... he's growlin' and pullin' at his leash." She gave a pleasant, throaty laugh. "You know what 'ol Reg done, Jack Wetzel?"

He leaned forward on the table, eye brows raised. "Run for his life?"

She laughed again. "No sirree. He just stood there an' looked thet dog over *real* casual like, and then he laid down right in front o' him and scratched his *cojones*!"

Wetzel's face broke into a grin. "You're kidding?"

She shook her head again. "Reckon not. Then he got up *real* slow-like an' headed back where he come from 'tother side of the house. Well ... they was all pissed off. The handler hollered an' let thet dog loose an' off he went after 'ol Reg! I yelled at 'em to call him off, but they jest laughed."

"What happened, Lacey?" Wetzel straightened in his chair.

She sat back, palms on the table, face solemn and looked at him with pursed lips then: "Well ... we could hear a lot o' commotion back behind the house, Jack, fer quite a spell. Them guys was all laughin', makin' smart aleck remarks 'bout what their dog was a doin' to mah cat. That's when lo and behold, here comes their dog hauling ass ... excuse my language, Jack ... an' 'ol Reg he's a straddle of him, a hangin' on like some bull rider ridin' fer eight seconds and a punishin' ride to git top score!" She pounded the table hard with her palms and laughed so hard, tears ran down her cheeks. "Reggie ... he ... was ... a hangin' on *real* good and raking thet sumbitch ... excuse my language, Jack ... thet ...dog one side o' his face an' eyes then 'tother."

Wetzel sat back in his chair and laughed heartily. Then he leaned forward. "You're kidding me now."

She swallowed the last of her coffee. "I reckon not. 'Ol Reg, he cleaned thet dog's plow, fair an' square. Them thugs was hollaring fer *me* to call off mah cat! Can you believe thet, Jack?"

Wetzel's face sobered. "That's a bad bunch at the Silver Cell, Lacey. I'd steer clear of them."

"Last I saw 'o 'em, they was a runnin' down the road behind their sumbitch dog ... excuse my language, Jack ... an' 'ol Reg, he was a givin' it to him, right an' left. They ain't been back since."

"How did their dog fare?" asked Wetzel.

She pursed her lips in thought. "I don't rightly know. He's not been back neither." She thought some more about the incident and then laughed. "You want more coffee, Jack?"

"No thanks, Lacey."

She stood. "Aw'ight then. Let's go see if Daniel brought them sheep in."

Wetzel stood and walked out onto the porch. He reached in his shirt pocket and pulled out a package of cigarettes, shaking a Lucky Strike out and stuck it into the corner of this mouth. The sunlight had reached the valley floor; he lit the cigarette and smoked while watching a long line of sheep slowly descend a mountain trail toward the barn and corrals. Lacey stood beside him for several minutes, peering up at him. "How long you been with the Forest Service, Jack, if'n ya don't mind my askin'?"

The cigarette in the corner of his mouth began a slow progression from one corner of his mouth to the other, and smoke drifted from his nostrils; he smiled at her, the cigarette wavered slightly. "Not at all, Lacey; it's been a few years now. I got out of the army, went to New Mexico State on the GI bill and graduated with a degree in range management." He shrugged, "When I applied for the government job, it probably didn't hurt that I was an Army vet."

"What'd ya do for the army, Jack?"

Wetzel thought for a moment, drew on the cigarette. "I was a Scout Dog handler."

"You trained dogs for the army?"

"No. I trained *with* Smoky ... he was the German Shepherd they gave me at Fort Benning, and me and him ... we ... were a team in Nam. They had us working point on patrols."

Lacey tucked her thumbs in jeans pockets and watched him again as he smoked his cigarette. "Was he a good dog, Jack?"

Without hesitation, Wetzel nodded. "The best friend I *ever* had, Lacey." He turned, and as he looked into her somber brown eyes, his own softened and gathered moisture. "He never *once* failed to be there for me; he saved my life and those of other American soldiers numerous times. I asked if I could bring him home with me when my tour ended, but the 'ol man ... my CO ... said Smoky belonged to the Army and was needed in Nam." He tossed the cigarette to his feet and ground it out with his boot heel.

"Is he still over there?" Lacey asked softly.

Wetzel pushed the Stetson back on his head with his thumb. "Maybeso; I think about him often and pray that he's okay."

"Maybe the war will be over soon." A puzzled look of hope appeared on her face.

Wetzel didn't answer. He watched from the porch; the sheep entered the corral, each one following the others. They milled around inside. An older, white-haired man closed the gate and then drank from a canteen strapped around his shoulders. Wetzel walked to the corral with Lacey.

The man smiled through his gray and white beard as he extended his hand to Wetzel. "How do you do, sir? My name's Daniel Reagan." Wetzel observed a firm handshake, the baggy work clothing that barely fit the trim older man, the green eyes peeking out beneath bushy white brows. Without the help of a sturdy belt, the pants would have had difficulty hanging on his hips. The man seemed oddly out of place in the wilderness setting and yet he carried himself with the confidence of a man accustomed to handling adversity in life.

"Jack Wetzel, Mr. Reagan."

Lacey interceded in the conversation. "Daniel has only worked for me a short time, Jack."

"Where do you come from, Mr. Reagan?"

"I never asked him o' his whereabouts," Lacey said icily, "ain't nobody's business."

The old man laughed a light, pleasant laugh. "It's quite all right, Lacey." He turned to Jack. "Mr. Wetzel is a law enforcement officer and has a right to know who I am and where I come from." He walked to the aged, wooden gate he had just closed, and leaned against it, taking in the clean, fresh mountain air. "I was raised in the mid-west, joined the army right out of college. Just a young lad then ... but I grew up fast." His eyes narrowed, remembering.

Interested, Wetzel leaned forward. "World War II or Korea?"

The old man sighed, "Both wars, son; Viet Nam, too."

He laughed as he looked into Wetzel's questioning face. "I was with a different agency in Nam." The old man rubbed his beard. "Wetzel? Hmmm ... yes! There was a Wetzel in my company at Omaha Beach—a Tom Wetzel." He peered at the law enforcement officer standing near him. "You look a lot like him, only more slender."

Wetzel stared at the old man, unable to speak. Finally, he said, "My dad served in the 1st Infantry Division at Omaha Beach."

CHAPTER FIFTY-THREE

THE OLD MAN STOOD LOOKING UP AT THE MOUNTAIN BUT NOT REALLY seeing it, hands at his side, jaws tight, as memories from a time long ago replayed in his mind.

THE LANDING CRAFT bounced in the waves, the cold sea water spilling over to where the men were hunched forward, wet helmets glistening, some of the men retching from the rough ride across the English Channel. He was not sea sick, only scared out of his wits as he heard the Navy pounding the shore line with their big guns. Suddenly, their heavy barrage ended with an eerie quiet that made a man want to talk, say anything just to break that damned silence. The man next to him placed a hand on his shoulder. "You all right, Danny?"

Reagan nodded as he pulled at the leather strap on his rifle slung on his shoulder.

Tom Wetzel had become his best friend and they shared some good times together while stationed in England prior to Operation Overlord commencing. "Won't be long now, pard." He had found Tom Wetzel to be a strong man, both physically and mentally, and a good, honest one as well.

Reagan nodded again, willing but unable to converse. He looked at Wetzel and smiled just as the landing gate opened with a loud splash. Someone shouted for them to disembark. Men began tumbling out ahead of them; some disappearing beneath the sea with their heavy packs and gear. Then to their horror, the men in front were cut to pieces. Machine gun fire, mortar and artillery fire!

Both men dove off into the water clutching their rifles, the heavy weight of their packs taking them deep into the sea. Machine gun bullets streaked deep into the water, hitting several men close to them. Reagan struggled to remove his pack, reached down and withdrew the bayonet from the scabbard at his belt and cut the straps while still holding onto his rifle. He kicked and swam to the surface for badly needed air. Bullets slapped into the water over his head and next to him as he swam hard and finally found footing on the beach.

Bodies bobbed like corks in the sea and corpses littered the beach. The German 325th Division commanded the steep bluffs overlooking the beach and continually poured heavy fire down on them. Reagan held tightly onto his rifle; he ran as fast as he could, zigzagging as he went. He saw Tom Wetzel's broad back just ahead of him, running hard. Men were cut in half, mowed down, blown literally to pieces in front of them, beside them, behind them. Miraculously, the two men weren't hit as they forced their weak legs and depleted lungs to function beyond anything humanly possible—on toward safety and the base of the steep cliffs ahead. Exhausted, they dove behind a small sand hill for cover. They both had made it past the open killing grounds of the German machine guns. God! It felt like an eternity.

The few men who had made it lay there for the first few hours and hunkered down, not knowing what to do. No leadership to advise them. Then mortar rounds began hitting near their positions. A loud authoritative voice said, "Two kinds of people are staying on this beach—the dead and those about to die!" They arose together and followed the officer, charging forward, taking out cement fortified machine guns, sustaining heavy casualties but slowly moving off the beach, eliminating their enemies and on to better cover.

Sweating profusely Reagan tossed a grenade into the pill box from below, and then ran, zigzagging back toward cover and safety. As the loud explosion from the grenade deafened him, he was hit hard, the impact knocking him to the ground; a deep burning sensation in his chest as the heavy bullet entered, ripping and tearing its way through his body.

He lay there for some time, immobilized and in shock. Then Tom Wetzel was beside him, ripping at his fatigues, checking his wound. His voice was quiet and calm which seemed surreal in the midst of intense rifle, mortar, and artillery fire.

"I gotcha, Danny. You'll be all right, amigo." Strong hands and arms lifted Reagan body and he was draped over Wetzel's broad shoulder as he began a slow run. Bullets zinged overhead and into the sand at their feet; one

round passed through Reagan's fatigue pants, another took the heel off one of his boots, but a panting Tom Wetzel somehow carried him to safety.

THE OLD MAN SIGHED DEEPLY. His tired, green eyes peered at Jack Wetzel. "Your dad was one of the finest men I've ever known and a real soldier, son; I owe him my life."

"I didn't get to know him very well, Mr. Reagan. He was killed in a forest fire in 1955 when I was just a kid."

Reagan's brow furrowed. "I'm sorry to hear that, Jack. Did he work for the Forest Service as well?"

Jack Wetzel nodded. "Yes sir. He was the Mimbres District Ranger before the war; they gave him his job back when he returned." Changing the subject, Wetzel turned to Lacey, "Your grazing permit shows fifty-one head of sheep. That about right?"

"We've lost a few head to the coyotes, but that's close, Jack. My male rams is up near Daniel's place. I keep them in another pasture away from them ewes till breeding season."

Wetzel climbed up on the log corral fence and began counting.

The old man sat beneath a shady pine tree and drank cool water from his canteen. He watched as Wetzel patiently counted the animals. *Damn if he doesn't look a lot like Tom.* A smile tugged at the corner of his mouth as he observed Lacey looking at the young law enforcement officer. He could tell she was definitely interested in him, and the boy had no idea. The old man's daughter would have been about their age ... if she had lived. A lump rose in his throat as he remembered another incident from his past.

The arrest and assassination of Ngo Dinh Diem, the president of South Vietnam, had marked the successful culmination of a CIA-backed coup d'état led by General Durong Van Minh in November 1963.

When the rebel forces entered the palace, Diem and his younger brother and advisor Ngo Dinh Nhu had agreed to surrender and were promised safe exile. But Reagan knew all this and much, much more. He was the responsible CIA agent at the embassy and had accompanied the two brothers after their surrender in the back of an armored personnel carrier headed back to military headquarters at Tan Son Nhurt Air Base.

Captain Nguyen Van Nhung and Major Durong Hieu Nghia had guarded the brothers with Reagan on that fateful day of November 2, 1963. During the trip to the base, Nhung nodded to Reagan. Reagan raised his arm, clutching a semi-automatic pistol and shot both brothers multiple times in the head. He would have nightmares of the incident for many years, and he never forgot the shocked, betrayed looks on both brothers' faces as he shot each of them. But orders were orders, and he had always obeyed them.

Hand-picked by the United States to be more amenable to their wishes than his predecessor, General Durong Van Minh, would now be in charge. Reagan stepped out of the blood-splattered armored personnel carrier and vomited.

THE OLD MAN had lost his wife and daughter in Viet Nam just last year; casualties of a war torn country. They had wanted to be close to him after being apart for so many years. But an explosive device hidden in a restaurant in Saigon frequented by Americans had taken both of them from him. Shortly thereafter, he resigned from the CIA. And now ... he was alone and tired ... very tired. He wanted only to find peace and quiet, real meaning to his life again.

As the old man watched the young couple talking and laughing, he broke into a grin. *Maybe I've finally found a reason after all. Maybe, just maybe, it's not too late for me.*

Lacey yelled, "Come on, Mr. Reagan! Shake a leg o'er heah. Them sheep ain't gonna git sheared by theyselves. I've talked Jack heah into helping us in exchange fer a helluva ... excuse my language, Jack ... a good supper!"

Wetzel just shook his head and grinned as he headed over to his Forest Service truck and removed his gun belt and uniform shirt.

CHAPTER FIFTY-FOUR

The man in black waited patiently as he lay on the roof of the apartment building. Total darkness enveloped him as the moon was but a mere slit in the star-studded sky. His hands worked quickly in the dark. With the dexterity and training of a professional, he assembled the sniper rifle in minutes. He pulled the bolt action back slowly so as to not make any discernable noise. Then he placed a shell from his pocket in the breech and slid the action forward, locking it into place in the chamber.

A pickup truck drove by on Market Street, backfired and startled a cat hidden in a shrub nearby. The man in black decided to maintain surveillance on the apartment for awhile. He had hoped the window curtains would be open for an easy view inside but was only slightly disappointed when they were pulled to. The small, single-story, flat-roofed apartment stood out in the darkened night as the porch light came on. Across the street, the high domes atop Saint Vincent de Paul Catholic Church stood like sentinels guarding the sacred premises.

Ten minutes passed; another vehicle approached from Bullard Street up Market Street to where the man waited. The blue, Dodge sedan stopped at the stop sign, brakes squealing, crossed to the apartment, and parked in front. The passenger door creaked open; a tall, Hispanic man stepped out, laughing as he did so. He walked with difficulty, dragging a leg as he walked around the car to the driver side door. The driver stepped out and the man in black immediately recognized him as one of his drug dealers. *Jose!* The two men laughed and talked in quiet tones for some time. Jose passed something to the disabled man. Suddenly, the apartment front door flung open and a young woman stepped out. The disabled man slipped the item into his shirt front.

Hands on her hips, the woman shouted, "Juan Garcia! Come in here this instant! Robbie and I have been waiting for you for hours." The attractive woman's red hair hung in a pony tail; she wore a white, cotton blouse and blue jeans; her feet were bare.

The man in black rested his cheek softly against the rifle stock and looked through the attached scope. He focused his sight through the rifle scope on the woman. She was shapely, good looking, and clearly agitated. He grinned as he changed his focus solely on the doorway, waiting for the boy to appear.

"I'll be there in a minute, dammit," Garcia snarled at the woman.

The red-head stamped her foot. "Now, Juan! I mean it."

Garcia started around the blue Dodge. "God dammit, Maggie! *Como chingas."*

"Who's that with you, Juan?" She strained as if to see who it might be.

"A friend ... shit!" Garcia struggled with walking as he dragged his leg up onto the sidewalk.

Jose got in the vehicle. "Later, man."

The woman leaned forward, pointed, and shouted, "You stay away from my husband!"

The Dodge started to pull away from the curb. The woman wasn't finished, not by a damned sight. "You hear me! You come around here again, I'll call the cops."

Garcia snapped at her, "Don't you talk to me like that in front of my friends, Maggie."

"Friends! That man is no friend of yours. He's trash, Juan, and he's going to get you into trouble."

Garcia ignored her, "Where's Robbie?"

The man in black concentrated on the doorway, slipping his finger into the trigger guard, caressing the trigger; he waited.

The woman stood there looking at her husband. "He waited up for his daddy for a long time and then went to sleep on the couch."

Garcia shook his head and walked into the apartment.

The woman stood alone on the porch, sobbing.

The man in black laid the rifle gently on the roof. It would be a long wait, and if his target did not show by early morning, he would have to wait for another opportunity. No matter, he had all the time in the world. His boss had ordered him to kill the boy, and he always obeyed orders.

Why the hell did he have a problem in killing him? The boy was nothing to him. True, when he'd kidnapped the boy after killing the old woman, he had hesitated in deciding what to do with him. He had admired the boy's toughness. Maybe the boy had reminded him of himself? Then the boy had escaped in the wilderness and the opportunity was gone. The boy had been guarded closely for a long time after the kidnapping. And anyhow, he knew the boy could not identify him. He had been careful and worn a ski mask.

But if he failed to follow direct orders from Pablo Enrique and not kill the boy? The man in black knew the answer to that question before it had even formed in his thoughts.

CHAPTER FIFTY-FIVE

WILDLIFE OFFICER BOB MCMURTRY WAS TIRED; PLUMB TUCKERED OUT. He had ridden all the way in, to the Heart Bar Ranch from Miller's Spring in the Gila Wilderness pulling two pack mules that were stubborn and a pain in the ass the whole trip. He grunted as he tossed flakes of hay to all the horses and mules in the barn. Picking up the pack saddles and panniers, he strode to the tack room and hung the saddles on the racks and the canvas panniers on wooden pegs.

As he started toward the house from the barn, a red F-100 Ford truck drove in from the highway. The speeding vehicle bounced high in ruts in the road and squealed to a stop near him. As three men stepped out, McMurtry reached down, quickly removed the chain from a stake that had been attached to one of his hunting dogs; he jerked the long metal stake from its anchor in the ground.

The first man to approach him was a young, Hispanic male. He was a big man, over six feet tall and probably 220 pounds with biceps as large as most men's legs. His long, black hair hung to his shoulders. What interested McMurtry most was the baseball bat he carried in his right hand. The ape spoke. "You McMurtry?"

"Who wants to know?" The other two men separated and begain to flank him on either side. He stepped back so that his back was against the barn.

"We'll ask the questions." The Hispanic man slapped the bat in the palm of his left hand and stepped closer.

McMurtry wished he hadn't been in such a big hurry to leave his service revolver in the house when he'd returned from the field. The other two men did not advance any closer as they eyed the heavy metal stake in the wildlife officer's hands.

The ape spoke again. "You drop that stake and we'll talk, *guero*."

McMurtry threw back his head and laughed. "Why, back in Tennessee where I come from, boy, they'd say you was plumb white-eyed."

The ape just looked at him. McMurtry spoke sharply. "Y'all know what I'm talking about ... scared to death." He was ready when the man charged him. As he had anticipated, the ape swung the bat right-handed. He ducked his head and felt the swoosh of the heavy bat as it passed overhead then he swung left-handed with the metal stake, as he was different than most at bat, and hit the man hard on his neck below the ear. The stunned man stumbled, tried to catch his balance. His eyes rolled back in his head, and he fell solidly to the ground.

McMurtry looked at one of the men and then the other. "You boys want some o' this?" He smiled and shook the stake out in front of him. The two men looked at each other as if not sure what to do.

McMurtry shook the stake again. "You boys stand together. I'll not be lookin' sideways at one o' ya then the t'other."

Both men just looked at him, one tall and skinny, the other a short, small man.

"Move! Damn you." He pointed with the stake to where he wanted them to stand.

The moved in unison and stood directly in front of him illuminated in the pickup's headlights.

McMurtry's eyes blazed as he spoke. "You boys had best start explainin' what this is all about. Don't reckon I know any o' ya. Don't recollect writin' any tickets fer game violations neither, so what gives?"

One man spoke suddenly. "We was sent to tell you to stay away from Juanita Flores," He looked down, "and to make sure you understood the message."

McMurtry's jaw dropped. "Juanita Floor-ezz?"

The short man spoke up. "Her husband wants you to know if you keep seeing her, you'll get worse than a baseball bat."

McMurtry raised the metal stake and stepped quickly forward. "*Ex*-husband, I says." He shook his shaggy head, removed the ball cap and then placed it back on his head, cocking it slightly to the right. "I'll be dadjimmed; thet yella livered sumbitch sent you boys to do his dirty job fer 'im." He laughed out loud, motioning toward the Hispanic man lying prostrate on the ground. "You git yore buddy and git the hell outta here."

He walked up close to both men and looked them in the eye. "You tell that worthless bastard of an ex-husband if'n any o' you set foot here again, I'll kill ya! And as to the lady you mentioned, you tell him thet I plan on marrying her ... the sooner the better." He shook the metal stake menacingly. "Now *git*!"

CHAPTER FIFTY-SIX

Jack Wetzel sat quietly on the porch, leaning back against the log wall, his legs and back feeling the fatigue; an aching, muscle soreness setting in. His dog lay sleeping beside him. Montie had lain in the shade most of the day and done nothing in the way of work. Wetzel thought maybe the dog figured somebody needed rest and it might just as well be him.

He'd learned that shearing sheep was no easy task. After insisting on helping Lacey with fixing supper, Dan Reagan was in the kitchen. Wetzel smiled; the old man had held his own with the shearing. He was obviously in excellent health for his age and willing to do more than his share of the work. Furthermore, he was a likable character. Wetzel wondered though about his work in Vietnam. He had seen a few CIA operatives when he served during the war; none of them were likable and most had become hardened killers.

The door to the cabin opened behind Wetzel and the Whippit brothers stepped out onto the porch. They were twins and looked alike in most ways, and yet it was easy for Wetzel to tell which one was which. The men were in their early thirties, shaggy brown hair covered with faded, well-worn baseball caps. Sporting thick, scruffy beards, Lattimore and Larrimore Whippit wore no shirts beneath their dirty, denim coveralls. Dusty leather work boots covered Lattimore's large feet while Larrimore's bare feet protruded out from below his coveralls.

Larrimore walked to where Wetzel sat. He handed Wetzel a large fruit jar. He grinned, showing his tobacco-stained teeth. "Heah, Jack boy I kin see y'all need something cool to drink." He laughed and took off his cap, running his hand through thick, unruly hair. Wetzel saw the cowlick at his hairline next to his forehead and confirmed that it was indeed Larrimore. Lattimore had no such cowlick. Further, Wetzel had noticed that Larrimore's right eyelid and face twitched as he spoke. His brother had no such affliction. Wetzel thanked him for the cool beverage, tilted the fruit jar and took a good drink. He immediately regretted it, feeling the deep burn of home-made whiskey in his throat and then back up into his nose. He gagged, coughed and then wheezed out in a tight voice, "*Moon ... shine*?"

The brothers slapped their legs and laughed so hard, tears ran down their cheeks. Finally gaining composure, Larrimore tucked his large hands inside the open sides of his coveralls. "Law a mercy, Jack! Y'all need to take it easy on thet there moonshine."

Lattimore quipped, "Now, Jack, ya'll got to remember this heah's *sippin'* not gulpin' whiskey. Haw, haw!"

Wetzel straightened up, swallowing hard. He grinned, appreciating the joke played on him. "I reckon I'll remember to sip from now on, fellas." He took a small sip and licked his lips. "You know ... it's not too shabby at that."

It was Lattimore's turn to insert his large hands inside the open sides of his overalls. "Best moonshine plumb west 'o the Mississippi, Jack."

Wetzel took another swig of the moonshine; it warmed him inside and the aches and pains began to dissipate. *Not bad.* He finished the contents in the fruit jar and was feeling somewhat better about not only his aches and pains but hell ... life in general. In fact, he didn't give a hoot 'n hell about much of anything when Lacey stepped out on the porch to announce that supper was ready.

"Jack?" She frowned and then turned to her brothers, hands on her hips. "What have you boys done to our guest?"

"Aw ... nothin', sis," Larrimore sputtered, "we was just haffin' a little fun."

"Damn you, I'll tan yore hides!" She threw a quick glance at Wetzel. "Excuse my language, Jack."

Wetzel looked up from his perch on the porch; his first attempt at standing failed, the second succeeded with Lacey's help. Montie sauntered over. As Lacey stood next to him, Wetzel enjoyed the feeling of her body close to him and her sincere interest in his welfare. He noticed for the first time that she was very pretty and said so. She blushed and helped him inside to the table. With everyone seated, she had the old man say grace and everyone filled their plates with lamb chops, mashed potatoes, gravy, and green beans. With his stomach full, Wetzel felt much better. A slight breeze from the opened front door rustled his hair and cooled his cheek.

Lacey stood up from the table and looked over his direction, "Anyone for peach cobbler?"

"You bet!" he said almost too eagerly.

"Aw 'ight then."

Dan Reagan peered at Wetzel beneath bushy white eyebrows. The green eyes were twinkling.

Larrimore stood, stretched his lanky frame. "Keep my dessert till I git back, sis. I plumb forgot to lock the gate up at the mine. Be right back."

* * *

LARRIMORE WHIPPIT DROVE the old pickup truck slowly along the narrow, rough road, bouncing high on occasion shaking his full stomach much more than he would've liked. Rounding a corner in the road, his headlight beams illuminated a black van blocking the road ahead. Stopping the truck, he put the transmission in neutral and set the hand emergency brake. He stepped out, his bare feet feeling their way toward the black van.

Two men stepped out, one from each side. The driver was a large man, well over six feet in height, and his thick, heavy torso indicated maybe 230 pounds. Larrimore Whippit felt like a skinny runt beside the giant. The other man folded his arms across his chest, leaned back against the van, and grinned insolently.

The large man took a step toward the advancing Whippit. "It's a bit late for you hillbillies to be out wandering around, ain't it?"

Whippit stopped within a few feet short of the man, rubbed his beard, and then spit tobacco juice staining the sandy soil by his bare feet. He tucked his hands inside the open sides of his patched, denim coveralls. "Ya'll need to move yore van o'er yonder so's I kin pass along."

The giant laughed, looked at his partner, who then laughed with him. *"Y'all?"* He grunted. "What the hell *are* you; some kind of goddamned, ignorant hick from the backwoods of nowhere?"

Whippit spat again, shuffled his feet, but did not answer the question. In a quiet voice he said, "I'm askin' ya kindly, mister, to let me pass." His right eye and the right side of his face twitched.

"And I'm telling *you,* you goddamned hillbilly that you ain't coming through ..." He hesitated, thought a moment, grinned, "Unless you got fifty bucks. That's the toll for passing through."

"This here's a Forest Service road, mister. You cain't—"

"Shut the hell up, you ignorant son-of-a-bitch! And get the hell outta here." The big man motioned with his hands in a sweeping motion, "Go on. Git!"

Whippit's right eye and face twitched; he spat tobacco juice out of the corner of his mouth, nodded and turned around, walking back toward his old pickup. The two men near the van laughed at him as he walked away. Larrimore Whippit opened the driver's door, retrieved a .30-.30 Winchester rifle from the rifle rack, levered a round into the chamber, took a rest on the door and fired.

The first and second rounds hit the van's windshield. The third passed through the big man's baggy pants just below the crotch, the fourth round knocked the second man's baseball cap from his head creasing his skull. Whippit walked toward them, loading three more rounds in the tubular magazine from his coverall pockets.

Both men threw up their hands and shouted simultaneously, "Don't shoot. *Don't shoot, goddamn it.*"

Whippit pointed the rifle at one man then the other. "Back home in Nawth Carolina, I'd kill the both o' ya ... bury ya back in a holler somewheres." He spat tobacco juice; some remained on his bearded chin. The right eye and face twitched uncontrollably. Finally, he shook his head. "Naw, won't do. Sis'd be maddern' a wet hen."

He pointed the rifle at both men again. "Shuck them clothes boys."

"W...hat?" the giant stammered.

Whippit fired a round each at the men's feet. Both men jumped, eyes wide. "Don't reckon I'll be askin' y'all agin."

The men quickly removed their clothes and stood before the determined mountain man in their underwear. He spoke softly. "Them skivvies, too, boys."

"Wait a damn minute here ..."

Whippit raised the rifle.

"Wait, hold on now."

Whippit aimed his rifle at the big man. The shorts came off and both men stood naked in the dark forest. Whippit pointed back down the canyon with his rifle. "You boys start a runnin' on down Whiskey Crick, an' don't you stop till ya git to the highway, ya heah?"

The naked men just stood there covering themselves with their hands, unsure of what to do.

Larrimore Whippit's tone was icy. "I ain't a gonna tell y'all again. *Git!*"

The men turned and ran down the canyon, yelling out when bare feet stepped on a sharp rock or pine cone. Whippit fired two rounds in the air to keep them moving, and then he turned and shot all four tires, flattening them. Removing the keys from the van's ignition, he threw them as far as he could. He walked back to his truck, placed the rifle back in the rack behind the seat. Releasing the hand brake, he stepped down hard on the gas pedal and sped toward the van, hitting it squarely in the middle of the passenger side, driving it off the road. He backed up, stopping only long enough to spit tobacco juice out of the driver's window. Then slowly the old truck continued on up the canyon toward the mine.

CHAPTER FIFTY-SEVEN

A DISHEVELED JUAN GARCIA SCOOTED ALONG THE FLOOR ON HIS BOTTOM to the coffee table and retrieved a hidden marijuana pipe. The prosthesis for his missing leg lay discarded close by. He filled the pipe with contents from a plastic bag that he had taken from his pants pocket then lit it, drawing the smoke deeply into his lungs. Closing his eyes, he drew on the pipe again, this time even deeper. *Jeez, this is sooo goddamn good! I can forget everything—all of it.*

But it would not be so for him. The past erupted again, violently, as it always did:

THE NORTH VIETNAMESE interrogator grinned and then laughed out loud as he stomped Garcia's severely injured leg. Garcia screamed in excruciating pain. The interrogator sat on his heels and slapped him in the face, once, and then again harder. "You piece of shit Yankee soldier. What American unit are you from? What are your orders?"

Sweating profusely in agony, Garcia rasped, "I need … medical … help. My leg—"

The interrogator laughed again. "You mean this leg?" He stomped hard on the leg again. Garcia screamed even louder.

"No one gives a shit about you, Yankee; no one. You're forgotten by the Americans, by your family. No one cares." The voice became conciliatory.

"Talk to me. I can get you medical help, but you have to talk. How about it, Yankee?"

Garcia gave his name, rank, and serial number.

The North Vietnamese stood abruptly. Shouting obscenities in Vietnamese, he kicked Garcia hard in the face, the ribs, and stomped on his leg again. "You stupid Yankee! Your leg is beginning to smell, Yankee. Gangrene …" He paused, leaning forward. "You ready talk now?"

His face contorted with pain, Garcia spat directly in his face. The North Vietnamese stood and kicked him hard in the side of his head; he blacked out.

JUAN GARCIA HEARD someone speaking to him, "Daddy … Daddy, are you okay?" Small hands held his unkempt face; days without shaving. Garcia opened his eyes. A small boy, soft brown hair with long dark eye lashes, knelt next to him. Big, brown eyes looked into his bleary ones. The voice laced with sadness spoke again. "Oh, Daddy, Momma will be so mad at you."

Garcia sat upright. Dizziness encompassed him, his head swirled round and round, but he saw his son Robbie clearly now and his school backpack lying nearby. He saw the compassion and love in those brown eyes. Tears rolled down his cheeks and he sobbed openly in front of his son. "I'm so sorry, Robbie. I … I just … the nightmares—"

"It's okay, Daddy. I understand. But Momma, well, she won't. We've got to get you cleaned up before she gets home from work," Robbie looked around, "and air the apartment out, Daddy. That stuff you're smoking stinks up our house."

Garcia struggled to move, scooting toward the bathroom on his bottom.

"You want your leg, Daddy?"

Garcia snarled, "No! Goddamn it," and hit the boy with the back of his hand, knocking him down. Frightened, Robbie got up and ran out the front door. "Wait Robbie, I didn't mean it, son." He scooted hurriedly to the front door and out onto the porch.

The boy cowered near the street, holding his face.

Garcia scooted toward him. "Look … Robbie. I never meant to hit you, son. I am so sorry."

The boy stood his ground, pointing at his father, *"You stay away from me. You … you meanie!"*

* * *

SOUTH OF MARKET Street directly across from the apartment up on the roof, the man in black smiled, a crooked smile, as he placed his cheek softly against the rifle stock, his finger slipped inside the trigger guard. He aimed carefully through the rifle scope at the boy's head.

Garcia pleaded with his son, "Please, Robbie. Come back inside." Wetting his lips, he begged, "Please son," and motioned the boy toward him, "come back inside the house."

The man in black heard the sound of an approaching vehicle as it sped west on Market Street toward their location. Irritated, he removed his finger from within the trigger guard and swung his rifle and scope to the east and the oncoming vehicle.

He clearly saw the overhead police lights and green truck approaching and swore, *"Dammit! ÍComo chingan!"*

The Forest Service truck slid to a halt in front of the apartment and a slender, tall man stepped out wearing a gray Stetson hat, beige uniform shirt and green pants. A .357 S&W revolver was strapped to his waist in a Sam Brown belt and holster. A black and white Border Collie dog sat in the back of the truck.

"Jack Wetzel!" the little boy exclaimed.

The man in black recognized the ranger as the man who had tracked him in the wilderness after he'd kidnapped the boy months ago. The ranger walked quickly to the boy and they embraced. The ranger spoke. "What's the matter, Robbie?" He examined the reddened cheek on the boy's face then turned to Juan Garcia, "What the hell's going on here, Juan?"

"Jack ... look ... I ... we had a little misunderstanding is all."

Wetzel stared at Garcia, his face darkening. The boy said, "It's all right, Jack. Daddy didn't mean it."

The man in black lay on the roof top his finger off the trigger, pondering what to do. *Kill them all?* He sighed, his hand moving in close to his body, the thumb and forefinger touching as if holding a cigarette, the little finger flicking at ashes from the cigarette that did not exist.

Kill everyone? He'd want to take the boy out first, as ordered, and if he did, the ranger would react. And if he was well trained, he would be difficult to kill and could complicate his precarious situation on the roof. Better to wait. He laid the rifle down on the roof and rested on his elbows. The dog apparently sensed his presence and looked directly at him, sitting up higher in the back of the truck.

Wetzel's voice had a metallic ring to it. "Juan, you're my best friend, but if you *ever* lay a hand on Robbie again, I'll beat you within an inch of your miserable life." The little boy hugged Wetzel's leg.

Garcia said nothing and scooted toward the apartment. Wetzel blurted out. "You need professional help, Juan, before things get worse, dammit."

Garcia turned back toward his old high school friend, his eyes blazing, "What *I* need is my leg and my life back *before* goddamn Vietnam, Jack." He pointed at Wetzel, "Can you or anyone help me with that?"

Wetzel hesitated before he spoke.

"I thought so," Garcia turned and scooted past the threshold of the apartment door.

"Hold on, damn you!" Wetzel moved as he spoke, holding Robbie's hand. He caught up with Garcia just inside the door. "Quit sitting around feeling sorry for yourself and thinkin' that everyone owes you something. They don't owe you shit. I don't owe you anything either. I spent a year over in that hell hole myself, and I suffer from nightmares, too."

Garcia stared at him; he was listening.

"That's right, Juan, me too." Wetzel rubbed Robbie's hair then hugged him. "There's a fella over in Las Cruces that I go see. I'll give you his name and number if you want."

"What is he? A goddamn shrink?"

"He's a man who knows post-traumatic stress and how to deal with it." Wetzel clenched his jaw.

Garcia sighed, shook his head.

"You think on it, Juan." He sniffed the air inside the apartment. "Jeez, Juan, what the hell are you doing smoking pot in here with Robbie coming home from school and all?" It was his turn to shake his head, "And Maggie ... she'll be madder'n a wet hen."

Wetzel walked into the apartment. "Give me your marijuana and the pipe, Juan. *Now!*"

He did not see the man in black unload the rifle quickly and deftly take the sniper rifle apart, place it in the carrying case and disappear quietly from the roof of the house across the street, but his dog Montie did. The dog bared his teeth and a low growl preceded him standing up with his paws on the tool box in the back of the truck.

The man in black stood silently in the shrubbery adjacent to the house; his thoughts were of the boy, Robbie. He had to admit the kid had guts. The boy did remind him of himself in a time long ago. Hell, maybe he wouldn't kill him after all. The thought made him laugh. He bit his lower lip. What the hell was he thinking? If the kid lived, *he* would die. It was as simple as that. Pablo Enrique was a very dangerous man to cross.

CHAPTER FIFTY-EIGHT

Gray and black clouds swirled in an overcast sky. The windshield wipers of Steve Hunt's New Mexico State Police car were on high speed, whipping the heavy down pour of water off the windshield. Hunching over the wheel, he maneuvered his car down Hudson Street in Silver City, New Mexico. He turned onto a side street adjacent to the Fire Station, drove around to the rear and parked in front of the Police Department side of the public safety building.

After turning the ignition off, he placed a rain cover over the black State Police cap, grabbed his yellow rain slicker and his brief case from the front seat, took a deep breath and stepped out into the deluge and strong winds. He swung his slicker over his shoulders and jogged to the entrance of the Police Station.

A grinning Don Ramirez, chief deputy for Grant County Sheriff's Office, held the door open for him. "Howdy Steve! Helluva storm, huh?"

Hunt managed a weak smile back at his friend, "Yes, it is. Thanks, Don." He swung the wet slicker off, hung it on an empty peg near the door and placed his cap there as well. "Is everyone here?"

"*Sí, jefe*. Everyone accounted for except—"

"Let me guess. That damned hillbilly from Tennessee."

Suddenly the door to the Police Station flew open, lightning flashed across the sky and thunder boomed as a heavy-set man wearing camouflage clothes, soaked hunting boots, a wet, old ball cap atop his head, and a .357 revolver encased in a shoulder holster under his left arm rushed in. Wildlife Officer Bob McMurtry grinned broadly. "Howdy boys! Helluva day, ain't it?" Not waiting for a response, he continued, "Why, I'm sure proud to be sharin' some fellowship with you fellers today." He headed toward the conference room, his tracks staining the carpet with every step. Sitting down heavily in a chair, he plopped both muddy feet up on the table in front of him.

The two men grinned at each other as they followed him into the room. Hunt walked to the closest table near the front of the room, set his brief case down and looked around the room. Forest Service LEO Jack Wetzel was talking to the newly sworn in Silver City Police Chief, Bill Rogers; a deputy sheriff Hunt did not recognize sat alone in the back of the room. He wore dark sunglasses and his crisp uniform appearance exuded a quiet confidence.

Hunt walked to the blackboard, picked up a piece of chalk, and wrote, "OPERATION PIPE CLEANER" on the board. The room quieted down. Hunt turned to the men in the room, "Have a seat, gentleman." He looked at Ramirez. "I didn't ask for anyone but you to be here representing the sheriff, Don." His voice had an edge to it. "Who's your friend?"

"The sheriff insisted that Ramon be here, Steve. Not my call."

Hunt's sharp gaze settled on the deputy. "Why don't you introduce yourself deputy and tell us a little about your past history?"

The deputy grinned, stood up and removed his dark sunglasses. "Yessir; you bet."

Hunt saw that he stood easily, hands at his sides, relaxed in his posture. His short black hair and clean-shaven brown face accentuated a handsome look and the dark brown eyes locked with Hunt's. The uniform was immaculate, clean and pressed. "I'm Ramon Perez. I worked for the El Paso Police Department for several years, Sergeant. There's really not much to tell." He shrugged his shoulders as he looked around the room.

Hunt persisted. "Why come here? The pay's not what it is in El Paso."

Perez's eyelids shuttered and then he looked at the blackboard. "A little peace and quiet, I guess."

Hunt's brow furrowed. *I'm not finished with you.*

"All right; let's get to it." He opened his briefcase and passed out copies of papers to each of the men in the room.

"Go on and take look. Operation Pipe Cleaner is a State Police initiative to clean out all the corruption, crime, especially the drug problem that we've all seen escalate here in the Silver City area since the gold strike." He held up a copy of the operation plan he'd handed out and then tapped on the blackboard for emphasis. "The operation name and accompanying information is never to be mentioned other than to the folks present in this room until culmination of certain events and arrests are imminent."

Hunt pointed at Wetzel and McMurtry. "I have you two in on this because you're out there in the boonies every day and most likely have or will run into these bad guys." He walked closer to the men he was addressing. "And we'll most likely need you to help track some of the bastards before it's all over."

Hunt looked directly at McMurtry. "Mac, take your damn muddy boots off the table for Christsake."

McMurtry grinned, tilted the ball cap to the right on his head, and removed his feet from the table. "Law a mercy, Steve; you're nit picky today, ain't ya?"

It was Hunt's turn to grin. "You and the Whippits up on Whiskey Creek are cut from the same damn cloth."

McMurtry leaned forward on the table. "I heerd tell o' them. Sounds like some fine country folks. Only they ain't from the great state 'o Tennesee. They're next door neighbors, I reckon." He turned and found Wetzel sitting directly behind him. His eyes smiled. "I heerd tell you was a sparkin' thet gal up yonder, Jack. Thet so?"

Wetzel blushed and said nothing.

Hunt cleared his throat. "We're here for business. Cut the chit chat and let's get to it."

"In the event some of you have a poor recollection of what's transpired here in the Silver City area during the last year, let me refresh your memory. Rancher Roger O'Brian was murdered while riding down on the Gila River and his body burned beyond recognition. Silver City Police Chief Thompson gunned down here in town. Police officers allegedly involved in corruption. All fueled by the drug trade. And the discovery of gold in Pinos Altos has only made things worse."

McMurtry stuffed chewing tobacco in his mouth, placed his muddy boots back on the table and leaned back in his chair.

"We've not solved these murders, but I have a good lead from my DEA source in El Paso." Hunt hesitated briefly as he looked at Deputy Perez. "Then a week ago, someone murdered a drug dealer on Highway 90 south of town, and it appears that the dope load was taken following the murder of an unfortunate passer-by." He sighed and sat on a table.

Chief Deputy Ramirez said, "That van that was robbed … was that William Bonney's dope?"

Hunt grunted. "It appears so."

Ramirez clasped his hands. "So now what? A drug war?"

"I'm afraid it's shaping up to become just that, Don."

Silver City Police Chief Bill Rogers blurted out, "Holy shit, Steve. I've already got more crime than my small staff of officers can handle —robberies, burglaries, assaults, thefts, illegal brothels dealing in dope."

"I know, Bill. That's why we've got to nip this in the bud before it gets worse."

Wetzel cleared his throat. "Operation Pipe Cleaner?"

Hunt stood. "Yes. Operation Pipe Cleaner is designed to do just that, Jack."

Rogers rubbed his chin. "I assume you've got inside intelligence on both Pablo Enrique's cartel and William Bonney's bunch of local thugs?"

"I do for Bonney, and I hope to soon for Enrique."

"Undercover or snitch?"

Hunt's eyes locked with Rogers'. "I'm not ready to elaborate on that now, Bill."

Rogers nodded.

Wetzel spoke up. "That bunch out at the Silver Cell Mine are a bad lot. Are they mixed up with either group?"

"Could very well be, Jack," said Hunt.

Lightning flashed outside, thunder boomed and then a steady downpour of rain. The law enforcement officers in the room said nothing. Deputy Perez broke the silence. "It looks like from your operation plan you want us to crack down hard on violators, get them to snitch."

"That's right, Perez. If we can establish these guys' base of operations and enough information for a search or arrest warrant, we'll be headed in the right direction to crush the drug trade." He paused, "When the illegal drug trade goes, most of the other crimes go as well."

McMurtry rubbed his bearded jaw. "Cut the head off and the rest dies, eh?"

"Exactly, Mac."

Hunt peered at Wetzel. "When you're out and about with your duties in Whiskey Creek—"

McMurtry interrupted, "You mean when he's sparkin' thet lil gal up yonder?"

Wetzel's face reddened. "Why don't you pay a little more attention to your *own* damn business, Mac?"

McMurtry face showed hurt. "You don't have to be so testy, Jack. Wasn't meanin' no harm."

Hunt interjected, "You boys settle your love lives on your own dime. Jack, see if your boss will allow you to patrol up there on Whiskey Creek on a more frequent basis—put the pressure on those guys and see what they do in response," He nodded his head toward McMurtry, "and take the hillbilly with you."

Wetzel hesitated before answering. "Okay, Steve."

"And when we get something we can really work with, I have a special task force of State Police officers assigned, ready to go in and kick butt once we get probable cause."

Rain pounded on the metal roof of the police station. Hunt looked at Police Chief Rogers, "Looks like the storm's not going to let up for a while, Bill." He smiled. "Have you got any hot coffee?"

Rogers returned the smile. "Yessir, we do … and fresh donuts."

CHAPTER FIFTY-NINE

DISTRICT RANGER BILL HOOD WAS IRATE. IN FACT, WETZEL HAD NOT SEEN his supervisor more upset during his long, tenuous experience in working for the man. Hood stomped over to the office window overlooking the visitor parking lot at Gila Center near the Gila Cliff Dwellings. His large, bulbous nose and surrounding face were beet red, the dark, horn-rimmed glasses had slipped down on his nose. He turned suddenly from the window, "Goddamn it, Jack!"

He slammed his fist down on the government issued metal desk, winced from the pain then held the hand gingerly as he continued around the desk to where his subordinate stood easily near the wall. The few hairs on Hood's closely cropped crew-cut stood up in the still, hot summer air. "I want a *full* investigation of this incident." He pointed his finger at Wetzel, inches away. "Do you hear me? I want nothing unturned in your investigation. Is that clear?"

Wetzel nodded, "Yessir. But what exactly am I investigating, Bill?"

Hood's eyes almost imploded. "What the hell do you think?" He took a deep breath then headed out the door of the office; he waved for Wetzel to follow. They continued down the hallway and out the door to the employee parking lot on the north side of the Visitor Center and office complex.

Hood pointed forcefully at orange flagging attached to a metal sign designating his exclusive parking spot titled "District Ranger". His hand shook uncontrollably as he shouted, "*Look at this!* The audacity! The unmitigated gall!"

Not understanding the gravity of a situation involving orange flagging blowing in the breeze, Wetzel stood and said nothing.

District Ranger Hood pushed his dark, horn-rimmed glasses back up on his nose, patted his belly protruding over his belt. It was obvious he needed to explain.

"On a recent field trip, I inspected a variety of signs and marked those I felt needed replacement with orange flagging." He paused as Fernando Cortez, a member of the helitack fire crew strode past them. Cortez said, "Evening, sir." Hood arrogantly said nothing to him. Once behind Hood, Cortez looked directly at Wetzel, winked, and entered the building.

District Ranger Hood continued, "As I said, there were several signs that I deemed necessary to replace here in the Wilderness District."

"I thought the sign committee—"

Hood's eyes hardened. "I don't need anyone's permission to do my job. I know what needs to be done."

"Yessir."

District Ranger Hood stepped closer to Wetzel. "You find out who did this, Jack. Who's responsible for trying to undermine my position by placing orange flagging on *my* parking sign?" The summer breeze played at the three solitary hairs near his forehead. "I'm giving you a direct order to find who it was that did *this*." He pointed again at the orange flagging attached to the sign.

"I'll get right on it, Bill."

"Highest priority", said Hood hotly.

"Yessir."

Hood started back into the building, turned. "Good man."

Wetzel bit his lower lip. "Bill ... I ... uh, need to check more frequently on the sheep allotment in Whiskey Creek if it's all right with you."

"Why? Is there something illegal going on with those people up there?"

"I need to ensure they're in compliance with their grazing permit, sir."

District Ranger Hood shook his head. "Good man, Jack. Can't have violation of forest—"

"—policy and regulations. Exactly, sir," Wetzel finished.

Hood placed his hands on the door sill, looking at Wetzel. "You're finally learning what we're all about, son." He turned and spoke over his shoulder, "Spend whatever time you need up there, Jack, but this investigation here has priority."

Wetzel smiled. "Yessir."

* * *

IT WAS ALMOST DARK; Wetzel guided his old truck down Highway 15 from Pinos Altos south then onto Highway 180 or Silver Heights Boulevard toward down town Silver City, New Mexico. Merle Haggard was crooning on KSIL, the Silver City radio station. The windows were down, allowing the cool, summer breeze into the interior of the truck. He drew deeply on a Lucky Strike tucked in the corner of his mouth; smoke drifted lazily from his nose. Ever slowly, the cigarette bobbed from one side of his mouth to the other. His brow furrowed as deep thought almost made him miss the turn into Dottie's Café, located on the south side of Highway 180 just north of the turnoff onto Hudson Street. He parked the truck, shut off the engine and stepped out, pulling his Stetson hat down on his head. Sighing, he made his way to the entrance to the cafe.

Wetzel tossed the remnants of his cigarette. A bell attached to the door signaled his entrance. As he looked for his special booth, he pushed his hat back on his head with his thumb. Luck was with him; the booth was empty. He headed for it and sat down heavily and picked up a menu.

He'd about decided on enchiladas with red chile and, of course, an egg on top when he heard soft footsteps and looked up into pretty green eyes set in a freckled face surrounded by a head of shoulder-length red hair. *Maggie O'Brian Garcia!*

His heart thumped in his chest. *God! She was so beautiful and God help him, he still loved her so.*

"Hi, stranger! Long time no see. Where have you been hiding, Jack?"

He fumbled with an answer, captivated by her very presence. He knew why he had stayed away. *She's my best friend's wife. Stop it, dammit.*

He looked into her green eyes. "Hi Maggie; you're looking great, kid."

She stood without replying, meeting his gaze.

He cleared his throat. "I … I've been really busy."

Maggie shifted her weight from left to right. "You haven't been by to see us since Juan returned from Vietnam; that's over six months ago. I thought we were friends, Jack."

"We are—I came by last week."

"I heard. You need to come by when we're *all* home. We'll have a cookout or something."

"Sure, Maggie; sounds good."

The cafe owner yelled out, "Hey, Garcia, get a move on. You've got other customers."

Maggie rolled her eyes, shouting over her shoulder, "Movin' on, boss." She smiled at Wetzel, "What do you want to eat?"

"Enchilada special, red chile and an egg on top."

"Over easy?"

"You bet, and can we talk when you get off work tonight?"

Her eyes softened as she gazed at him. "Sure, Jack. It'll be another hour though."

"I'll wait." He smiled at her.

CHAPTER SIXTY

WETZEL DROVE MAGGIE HOME FROM THE RESTAURANT AFTER WORK. IT WAS late; a full moon lit up his old truck as it turned onto Market Street. Maggie sat with folded hands in her lap looking straight ahead. Creedence Clearwater Revival sang "Have You Ever Seen the Rain" on the radio. He pulled the truck over next to the curb after exiting Bullard Street.

Maggie turned to him, her eyes soft, questioning. He wanted so much to pull her to him and kiss her, but he knew it was never to be. Reaching out, he took her hands in his own. "Maggie, has Juan ever hurt you in any way?"

"No. Why do you ask?" Her eyebrows rose.

Wetzel stammered, "He … he's not himself these days."

Silence, then she answered, "That damned war. It's killed or ruined so many of our boys, Jack." She let out a big breath, shaking her head, the pretty red hair bouncing on her shoulders. "Juan's depressed. He lost his leg, and I think he's had unspeakable things done to him in captivity."

"I know. He's suffering from PTSD, Maggie."

"From what?"

"Post-traumatic stress disorder." He shrugged. "You know. They called it 'shell shock' during World War II."

She nodded slowly.

"Anyhow, he needs professional help, and he needs it *now*."

"Oh, Jack. He just needs rest—*lots* of rest and support from all of us."

Wetzel gripped her hands more tightly. "Yes. He needs all that but much more, Maggie." He licked his dry lips. "He needs to be seeing someone who can truly help him professionally to get through all this."

She turned the radio off and looked into his eyes. "Do you know of someone for him to see?"

"Yes. I go see a gentleman once a month in Las Cruces."

Maggie turned in the seat. "Does he help you, Jack? You know—with the terrible nightmares, the hatred?"

Wetzel exhaled. "Yes, he's helped me, but I won't lie to you. I still have occasional nightmares of the war, the killings, and the hopelessness of being in a war that had no objectives, no end game; the stupid policy of not pursuing the enemy into Cambodia and Laos, of no total victory. We've won all the battles, but sadly we're losing the goddamn war." His eyes misted over. "I think of all those servicemen that have died or been crippled and for what? And I think of my scout dog, Smoky."

Maggie nodded. "They've turned the war over to the South Vietnamese for the most part."

"They can't beat the NVA, Maggie. Not without American leadership."

Silence.

Wetzel cleared his throat. "I'm afraid for you and Robbie. And that Juan might even hurt himself if he doesn't get some help."

"He won't want to see a 'shrink', Jack." Maggie pulled her hands from his.

Wetzel reached for a cigarette from the Lucky Strike pack in his shirt pocket. He stuck it in the corner of his mouth and lit it with his lighter. Maggie sat looking straight ahead, hands folded in her lap. The night was quiet and had cooled down from a hot, summer day. A Chevy sedan lumbered past. He smoked in silence, thinking.

Wetzel removed the cigarette from his mouth. "We've somehow got to convince him, Maggie, before it's too late."

"I love him, Jack. You know I'll do *anything* to help, but he's not listening to me anymore." She clenched her fists. "He just gets mad and leaves me when we get confrontational." Her eyes misted and then real tears flowed down her cheeks.

Wetzel turned to her; he felt so bad for her. "We'll think of something. You can count on that, kid." He tossed the cigarette and headed the old truck westbound for her apartment.

They drove past the building and parked alongside the curb. A white van was parked in front; the porch light was on with the front door left open to assist in cooling the interior. A wooden screen door near the outside light prevented the swirling insects from entering. Mexican music pierced the night quietness and loud laughter rumbled from within the apartment.

Wetzel led the way inside. Juan Garcia lay sprawled on the living room floor, a Tecate beer in his right hand, a marijuana cigarette in the left. He peered hard at his high school friend as he entered. "Well, look at what the dog drug in, Jose." He sneered and drew deeply on the marijuana cigarette, holding the smoke deep in his lungs.

"Where's Robbie?" Wetzel's voice had a metallic edge to it.

A slender, dark man stood from the sofa. Black hair flowed over his shoulders. A slim black mustache accentuated a pinched, gaunt face. He wore a black tee shirt and bell bottom jeans. "Hey, *guero*. Lay off mah main man here." He stepped closer and jabbed a pointed finger in Wetzel's chest. Jack hit him on the point of his chin with a hard right-hand punch, knocking him flat to the floor. Stepping over the prostrate Jose, he strode to Juan, grabbed him by his shirt front and hauled him up from the floor. "*Where's Robbie? Damn your hide!*"

Maggie screamed. "Stop it, Jack. You'll hurt him."

Garcia's eyes showed fear. He stuttered a reply. "He's ... in ... his bedroom." Pushing at Wetzel to no avail, he added weakly, "Leave me be, Jack." Wetzel dropped him to the floor, turned and walked to Robbie's room. Maggie knelt and tried to hug Juan, but he pushed her away. The remnants of his marijuana cigarette fell from his trembling hand to the floor; he threw the can of beer to the far corner of the room. It fizzed loudly, the contents spilling out on the carpet.

"Dammit, Maggie, leave me alone." He scooted on his buttocks to the couch and pulled himself up. Pointing at the unconscious Jose sprawled on the floor; he said thickly, "What the hell did you bring Wetzel for anyhow? Goddamn."

Maggie stood, hands on her hips. "He was kind enough to bring me home from work."

"Shit!"

Wetzel appeared holding Robbie's hand.

The little boy's eyes were sad. "I told you, Jack. It's okay. Daddy's just not feeling too well today is all." Tears trickled down his cheeks. He hugged Wetzel's leg.

Wetzel looked at Garcia, a long hard look. "I told you to get help, Juan."

"I don't—"

"Shut up, Juan. From now on, you do as you damn well please, but I'm taking Maggie and Robbie to stay at Mom's house. They can't stay here anymore. It's unsafe."

"You can't just ... walk in my home ... and tell me—"

"I just did." He looked at Maggie and then the boy. "Get some clothes together. We're going. *Now!*" Both moved as directed.

Wetzel walked over to the kitchen table picked up a pencil and wrote on the tablet lying there. As Maggie and Robbie entered the living room with their belongings, he said to Juan, "I left you the name and phone number for the man who can help you with PTSD. Call him," He pointed to Jose who had begun to return to consciousness, "and stay away from trash like him." Wetzel looked at his friend, his hazel eyes softened. "They're not your friends, Juan. They're using you, amigo, and they'll keep on using you if you let them."

Robbie looked at Garcia. "It'll be all right, Daddy. It'll be all right." He scurried out behind Wetzel with his mother behind holding his little shoulders. The screen door slammed shut.

The old truck started up and drove off. The Mexican music continued playing. Jose stirred on the floor. Garcia lay back on floor and cried.

CHAPTER SIXTY-ONE

Wildlife Officer Bob McMurtry yawned as he steered his New Mexico Game and Fish truck north on Highway 15. As he passed Gila Hot Springs and Doc Campbell's store, the truck's headlight beams sliced through the darkness cloaking the night. Stars twinkled overhead with the North Star leading the way.

McMurtry turned off the highway into the Heart Bar Ranch headquarters. To his surprise, he saw the porch light on and a blue sedan parked near the housing area. The vehicle belonged to Juanita Florez. Worried, he stepped out and walked quickly to the house. The aroma of refried beans, chili, and rice cooking helped settle his anxiety as he strode into the log structure that had been built decades ago.

A tall, pretty woman turned from the stove and smiled at him, displaying even, white teeth. "*Roberto!*" Black hair tumbled on her small shoulders. McMurtry's tension softened as he gazed upon the woman he loved.

"Juanita Floor-eez. You are a sight for sore eyes."

She stepped away from the stove, walked tentatively over to him and gave him a hug and a peck on his bearded cheek. "*Te amo, Roberto,*" she said softly.

Blushing, he stammered, "Wel-l-l ... I'll be dadjimmed." He held her close, beaming. "I love you, too, Juanita." He peered around the kitchen. "Where are them boys o' yourn anyways?"

Juanita pulled away, headed back to the stove, and said over her shoulder, "*Los ninos* are een ... the back yard, *Roberto*."

He hesitated. "When are we gittin' married, Juanita?"

She laughed out loud. "Go on. I weel haf supper ready soon."

Placing his burly hands in the pockets of his camouflage pants, he sauntered out of the kitchen, through the living room and out to the back yard. Juanita's boys were wrestling on the ground near the bank of the Middle Fork of the Gila River. McMurtry stood there watching the boys play and listened to the murmur of the river. The sunset lit up the few cirrus clouds in a once blue sky that became a fiery red glow in the west. A slight breeze stirred the leaves in the cottonwood trees near the river.

The boys quit wrestling and suddenly realized they were not alone. They squealed out together, "Mac!" and ran toward him.

McMurtry grinned broadly. "Elfigo! Jose! How are you boys anyways?" Each of them hugged a leg. He reached down and ruffled their hair.

"I'm fit as a fiddle, Mac." Jose, the eldest, tried to imitate the wildlife officer.

"How 'bout you, Elfigo? You doin' all right, boy?"

The younger boy didn't respond. McMurtry knelt near him and placed his hands on the boy's shoulders. His rough voice had softness in it. "You okay?"

Jose spoke. "He's not feeling so good, Mac."

"Oh? An' why is that, Jose?"

Jose clutched his jeans. "I got to go pee."

McMurtry laughed and pointed at the closest tree. "Well, that tree yonder ought to do for ya."

"Mom doesn't like us to pee outside, Mac." He clutched his pants more tightly.

"Wel-l-l, don't reckon we'll be tellin' your mom, an' I'm guessing you'll never make it to the bathroom." He waved toward the tree. "Go on son an' git the job done afore you wet your breeches."

Jose scurried off. McMurtry turned to the younger boy. "Now what is it, boy? What's goin' on?"

The little boy looked down at the ground. He placed his hands in his pockets, shrugged. "I'm kinda embarrassed talking about it, Mac."

"I garntee ya, I kin keep a secret, son."

Elfigo's big brown eyes brightened. "You won't tell *anybody*?"

"Nary a soul."

Elfigo sighed, took a deep breath and then sighed again. "There's this kid in school." He chewed on his lower lip. "He's picking on me, Mac." Elfigo threw up his hands. "an' I don't know *what* to do."

McMurtry rubbed his whiskered chin thoughtfully. "What exactly is this feller doin' to ya?"

The boy pulled his hands from his pockets, folded his arms and then put his hands back in his pockets. He leaned close and whispered, "He pulled my pants down when I was peeing at school."

McMurtry whistled low, continued rubbing his chin. "Why, that lowdown yeller sumbitch."

Jose returned from the tree. "Mom doesn't let us swear, Mac."

McMurtry ignored Jose's chastisement. He looked at the younger brother. "I reckon he's done this more'n once?"

"Yessir."

"An' you want to know what to do?"

"Yessir."

McMurtry stood. "I'd say he's most likely doin' this while you boys are peeing at the urinal."

"Yessir. He stands there and watches us and then pulls my pants down."

"Uh huh." McMurtry motioned for Jose to come closer.

"When you boys git back to school make sure you go to the bathroom together. Stand next to one another an' when this kid comes up behind Elfigo, Jose, you turn and punch him in the face as hard as ya kin, then both o' you'uns grab him by the hair and drag him to one o' them toilets and stick his head down in the water. Hold him down there awhile, but don't drown him, ya heah?"

"B-but—" Elfigo stammered.

"I ain't finished." McMurtry pointed at Elfigo. "Then you look that sumbitch in the eye, eyeball to eyeball, son, and hit him as hard as you kin right smack dab in the nose. *Bust it wide open.* An' tell him if'n he *ever* picks on anybody again, he'll git more o' the same."

"We aren't supposed to fight in school, Mac. What do I say if they ask me about the fight?"

"Well, for starters, in my book it ain't no fight, jest a whippin', I'd say. You tell 'em you don't know nothin' 'bout a fight."

The little boy's head dropped. "But ... that's lying, Mac." He kicked at the ground with his foot. "Shucks, you know Mom doesn't allow us to lie."

McMurtry's smiled. He took Elfigo by the shoulders and looked over at Jose. "If you don't give him the opportunity to fight back, wel-l-l, it ain't no fight, *is it*?"

The boys looked at him mischievously and then at each other. A smile crept over their faces.

McMurtry smiled back, his eyes twinkling. "Good boys. Now let's go git some o' them vittles yore mom's making for us, huh?" He placed a hand on each boy's shoulder and guided them toward the ranch house. *Dadjimmit. I sure hope they all stay over tonight. I've been feelin' a mite lonely these days.*

* * *

McMurtry stood silently on the porch of the old ranch house, hands in the side pockets of his old coveralls. A full moon displayed the looming outline of the barn below and the ragged contours of the riverbank; the river murmured softly to the lonely wildlife officer, an owl hooted in the distance.

Sighing, he closed his eyes. Suddenly, soft arms encircled him and Juanita hugged him. "Oh, *Roberto, mi querido,* whatever am I to do with yew?"

McMurtry smiled. "Wel-l-l, for starters, Miss Juanita Floor-eez, you kin marry me."

Her soft voice reached out to him as she hugged him, "Do yew love me, *Roberto*?"

He turned to face her, his coarse, rough hands gently holding her so as to see her pretty up-turned face in the moonlight. "I reckon more'n anything, Juanita." He pressed his lips lightly on hers and then kissed her more fervently, parting her lips. She returned the kiss and held him tighter.

"Would you consider joining the Catholic Church, *Roberto*?"

He laughed out loud. "Them's fightin' words where I come from—Baptist country an' sech. From a young'un on up, I was told you Catholics were the devil himself; why, complete with horns, tail, and hooves."

It was her turn to laugh. "Oh, my! Well, I can show yew I haf no horns and no hooves, *Roberto,* but as for the tail ... well ... maybe when we are married."

McMurtry's face heated. "I'll be dadjimmed. Did you just tell me we kin git married?"

"*Sí, Roberto, pero* plees promise me yew weel consider joining the church and allowing *mis niños* to go to church."

He hugged her tight. "You have my solemn promise. I'd be right proud to have a good Christian woman as my wife."

"Bueno, Roberto."

A poor will broke the silence with its night call as they held each other. *God, I know a rough, ole' codger like me don't deserve this purdy gal, but I hope nothin' goes wrong to keep me from marryin' her.* He grinned. *Dadjimmed if she didn't say, "Yes."*

CHAPTER SIXTY-TWO

THE OLD MAN TOOK HIS TIME WALKING UP THE STEEP RIDGELINE, PAUSING occasionally to rest on his walking stick. He didn't labor as hard these days as he had when he first hired on working for Lacey Whippit. His heart, lungs, muscles had all been strengthened but most importantly, his mental state, a feeling of peacefulness had encompassed his whole being; a life in the outdoors had transformed him in so many ways. The stress was gone, his deeply tanned face and hands replaced the pallor of the city life.

A slight breeze moaned softly through the ponderosa pine trees and Reagan felt it stir the whiskers of his beard. It was the beginning of summer with warmer days but the nights were still cool and pleasant for sleeping.

He peered down slope at the sheep grazing below him; his sharp gaze saw nothing that looked out of place or did not belong in the natural setting, no predators lurking about looking for an easy meal. Most of the ewes had lambed and it was a never-ending job now to keep an eye out for the little ones. Coyotes were the major problem, with an occasional mountain lion intruding onto ranch property. The old man's right hand grasped the leather rifle sling on his shoulder as he continued up the steep grade. He carried a .30-.30 Winchester carbine that Lacey had given him for "killing coyotes and sech".

Smiling to himself, he recalled she had been concerned that he would hurt himself with the rifle or not know how to use it safely. She showed him how to load the magazine, lever a round in the chamber, and shoot while aiming properly. He thought briefly about all the weapons he had become deadly proficient with during his lifetime; far too many lives taken at his hands. Shaking his head, Reagan withdrew from his thoughts of the past and continued up to the top of the ridge. The morning sun blanketed the trees on the ridgeline and then began its slow descent into the recesses of the canyon bottom, the start of another day in the wilderness. Placing the rifle against a tall pine tree, he lowered himself into a comfortable sitting position in a thick bed of pine needles. The serenity, the awesome tranquility of the wilderness overwhelmed him as it had the first day of his arrival.

What did the future hold for him? Would he stay here for the foreseeable future or move on? And to where—and for what purpose? He sighed deeply. No, he would stay as long as Lacey needed him; he had no other purpose in life. And there was the wilderness ... ahh yes! He had found no place on this earth of more liking to him than where he was at this very moment in time. Reagan's eyes narrowed as he detected movement below in the canyon. Then he observed a lone horseman riding slowly around the perimeter of the grazing sheep. Lacey Whippit!

He stood and waved as he called out to her in the clear morning air. Standing in the stirrups, she waved for him to come down off the ridge.

* * *

LACEY WHIPPIT TIED her horse to a small pine tree and retrieved the lunch she had brought from the saddle bags. Looking around, she found a boulder that was flat enough to lay out the sandwiches, can of peaches, and remnants of the cake she had baked the previous day. She swiped at several large ants atop the boulder, walked to the horse and removed the canteen of cold water from the saddle horn. As she sat on the pine-needled ground nearby, the horse pawed anxiously at the ground with its front hoof stirring and scattering the ground litter. The scent of the pine needles and the warm sun was pleasing to her.

Hearing footsteps nearby, she looked up to see the old man approaching. He called out, "Howdy, Lacey; didn't expect you up here today."

She stood, smiling. "Thought I'd get outta thet filthy mine and bring ya a bit o' lunch, Mr. Reagan."

Her pretty brown eyes sparkled with excitement. Reagan imagined her at some of the Washington, D.C. parties he had attended years ago wearing an elegant dress and expensive jewelry. In his mind, he took her hand and danced with her as he had with his wife in the grand ballroom. The old man's eyes softened; no, he truly liked her just as she was, here and now; the dusty hat and work clothes used to make an honest living, the beautiful tanned face that displayed an honesty and sincerity about life.

He returned the smile. "Well, thank you, Lacey, for thinking of me." He tapped the walking stick against the boulder. "Your lunches somehow always outdo mine."

"Have yoreself a seat, Mr. Reagan an' let's et."

As he settled down next to her, she handed him a sandwich. "Hope you ain't tired o' mutton, Mr. Reagan. Hit's about all we et around heah."

Accepting the sandwich, he took a big bite and replied with his mouth full, "Not at all. I have come to appreciate mutton."

She laughed heartily, a throaty laugh. "How are them sheep doing, Mr. Reagan? Lost many o' the lambs?"

The old man ate more of the sandwich and washed it down with a swallow of water from the canteen she had brought with her. "We lost two to coyotes before I brought them into the pen close to the house at night. I killed a coyote the next night, and I've shot at two more since then."

Lacey munched on her sandwich as she listened. "Yore doin' a fine job, Mr. Reagan. I'm much obliged to ya." She reached for the can of peaches and opened it with a small metal opener, a P38, found in military and firefighter C rations. "All but four o' the ewes lambed out so we got the best lamb crop we've ever had, and thanks to you, we've not lost many this year."

The old man nodded his thanks, retrieved his pocket knife and stabbed a couple of peaches from the tin can and ate them.

Lacey cleared her throat. "Mr. Reagan ... I, uh ..." She shuffled her dusty boots in the pine needles and looked down the canyon.

The old man swallowed the peach in his mouth, wiped the pocket knife blade on his work jeans and returned it to his pocket. "What is it, child? Is everything okay?" He said nothing further; his quiet manner indicative of someone fully intent on listening rather than talking.

Lacey sighed deeply then picked up a stick from the ground and slapped her leg with it. "Aw 'ight then; I hate to bother ya with mah personal problems, Mr. Reagan." She flung the stick away. "I ain't got nobody to talk to 'bout sech things. Them brothers o' mine are good men but neither one o' them's worth a tinker's damn—excuse my language, Mr. Reagan—for listening to me 'bout much o' anything." She bit her lower lip.

The old man said nothing.

The young woman folded her arms across her chest. "It's jest that all mah life, I've been happy living with mah family and working outside. Mah daddy was a good man, too, but you've been more o' a father to me than he ever was, Mr. Reagan." She peered down the canyon again. "And you've no idea how much I truly appreciate it."

The old man started to reply, and then decided against it.

Lacey unfolded her arms and clasped her hands tightly. "Aw 'ight then; Mr. Reagan, I speak plumb awful. I know I do, and I jest *hate* it." Pretty brown eyes locked with his.

"Would ya ... be willin' to teach me how to talk proper-like?"

It was Reagan's turn to look down the canyon.

Lacey quickly said, "I figgered it'd be too much to ask, Mr. Reagan."

The old man smiled and then rubbed his beard. "I would be honored to help you, Lacey."

Her eyes brightened. "Oh, Mr. Reagan! Would ya help me? I kin pay ya; I've got some money saved."

An ewe sheep bleated in the distance. A Mexican jay flew from a Gambel oak tree to a much taller Ponderosa pine tree. The warm afternoon sun burned through the tree foliage.

"I have no use for money, Lacey, and friends help friends because they want to; it makes them feel good to assist."

"But Mr. Reagan—"

"However, I do have two questions that I'd like to ask of you before we finalize our ... agreement."

Lacey leaned forward. "Why shore, Mr. Reagan. What is it?"

The old man stroked his beard thoughtfully. "The first question is why? What's changed in your life that makes you want to improve your speech? Why now?"

"Ah reckon, I'd rather not say, Mr. Reagan."

The old man smiled. "It wouldn't have anything to do with a young Forest Service ranger who's been out here lately on a frequent basis, would it?"

"Aw … heck, Mr. Reagan." Lacey smiled.

Reagan nodded. "Jack Wetzel is a good man, Lacey. I think he likes you just the way you are—the way you talk and everything about you. You're a beautiful woman."

"Uh-huh." She shuffled her feet, and then grinned. "Mr. Reagan, you an' ah both know I sound like a damn hick hillbilly. Admit it."

The old man grinned. "You do have an interesting way of talking. To be honest, Lacey, I rather like it. You, your manner of speech, everything about you is refreshing to me, and I've no doubt it is to Wetzel as well."

"Do ya *really* think so, Mr. Reagan?"

"Yes, I do. Now, please permit me ask the second question. Are you in love with Jack Wetzel?"

The young woman bit her lower lip, struggling with an answer, "Ah don't rightly know, Mr. Reagan, but ah shore like bein' around him."

The old man smiled. "Good, Lacey. What do you say to us starting your lessons today, right now?"

Grinning, Lacey nodded. "Aw'ight then."

"Okay," he said. "Your reply should be, 'okay' or 'all right.'"

Lacey frowned, wrinkling her brow and ventured a reply, "O … kay."

The old man continued, "And in lieu of 'Ah', use 'I.'"

"O … kay, Mr. Reagan. Ah … *I* would like ta … *to* know where you come from an' what you done in yore … *your* life to be the man you are heah today."

The old man looked down the canyon at the sheep still grazing contently on the abundant grama grass. "Here, Lacey, not heah."

"Yessir. *Here*."

His lips formed a thin line as his jaw tightened before speaking. "I am not the man I seem to be, Lacey." He shook his head. "What I mean to say is … I've done horrible things in my lifetime." He hesitated as he stood facing away from her. "Unspeakable things that would turn your stomach if you knew of them. Although I was acting under orders, I should not have complied." Sighing, he swallowed hard as he turned to her and took her gently by the shoulders, his gaze softening. "I have to believe that I've changed, Lacey. That I am truly as good a man as you would believe of me." He dropped his arms resignedly.

"What exactly did ya ... *you* work at, Mr. Reagan?"

"I made a career out of the army, Lacey; two wars—World War II, the European Theatre then Korea, the Chosin Reservoir." He tucked his arms against his chest. "Then I was recruited with the Central Intelligence Agency and until recently served in the Viet Nam War."

Lacey smiled. "That's honorable, Mr. Reagan, to serve yore country."

"Your, child, not yore," the old man reminded gently.

"Yessir ... *your*."

He smiled and picked up his walking stick. "Let us continue with your lessons as we check on the sheep, Lacey. You ride and I'll walk."

CHAPTER SIXTY-THREE

WETZEL PUSHED THE STETSON BACK ON HIS HEAD WITH HIS THUMB. HE shook out a Lucky Strike from the packet in his shirt pocket, stuck it in the corner of his mouth and lit it. His old Chevy truck rumbled down the gravel road toward his mother's ranch house. Thunderheads had been forming most of the day, and he peered out the open window at the clouds to the west darkening to a menacing state. The wind had increased in velocity, filling the air with a fresh smell of impending rain. He looked over at the Border Collie riding in the seat beside him. "What do you think, Montie? We gonna to get some much-needed rain?"

The dog shuffled over to the opposite window, stuck his head out, opened his mouth, smiling as he enjoyed the wind blowing on his face. Thunder rumbled in the sky, lightning flashed in the distance. The air seemed to come alive. *It's July 4th and the monsoon rains have appeared right on cue this year.*

As he pulled into the driveway leading to his mother's house, Wetzel noticed a brand new 1973 red Dodge Dart parked next to the house. It was a vehicle he did not recognize. He parked his old truck, let Montie out, and walked to the back door leading to the kitchen. Robbie Garcia charged out the door careening into him.

"Jack! Jack!" the little boy shouted, hugged Wetzel's leg, and patted Montie on the head.

Wetzel knelt down and hugged him back. "It's sure good to see you, Robbie. Where's your momma?"

Robbie frowned. "She went to find my daddy, Jack." He pursed his lips, "She's been real worried about him."

Wetzel stood. "Come on partner, let's go see Helen."

"You mean Gramma, Jack?"

Wetzel grinned. "Yes, Robbie. I mean Gramma."

He entered the kitchen with the little boy in tow holding his hand. A middle-aged man with gray hair combed straight back on his head and held into place with some kind of hair cream sat at the kitchen table talking to his mother. He wore an expensive navy-blue business suit, a bright red tie, and highly-polished black leather shoes. Wetzel recognized him as Bert Newell, one of the defense lawyers from town, a man who had grilled him in the courtroom on several occasions, made insulting personal remarks, and then had the audacity to walk up to him, hold out his hand and say, "No hard feelings, huh?"

The man looked up when Wetzel entered the room and smiled, displaying white even teeth. "Why, hello, Jack. How are you, son?" He stood and extended his hand.

Wetzel ignored him; instead he gruffly addressed his mother. "What's *he* doing here?"

Helen Wetzel set her coffee cup down on the saucer. "He's a guest in *my* house, Jackie." Her steady blue eyes peered into her son's eyes, "And you'll show Mr. Newell respect while he's here."

Wetzel turned to Newell, sighed and shook his hand, "Howdy, Bert." The man's hand was limp and moist. "What brings you out to the ranch?" He tried very hard to control his seething dislike for a man who defended drug dealers and murderers as a way of making his living.

Newell smoothed back his hair with both hands. "Your mother and I have become ... friends." He smiled at Helen Wetzel, his pearly, white teeth displaying a handsome grin.

"Oh." Jack Wetzel's eye twitched. Robbie Garcia clutched his hand tightly.

The silence grew awkward. Newell placed his hands in the pockets of his expensive suit pants. "I advised your mother and Maggie Garcia this afternoon that I successfully defended Juan in court this morning. He was acquitted of charges stemming from his arrest a month ago of trafficking drugs."

Wetzel looked at his mother. "Maggie left to look for Juan?"

"Yes, as soon as Mr. Newell advised us of his release."

"But it's not safe for her at their apartment."

Newell said, "Now Jack, that's just not so."

Eyes blazing, Wetzel turned on him. "Who the hell pulled *your* chain, Bert."

Newell's eyes showed fright; he held up both hands.

Helen Wetzel stood and walking between them, took Newell by the arm and directed him toward the door. She smiled. "Thank you, Bert, for coming all the way out here to let us know about Juan." She looked at Jack. "And *all* of us appreciate everything you've done for Juan. He's very special to us."

She steered Newell out the door and toward his vehicle. He climbed in and the car roared to life. Waving, Newell backed up and headed down the driveway.

Helen Wetzel stormed back in the house, slamming the screen door behind her. "Just what was that all about, Jackie?" Her face was set, eyes squinting and her pretty face lined with anger.

"You know what he is, Mom; what he does for a living for Pete's sake."

She wagged an angry finger in his face. "Don't you Pete's sake me, Jackie!"

Wetzel took her by the shoulders and hugged her. "I'm sorry, Mom. I love you."

Robbie Garcia chimed in, "He's real sorry, Gramma. Please don't be mad at Jack."

Her eyes softened. "Maggie had to go to him, Jackie. She loves him."

"I know it, Mom, but it's not safe for her there." He looked at Robbie. "It's not like it used to be."

His mother nodded. "That's why I insisted that Robbie stay here with me for the time being."

Wetzel's lips trembled. "But—"

She held her son's hand and murmured softly, "You've got to let her go, son." Her eyes moistened. "She's an adult, and she belongs to *him*, Jackie."

"I know, Mom. It's not *that;* I reconciled that some time ago." He looked down at the little boy who still hugged his leg. "I just worry for her safety is all."

Robbie said, "Momma will be all right, Jack. Don't you worry about her; she can take care of herself."

Wetzel smiled. "Maybeso." He looked back at his mother, a lump formend in his throat, and a worried look returned to his face.

CHAPTER SIXTY-FOUR

THE MAN IN BLACK STOOD TO THE SIDE OF THE PHONE BOOTH IN THE shadows facing the street. He glanced in all directions taking his time, and then reviewed the entire scene again. Satisfied, he used the rotary pay phone to dial the desired number. The phone rang, his dark eyes continued to survey his immediate surroundings. His left hand held the telephone, his right hand hung by his side, cupped with the thumb and forefinger touching as if holding a cigarette and the little finger moving as if dusting the ashes of the invisible cigarette.

Someone spoke into the phone. "*Quien es?*"

"Carlos?"

A moment of hesitation. "*Si.* Tomas?"

The man in black replied, "Let me speak to Enrique."

"I will pass the information—"

"*Now! Cabron!*"

THE PHONE WAS silent for several minutes. The voice of a powerful man spoke, his unquestioned authority exuded through the phone line. "Tomas, *mi'jo, w*hat is going on down there?"

"We are being challenged by the opposition—a bunch of *gringos.*"

"Who are they, and why have you not eliminated them, Tomas? This is what I pay you the big dollars for."

"I have been working on them, but they are many. And the head of the group is well guarded. He calls himself William Bonney."

"William Bonney? I have heard that name before, have I not?"

"*Si, patron;* he has taken the name of an outlaw."

"I don't give a damn what his name is ... *kill him*! And eliminate our competition."

"I have been told they are planning a raid on our operations center on Whiskey Creek."

"When?"

"Soon. I have alerted the center and made several attempts at killing Bonney. I will get him just as I have all the others, *patron*."

"I will send Carlos with some men."

Tomas surveyed his surroundings; his eyes fixated on a slow moving blue van headed his direction up Broadway Street. His right hand disappeared inside the backpack hanging from his left shoulder; his eyes never left sight of the van.

"No. I have everyone I need, and I don't trust Carlos."

"And is the boy dead as I ordered?" queried Enrique.

The phone went dead as the man in black replaced the receiver and melted away into the night. Slowly, the blue van passed the public telephone booth near the Post Office then quickly sped up the street toward the courthouse squealing the tires; the tip of a shotgun barrel protruded from the passenger window.

An irate Enrique screamed into the dead phone, "*Goddamn you!* No one hangs up on *me*!"

He knocked the phone off the desk, stomped to the door yelling, "Carlos*! Ven!*"

The blue van made a U-turn at Cooper and Broadway and descended toward Bullard Street and downtown Silver City. Once again, it cruised along slowly. As the van approached the intersection at the corner of the Murray Hotel, a muted pistol shot rang out; the driver slumped over the wheel shot through the head. The passenger attempted to bring the shotgun barrel around to face the threat to his immediate left. The man in black walked swiftly from the shadows to the driver side window, a black automatic pistol with an attached silencer in his right hand and shot the passenger twice in the chest and once in the head. As the car careened toward the cement curb in front of the Palace Hotel down the street, the man in black disappeared into the shadows from whence he had come.

CHAPTER SIXTY-FIVE

WILDLIFE OFFICER BOB MCMURTRY FELT TOTALLY OUT OF PLACE IN A newly rented tuxedo complete with a fancy bow tie, as he stood beneath the Chinese elm tree in the parking lot of St. Vincent de Paul's Catholic Church. He pulled a cigarette from his shirt pocket, lit it, and drew smoke into his lungs. The church wedding had gone much better than expected. Well, except for the hour-long sermon. Law-a-mercy! That priest could talk a man's leg plumb off an' not even wind himself in the process. The wedding ceremony, a mass just as Juanita had wanted, had come off without a hitch.

The Catholic Church service was entirely alien to him. He was used to what his father had called "jumping out-of-the brush" preachers who conducted fire and brimstone revivals within huge tents back home in Tennessee. He recalled attending the revivals as an adolescent, dumbfounded as the ranting and raving reached a crescendo and then some folks began to recant all their sins *in front of everybody*.

Maybe someday he'd want to tell his grandkids about his special wedding day. Them Catholics had a feller who was called a priest; this here priest presided over the whole kit an' keebuttle, talking and gesturing with the congregation joining him in prayer occasionally. Then to McMurtry's dismay, the priest drank some wine, broke some bread, and drank some more wine. When he was all done eating and drinking, why, he gave everybody else some bread, too. The priest never ranted or raved, but lordy, he could talk a man plumb to death about marryin', and responsibilities of raising them kids Catholic, an' sech.

An' Juanita Floor-ezz—why, she never looked purdier to him than in her white wedding dress and veil. Jack Wetzel as his best man sure looked snazzie in his fancy suit, though a mite uncomfortable all duded up like McMurtry himself. Juanita's boys Elfigo and Jose were there grinning from ear to ear; Mac didn't know if it was because their mother was marrying him or that they had beaten the hell out of the bully who had been picking on Jose at school and gotten plumb away with it. He smirked.

The drive out to Lake Roberts to the reception took less than an hour. Juanita snuggled up close to him, hanging on his arm as they drove past the Santa Rita copper mine and then along the Mimbres River in his old pickup. Juanita's family had a large picnic area prepared at the lake. *Tio* Beto had been preparing a pig in a pit since the night before. The Mariachis were playing Mexican music as they arrived. McMurtry grinned thinking again about Elfigo and Jose.

Wetzel met them as they exited the truck. His new friend, Lacey Whippit, from the head of Whiskey Creek stood behind him.

Wetzel grinned. "And how's Mr. and Mrs. Robert McMurtry this fine afternoon?"

"Couldn't be better, Jack boy," said McMurtry, "an' how 'bout you?"

"I'm doing well, Mac, but my boss, Bill Hood's not happy that I haven't solved the mystery of orange flagging on his parking sign at headquarters."

"I reckon one day, Jack, he'll git o'er it."

Juanita smiled and said, "*Estoy muy contesta,* Jack," and looking at Lacey Whippit asked, "How are yew Lacey?"

Lacey looked uncomfortable in the blue cotton dress and flat black dress shoes. Her brown hair cascaded to her shoulders and was pulled back on each side with a pearled hair comb. She smiled a genuine smile. "I reckon I'm fine; thank ya, Juanita."

McMurtry had never seen the girl dressed up before, meeting her on several occasions always in her work clothes while patrolling with Wetzel up Whiskey Creek. She looked beautiful and he told her so. She blushed as Juanita gave her a hug. Family and friends wished the newlyweds well, among them Juan and Maggie Garcia. McMurtry shook Juan's hand and hugged Maggie, who congratulated Juanita on her marriage.

As they made their way to the festivities and the food, they met Juanita's aunt or *Tia* as she was called. *Tia* Josie hugged Juanita and gave McMurtry an evil glare. He smiled broadly at the slender older woman, wearing wire-rimmed glasses, her gray hair pulled back into a tight roll at the nape of her neck. For some reason, she had never cared for him and had made it quite obvious that she did not want her niece to associate with him much less marry him.

"Why, howdy *Tia!* How are ya this *fine* day?"

She continued to glare at him and said under her breath in Spanish, "You treat her well, *cabron*, or I'll have your *cojones* roasting over the fire in my fireplace come fall."

McMurtry wasn't exactly sure what the woman said, but he did get the general drift of the message. He nodded. "Yes, ma'am. I'll take good care of her."

Tio Beto sauntered over holding a cold beer out to them. "Haf a beer, man; the pig has been cooking in the ground and is *muy bueno, amigo.* Holding the fingertips of his right hand together, he touched his lips as if savoring the flavor; his eyes rolled back in his head, and he lost his balance momentarily as he turned to go back to the ice chest containing the beer. He shrugged and grinned at them.

Several tables of food for the large crowd of well-wishers included plates of pork, tamales, beans, enchiladas red and green, salads, salsas of several types, and rice. Someone had brought blueberry, cherry, and apple pies in lieu of the wedding cake due to worries over transport and ants. McMurtry's salivary glands worked overtime as his eyes feasted on all the food and desserts.

Wetzel strode over to *Tío* Beto, took a Tecate beer from him. "Beto, I sure hope you didn't dig a hole and cook that pig here on Forest Service property without authorization."

"Jack ... I—"

"Never mind, Beto! I don't want to know about it." Wetzel turned to Lacey Whippit next to him and said, "Have you met Lacey?"

Beto bowed graciously. "*Tanto gusto, senorita.* It's a pleasure to meet you, ma'am." He motioned toward the ice chest. "Beer?"

"Shore ... ah ... *sure.* Thank you." She smiled sweetly. "Tecate please."

McMurtry and his bride appeared at the ice chest. "Beto, gimme and Juanita one o' them beers, would ya, ameego?"

"*Sí,* Roberto. *Como no!*"

* * *

THE NIGHT WAS QUIET—STILL, peaceful to a thoughtful Wetzel as he stood on the mesa overlooking Lake Roberts. The moonlight shimmered below from the lake surface; a coyote yipped in the distance across the lake and was answered nearby. The stars shone brightly in the darkened sky overhead as he removed his tie and unbuttoned the top button on his rented tuxedo. Turning to the girl standing next to him, he took her in his arms and held her tightly for some time and then kissed her.

Lacey Whippit returned the kisses then placed her hands on Wetzel's chest as she stepped back a step. "Jack, are ya ... *you* ready for a relationship? I mean ... well, how ya feel about ... Maggie n' all."

Wetzel looked back toward the lake. "I'm over all that, Lacey." He sighed into the night. "It shouldn't have ever been in the beginning for Pete's sake." Shaking his head, his jaw clenched, and he exhaled. "My God, Lacey, she was ... *is* another man's wife!"

"Jack, you don't owe me—"

Wetzel turned quickly and brought her into his arms again. "Yes, I do, kid! I do." His eyes locked with soft brown. "I don't know how it happened. We were all such close friends in high school and then after several years, I just ... didn't think Juan would ever return from Nam. And ... I fell in love ... I guess."

He took her by the hand, led her to his old pickup truck and helped her get in on the passenger side. Then he got in on the driver's side, slamming the heavy metal door shut. Reaching over, he gently pulled her to him and kissed her again. She returned his kiss as he moved closer and held her more tightly. The Mariachi music seemed distant to Wetzel.

Lacey pulled slightly away from their entanglement within the small confinement of the truck cab. *"Jack ... your—"*

Wetzel's face blushed as he looked down. "Oh! It's ... just ... the gear shift Lacey."

"Uh-huh."

He grinned sheepishly. "Maybe this idea of making out in my truck wasn't such a good idea, huh?"

Lacey pulled him to her and kissed him softly on the lips. "If you don't mind me sayin' so, Jack, I never said nothin' bout it bein' a bad idea."

CHAPTER SIXTY-SIX

Bob McMurtry held his new wife Juanita tightly as he whirled and danced to the music. He leaned closer to her. "If'n I had some *real hoedown* Tennessee mountain music, I reckon I'd dance a jig fer ya, Juanita."

She laughed. "I'd like to see *that,* Roberto."

He grinned broadly. "We'll head back to Tennessee one o' these heah days an' I'll show ya how it's done, gal … by the *master* himself." Taking her hand, he led her away from the dancing to where the food was located. "You hungry?"

"No, yew go ahead and eat, Roberto. I want to talk to Maggie."

"You shore?"

"Sí." She smiled at him and walked to where Maggie and her husband were standing and began conversing with them.

Suddenly, a loud voice behind her said, "*Mire,* Jose. Take a close look at what a real slut looks like, huh?"

Juanita turned and saw her ex-husband standing a short distance away. His black cowboy hat was tipped back on his head. The dark face with the black pencil mustache had a hard, mean look to it, his dark eyes flashing with anger. His stocky frame was attired in western shirt, Wrangler jeans, and black cowboy boots. Several men stood alongside him staring at her. One in particular had long, black hair to his shoulders; he was slender of build, dark-complected as well, and wore a dirty black T-shirt and bell bottom jeans. He grinned as he purposely took her in fully within his leering gaze, slowly from head to toe.

"Aw, she ain't so bad, man. I've seen a helluva lot worse."

Juanita's eyes blazed at her ex-husband as she shook her head. "Don't do thees—"

"Or you'll do *what*?" He sneered.

McMurtry appeared behind her, full plate of food in hand. He had not missed the number of men or the concealed weapons they carried. "Why don't you boys git some o' thet good grub over there an' *relax*, enjoy yourselves?" He grinned as he pointed toward the prepared food, but he moved forward in front of Juanita maintaining eye contact with her ex-husband.

They locked eyes and for a moment nothing was said, and then the ex-husband spoke. "I'm going to teach you a lesson that you'll never forget, *cabrón*."

Maggie Garcia leaned down to Robbie and whispered, "Find Jack Wetzel, son. Bring him here quickly." She pushed him away. "Run Robbie! Run!"

McMurtry's set face broke into a grin again as he stepped closer. "Wel-l-l, how bout we take a rein check on yore lesson plan for another day? As you can see, this here's a party. Why not enjoy it?" He peered casually at Jose and the other men standing next to the ex-husband.

McMurtry's peripheral vision viewed Juan Garcia limping up beside him. Garcia spoke to the slender man. "Jose, please take these men from here, my friend. Let this man enjoy his wedding."

Jose laughed and looked around at the men he'd come with. "Well, lookee here. It's the town's crippled pot head telling *us* what to do." He laughed again only louder.

Garcia started to speak; McMurtry said softly, "It's okay, Juan. Somehow, I don't think this sumbitch gives a good damn 'bout what ya have to say."

Garcia limped closer to McMurtry then beyond him to face Jose. Maggie pushed forward to stand next to her husband, hands on her hips. A slight breeze cooled the night air and stirred the red curls in her hair. A dog barked and was immediately answered by a howling coyote.

Garcia pleaded with Jose. "Please, take these men from here. Leave now."

Sneering, Jose spit in his face and shoved him hard. Garcia stumbled backward, almost losing his footing if it had not been for McMurtry standing behind him. Jose turned and slapped Maggie hard, a stinging slap and then back-handed her to the ground. Juan Garcia screamed, his face purple with rage, as he charged into a stunned Jose. His momentum carried him and Jose to the ground with Garcia on top. As Garcia straddled the man, he pounded his face again and again beating him to a bloody pulp. He wrapped his hands around Jose's neck. "Don't you EVER touch my wife, you son-of-a-bitch!"

A shot ran out; the back of Garcia's head exploded. He slumped over, his face puzzled, as he rolled away from the prostrate body under him.

McMurtry shouted, "No, Maggie!" As her horrified face realized her husband's fate, she rushed Juanita's ex-husband, who stood with raised pistol to fire again. "No!" she cried. "Stop it!" Grabbing his arm holding the deadly gun, they grappled. He attempted to shoot her, but Maggie's adrenaline and strength prevented it and his shot went astray. Someone in the crowd cried out.

McMurtry sprang forward grasping the gunman's wrist that held the gun. As he did so, he shoved Maggie back. Twisting the wrist back then outward, he broke the man's trigger finger. The man screamed. As they wrestled for control of the gun, a shot was fired. The gunman groaned and McMurtry felt him shudder and collapse to the ground. Taking full control of the pistol, McMurtry turned toward the other four men who had arrived with Juanita's ex-husband. Too late he saw one of the men pull a knife, step close to Maggie and stab her in the back. McMurtry tried to shoot but could not as the man took cover behind Maggie and in front of a crowd. Grinning from behind cover, he stabbed her again.

McMurtry charged forward, pulling Maggie to him and swung the pistol hard against the man's face, dropping him to the ground. He held a slumping Maggie to his breast as he fired two shots into the man lying on the ground.

As he turned toward the other attackers, he heard a hard voice ring out in the night. "Hold it right there! Forest Service Law Enforcement, don't anyone move!" Wetzel stood, knees bent, with his revolver pointed at the remaining attackers. One of the men reached for a gun beneath his shirt; Wetzel shot him twice in the chest and then swung his weapon at the others. "Hands up! All the way up and spread those fingers." The two men complied. Wetzel ordered them down on the ground, removed their weapons and then used his belt to bind one of the men from behind. Using a bystander's belt, he secured the other man.

He looked at Juanita standing there, hands to her shocked face, trembling. Quietly, he said, "Get someone to drive you down the hill to the store, Juanita. Use the phone to call Grant County Sheriff's Office. Advise them we have at least two men in custody, several wounded and deceased. We'll need an ambulance."

She stood there not moving. Wetzel took her by the shoulders and said firmly, "*Now* Juanita! Maggie needs help."

Juanita slowly nodded her head. Wetzel turned to a bystander and ordered, "Drive her to the store, dammit. *MOVE*!"

McMurtry held Maggie in his arms. "Hold on, gurl. Hold on." He felt blood running down her back and over his supporting arm. Blood trickled out of the corner of her mouth. Beads of perspiration covered her pale face.

Wetzel knelt beside her and with McMurtry's assistance, held her upright while stripping the back of her dress off. Two two large knife wounds were bleeding profusely. He took a table cloth he had ripped from a table and bound it tightly around her torso and then gently laid her back on the ground with her head in his lap. Tears filled his eyes and ran in rivulets down his cheeks. "Oh, Maggie ... Maggie girl," he sobbed.

She groaned, closing her eyes only to open them again to look directly at Wetzel. "Jack, take—" She coughed; bright red blood appeared on her mouth and chin. Swallowing with difficulty, she continued, "Please take care of ... my ... Robbie."

Wetzel held one hand, McMurtry the other. Maggie struggled again to speak but could not. Wetzel whispered, "I love you, Maggie." He smoothed back her red hair from her dampened brow and kissed her forehead. Lacey Whippit stood quietly with a hand covering her mouth, eyes widened with fear and softened with the knowledge of a forlorn love.

Maggie's saddened green eyes peered into Wetzel's horror stricken gaze. She smiled and nodded; her body shuddered and she was gone.

Wetzel wept uncontrollably. He laid her head gently on the ground and stood. Then he strode over to where the two restrained men were lying and began kicking both men with as much strength as he could muster. Then he reached for the revolver at his side. Strong arms grasped him from behind, pulling him back. "Easy, Jack. It's me, Mac."

CHAPTER SIXTY-SEVEN

It was sunset and the bright azure New Mexican sky transformed into clouds of a golden hue so beautiful to the five-year-old boy that he had to stop and gaze westward with his mouth open. Robbie Garcia did not dare tarry too long at the view before him for he knew that he must get back to Gramma Helen's ranch house soon or be in big trouble.

He reined in the little pony. "Whoa, Buck. Just take a look at that, boy!" The horse came to a standstill but pawed at the ground, anxious to return to the barn for a well-earned portion of oats and maybe a flake of alfalfa hay, if he was lucky. Panting, Wetzel's dog, Montie, lay down under a large juniper tree for a quick respite. Wetzel had insisted that the dog remain with Robbie while he worked in the Gila Wilderness and away from his mother's ranch.

Finally, the boy allowed the buckskin to take a shortcut through a rough canyon laden with rocks and boulders. As they topped out on a ridge covered with oak, piñon and alligator juniper trees, he turned to look back one last time at the fading sunset. It had been almost six months since the deaths of his parents but he still had difficulty in believing they were both actually gone from his life. He believed in his heart that one day he would be with them again and that his daddy would have a good job so his momma wouldn't have to work. And his daddy would not be taking any drugs or be friends with bad people. They would be together—a family again.

Robbie sighed as a big tear ran down his cheek. Gramma Helen and Wetzel were so good to him, making him feel at home, but he missed his momma and daddy so much that he ached for them to be with him again.

With the sun now gone from the distant horizon, the sky began to darken and Robbie knew he needed to move on. As he turned in the saddle, he heard Montie growl deeply in his throat; teeth bared, the hair stood up on his back as the dog moved to the front of the horse.

"What's the matter, Montie?" Robbie frowned. He looked in the direction the dog was facing but saw nothing to alarm him. He touched his spurs to the pony's flanks but as the horse trotted ahead, the dog intervened again, stopping their progress. Realizing it was late, he admonished, "Stop it, Montie! We've got to get on home."

Looking up from the growling dog, he saw a man step out from behind a large juniper tree. The man held a rifle with a scope; the rifle was supported by a sling on his broad, muscular shoulders. His dark hair hung down his back. He was swarthy and dark of complexion, a large, ugly scar ran along his face from his right eye down the entire cheek to his throat. He wore dark clothing and boots, all of which appeared to be worn and dirty from recent travel.

In a gritty, deep voice, the man said, "Get off the horse, boy."

The dog charged, quickly and aggressively, but not fast enough. The man slightly raised the rifle, firing a three round burst that hit Montie. He cried out as he fell in mid-stride, and though mortally wounded, the dog continued crawling with all the strength he had left in his body toward his adversary and threat to the boy he was ordered to protect.

Another burst from the rifle silenced the dog. The man's impassive face turned to the boy again. The gruff voice was hard this time, "Damn you! I said, *Off. Now!*" He pointed the rifle at the boy astride the pony.

Robbie dismounted, and as he did so, he swung the horse in front of him and the man with the rifle. His voice shook with fear. "Wha … what do you … want with me, mister?"

"Get out from behind that horse, boy."

Robbie whimpered. "Why did you shoot my dog, mister?"

"I'll kill your horse if you don't move out from behind him."

Robbie cried, but hung on to the reins and stirrup on the left side.

Another soft voice spoke suddenly. "Don't move, Robbie. Stay right where you are."

The boy looked to where he thought he'd heard the voice coming from but could see nothing. "Who ... who ... *are you*?"

The man with the rifle jumped behind the tree. "Tomás? *Eres tú*?" "Is that you?"

The voice in Spanish seemed to come from another direction than before; it was calm and direct without any urgency. "Carlos, what are you doing here?"

Fear exuded with the reply. "I am under orders to sanction the boy. Enrique has decreed this to be." Carlos waited to determine the direction his adversary's voice had come from. But it came from yet another location. Robbie could not see anyone although he strained his eyes to do so.

The voice continued, "This is *my* territory, Carlos. No one does anything on my turf without *my* approval *cabrón*."

Carlos moved around the tree to cover the location where he thought the voice had come from. He held the rifle to his shoulder, listening intently. Heavy perspiration formed on his forehead and sweat ran along his torso from his underarms.

Robbie held tight to the reins and stirrup as he sobbed.

The soft voice again, "But you knew that, eh, Carlos?"

"Come out and fight me like a man!" shouted Carlos. He turned swiftly, at a noise behind him. He started to bring the rifle up to firing position and was stopped with a thud as an arrow entered his right eye, slamming his head into the tree trunk and pinning it there. Carlos' lower body and arms flopped and quivered uncontrollably as he inadvertently fired several rounds into the ground then the rifle clattered to the ground.

Robbie gasped.

The man in black stepped out from behind a heavily foliated oak tree, and Robbie recognized him as the man who had kidnapped him. Dark cropped hair with dark sunglasses covering his eyes, he moved lithely but did not appear overly muscular. He laid his bow and quiver of arrows on the ground. Quickly, he moved to the impaled man. Softly, he whispered, "And I was next? Hmmm ... Carlos?" He drew the knife at his belt and slit Carlos' throat from ear to ear. Wiping the blade on the dead man's shirt, he sheathed it, and walked over to the boy.

"Remember me, Robbie?"

Robbie shook uncontrollably, more terrified than he had ever been in his entire life, but he stammered out a reply, "Y-y-yes ... sir."

A smile flickered on the man's face for just an instant. "You don't have to be afraid of me, Robbie. If I had wanted to kill you, it would have already been done." He looked off in the distance, a quizzical look on his dark face. His right forefinger touched his index finger while the small finger flicked at the cigarette that wasn't there.

"You somehow knew to hide behind the horse." The man in black removed the dark sunglasses and turned toward the boy. "I like that in a man."

Robbie looked into the dark, smooth-shaven face and the sharp blue eyes peering down at him. Robbie stammered, "Why ... he-help me, sir?"

The man in black looked directly at the boy standing in front of him. The dark eyes softened then hardened again, and he replaced the dark sunglasses. "You remind me of someone, Robbie; in another life—long ago." He walked back to the tree and picked up his bow and arrows. He strode away, and in Spanish, he said softly over his shoulder, "Damned if you might be worth dying for, boy." Then he disappeared in the darkening landscape.

Not understanding what had been said, Robbie leaped astride the pony and rode hard for the ranch house.

CHAPTER SIXTY-EIGHT

District Ranger Bill Hood scratched his head, yawned and pulled off his horn-rimmed glasses rubbing his eyes. He stood up from his desk and stretched his bulky frame. His uniform shirt pulled taunt over his huge belly and the bottom button burst and sprang across the room. Hood swore as he shuffled over and bent to retrieve the missing button. He grunted and then swore again as he felt the seams of his pants give ever so slightly in the back.

Returning to his desk, breathing heavily, he sat down and replaced the glasses on his nose. Swiveling his chair around one hundred eighty degrees, he peered through the window outside the Gila Center Visitor Center and office complex. He adjusted the heavy glasses as he observed several cars parked in the public parking lot. Two wilderness rangers appeared on horseback, herding mules across the parking lot toward the forest service barn below the parking lot and adjacent to the confluence of the Middle Fork and the West Fork of the Gila River.

Hood turned back to his desk, scratched his head again and pulled at his shirt near the missing button, shrugged and reached for the blue envelope in the in-box. It was marked "Confidential for District Ranger." Ripping the envelope open, he read the heading "Investigative Report" and to the right "Vandalism-District Ranger Sign."

He smiled broadly. *Finally!* It was way past time for Wetzel to complete the investigation and get the report to him. He would make whoever was responsible pay dearly for trying to make a fool out of him. After all, as District Ranger, he had the right to do as he damn well pleased with regard to flagging signs that he deemed needed removal. And to hell with the sign committee or other staff who felt it was their right to decide what needed done on the district. Hood grinned, licking his lips as he thought of the severe discipline he had in mind. Leaning back in his chair, he propped his large feet up on his desk and read the report:

On the night of May 25, 1973 at approximately 1210 hours, several perpetrators, most likely four individuals as evidenced from sign left at the scene of the crime, entered the parking lot to the rear of the Visitor Center and office complex. Ensuring that no one was nearby to view said criminal act, two of the individuals stood guard, one overlooking the parking lot and the other facing the trail coming down from the mesa above the Visitor Center where the housing is located. This was ascertained by the discovery of footprints in and around the location where these individuals were stationed. Of special interest, it is noted that both lookouts were bare footed with one perpetrator displaying four toes on one foot and five on the other.

Grunting, Hood removed his feet from the desk, pushed the heavy, thick glasses up on his nose, and scanned the remainder of the document with a frown.

The two perpetrators then proceeded to defecate and urinate with audacity and unmitigated gall in their area of surveillance.

Hood slammed his palm down hard on his desk. "Those sons-of-bitches! I'll throw the book at them, by God." Eyes wide with excitement, he continued reading the report with renewed interest:

The other two perpetrators proceeded to the sign designated as "District Ranger Parking Only", their footprints indicating that they stopped near the metal post supporting said sign. These individuals both had five toes each as evidenced by tracks in sandy soil at the base of the post. It appeared the toes were poorly developed and indications that the toes might have soft pads on the underside.

An attempt at taking legible fingerprints failed, but it appeared from the smudges on said sign that one of the perpetrators had jumped to the top of said sign while his accomplice operated from lower on the post just below said sign. Together, they were able to tie the orange flagging onto said sign.

Hood's mouth flew open, his brow wrinkled; he stood holding the report clenched in his fist. Aloud, he said, "What the ..." His mouth contorted as he read the rest of the report:

"It appears the perpetrators were able to gain access to the fire cache in order to obtain orange flagging used in the crime scene. The investigator found a roll of flagging in the cache that had a six foot section missing. The end of the flagging on said sign matched one end of the roll.

The investigator interviewed several members of the helitack crew in regard to the missing flagging in the fire cache. No one observed anything unusual in the days preceding the incident on the 25th of May. Further, no one has observed the four small individuals, one of which has only four toes on one foot. The investigator will advise all Forest Service personnel to be on the lookout for these individuals. Case closed until such time new leads surface.

Jack Wetzel

Law Enforcement Officer

District Ranger Hood's head pounded with an intense headache; his face turned red then mottled purple as he strode from his office still holding the incident report tightly in his fist. *Squirrels?* He yelled, "WETZEL! Where the hell are you?" He passed one of the helitack crewmen in the hallway. "Where's Wetzel?"

The crewman shook his head, "Not here, sir. He headed out to the field early this morning."

Hood shouted, "Well, where the hell was he going, dammit?"

Taking a step back, the crewman replied tentatively, "I think he said he was going to Whiskey Creek, sir."

Clenching his jaws, Hood stood for a moment, his nostrils flared, eyes wide and flashing with anger. "I want that son-of-a-bitch in my office the minute he returns. *You hear me?*"

CHAPTER SIXTY-NINE

THE WESTERN SKIES BOLSTERED LEAD-COLORED CLOUDS SO LADEN WITH rain that their fingers strained downward appearing to obliterate the magnificent New Mexico topography from sight. Wetzel steered the green forest service truck along the rough dirt road that traversed Whiskey Creek. He cruised slowly past the Silver Cell Mine, noting an increase in the number of vehicles. The mine served as a front for the Enrique cartel, and it worried him that Lacey and her brothers lived so close to it. The wind increased in velocity, lightning flashed illuminating the black sky; within seconds thunder rumbled deeply.

Wetzel had not been the same since the deaths of Juan and Maggie Garcia. He awakened in the middle of the night, thinking it had all been a bad dream only to realize that his friends had been murdered, and he had failed to protect them. He had become irritable of late, the war images had returned, and there was less joy in life.

The radio crackled with fire dispatch traffic, "207 ... Dispatch; do you copy?"

Wetzel keyed the mic. "Dispatch ... 207."

"You have orders from District Ranger Hood to return to base ASAP."

Wetzel grinned. "Copy. It may be awhile. We're getting heavy rains in Whiskey Creek." Hood had read his report. Wetzel slammed the palm of his right hand on the steering wheel. It served him right. The pompous ass!

He sighed deeply as he turned the truck sharply to the right to avoid a large hole in the road. The thought of losing his job he had worked so hard to get and keep didn't seem to be important to him anymore.

"207 ... Dispatch; District Ranger Hood's orders are for you to return NOW!"

Wetzel hesitated before responding, "Weather's ... bad ... can't ... copy." He turned the radio off and slouched forward in his seat. The rain pattered tentatively on the roof, hood, and windshield and then began a ferocious barrage, pounding the vehicle incessantly. The wipers hummed at top speed, but Wetzel had difficulty seeing the road ahead and made slow progress toward the head of Whiskey Creek.

Lightning flashed in the darkened sky, illuminating the narrow, eroded road. The rain continued unabated with water rushing down the center of the road causing further erosion. Wetzel maneuvered the green truck along the winding road; lightning flashed again, this time in close proximity and immediately thunder roared in the forest dominated by towering, swaying Ponderosa pine trees. Suddenly, the small cabin owned by the Whippits appeared within his vision. He braked the truck to a stop in front of the cabin, turned off the ignition, but remained in the cab while the wind whirled and blustered and the rain came down in torrents, pounding the truck.

Wetzel closed his eyes, leaned his head back and breathed deeply, holding his breath for a few seconds, and then exhaled slowly. He continued with the exercise for several minutes and calm returned to his being. He had used the technique during his tour in Viet Nam. It had been the only thing that had ever really helped him relax over there.

The rain began to lessen in intensity; he pushed his Stetson down on his head, opened the driver's door, and stepped out into the driving wind and rain. Leaning forward, he sloshed through standing water and up onto the porch.

"Howdy, Jack." Larrimore Whippit stepped out on the porch from the cabin, grinning. "Long time since we seed ya heah." Whippit tucked his large hands in the sides of his patched, faded demim coveralls. He had no shirt on under the coveralls and his bare feet extended from below tattered coverall pant legs.

"Howdy yourself, Larrimore." Wetzel shook hands. The cowlick in Larrimore's hairline amply displayed his identity from his twin brother.

"You've not been around much lately." Larrimore ran a coarse hand through his unruly thick brown hair. Placing the hand back in the side of his coveralls, he added, "Come on inside. Sis'll be tickled to see ya."

Wetzel removed his wet hat, shook the water from it, and stamped his Packer boots before following Larrimore into the dimly lit log cabin. Lacey Whippit sat at the kitchen table; what appeared to be ore samples lay on the table under her intent gaze. She looked up as the two men entered, and a smile appeared on her lips. Pushing back the wooden chair, she stood. "Wel-l-l ... would ya look at what the cats drug in?"

Wetzel grinned, his heart warmed at the sight of her. Stepping forward he shook her outstretched small brown hand. Her firm handshake pleased him. "It's always good to see *you*, Lacey." She wore her usual worn work garb, her dark brown hair pulled back in a ponytail.

Wetzel pulled at his wet Stetson. Their eyes locked. "You look great."

"Uh huh." The eyes twinkled.

"Well, I ... uh ... I thought I ought to check on the sheep allotment."

"Uh huh."

Wetzel looked at the rough wooden floor and then back into her smiling, pretty brown eyes.

She laughed. "Them sheep are being watched by Mr. Reagan, the best man in the business. We can take a run up on the mountain in the mawnin' if'n you'd like, Jack."

It was his turn to laugh and it felt good. "In the mornin' then." He turned to go.

Lacey reached out a hand to his shoulder. "Ah reckon there's no need to rush off in this heah storm." She reluctantly removed her hand. "Why don't ya stay awhile and visit? I kin put coffee on an' vittles are already on the stove."

"Stay overnight with us, Jack. The couch sleeps pretty darn good, leastways for naps." Larrimore grinned, displaying his tobacco-stained teeth, and turned to Lacey. "It's time I watched the mine and let Lattimore come on down to the house for something to eat and rest." In the living room he put on old boots without socks, a canvas jacket and slouch hat, walked to the porch, and said over his shoulder, "See ya in the mawnin', Jack boy."

An awkward silence ensued. Then Lacey motioned to the table. "I want ya to take a look at this heah ore on the table." She took hold of his arm and steered him to a chair at the table. "I'll fix us a cup 'o coffee, Jack, whilst ya take a looksee at them samples."

Wetzel peered at the ore samples and picked up one, looking more closely at it; the sample didn't particularly impress him, but then again he knew nothing about mining. He placed it on the table and picked up the remaining two samples, turning them over in his hands. Part of one sample appeared to have a somewhat malleable surface. He could not resist the urge to poke at it and eventually bite it with his teeth. He was surprised to find that he could leave evidence of teeth marks.

He heard Lacey laugh and looked up to see her standing near him, a steaming cup of coffee in each hand. "You ain't too bad a miner at thet, Jack. That's what I done, too." She set the coffee down and sat in the chair opposite him with elbows on the table, her hands cupping her face on both sides. "Soft, ain't it?

Wetzel peered intently at the sample in his hand.

Lacey placed her palms down on the table and leaned forward, grinning. "It's *gold*, Jack! An' me an' the boys ... we've plumb found the vein."

Wetzel's mouth opened in astonishment. He stammered, "That's ... that's ... are you sure it's all real gold, Lacey?"

She smiled at him, sat back in the chair, and drank from her coffee mug. "Jest as you say, Jack, 'Yessir, ah reckon so.'" Drinking more of the hot coffee, her brown eyes locked with his widened stare.

He grinned and looked out the picture window in the living room as the lightning flashed illuminating the darkness briefly, thunder rolled. He leaned back in his chair and let out a loud yell, jumped up, raced around the table, and in one swift move, scooped up Lacey in his arms and hugged her. "I'm so glad for you and your brothers, Lacey!" He held her out in front of him by her small shoulders. "My God! You've struck it rich, girl."

She moved toward him and hugged him tightly around his waist.

Her head rested on his chest, but she said nothing. Awkwardly, he placed his arms around her, withdrew them, then held her tightly again. Slowly, he brought his hands up and turned her head gently upward, bent his head down until their lips met; ever so slightly they kissed. Wetzel leaned in further, this time kissing her again. He reached down with his hands on her slim waist, held her while peering into her eyes. He gasped, "Lacey … I …"

Before he could say more, she kissed him, parting his lips. He returned the kiss much more passionately, savoring the moment with her in his arms. Then he reached down and taking her hips in his hands he pulled her close, hugging her tightly. They were both breathing hard when they heard the front screen door open and slam shut with a bang.

Lattimore Whippit stood there, dripping water and grinning from ear to ear. "Howdy, Jack boy. I'd shore tell ya ta make yourself ta home, but … uh … I reckon you already done thet. Ha! Ha!"

The couple jumped back from each other, and they said nothing. Lacey straightened her clothes, and Wetzel not knowing what to do with his hands, placed his thumbs inside his jean's pockets. Finally, he said, "Howdy yourself, you ol' hillbilly!"

Lattimore apparently liked that, and stepping forward, he shook hands with Wetzel, laughing heartily. He whispered as he passed Wetzel, "Ain't nothin' to be embarrassed about, jest part o' sparkin' a gal is all."

He walked to his sister, gave her a hug, and then proceeded to the kitchen. "You got any vittles fer a cold, hungry brother of yore'n?" He turned, "I'll bet ol' Jack heah is as hungry as I am. Ain't thet right, Jack?" He was still grinning while looking at both of them.

Impatiently, Lacey moved toward the kitchen. "You get cleaned up afore supper, Lattimore, or you don't get any of them lamb chops that I got cooked up ready to eat. And another thing, get outta them wet clothes and quit dripping all over the house." She waved toward one of the bedrooms. "Go on, git!"

Lattimore wasted no time in heading to the bedroom. His sister wasn't finished yet with him. "An' put on shirt an' some shoes for Christsake."

He answered, "Yes ma'am."

CHAPTER SEVENTY

THE OLD MAN AWOKE; THE COOL MORNING SMELLED OF RAIN. He stretched leisurely under warm blankets and looked out the line shack's foggy windows. It was late summer and the monsoon rain would soon be over. He had slept in, enjoying the warm bed; the sun was already up and he heard the rooster crowing several miles down Whiskey Creek at the Whippit place. He lay there, reluctant to get up for some reason he was unaware of. He placed his hands under his head and thought of the day ahead. Lacey had advised that the young Forest Ranger might arrive to check on the allotment. Reagan smiled as he thought of her looking forward to Wetzel coming to Whiskey Creek.

Lacey had done well in her speech classes, improving her correct language skills for several months and then for whatever reason had failed to come back for more lessons, falling into her old manner of speech. Frowning, he thought it had occurred after the Garcias had been murdered. He had come to love that girl as if she was his own and had taken a real liking to her brothers even though they were eccentric to say the least. They worked hard, kept to themselves and were sincerely good folks. He had worked with so many greedy, mean and corrupt people in his work with the CIA. Some within the agency and others in countries where he had been stationed cared little for anything other than power, gain, and personal profit.

Throwing back the covers, he sat up on the old metal cot and watched a beam of sunshine slither through the foggy window and onto the rough wooden floor. It had rained hard most of the night with boisterous thunderstorm activity. Unusual for him, he just sat there on the cot as the image of his wife and daughter flashed into focus before him. Inadvertently, he cried out, "Please, not again." But his wife's face remained. She smiled at him, that special smile that he loved so, the eyes twinkling, her soft lips parting to display even white teeth. She spoke softly, "Danny ... oh, my Danny. You worry me so, my dear." She looked at their daughter, who stood beside her. "Beth and I want you to know that we love you—always will. Our deaths were not your fault." She gazed directly at the old man. "You must move on from all the chaos and death."

Reagan cried out and reached for his family, but they were gone as suddenly as they had appeared. Sobbing, he stood next to the bed, not moving. He closed his eyes and covered his mouth. Then he took a deep breath remembering that fateful day. Saigon streets were teeming with cars, carts, pedestrians. He had been late in meeting his family at the restaurant due to the congestion. Parking a half block from the restaurant, he exited the car when the explosion nearly knocked him off his feet. Stunned, he saw the restaurant was gone, obliterated in an instant. Then he saw a thin Vietnamese man, wearing shorts, sandals, and an open cotton shirt placing some kind of device in his pocket. The man had not noticed Reagan behind him as he watched the carnage and destruction.

The Vietnamese man smiled and then turned quickly to enter the small Volkswagen sedan parked near the street, but he was not fast enough for the CIA agent, who drew his automatic pistol from his shoulder holster and shot him multiple times in his back and the back of his head. Reagan did not stop to watch the man slump forward but ran toward the scene of hell itself. "*Nancy! Beth!*"

Trembling, the old man took a deep breath, and unable to stand, remained sitting on the cot. Suddenly cold in his T-shirt and boxer shorts, he lay back and covered himself with the woolen blanket. He lay there with his arms at his sides, not moving, eyes straight ahead. Then tears trickled slowly down his tanned face to patter softly on the pillow.

Minutes passed. Finally, he stood and dressed in his faded blue jeans and work shirt, leather work boots. He walked to the wash basin near the wood cook stove, washed his face, and combed his hair. Turning his attention to the stove, he placed paper and kindling in the fire box, started a fire and added more wood. Next, he retrieved two eggs Lacey Whippit had brought over the previous day and a cast iron skillet that he set over the fire. After pouring water and placing coffee in the old coffee pot on the stove, he stepped out on the porch.

As he stood there, the sun broke through the trees spilling warm sunshine on his face. A soft breeze caressed his hair and beard. He took a deep breath, inhaling the fresh mountain air and then slowly exhaled. During the months Reagan had been tending the sheep, he had never felt so full of life nor loved living as he had here in the mountains. And he had grown strong and healthy, with tanned face and arms where he had rolled the sleeves in the summer heat. He knew his cardiovascular and muscle strength had never been better given his age.

He had seriously taken on the task of caring for the sheep, guarding them from their predators—mountain lions, bears, and coyotes. And in doing so, he had found his inner being and a reason to live again. If he could only do away with the nightmares! Sighing, he knew it would take time. He felt so responsible for the deaths of his wife and daughter and many of the killings he had orchestrated while employed with the CIA. Reagan had reconciled himself that the past was just that—the past, and there was nothing he could do to change it now. But he did have control over today and any future days he had left in his life on earth.

The sound of the coffee pot gurgling interrupted his thoughts, and he turned to re-enter the cabin. He strode to the stove, added more wood, placed cooking oil in the warmed skillet, and cooked the two eggs for breakfast.

After eating, Reagan retrieved his rifle, checked to ensure that the magazine tube was fully loaded with .30-.30 cartridges. He returned to the porch, called to the sheep dogs, released the sheep from the pen near the cabin, and together they herded the sheep toward a meadow some two miles distant for adequate grazing and water. He had previously stayed away from the meadow as it was in close proximity to the Silver Cell Mine. But the abundant grass and forbs and a spring fed creek made it a suitable choice for the day.

Once there, the sheep fanned out in the meadow under the diligent watch of the sheep dogs and the old man. Pursuant to his watchful habit of securing an adequate view of the herd, he climbed part way up the west side of the steep canyon, removed his pack, and sat down amongst the pine leaves littering the ground with his back against a large Ponderosa pine tree. He set the rifle next to him and withdrew his canteen of water from the pack. He drank his fill and watched the dogs circling the sheep, never barking but occasionally biting at their heels to keep them in the meadow.

White, thin clouds raced across a bright blue sky as the darker, gray clouds slowly slipped from the horizon. The old man sat for a spell and then seeing the dogs were doing a good job with the sheep, he decided to take a short jaunt down the canyon. As he stood dusting the pine needles from his pants, he reached for the rifle and pack. Laughing, he knew he would be back within a few minutes with no need to carry a rifle and pack. Besides this was an excellent location from which to watch the sheep grazing in the meadow below.

The old man walked slowly mid-slope enjoying the morning as he contoured the canyon in a southerly direction. He was careful in traversing the rocks and steep slope without mishap. Pausing to observe two Mexican jays chase each other first into the foliage of a gambel oak then higher upslope to a much larger pine tree, he heard voices on the other side of the ridge. As he listened, it appeared to him that someone was in distress. He thought possibly whoever it was had fallen or injured themselves in some way. Reagan climbed up the steep slope of the canyon wall, zig sagging back and forth until he reached the ridge top. Breathing heavily, he took a short rest and noticed an old narrow logging road that ran from the ridge line down into a smaller canyon to the north. He heard voices more clearly now; someone was pleading for help.

He hurried along the overgrown road as it traversed down into the small canyon. Suddenly, he stopped in his tracks as he saw several men surrounding another man lying on the ground with his hands bound behind him. His bloodied face exuded fear as he asked for mercy; one of the men laughed and kicked him in the face.

The old man reached instinctively for the rifle that was normally slung over his shoulder as he wandered the hills. With no rifle, no cover, he stood there in the road contemplating what to do. He felt a tightening down deep in his belly, conscious stirring of honed survival skills long since buried in his past. Fight? No firearm. Flight? It was too late to run.

One of the men saw him, pointed his automatic rifle at him and shouted for him to come to their location. The others aimed their rifles and handguns at him. He was trapped; he knew it and reluctantly accepted it as he walked toward them with his hands in the air as commanded.

As the old man approached them, his quick eye observed there were five men standing, two with what appeared to be assault rifles and three with handguns. A heavy set man with a pock-marked face wearing a black T-shirt and blue jeans approached, pointed a revolver at him and shouted, "Who the hell are you?" He shoved Reagan toward the others. "What are you doing out here?"

The old man looked at him. "I might ask *you* the same question."

The man snarled at him. "Don't get smart with me, you old bastard." He grabbed the front of Reagan's shirt, pulled him close with the gun inches from his face. Instinctively, the old man reached out, clutched the revolver hand as he moved sideways out of the line of fire and twisted the revolver sharply backwards breaking the man's trigger finger caught in the trigger guard. Taking possession of the handgun, he wheeled about pulling the screaming man in front of him as cover.

Reagan then fired at the man closest to him, shooting him twice in the chest and once in the head. As he turned searching for the other man with a rifle, he felt pistol rounds hitting the injured man he held tightly in his grasp. *There he is!* As the man with the second rifle took aim, Reagan fired at his adversary as rapidly as he could pull the trigger. The man he was holding sagged to the ground. The old man heard something behind him, and as he turned he was hit hard on the back of his head. Everything went blank.

As Reagan lay on the ground, he slowly gained consciousness. His hands were tied securely behind his back. With a splitting headache, he lay there trying to get his bearings. Another man he had not seen before placed a noose around his neck and dragged him, choking and gagging, under a large oak tree to where the other bound man lay with a noose around his neck.

The bound man peered at the old man through swollen eyes that were closing shut. "*Buenos dias, Senor.* Francisco ... Cordova ... at ... your service." Cordova struggled to see the old man. "You must be the sheepherder from up Whiskey Creek." Blood dripped from his swollen mouth. "For a sheepherder, you do well, *amigo*. Three of these *cabrones* are dead."

Reagan's head throbbed with pain. "Who *are* these men?"

Cordova attempted a smile. "These men work for ... William Bonney. I ... on the other hand ... work at the Silver Cell Mine."

A large, tall man strode over to the prostrate men. His brutal face was accentuated by piercing black eyes; long brown hair fell to his massive shoulders. He said, "Shut up!" and grabbed the rope attached to the noose around Cordova's neck, tossed it over a large limb of the tree overhead. Then taking hold of the rope he hauled Cordova up and off the ground. He tied the loose end of the rope to an adjacent tree trunk and grinned as the man kicked and struggled for breath.

He then stood over Reagan. "I'm William Bonney, and you'll get the same goddamn treatment, you old bastard, for meddling in my affairs." He viciously kicked him. "You killed three of my men, you son-of-a-bitch!" Saliva trickled from the corner of his mouth. "Who are you? What are you doing out here in the hills?"

"I am Daniel Reagan ... a sheepherder," replied the old man evenly.

"A sheepherder? Like hell you are. You work for Enrique?"

"I do not know anyone with that name."

"You're a goddamm liar!"

Bonney spit on the old man and then dragged him under the oak tree near the struggling Cordova. He jerked and then hoisted the old man off the ground. Bonney then bent to tie the rope off on the adjacent tree trunk. Gasping for air that was not there as the noose violently choked his airway, Reagan heard what sounded like a rush of air fly past his face. His bulging eyes followed the sound and saw the rope holding Cordova separate and heard Cordova grunt as he hit the ground. Almost simultaneously, Bonney cried out and let go of the rope he'd held in his hands; the old man fell to the ground.

His mouth wide open and wide-eyed, Bonney stood looking incredulously at an arrow imbedded in his right arm. The old man heard a piercing scream and a firearm discharged. He espied one of the men grasping at an arrow in his throat and heard another thud as a second man dropped his rifle, took a step, and fell over with an arrow embedded in his chest. Bonney pulled a pistol from the back of his pants with his left hand and began shooting in several directions as he ducked behind cover of an oak tree. Then he turned and ran down the canyon, tripped and fell several times, but eventually disappeared from sight.

A deep silence ensued in the steep canyon; the wind billowed through the trees moaning softly, accentuating the now strangely quiet setting. Reagan struggled to sit up, and then scooted on his bottom to Cordova who lay silently on the pine needled floor of the forest. He leaned down and used his teeth to loosen the tension on the rope around Cordova's neck. When he had at last succeeded, he heard a soft step behind him. He whirled around to confront the threat.

The man in black stood with both hands on the bow propped in front of him, a smile on his face, eyes twinkling. He spoke softly. "Danny … Danny Reagan. *Què tal, amigo*. It's been a long time, my friend."

CHAPTER SEVENTY-ONE

REAGAN BLINKED HIS EYES TO CLEAR HIS VISION AS HE GAZED UP AT THE man towering over him. Licking his lips, he said incredulously, "*Tomás*?"

The man in black laid his bow and quiver of arrows on the ground and drew a knife severing the rope on Reagan's wrists. He strode to Cordova doing the same for him.

Cordova coughed and sucked more air into his lungs, savoring the breath of life. He lay back on the forest floor while attempting a grin at the man in black. "Just … in … the nick of time, eh, Tomás?"

The man did not answer; he sat down under the oak tree with his back against the trunk. He peered through dark sunglasses at the old man, who gingerly rubbed his raw neck while surveying the dead men lying on the ground. Moments passed; finally Tomás said, "What is it, Danny? No words of wisdom for a friend from the old days?" His arms rested on bent knees as his left forefinger and thumb met with the little finger seemingly flicking ashes from a non-existent cigarette.

As he observed the dead bodies with protruding arrows, Reagan swallowed hard feeling soreness in his throat as he spoke, "I … ah … I … was just wondering how in the hell we defeated the Indians back in the day."

A smile curled around the man in black's mouth then disappeared as quickly as it had appeared. "I like the bow and arrows, Danny. It's a quiet, proficient weapon that I have honed to perfection."

"I can see that my friend." The old man stood stretching his frame then his arms. "What are you doing here, Tomás, in this wilderness?"

"I work here at the Silver Cell Mine." The man in black turned toward Cordova. "*Un momento*, Danny." He stood, walked over to Cordova, knelt beside him and whispered to him with his back to the old man.

Daniel Reagan's mind flashed back to a forgotten time long ago: The CIA's covert operations in Vietnam—assassinations—too many to remember. He had hired Tomás for the most difficult, the toughest assignments deep in enemy territory. The man had never failed to accomplish any task and he always brought back souvenirs to substantiate the kills. Reagan had always paid him with CIA cash, double what he paid other contractors. One of his impeccable intelligence sources had advised him that there was no better hitman than the Mexican Tomás Perez, who worked for one of the Mexican drug cartels.

Reagan accompanied the man on several of the missions and found him the best operative he had ever contracted in his career with the CIA; deadly, cold, brutal, uncaring, but with an unmistakable trait useful to Reagan—loyalty.

Cordova stood unsteadily with Tomás supporting him as he smiled and spoke to the old man, "Well, my sheepherder friend, I owe you a debt of gratitude for your assistance. *Muchas gracias!* I must return to my work at the mine."

"Of course, *Señor Cordova*," replied Reagan.

"Be careful, old man. Times are dangerous." Cordova turned to the man in black. "Will you track Bonney and kill him?"

The man in black stood as he peered out from the ridge top toward the mountain beyond. The sun had set, staging a picturesque backdrop in the sky; a golden hue exemplified the billowing clouds. "No, Francisco. Not today," he said over his shoulder. "He will return when he has regained his courage and has more men." Tomás pursed his lips and spat out from where he stood. Grinning, he turned to Reagan. "Then I will kill him. It is long overdue."

Cordova said nothing as he walked down the canyon toward the Silver Cell Mine. The man in black returned to the oak tree and took a seat, leaning back against the large trunk. Drawing up his knees.

"Danny, old friend, I could use someone of your talents." He laughed, "We are relics … you and I. These so called killers today; they are lazy, out of shape, and they have no professionalism, no pride in their work, *amigo*."

Taking off the dark sunglasses, his bright blue eyes bored into the old man's eyes. "Why are *you* here … in … this place? What could the agency possibly be doing *here*?"

Reagan moved over to the tree and sat next to the man in black with his back to the trunk. He told him what had happened to his family in Vietnam and how he had resigned from the CIA. How he had traveled out West eventually to New Mexico and happened to find work herding sheep at the Whippit place.

He continued with his story, "Until today, I thought I had finally found peace and real meaning in my life, Tomás. A *normal* life without violence and bloodshed."

The man in black replaced the dark sunglasses and sighed. "I'm sorry about your family. I know about losing someone close—my brother. I blamed an old woman for his death—a *bruja,* a witch. I was told by the man I work for that she had poisoned him and he had drowned in the river, so I shot her in the head." He sighed more deeply. "Now, I don't know. I don't trust my employer, and the more I think about it, I tend to believe the old woman that the one responsible was Pablo Enrique."

Reagan leaned forward then back against the tree repositioning. "Are you still working for the cartel?"

"Yes. This is my territory."

"Sooo … the Silver Cell Mine is a front for the drug trade?"

The man in black did not answer. "There's a big war brewing between us and Bonney's bunch. Come work for me, Danny! It'll be just like old times."

The old man shook his head, "I'm done with all the killing. I want no part of it."

"And yet today you did not hesitate to kill."

It was Reagan's turn to not answer.

A red-tailed hawk soared overhead, riding the wind currents, looking for something to eat. The wind moaned softly in the trees stirring the upper limbs and branches.

"What is this Whippit place to you? I understand there's a bunch of hillbillies up there trying to mine a nothing claim. And these sheep?

Jesus, Danny. *You* a sheepherder? You were head of black operations for Christsake!"

The old man's voice was sharp, "I'll kill any man who tries to harm the Whippits. The girl means … a lot to me."

The man in black's eyebrows arched momentarily. "Ahh … a girl friend?"

"*No.* Lacey's like a daughter to me."

A moment passed in silence.

The man in black said, "I see. Well, I certainly have no interest in them, to harm them in any way. But—"

"But what, Tomás?" the old man said tersely.

"I heard William Bonney had an axe to grind with them over one of the Whippit boys herding two of his men off the mountain at gunpoint some time back … naked, mind you."

"Would Bonney harm them?" Reagan's eyes narrowed.

"Hell yes, Danny. He doesn't give a shit about some damn hillbillies any more than I do." The man in black leaned his head back against the tree trunk listening to the mournful wind blowing through the trees.

The old man said nothing but sat thinking about what had been said.

The man in black said, "What's the name of that ranger whose been patrolling up here lately?"

"Jack Wetzel."

"Wetzel … yeah, that's right. You might want to tell him and that hillbilly game warden to help you with Bonney. They're both capable." He reached down and picked up a pine cone lying next to him. He laughed a short laugh. "I attempted to kill both of them awhile back and failed." He looked intently at the pine cone as he spoke. "They are the *only* men who have ever escaped death from me, Danny."

"When do you think Bonney might make his move against the Whippits?" queried the old man.

"Anytime; a few days … a week … a month maybe."

Reagan considered what had been said as he looked out over the mountain side watching the white clouds sailing softly by in a blue sky.

The man in black interrupted his thoughts, "Hey Danny, you remember that time in Nam when we killed those high ranking North

Vietnamese officers and then made a run for it? We made it to the water, and you pulled me half dead at least two miles out to the Navy craft waiting for us."

"I remember," replied the old man softly.

Tomás laughed a quiet laugh. "How many bullet holes did I have in me?"

"*No recuerdo,* Tomás, *pero eran muchos.*"

"That's the only time in my life that I thought I wouldn't make it." The man in black paused. "As I lay there on the deck, bleeding out, struggling to live, I saw ... a trail leading up to what appeared to be a misty green mountain pass, high up on the mountain; and beyond it in the distance a ... soft, bright, radiant light shining there for me to follow."

Reagan whispered, "Lambent Pass."

The man in black turned to him. "Have *you* ever seen it, Danny?"

"Yes," said the old man so softly he was barely heard.

The man in black tossed the pine cone down in the canyon after realizing he had inadvertently squeezed the sharp needles into his hand. "Was it like I described, Danny?"

Reagan answered after a few minutes of silence. "Yes, Tomás—just as you described it."

"Were you dying?"

"It was 1950—in Korea at the Chosin Reservoir; the Chinese had overrun our position with overwhelming numbers. I was shot in the leg and a bullet had grazed my scalp leading to profuse bleeding affecting my vision. A Chinese soldier appeared suddenly to bayonet me as I lay there. He must have thought I was dead and not worth the effort; he took my wrist watch, combat boots and heavy parka and left me. As I lay there in the bitter, subzero cold of North Korea freezing to death, I, too, saw the lambent pass."

Both men sat in silence, leaning against the large oak tree listening to the silence of the wilderness; the wind moaned softly in the trees showering pine needles from the ponderosa pine tree nearest them to the ground. An Abert squirrel scampered along the forest floor, stopped momentarily, stood on his hind legs looking over his shoulder toward the men, and then disappeared up the pine tree.

The old man looked at his companion. "I notice you don't smoke anymore."

Tomás smiled briefly, "No, not for a long time. They say it's unhealthy for you, Danny … even *dangerous*." The dark eyes twinkled beneath the sunglasses.

A woman's voice startled both men. It was Lacey Whippit calling for the old man, "MR. REAGAN! MR. REAGAN!"

The man in black gathered his compound bow and arrows. "I'll dispose of the bodies." He started down the canyon toward the Silver Cell Mine. "We'll meet again, Danny." He turned and said quietly, "Maybe … maybe at the pass, *amigo*."

Reagan smiled ruefully and then walked in the other direction.

CHAPTER SEVENTY-TWO

JACK WETZEL PARKED HIS GREEN GOVERNMENT TRUCK NEXT TO THE GILA National Forest Supervisor's office on College Avenue. Further up the street within view of the Forest Service building, Western New Mexico University campus sat perched on the hillside overlooking the town of Silver City. Wetzel exited the truck, slammed the heavy metal door shut and thoughtfully rubbed his freshly shaved chin. He sighed deeply as he stood there leaning against the truck polishing his boot tops on his pants legs.

He was to attend an administrative hearing with his boss, District Ranger Hood, Forest Supervisor Warren Carter, and the head of the Human Resources Department. Evidently, his boss had not found his report on the investigation of flagging placed on the district ranger's parking sign at the Gila Wilderness District office amusing. Nor had Wetzel thought that he would. He was just fed up working for Hood, who appeared to have no clue as to the important issues for the district. Wetzel felt that Hood deserved the orange flagging on his individual parking sign by unilaterally deciding which signs should be removed without any consultation with the sign committee or anyone else on the district.

As he stood next to the truck, he thumbed his Stetson back on his head and reached for his pack of Lucky Strikes in his shirt pocket. He shook out a cigarette and placed it between his teeth, lit it with his lighter and drew the smoke deeply into his lungs. Leaning his elbows on the side of the truck, he watched traffic on College Avenue. Students driving up the hill to attend morning classes; a van load of hippies, men with long hair, scraggly beards, and sallow faces, and the girls with even longer, disheveled hair giggling and then laughing loudly as they passed by with the windows open.

The cigarette made a slow progression from the left side of Wetzel's mouth to the right side as smoke drifted lazily from his nostrils. He had a good chance of being fired today and was saddened at the thought of no longer having a job that he thoroughly enjoyed working in the wilderness. He had known when he wrote the report that it would cause serious consequences for his career, and it was time for him to deal with it, one way or the other.

He took his time finishing the cigarette and then entered the rented government building, smiled at the receptionist behind the front desk as he passed by, heading for the supervisor's office down the hall. The smile faded immediately as he made the turn. Hearing voices inside the office, he removed his hat, hesitated for a moment, and then knocked on the closed door.

Forest Supervisor Warren Carter answered the door with a smile. "Come on in, Jack, and have a seat." He gestured toward a chair in front of his desk. District Ranger Hood was seated in an adjacent chair and an individual from Human Resources was seated off to one side of Carter's desk. Hood did not look at Wetzel or acknowledge that he was in the room.

Wetzel sat with his hat in his hands as he directed his gaze toward Warren Carter. Carter was highly respected by virtually all the Gila National Forest employees as a firm but fair Forest Supervisor, and he was well liked within the Silver City community. He had worked his way up the chain of command within the organization from Range Conservationist to District Ranger to Forest Supervisor and knew the forest service inside and out. He was in his late fifties with thinning gray hair, barrel chested and a stocky build. As usual, his uniform was immaculate and he exuded confidence in his stride back to the chair behind his desk.

He put his feet up on the desk and leaned back in the chair as he nodded for Hood to present his case for insubordination and the firing of a member of the permanent staff within the forest. Hood outlined the turbulent history betwen Wetzel and him for several years and their inability to get along. He articulated the incident of someone placing flagging on *his* parking sign at the Gila Wilderness District Office and that he had directed Wetzel to investigate the matter post haste. Further, he noted as he handed Carter a copy of the investigative report Wetzel had done on the case, that the investigative report itself was a joke and meant to undermine him as a supervisor. He paused as Carter read the investigative report.

Carter scanned through the two-page report, showing no emotion or facial expression as he stood and handed it to the Human Resource representative. Hood began to speak again but stopped as Carter held his hand up, palm facing him. Then Carter stood and walked to the large window behind his desk seemingly to view the grove of juniper trees swaying in the morning breeze. As he turned toward Wetzel, Jack caught a glimpse of a twinkle in his eyes and a brief smile that disappeared quickly. His sharp blue eyes locked with Wetzel's. "Well, Jack. What do you have to say for yourself, son?"

"I can honestly say that I did my best in completing an investigation with no leads whatsoever." He clutched his Stetson tighter in his hands. "However, it most likely was a bit ... *trivial* in the summary statement—"

"Trivial!" shouted Hood, the wide-rimmed glasses slipping down to the end of his bulbous nose, his reddened face displaying outrage.

Carter sat in his chair with elbows on the desk. "Bill, if you can't maintain a calm, professional demeanor in here, I'll ask you to leave."

Hood readjusted his glasses and his seat in his chair. "Yes sir."

"Good. You had your say in the matter. Now it's Jack's turn." He chewed on his lower lip. "Do you have anything else to say, Jack?"

"Yessir, I reckon I do. In response to the charge of insubordination, I have not been insubordinate; I completed the investigation as ordered, such as it was. And—"

Carter leaned back in his chair. "And *what*?"

"Well, sir. Bill and I have never gotten along. We just don't see eye to eye on much of anything."

"Uh huh." Carter shifted slightly in his chair. "You two were in here awhile back with similar issues, weren't you?"

District Ranger Hood swallowed hard and nodded; Wetzel said, "Yessir."

Carter slapped his hands down hard on his desk. "The charge of insubordination doesn't appear to hold water, Bill. The boy did complete what you asked him to do. He didn't refuse orders." Looking at the human resource representative, he asked, "You concur?"

The human resources representative nodded.

Carter looked hard at Wetzel. "As for your *trivial* report as you have described it, it seems to me you're trying to be a smart ass to your boss." He rubbed his square jaw while peering directly at Wetzel. "Is that the kind of employee you are Jack? A smart ass kid who is looking to undermine his supervisor at every turn?"

Wetzel squirmed in his chair clutching his hat.

"Is *that* what you've become?" Raising his voice, Carter repeated, "Well, *is it*?"

Wetzel sighed deeply and replied in a monotone, "No sir. I'm not that sort of employee."

Carter leaned forward on the desk with his elbows. "I would hope to God, not, son. I worked under your dad for years on the Mimbres District. Got to know him quite well, and I damned well know he wouldn't have raised a son that wasn't of good character, certainly not someone who was disrespectful and a smart ass."

"Yessir." Wetzel nodded. "I owe my boss an apology regardless of what you decide to do with me today."

"Uh huh," said Carter.

Wetzel stood with hat in hand and turned to Hood. "Bill, I'm sorry for my sarcasm in the report." His brow furrowed as he swallowed hard, searching for the words to say. "You're right. You and I have never gotten along or seen things the same way. I felt at the time and still do that you should have included the sign committee and staff in your determination of which signs to remove."

Ranger Hood started to reply but Carter's upraised hand stopped him. "Let the boy finish, Bill. *Jesus*!"

"I love this job of mine more than anything in the world. But if you feel I need to be fired for what I've done, I'll save you the trouble and resign."

His eyes wide, the human resources representative dropped the investigative report on the floor and then bent to pick it up.

Ranger Hood beamed, his face reddened. "Yes. We want you out of here. *Gone*!"

Carter's voice boomed across the room. "Shut up, Bill. When I want your damned opinion, I'll ask for it." He paused briefly. "As for apologies, Bill, when you return to your district, you will convene a meeting with all your staff—*everyone*, and you will apologize for not including them in your prior decision with regard to which signs stay and which go. Then you will ask the sign committee to give you recommendations as to your final decision in the matter."

Hood sputtered, "But, I've already made—"

"That's right, you did and by doing so, you've caused this whole damned mess. If you want to be a district ranger and a decent manager, involve your damned people."

He turned to Wetzel still standing. "Sit down, son." Wetzel sat.

"The problem with you two, as I see it, is you will never get along. You're about as far from peas and carrots as it gets." Carter scratched his thinning gray hair. "So here's the deal. Jack, you will have a letter of reprimand placed in your personnel folder for your actions in regard to this incident. If you so much as require my attention again in a personnel action, I'll fire you myself; is that *clear*!"

"Yessir."

"Good. If at the end of one year, you have behaved yourself, we will remove the letter from your personnel folder."

Carter looked at Ranger Hood. "Given that you two can't get along, and right now I badly need a Law Enforcement Officer here who knows the area, I'm re-assigning you to a new duty station. You have one week to make your apology and get your things together before heading to Beaverhead Ranger Station."

"*Beaverhead*? That's in the middle of nowhere, Warren."

"It's the only opening I have available, and you're not staying at the Wilderness District; is that *clear*!"

Hood nodded his drooping head, the thick rimmed glasses sliding down the bulbous nose.

Carter looked over at the human resources representative. "You capture all this?"

The man smiled. "Yes, I believe I have."

Carter stood. He looked squarely at each of the three men in the room. "Any questions?" No one spoke a word. "Good. Now get the hell outta here. I've got work to do."

CHAPTER SEVENTY-THREE

New Mexico State Policeman Steve Hunt maneuvered his personal pickup down the road; a new red 1973 Chevy he was very proud of. It was everything he had wanted in a personal rig except it wasn't four-wheel drive, but hell, he just couldn't afford that option and a two-wheel drive was all he really needed. As the headlights illuminated Highway 15, he passed through Pinos Altos and was amazed how much the town had grown with the discovery of gold. The town had extended south into the city limits of Silver City with houses, businesses, and bars.

He passed the small Catholic Church and headed up through the forest. The full moon provided enough light to allow a glimpse of Bear Canyon Lodge and some outbuildings a few miles farther into the forest of Ponderosa pines. A breeze cooled his face through opened windows.

Hunt did not wear his customary black hat and uniform, shoulder strap, black creased pants with stripes, and polished black boots. Instead he wore a T-shirt, jeans, cowboy boots and a ball cap with the insignia of a mustang and Western New Mexico University. However, he did carry a .357 revolver holstered on his belt and a backup .38 two-inch revolver on his ankle. He was to meet an informant who had called him earlier in the day about information regarding William Bonney's drug operation and plans of operation.

The man had advised Hunt to meet him at Copperas Vista parking area and to come alone at midnight when there would be little or no traffic. The man stated that he had important information for the NMSP Task Force of which Hunt was in charge.

Hunt descended to Sapillo Creek, ascended up the mountain, followed a small ridge line, and then began the greater ascent to Copperas Vista. He slowed, wary of an ambush, and turned his headlights on high beam. He unsnapped the keeper on his holster and withdrew the heavy revolver, laying it on the seat. At the vista pullout, he turned in and allowed his headlights to illuminate the full parking area. There were no vehicles parked in the lot. He slowly cruised through peering at the shadows in the trees on the down canyon side. Seeing nothing, he parked his truck on the north side, shut off the motor and lights, and with revolver in hand exited the vehicle.

Hunt moved quietly to the tree line for cover canvassing the landscape for something out of the ordinary. He paused beneath a ponderosa pine, listening intently, his eyes searching for movement. The clear sky sparkled full of stars and a half moon assisted in illuminating the terrain. He peered out in the eerie quietness from the vista vantage point toward the Gila Wilderness. It appeared to him as an endless space in the horizon, full of hills, valleys, the river below and the Mogollon Mountains in the far distance.

Hunt removed his cap with his left hand and stood in awe, allowing the breeze to pull at his short cropped sandy hair. He replaced the cap as he tried to remain vigilant, but thoughts of previous mountain men, prehistoric Indians, Apaches, and white settlers in the area clouded his mind. *Hell, Geronimo always bragged about being born at the headwaters of the Gila River.* What a country to behold! Thank God men like Aldo Leopold and others recognized the significance of the area and helped make it the first designated wilderness for future generations to appreciate and enjoy. He took a deep breath of fresh mountain air as his eyes strained to see the top of Mogollon Baldy far in the distance. It was one of the highest peaks in the wilderness and a fire lookout sat at the summit. He had camped just below the lookout one night a few years back, and it was one of the most miserable times in his life. A thunderstorm came in during the night with high, gusty winds and heavy downpour throughout the night. He, his horse and mule, all spent a restless night with no sleep.

As he stood there reflecting on the past, his ears picked up the sound of a vehicle approaching the vista. He moved quickly to squat down behind a large alligator juniper tree, revolver at the ready.

A car approached the parking area, slowed, but did not turn in as it continued past the overlook. It was a small green VW bug. He could not make out the driver or any occupants; the vehicle drove out of sight on Highway 15 headed north toward Gila Center and the Cliff Dwellings. Hunt stood, holstered his revolver but remained under cover of the juniper tree.

He stood there in the quiet and the darkness beneath the large tree with its sweeping branches extending outward and upward from the trunk. Maybe the informant wasn't coming. That thought provoked yet another thought which sent a chill up his spine. Was the informant compromised? Dead? Why would he not show as promised?

Again the sound of a vehicle interrupted his thoughts. It was coming from the north and as it rounded the curve, Hunt could see that it was the green VW bug. It slowed for the overlook parking lot, turned in and parked next to his red Chevy truck. The driver stepped out closing the door. The young man looked quickly in the interior of Hunt's truck then stepped in the shadows. He stood with his hand on a semi-auto handgun holstered on his right hip. He wore dark clothing, sunglasses tucked into the front collar of his T-shirt. Short cropped black hair covered a head that was held stationary momentarily to allow for listening intently for any sound. He stood thus for several moments.

"Steve?" he whispered softly into the night air. "Steve?" he asked again a trifle more loudly.

"Over here, Ramon." Hunt stepped out next to the big tree.

They met under the large juniper tree. Hunt shook hands with Grant County Deputy Sheriff Ramon Perez. "Everything okay?" He placed his hands on the shoulders of the lithe deputy sheriff. "Your cover's not blown, is it?"

Perez grinned. "Naw, Bonney thinks he's got law enforcement in his back pocket with the information I've given him."

"You be careful. Bonney's a mean son-of-a-bitch."

"He's a bad one for sure, but I was raised dealing with a much tougher crowd."

Hunt tucked his thumbs in his jeans pockets. "What's going on with Bonney and Pablo Enrique's crew at the Silver Cell Mine?"

"There's a drug war brewing, Steve. Bonney recently sustained a fairly serious wound to his right forearm and somehow lost several of his men. He blames Enrique's Silver Cell Mine bunch and plans to retaliate soon. He's got more soldiers coming in to help."

"Do you have a specific date?" asked Hunt.

"Unfortunately, no." Perez walked over to a boulder at the overlook and sat down. He looked at Hunt with his dark eyes squinting in the darkness. "However—"

Hunt folded his arms across his chest. "*What*?"

"He's upset with the Whippit family at Whiskey Creek and their sheepherder. I got the impression without asking too many questions that the Whippits had roughed up some of his men, and the old sheepherder may have as well."

"Does he plan to harm those folks?"

"Yes, this weekend; a night raid."

"My God." Hunt sat next to Perez.

Perez sighed. "I'll let you know the specifics when I get them, but you should alert your NMSP Task Force to be ready at a moment's notice. I'm afraid to notify the sheriff due to possible leaks in the department."

"Yeah, I need to warn the Whippits." Hunt thought a moment. "And get Wetzel and McMurtry on board and out there on-site. Damn it; this thing is spiraling out of control. A lot of folks could get hurt."

Deputy Sheriff Perez looked at him and nodded.

CHAPTER SEVENTY-FOUR

WILDLIFE OFFICER BOB MCMURTRY TOSSED FLAKES OF HAY TO HIS HORSES and mules at the Heart Bar Ranch. He sauntered over to the hunting dogs in the big barn a short distance from the headquarters buildings to feed them. Juanita hollered at him to come in for an important phone call. McMurtry grumbled as he finished feeding the dogs and walked the approximate 100 yards to the house. He tipped his old baseball cap back on his head and stuck his hands into the sides of his brown coveralls.

Stepping into the kitchen, McMurtry said, "Now Juanita, just what in tarnation is so dadjimmed important to pull me from the barn at feedin' time anyways."

His wife looked at him with hands on her hips, "Why don't you ask *Señor* Hunt with the New Mexico State Police what's so *dadjimmed* important?" She continued when he didn't answer her. "I hev supper ready so don't yew be such a grumble butt."

He grinned at his pretty wife and reached for her. "I'm shore sorry, honey bun."

Evading his grasp, she said, "Talk to *Señor* Hunt and wash up, *la comida* weel get cold." The hands went back on both hips. It was her turn to grin, "An' don't honey bun me, Roberto."

McMurtry found the telephone in the hallway and retrieved it. "Howdy, Steve."

"Howdy yourself, you ole hillbilly."

McMurtry laughed. "Now that's a high compliment coming from a state po-leece man."

"Mac, we're going to have trouble up at Whiskey Creek this weekend. I have good information that Bonney's bunch may attempt to harm the Whippit family. Can you get up there for a few days? Take your shotgun, rifle if you have one, and plenty of ammunition."

McMurtry leaned against the wall holding the phone close. "Did you get ahold o' Jack Wetzel?"

"Yes. He's already headed up there to stay the weekend."

"Okay. I'll head on over after supper."

"Thanks, Mac. I'll have the Task Force available to help. I don't know for sure if Bonney's bunch will show or when. We'll just have to cover the entire weekend."

"10-4." He hung up the phone on the wall and turned around just in time to have both boys each grab his legs.

Elfigo grinned as he looked up at McMurtry; his eyes wide he grasped his adopted father's leg tightly. His brother Jose held the other leg tightly with his head held close. "Hi, Daddy!"

McMurtry bent down and patted both boys on the head. "Wel-l-l, how are you boys doin' this fine evening?" He knelt down and hugged both of them. "We'd best git in there and eat afore your Maw comes after us with a rollin' pin."

The boys laughed and then ran into the dining room.

McMurtry stood there a moment peering out through the kitchen window. The darkness outside accentuated a dark mood enshrouding him as he thought of what might lie ahead for him and his family.

CHAPTER SEVENTY-FIVE

Jack Wetzel's green Forest Service truck bounced along the rough track in Whiskey Creek, over protruding rocks and deep erosion cuts in the road. Not being a county road, there was limited-to-no maintenance to provide some semblance of a smooth passage up the canyon. As he passed the Silver Cell Mine, he slowed to observe what appeared to be going on as he always did on his patrol in Whiskey Creek.

Wetzel observed numerous vehicles compared to past patrols; trucks, vans, as well as sedans parked at the mine. The increased activity made him to stop in the road and take note of several license plates displaying Texas registration. He reached over and retrieved a notebook to jot down the number of the closest vehicle plate. He paused to look up and see a man exit the mine office building and walk directly toward him. He laid the notebook in the passenger seat, watching carefully that the man did not have a weapon and that he kept his hands in full sight.

Wetzel exited his truck and stood waiting behind the cover of the truck door. He recognized the man as the alleged manager of the mine, Francisco Cordova. Cordova smiled as he approached, held out both arms with his palms open, "Ranger Wetzel, I believe. To what do we owe the pleasure of this visit?"

Wetzel tipped his Stetson back on his head with his thumb, and then placed both thumbs in his green jeans pockets. He grinned back at Cordova. "*Para servirle, Señor Cordova.*"

Cordova smiled broadly. "Ahh ... I wasn't aware you spoke Spanish."

"Just enough to get me in trouble, I reckon."

Cordova wet his lips and bit his lower lip. "I assure you, Ranger, you are in no danger; you will find no trouble here at the Silver Cell Mine."

Wetzel said nothing. He removed the pack of Lucky Strikes from his shirt pocket, shook two cigarettes out and offered one to Cordova, who reached out and took it.

"*Gracias.*"

Wetzel said nothing. He placed the second cigarette in his mouth, the pack back in his shirt pocket, retrieved his lighter, and lit Cordova's cigarette then his own. Cordova appeared to have recently sustained facial injuries. Wetzel drew deeply on his cigarette and removed it. "Just a routine patrol out here in the forest, *Señor* Cordova."

The cigarette returned to his lips, sat there precariously then moved slowly to the right side then back.

Both men smoked in silence, studying each other. Not in an aggressive, but rather a respectful manner. It was a bright sunny day with thin clouds sailing along in a blue New Mexico sky. A slight breeze rustled the leaves of a mountain mahogany shrub nearby.

Cordova's lips moved slightly, but he did not speak then he said, "May I make a ... recommendation for the Forest Service?"

Wetzel removed his cigarette. "The Forest Service is always interested in public input."

A smile began on Cordova's lips but then disappeared. "It has come to our attention ... to those of us here at the mine that the forest ... shall we say ... in *this vicinity* has become somewhat more dangerous." Cordova's dark eyes locked with Wetzel's.

He continued, "We at the mine request ... uh ... additional patrols from your agency— especially *at night*." Cordova drew smoke deeply into his lungs, blew it out slowly, the smoke wafting gently through the air. "And most importantly *this weekend*."

Wetzel dropped his cigarette and using the heel of his Packer boot extinguished it. He picked the butt up and placed it in his pocket. "Concern for the mine employees?"

Cordova smiled. "We can take care of ourselves, but there are *others* in the neighborhood who may be in danger of these … shall we say criminal elements."

Wetzel opened the door to this truck. "I'll be here, *Señor* Cordova." He stepped inside and closed the door. "All weekend."

Cordova nodded. "Say, hello, to my sheepherder friend." He turned abruptly and walked back to the mine office. Wetzel started up the truck and proceeded up the canyon, bouncing along over the rough terrain. Cordova's words hung in the hot summer air.

* * *

THE OLD MAN wiped perspiration from his brow as he brought the sheep in early from grazing. The sheep did not want to move, preferring to lay in the shade of the big ponderosa pine trees to escape the heat. The stock dogs proved their worth once again to the old man, who from months of experience, firmly believed in their importance. They nipped and harassed the sheep to get up and move in the right direction toward home.

Only when the last of the sheep had entered the corrals near his line shack did the old man relax enough to pet the stock dogs for their fine work in assisting him, sit on his porch, and drink from the old canvas covered canteen. He unslung the leather rifle sling from around his shoulders and leaned the rifle, a .30-.30 Winchester, beside him against one of the posts supporting the porch roof. He removed his backpack, heavy with all the extra ammunition he was carrying these days for the rifle. Reagan had never been one to not prepare for the worst to come in life. In this instance, he was very concerned about the lives of people he had come to know and deeply care about.

Removing his sweat-stained hat, he felt a cool breeze blow softly through his thinning hair. He sat there enjoying the solitude, the quiet, and the wonders of nature. Never in his entire life had he ever dreamed of such a place as this New Mexico wilderness, and being an integral part of it. Not only had he found a reason to live, but he was also thoroughly and completely enjoying his present life. He would help Lacey Whippit with the sheep as long as she wanted or needed his help, and he would protect her with every ounce of strength and ability he still had within his body.

He was aware that she and her brothers had found a large vein of gold within her father's old mine and one day she might leave this place for a life of luxury and travel. Reagan knew when that time came, if he were still alive, he would stay. He had already seen and done the other life and it was not to his liking. This stage in his life, living out here in God's own backyard was what life was all about for him. He had lost his family, committed atrocities for his government, and literally lost all meaning to life until the wilderness had claimed him. The cities, the corrupt people, the killings—all behind him now and he had no more taste for it. He shuddered as he thought of the issue at hand with Bonney. It clearly was not over for him, was it? He could leave this wonderful place that he had found, but where would he go? And what would happen to Lacey?

No, he could not leave, and he would do whatever was necessary to protect her. He had grown older and was not his former youthful self by any means, but he had actually grown stronger and fitter with the fresh air and exercise. He was still capable of killing men, if necessary, and without a doubt, it would come to that. He had no hard feelings toward Bonney one way or the other for what the man had tried to do to him; that was just business. But harming Lacey? Reagan would kill Bonney and anyone else without any hesitation if they attempted to harm the girl.

Sighing, the old man stood, stretched his aching limbs, replaced the backpack, slung the rifle over his shoulder, called his dogs and strode down the road toward the main ranch house. It was the beginning of a quiet evening, cooling down from the hottest part of the day. The smell of pine needles in the air caused him to pause and take in a deep breath of fresh mountain air.

CHAPTER SEVENTY-SIX

HELEN WETZEL EXITED HER PICKUP AFTER PARKING IT ALONGSIDE THE curb in front of the Palace Hotel near the intersection of Bullard Street and Broadway. She was to meet her friend, Bert Newell, a lawyer in town who had taken a romantic interest in her. They began their relationship durng the mitigation process of Juan Garcia' drug charges, the aftermath of his murder and his wife, and the subsequent adoption process for their son, Robbie. Helen appreciated the attention he always gave her. He had been very nice to her, but she had put a quick stop to his buying her expensive gifts, and he seemed to be jealous whenever another man spoke to her in his presence.

Robbie Garcia jumped out of the truck on the passenger side and closed the heavy door. He was five years old and very mature for his age. He smiled a happy face and helped Helen up on the steep sidewalk. She beamed at him. "Why, thank you, young man."

He replied, "You bet, Helen." He hitched up his new wrangler jeans she had purchased for him.

She laughed. "You *so* much remind me of Jackie at your age, Robbie."

The little boy's smile broadened on his face. He tipped his straw hat back on his head with his thumb. "I sure hope I can be as good a man as Jack Wetzel, ma'am."

Helen looked at the boy, a solemn look on her pretty face. "You're already there, Robbie." She placed a hand on his shoulder, steering him through the door into the hotel lobby.

The interior was dark in comparison to the bright sunlit exterior. As her eyes adjusted to the change in light, she saw Bert Newell with his back to her in a serious discussion with a big man who pointed his right forefinger in Newell's face. The man's dress differed from Newell's immaculate expensive suit, tie, and shoes. As Helen looked at the large man, a shiver ran down her spine. He wore dirty combat boots, worn and faded jeans, a black sweat stained t-shirt; his dark brown unkempt hair extended to his massive shoulders. A long scar on his face accentuated a growing ugliness about him. She heard the man say, "You better do your goddamn job or I'll cut your b---- off and toss 'em to my dogs."

The man noticed the woman and boy standing there; he pointed a threatening finger at them. "What the hell do *you* want?"

Shocked, Helen Wetzel's face reddened as she pushed Robbie behind her. Her voice rang out clearly. "I believe you need to watch your filthy language around children, mister."

The man stepped closer, his menacing face just inches away. He sneered. "Oh, you *do*? You know who *I* am?"

She looked directly into the fierce, blazing eyes and calmly said, "You're a loud-mouthed bully with filthy language, and you ought to be ashamed of yourself."

She saw Newell cringing behind the big man, saying nothing.

Robbie stepped around Helen Wetzel to stand by her side, hands on his hips. His angry expression was not lost on the big man. "You better apologize to Mrs. Wetzel, mister!"

The big man swung his full gaze to the boy who had challenged him. He grunted. "I don't apologize to anybody, you little shit. I'm William Bonney!"

Newell finally spoke from behind the big man, "Mr. Bonney—"

Bonney said over his shoulder, "Shut up!"

Helen Wetzel turned abruptly, taking Robbie by the shoulders, to leave the room.

Bonney moved quickly; he grabbed her and shoved her along with Robbie against the wall. His fiendish face with clenched jaws jutted out inches from Helen Wetzel's face. "By God, you'll apologize *to me*."

Helen Wetzel had never been more afraid in her entire life. She was paralyzed and unable to move or speak.

The big man grasped her blouse and raised her off the floor. His eyes wide, drool ran from the corner of his mouth and down his chin. "Let me hear you say, '"Ple-e-e-se, Mister Bonney, I am *so* sorry. I apologize.'" Bonney was so intent on his speech that he did not hear someone step into the lobby from the side entrance.

Bonney pulled Helen Wetzel close to him next to his ear. "*What's that*? I can't hear you. Cat got your tongue, missy?"

Strong hands took hold of Bonney from behind, jerking him around. Helen dropped to the floor and stared. A strong hard fist hit him in the face, knocking him backward toward the hotel desk. He landed on his back and slid against the desk. Grant County Chief Deputy Sheriff Don Ramirez stood tall over the man. Helen had known Ramirez since he was a boy and friend to her son Jack. Ramirez's bulging biceps strained at his uniform shirt sleeves, and thick strong legs supported a fit, stocky frame.

Bonney leaned forward, blood running down his face from a broken nose. He reached for the bulge at his ankle under his right pant leg. Ramirez's right hand went to his service revolver. "That's right, Bonney. Go for it!"

Bonney hesitated.

Ramirez unsnapped the keeper to his holster. "Go on, dammit. Pull that pistol, you son-of-a-bitch!"

Bonney sat back against the desk, hands away from the concealed weapon on his ankle.

Ramirez stepped forward, jerked Bonney onto his stomach and handcuffed him behind his back. Then he searched him, finding a knife as well as the small revolver in an ankle holster. Breathing hard, he said, "You're under arrest for assault and disturbing the peace."

He turned to Helen Wetzel. "I'm sorry I didn't get here sooner, Mrs. Wetzel." He looked from her to Robbie and back. "Are you okay? Did he hurt you?"

Newell stepped up from where he had been hiding against a back wall. "Yes, Helen. Are you all right?"

She slapped him hard across the face. "I don't want to *ever* see your cowardly face again."

"B-but—" he stammered.

Ramirez said curtly, "You heard her. Now get out."

Newell shuffled out the door to the street.

Helen Wetzel said nothing for a few moments, and then took a deep breath. "Jackie told me Newell was no good." She shrugged, "I don't know what I was thinking, Don. I should have listened and known better."

Ramirez turned toward his prisoner, "Now you know, ma'am. That's all that matters and that you and Robbie weren't seriously hurt."

Helen Wetzel looked at Robbie and smiled. "Thanks for standing up for me, Robbie."

Robbie held the door for her as they exited the hotel. "I had to do something; Jack wasn't here."

The bright sun caused them both to squint as they walked to the parked pickup truck. They got in, closed the doors. Helen Wetzel started the engine and then turned to the boy. "It's not *what* you did, son. It's that you did *something*."

The boy pushed his straw hat back on his head with his thumb and grinned, "Maybeso."

CHAPTER SEVENTY-SEVEN

In the western sky, soft, billowy clouds transformed slowly from white to pink then red portraying a landscape of such beauty that Wetzel had to stop the truck on the rough road in Whiskey Creek and gaze in wonderment at the picturesque scene.

As he watched the sun descend below the horizon, he continued up the canyon, rounded the last curve in the rough road and pulled to a stop in front of the rock house nestled in among a stand of ponderosa pine trees. He reached over and retrieved his .30-.30 Winchester rifle and a box of ammunition from the passenger seat.

The old man sat on the porch steps, his .30-.30 rifle leaning against a porch support post, his hat lying next to him. His green eyes twinkled and a smile formed on his bearded face as he watched him approach. "How the heck are you, Jack?"

Wetzel grinned and sat next to him on the porch as the evening shadows lengthened. He set his rifle and ammunition down and shook hands with the old man. "I'm fine, Mr. Reagan. Reckon I'll camp out here for the weekend if it's okay with Lacey."

"She's always happy when you visit, Jack."

Jack's face blushed warm as he withdrew a pack of Lucky Strikes from his shirt pocket, shook a cigarette out and lit it. The old man looked at him thoughtfully for a moment without speaking. "You know, Jack, you look more like your father each day."

Smoke drifted lazily from Wetzel's nose. "Thank you, Mr. Reagan. That's a real compliment in my book."

The old man leaned forward, a solemn look on his face. "Are you here because of a threat from William Bonney?"

"I am. According to sources, he'll try something this weekend."

The old man frowned. "What does *something* mean?"

"It means harm, maybe death to you, Lacey, her brothers, and anyone else in the way, I reckon."

Silence.

The old man said, "I'm not surprised, but I was hoping it would not be so. Bonney's a mad animal who does not think things through."

"What do you think he'll do, Mr. Reagan? What do *we* need to do?"

The conversation was interrupted at the sound of a motor vehicle, and then headlights appeared up the road toward the house. Both men scrambled for their rifles and cover behind porch supports.

The pickup parked next to Wetzel's ranger truck and lights were extinguished. Wetzel recognized it as the New Mexico Game and Fish truck belonging to Wildlife Officer Bob McMurtry. The driver door creaked open with fast food cups and wrappers falling out onto the ground. McMurtry stepped out. "Howdy, men!"

Dressed in camouflage coveralls, a faded baseball cap with "Vols" embroidered on it perched on his head with unkempt hair protruding from underneath, McMurtry wore a leather shoulder holster encasing a stainless four-inch .357 S&W revolver. He stepped back to retrieve a .223 Ruger Mini-14 rifle with two twenty-round magazines taped together, one upside down from the other.

As he trudged up to the porch, the other two men met him on the steps.

"Howdy yourself, Mac." Wetzel's eyes twinkled.

"Mr. McMurtry, how are you?" asked the old man.

McMurtry beamed. "Fit as a fiddle, fellers." He shook hands all around. "Thet little gal got any coffee for us?"

The old man said, "I'll fix us a pot; come on inside. Lacey will be back with her brothers shortly."

Wetzel followed everyone inside and placed his rifle and ammunition near the front door with the other men's armaments and gear. The old man made coffee while the other two men sat at the old wooden table. McMurtry sat at the end and casually placed his boots up on the table. "Well, Jack boy, we goin' to have a bunch o' pot smokin' druggies up heah tryin' to cause us problems?"

"Sounds like Bonney's bunch have it in for the Whippits, and as I understand it, for Mr. Reagan as well." Wetzel leaned back in his chair.

McMurtry shifted his gaze to the old man. "What are them boys so mad at you fer anyways?"

Reagan walked to the table and sat across from Wetzel. "I caused problems for some of his men at a recent encounter."

"Problems? What the hell can an ole sheepherder do to cause problems?" asked McMurtry.

Wetzel leaned forward and placed his elbows on the table. "Mac, Mr. Reagan is not … quite what he appears to be."

McMurtry removed his boots from the table to Wetzel's relief. "Uh huh." He locked eyes with Reagan.

Reagan said, "What Jack is trying to say is that I'm rather new at this sheepherder business."

"Uh huh. Just exactly what *have* you been doin', old man?"

"Working for the government … the CIA."

"You woolin' me?"

"No sir. I spent a life time in the military and most recently the CIA. I had an altercation about a week ago with Mr. Bonney and friends not far from here."

"Fight, eh? McMurtry's eyes beamed.

"Yes. I'm afraid I had to kill several of his men."

McMurtry slammed his hand on the table. "I'll be dadjimmed. If thet don't beat all."

Wetzel interjected, "And several months ago, one of Lacey's brothers ran into some of Bonney's men. He got the drop on them, had them disrobe, and then chased them down the mountain."

McMurtry chuckled. "I ain't surprised. Them mountain boys are tough, an' they don't take kindly to bein' shoved around."

The coffee pot finished perking. The old man got up, found three tin cups, and filled them with hot coffee. "I've thought about the threat and how to handle it if both of you are interested in what I have to say."

Wetzel straightened in his chair. "We're interested, Mr. Reagan."

"Please, call me Dan."

"Tell us what you've got in mind, Dan," replied Wetzel. McMurtry nodded as Reagan handed each of them a cup of coffee and sat down.

Reagan sipped at the hot cup. "I figure he'll come when we'd not expect it, most likely in the early morning hours when we're most vulnerable to attack." He looked intently at the two men sitting at the table. "He'll feint an attack on most likely the front of the house, and then send his main force in from the back in overwhelming numbers while maintaining an attack on the entire perimeter."

Wetzel blew on his coffee then sipped it. "How many men will he have for Pete's sake?"

"More than we can handle if we do this wrong," said Reagan. "My guess is if he doesn't finish us off in the initial assault, he'll employ a sniper during the day to reduce our numbers and keep us from getting any rest or sleep."

McMurtry drank the scalding coffee with some difficulty and cleared his throat. "Then we'd best figger out what *we're* gonna do to even the odds."

"I have a plan; when Lacey and the boys return, I'll go over it in detail. Then all of you can decide if it's what you want to do."

Wetzel spoke up, "Will they have automatic weapons."

The old man nodded, "But we should have the element of surprise and—" His green eyes twinkled beneath shaggy brows. "And we have the advantage of being expert marksmen, do we not, gentlemen?"

His face sobered. "When you think about, it only takes *one* well-placed shot to kill a man. Automatic fire is over rated in my opinion."

McMurtry nodded as he gulped more hot coffee. "Should we set up for them tonight?"

Reagan rubbed his beard. "The source said weekend; however, that being said, one of us should be awake and armed at all times. I'll volunteer for duty tonight. Everyone else can get some sleep in preparation for the entire weekend."

CHAPTER SEVENTY-EIGHT

THE OLD MAN'S SHEEPDOGS INTERRUPTED THEIR CONVERSATION. NOT prone to barking, they emitted deep growls to inform those inside the house that someone was nearing their location. Reagan quickly extinguished the light in the kitchen and listened intently.

He turned the light back on. "It's Lacey and the boys."

Moments later, the kitchen door opened; Lacey Whippit stepped into the light with her two brothers in tow. She wore a dust-covered denim blouse, blue jeans and boots. Her brown hair pulled back in a ponytail was also covered in dust. The Whippit boys wore faded and patched coveralls, dirty as usual from working the mine. Larrimore, determined as such from his twin brother by his hairline cowlick, crowded in past Lacey. He tucked his hands in his coveralls. "What's the occasion, boys? Somebody's birthday?"

Lacey placed her hands on her hips. "Lattimore, git them extra chairs from the porch." As he did as bidden, Lacey smiled at Wetzel, the old man and McMurtry. "Thank you all for coming. I haven't told the boys everything. We locked up the mine the best we could for the weekend."

Reagan smiled. "No worries about the mine, girl. We have our health and safety to be concerned about this weekend."

Everyone sat down and a brief discussion ensued describing the situation and how to best handle it. The Whippit brothers listened intently and said nothing.

The old man detailed the plan he had devised for the next two days. The two Whippit brothers would each melt into the woods early in the morning before dawn, one down the road to the front of the house, the other in the opposite direction to the rear of the house. The dogs would remain on the porch as vigil there. Wetzel and McMurtry would cover the rear of the house with the old man and Lacey covering the front.

Reagan paused and rubbed his whiskers thoughtfully; the room was silent, each person with his own thoughts. "Although our main concern is the early morning hours, if this situation is prolonged, I'm concerned about sniper activity during the day. We must keep under cover and out of sight."

McMurtry spoke up. "What 'bout these Whippit boys bein' out there in the thick of it and by their lonesome?"

Larrimore grinned with a wad of tobacco in his mouth. "Don't you worry none 'bout me and Lattimore, Mister Game Warden. Won't nobody be sneakin' up on us. We was born in the woods."

Lattimore slapped McMurtry on the shoulder. "Like as not, it'll be *us* sneakin' up on them tothers."

Reagan nodded. "They're best suited outside, free to roam; better for them and for all of us. Jack, phone Steve Hunt. Let him know what we've planned."

Lacey stood. "Aw 'ight then. I'll rustle us up some supper."

Wetzel walked over to the telephone sitting on a small end table next to the couch. He picked up the receiver to dial out. No dial tone. He punched the button several times. The line was dead. They were on their own.

Reagan looked across the room at him. His voice was calm. "They've cut the line?"

Wetzel nodded.

"Then a change of plan for us. They'll be coming soon … maybe early morning." He shrugged his shoulders. "May as well get it over and done with."

McMurtry walked into the kitchen. "Lacey, do you'ins have candles or an oil lamp when y'all lose power?"

She nodded and pointed toward a kitchen drawer. McMurtry

found candles, lit two of them, set them up in small saucers from the kitchen cabinet, and then turned the lights off inside the house.

They all ate supper in silence. Afterward, each of them tended to their weapons and ammunition. One by one, everyone but Reagan retired for the night to get a few hours rest. Wetzel spread blankets Lacey had given him on the living room floor. McMurtry lay on the couch, and the Whippit boys soon disappeared into their bedroom.

Lacey approached Wetzel. "Jack ... I ... uh, can I speak with you please?"

Wetzel stood. "Sure, Lacey."

She took his hand and pulled him into her bedroom and closed the door. She pulled him close. "Oh Jack, what's happenin' to us? My God!"

He held her close; a lump appeared in his throat. He couldn't speak so he just hugged her more tightly. "We'll be allright."

She peered up at him in the darkness. "I don't want anything to happen to you."

He kissed her, hugged her again more tightly. "I'll be fine, Lacey. You just keep your head down."

"The gold mine, Jack, we've struck it rich. If something should happen to me and mah brothers, I want you to have it all."

Wetzel laughed. "First of all, nothing's going to happen to you. I'll make sure of that." He held her by her slim shoulders. "What would someone like me do with money? I've never wanted to be rich."

"Aw 'ight then, give it away. But it's yours," she said.

"We'll talk about it later. Get some rest; it'll be a long day for us."

She pulled him to her and kissed him. "I love you, Jack Wetzel."

"I love you, too." He turned and walked back into the living room. His heart thumped so loudly in his chest he thought someone would surely hear it, but McMurtry was snoring loudly on the couch.

Wetzel lay in his blankets as darkness settled around him. He closed his eyes, but he could not sleep. The nightmares from the Vietnam War returned. He couldn't rid the image of the North Vietnamese soldier running at him, the sharp bayonet gleaming in the moonlight, the explosions, the screams of badly wounded soldiers, and the terror of a night he would never forget for the rest of his life.

He sat up hands trembling, his heart thumping in his chest. Closing his eyes tightly, he recalled a prayer from the early days of his childhood:

Saint Michael the Archangel, defend us in battle; be our protection against the wickedness and snares of the devil …

He hesitated, searching for the words of long ago. Maybe somehow with God's help, he could defeat the awful nightmares and fear from the war. *I'm not afraid of dying so what is it that I am afraid of? Failing? Failing what?* Wetzel had always believed in God, but he had not been someone to attend church on a regular basis. And he felt religion was a very personal relationship between a person and God, not to be touted in front of everyone at church to impress others.

An owl hooted in the distance behind the house; a coyote howled mournfully in the still night and was answered by yet another farther up the header canyon of Whiskey Creek. Wetzel lay back on his blankets, the trembling ceased. He closed his eyes; he felt at peace with himself and what was about to happen. A smile curled at the corners of his mouth, and then disappeared as sleep overtook him.

CHAPTER SEVENTY-NINE

WETZEL WAS AWAKENED BY A SOFT HAND ON HIS SHOULDER. MOONLIGHT shone in through the windows arching across the old man's features. Reagan smiled. "It's time, Jack." The cabin's interior was darkened, but Wetzel could see McMurtry was up tending to his rifle at the table. He stood, stretched his slender frame, and walked to where his rifle was leaning against the wall near the rear door. He picked it up and worked the lever action loading a round in the chamber, released the hammer gently, and loaded an additional .30-.30 shell into the magazine tube. Reaching down, he withdrew the .357 revolver from its holster, opened the cylinder and checked the six rounds of hollow point ammunition. He spun the cylinder closed, holstered the firearm, and ensured the two speed loaders on his leather belt were also fully loaded.

Next, he stuffed as many .30-.30 shells in the back pockets of his green jeans as he could. He walked to the table where McMurtry, the old man, and Lacey sat. In a hushed tone, he asked where the two Whippit brothers were.

The old man answered softly, "Went out two hours ago."

Wetzel nodded, smiled at Lacey, and headed to the coffee pot.

The sheep dogs uttered deep growls from the front porch.

Everyone stopped what they were doing.

Silence.

The old man motioned everyone down on the floor and to their positions. The dogs growled again.

Suddenly, a voice said, "He-ll-o, the house; anyone home?"

Silence. The voice spoke again, more loudly, "Anyone there?"

The old man motioned for Lacey to answer as he peered out the corner of the front window. A man stood just below the steps of the porch, dressed in a blue T-shirt, blue jeans, and a red ballcap.

Lacey switched the porch light on and dropped to the floor. "What do ya want?"

The man shielded his eyes from the light with his left hand; his right hand remained along his leg. "My car broke down. Can I use your phone to call for help?"

"Sorry, cain't help ya. Haven't had phone service fer months." Lacey immediately rolled over to where the old man was positioned.

Reagan peeked out the window. The man stood there momentarily, as if unsure of what to do. His eyes concentrated on the location where Lacey had been speaking from. Suddenly he reached behind his back, displayed a handgun, and began shooting into the house. He stood blazing away until a single rifle shot resounded in the darkness, and his head exploded; the man teetered forward and fell to the ground. Reagan muttered, *"Larrimore! What a shot!"*

Momentary silence. Then other unseen men began yelling in dismay, questioning what had occurred. The old man turned to Lacey. "When you fire, fire multiple rounds, and then move! If they're smart, they'll zero in on our muzzle flashes." They each aimed their rifles toward the front yard, illuminated by the porch light. A burst of rifle fire shattered the light and the porch and front yard returned to a darkened state with only moonlight to discern the scene.

Wetzel clutched his rifle as he flattened himself on the kitchen floor next to McMurtry. *If the old man is right, the main concentrated attack will be to our position.*

His thoughts were interrupted by a heavy broadside of automatic fire on the front of the house. Endless bullets ripped through the side of the house, breaking windows, pictures, lamps, tearing into furniture, some continuing through the house breaking the kitchen windows to the rear. The barrage thundered as it pounded the cabin without mercy. Wetzel's ears were deafened by the ensuing exchange of gunfire.

Then silence. It was so quiet that it seemed eerie to Wetzel. He wanted to scream with the built-up adrenaline in his system.

During a lull, Reagan asked if everyone inside the cabin was all right. Each stated they were okay.

Calmly, he said, "They'll try to take the front, and then their main force to the rear." He looked over at Lacey. "Crawl to the back and help the boys." She just looked at him, her eyes wide. He smiled. "Go on now; they'll need your help. I'll be fine here." Nodding, she crawled slowly to the rear of the house, dragging her rifle with her.

Outside the sharp crack of a rifle shot, and then another followed by angry yelling. "Get that son-of-a-bitch! Kill 'im!" Multiple shots followed then additional single rifle shots. Wetzel grinned. *Larrimore is picking them off one at a time.*

The old man interrupted Wetzel's thoughts as he opened up with three well-placed shots from from his rifle through the front window to the left of the door. He rolled on the floor to the window on the right side and fired three more times. Men screamed. Bullets ripped through an already shredded wall in the front of the house.

Suddenly Wetzel heard two distinct rifle shots to the rear of the house with grunts, and then a thump of bodies hitting the ground. He rose to his knees along with McMurtry and peered out through the shattered window. At least a dozen men converged on the house, carrying shotguns and rifles. Their forward progress was stopped as two of the men lay dead on the ground. Wetzel lined his sights on the nearest man and fired. As that man fell, he levered another round in the chamber, and fired dropping another. He vaguely heard McMurtry firing his Mini-14 rifle next to him till his magazine emptied.

Wetzel quickly dropped down behind the kitchen sink and scrambled to reload his .30-.30 rifle. His peripheral vision caught McMurtry yank an empty magazine from the magazine well, flip it upside down and insert the other twenty-round magazine. In the same instant the kitchen door flew open, with a man firing an automatic weapon on full auto sweeping the room. A shot from Lacey's rifle knocked him backwards. Wetzel finished loading the magazine tube and levered a shell into the chamber as several additional men stormed the house through the kitchen door. Others fired through the kitchen window from outside.

Bullets whistled past his head and embedded in the walls and wooden floor as Wetzel and the others returned fire. Wetzel heard

McMurtry grunt in pain. Sliding over in front of Lacey, he dropped an empty rifle and drew his .357 S&W revolver shooting yet another man entering the house. Bodies piled up inside and just outside the kitchen door, one atop another. The shooting paused momentarily; smoke hung in the air. He motioned for Lacey to remain with McMurtry, who was reloading his magazines.

Wetzel crawled to the door, over the bodies to the exterior. He rose quickly and ran to cover behind a nearby boulder. He espied a group of men a short distance away talking excitedly to a large man in a black t-shirt with hair to his shoulders. *Bonney!*

A savage rage roared within Wetzel. He rose from behind the boulder and strode toward the men, firing, dropping one then two, three men. His revolver clicked on an empty cylinder. Breaking open the cylinder, he dumped the shell casings, reached for a speed loader, reloaded, snapped the cylinder to, and brought the revolver up as a bullet struck his right side. The hot searing pain and force of the blow knocked him down. He saw Bonney turn away as the men rushed toward him, shooting. A bullet hit his left arm, another grazed his head. Blood poured down his face into his eyes. Wetzel could just barely see the two lead men approaching him hesitate, the first one fell, and then the second stood still. *McMurtry?*

No sooner than the thought of McMurtry helping him occurred, Wetzel observed an arrow protruding from the second man's chest just before he collapsed to the ground. Two other men were impaled with arrows. The onslaught of men to Wetzel's position wavered, broke, and then retreated from the house toward cover in the trees. As they ran, two other men went down with arrows in their backs.

As he attempted to sit up, Wetzel saw a man in black clothing kneeling beside him. He had not heard the man approaching. The man set his bow and quiver of arrows on the ground, and calmly said, "Do me a favor, Wetzel; don't shoot me. I'm a friend of Reagan's."

Wetzel looked incredulously at this man who had saved his life. The dark face looked familiar to him. The man wore a black shirt, black camo pants and black military boots. He carried a pistol belt, a bandolier of rifle rounds and rifle strapped to his back. Where had he seen him before? "Who ... *are* you?"

The man in black picked up his bow and quiver of arrows. Then he helped Wetzel up without answering. "We've got to make a run to the cabin if we're going to live. Can you do that?"

"Yes."

The man in black held him upright in a tight, strong grip as they rushed toward the cabin. They almost made it to the door before the shooting began again. Bullets zipped past them and splintered wood over the door frame. The man shoved Wetzel roughly inside ahead of him. Wetzel heard the sound of a bullet solidly striking the other man as he entered the cabin.

CHAPTER EIGHTY

THE MAN IN BLACK GRUNTED AS A SHARP PAIN SHOT THROUGH HIM. He shrugged it off as he called out tentatively, "Danny?" He dropped to the floor as a rain of gunfire came in through the kitchen window throwing splinters of glass shards into the interior. He peered into the smoke filled, debris strewn room. "Danny Reagan?" he asked more assertively.

A soft voice near the front door answered him. "Tomás?"

McMurtry struggled to his feet, his rifle extended forward. "Just who the hell are *you*?" His gaze had a hint of recognition in it.

Wetzel said, "I don't know Mac, but he saved my life just now, and he knows Mr. Reagan."

"The hell ya say," returned the wildlife officer. "He's the sumbitch who tried to kill me when I was trackin' him up from the river, Jack. Damn near made me look like a porcupine."

"Get down, Mac!" Wetzel rolled toward McMurtry and pulled him down to the floor. Another rain of gunfire tore through the kitchen interior.

The man in black crawled to Reagan, laying his bow and arrows on the floor. "You all right, Danny?"

The old man coughed. "I've … been better."

"You hit?"

"I got clipped a couple of times."

In the moonlight, the man in black noted the pile of bodies on the front porch and in the yard. "You've been busy, Danny."

The old man laughed and then coughed, blood spilling from his mouth onto his white beard.

The man in black unslung the rifle from his shoulders, set it next to him, and then leaned against the wall facing the old man. "I would have been here sooner, but they attacked the Silver Cell Mine when they hit you."

"Why did you come, Tomás? You don't owe … anyone here … anything." The old man coughed again. "Any debt you … may have ever felt you owed *me* … has been paid long ago."

Silence.

Tomás leaned in closely to Reagan and spoke softly in his ear, "You're the *only* real friend I ever had, Danny."

Then he moved along the floor on hands and knees, grunting as he did so. A trail of blood followed him as he moved. From the center of the room, he spoke. "How many do we have who can fight?"

Lacey spoke up from the corner below the kitchen counter. "Ah reckon I can, mister."

The man in black gazed at the slender woman with the pony tail. "You the Whippit girl?"

"Uh huh."

"Those boys outside … they your brothers?"

"Uh huh."

Silence.

"They're down. Didn't make it."

"Oh, my God," whispered Lacey.

Wetzel crawled over to her and held her tightly as she sobbed uncontrollably.

McMurtry said, "Count *me* in." A bloody handkerchief covered his lower leg below the knee.

Wetzel sighed deeply and flinched as a searing pain shot through his bloodied right side. He wiped at blood running down his face from a scalp wound with his right hand; his left arm hung useless by his side, a trickle of blood dripped to the floor. "Me, too."

The man in black grinned, just for second, his white teeth gleaming in the pale moonlight. It seemed unnatural for him. "They'll be coming at us with everything they have now. Bonney has to finish this and get the hell out." Tomás advised each of them what their assignments were; everyone nodded in agreement.

* * *

THE MAN in black sat up crossing his legs. A sharp pain ran through his back; he clenched his teeth and swallowed hard. *They've done well against overwhelming odds. Danny's right. I owe no one. I've always made it a point to never owe anyone for anything. So why the hell did I come up to the cabin? Why? And why not kill the boy when ordered to do so?*

The answer was simple. He had come to help his only friend in life. He had never felt obligated to help anyone except his brother who had died years ago. He had lived his entire life by impulses, gut feelings, intuition, and it had served him well. He was still alive wasn't he? He had killed men and women over the years without remorse, but he had always held the line at killing children.

He crawled back over to the old man near the front door. Using his rifle butt he knocked out the remaining window frame and glass, and then quickly rolled to the old man. His action brought swift rifle fire through the window.

"Still with me, Danny boy?"

The old man sighed then coughed up red blood. "Not ... much ... help, Tomás. I think they nicked a lung."

"Hang in there. I've seen you in far worse condition."

Reagan laughed. "I was a lot younger back then."

"I need your cover fire, Danny. Are you loaded and ready?"

The old man grimaced as he struggled to a sitting position at the corner of the window. "I am."

The man in black peered through the smoke-filled room at Wetzel and McMurtry. "If Bonney escapes, you'll have to track him down and kill him. If you don't, he'll be back."

McMurtry said, "Don't you want him?"

Tomás lowered his head. "I've seen both of you track." He winced at the sharp pain in his back. "I may have something else more important to do."

"If he gets past you, Tomás," replied Wetzel, "We'll get him."

The man in black nodded and touched the old man's shoulder.

"Maybe I'll see you at the Lambent Pass, eh, Danny boy?" Not waiting for an answer, he nodded to the old man, who began firing rapidly. Tomás slipped out and disappeared into an inky darkness that sporadically lit up with muzzle flashes.

CHAPTER EIGHTY-ONE

THE MAN IN BLACK PUSHED THE BODY OF A DEAD MAN FROM THE PORCH IN front of him as he crawled on his belly toward the end of the porch. Bullets thudded into the body shielding him and whizzed over his head. Reaching the end of the porch, he dropped flat to the ground, lay there among the dead, listening intently as his eyes adjusted to the darkness.

When the firing lessened, Tomás crawled again silently through the dead bodies littering the front yard. He clutched an automatic pistol in each hand, a silencer attached to the end of each muzzle. Hearing the sound of voices in the distance, he visually located the position and moved stealthily in that direction, pausing every so often, listening, straining his eyes to see, but ever so carefully, so as to not allow his adversaries knowledge of the impending danger.

He crawled noiselessly to within a few yards of four men who stood holding automatic rifles pointed at a fifth man with his hands held over his head. One of the men spoke. "You're a goddammed undercover cop! I trusted you ... you son-of-a-bitch." The man in black recognized the voice of William Bonney.

The man with raised hands replied calmly, "Bonney, you actually *believe* that?"

"Goddamned right, I believe it!"

"You're misinformed."

The man in black listened intently to the voice of the man with raised hands. *That voice? Where have I heard that voice? Back in my past … but when?*

Without warning Bonney struck the man with his rifle butt, knocking him to the ground. Then he fired three rounds from his rifle into the prostrate form on the ground.

Instinctively, Tomás stood and methodically shot each of the men. No sound other than a quiet, muffled response from the silencer; one head exploded in a red mist then another before the third man turned and looked quizzically at the man in black yards away. Then he, too, died instantly, shot between the eyes.

Tomás dropped to the ground as Bonney spread automatic fire in his direction. Then he fired hurriedly at Bonney, who had turned and fled. He sprang forward in pursuit. "Turn and fight; damn you, *culero!*"

He lept over the prostrate form of the man Bonney had just executed. As he did, he heard the man say weakly, "Tomás?"

The man in black hesitated, shifting his pistols toward a possible new threat. He moved cautiously toward the inert form of the fallen man. He knelt down and searched for weapons, finding one in an ankle holster. He tossed the .38 revolver into the darkness.

He looked impatiently in the direction where Bonney had fled, and then leaned forward trying to ascertain who it was that lay dying. A sharp pain tore through his torso. The face looked familiar somehow to him. "Who are you?" he asked sharply.

The man whispered, "I … am … Ramon …" He struggled to speak. "Perez … Ramon Perez … *your brother*, Tomás."

The man in black strained his eyes to see who said such outrageous things. *My brother is dead! Murdered, poisoned by an old woman, the bruja, the witch.*

He dropped the pistols, and carefully, he raised the man's head closer to him. He locked eyes with the man. *Ramon! My brother … is alive?* Tomás uttered a strangled reply, "Ramon? Is it you, *hermano*?" Not waiting for an answer, he said, "*My God!* He looked deeply into the man's dying face. "It *is* you."

Ramon whispered, "*Sí, es verdad.*"

"I've got to get you medical attention … get help."

"I'm almost bled out ... too late." Ramon raised his head closer.

"But ... but ... you were poisoned by Doña Consuelo Vasquez and drowned in the river."

"No. She had nothing to do with it. Pablo Enrique ... ordered my killing. To be carried out by ... Carlos."

"What?"

"The current carried me ... down the river several miles ... I was found and ... lived for another day."

Silent, Tomás thought of his reluctance earlier to intervene before Bonney shot the man who turned out to be his brother. And he had killed the old woman thinking she had murdered his brother. He clung tightly to Ramon as he remembered the old woman saying, "I tried to protect your brother and you from the *brujo* you work for." Then he had shot her dead. Pablo had lied to him!

"I became a cop, Tomás." Ramon tried to laugh, but it hurt too much. "And a damned good one, too."

Tomás wept bitterly as he held his brother tightly. He felt the life slowly ebb from Ramon's body. He failed to notice the shooting had stopped, sirens were screaming up from the canyon below, and to observe a tall, slender man approach him from the cabin.

Wetzel's head and face were covered in dried blood, his left arm bloody and hanging uselessly at his side, his right side and leg covered in blood. He stood, swaying slightly, trying to understand what had transpired prior to his appearance.

"Tomás?" he asked tentatively as he holstered the .357 revolver.

The man in black looked through him at ... nothing. Gently laying his brother's head on the pine needled forest floor, he stood.

His head cleared, and he quickly returned to operational mode. He noticed the darkness fading as the gray dawn of a new day took over. He looked at Wetzel and pointed in the direction Bonney had fled.

"He ran that way just moments ago." Reaching down, he retrieved the two pistols with silencers, and then gave the fully loaded one to Wetzel. "Track and kill him."

"What about you?"

"No, you take him, Wetzel. I have something else to do that can't wait."

Tomás looked one last time at his brother, sighed, and disappeared into the forest. The lead state police vehicle burst into sight, siren blasting, emergency lights flashing. It screeched to a halt, and SWAT team members spilled out.

Wetzel heard Steve Hunt calling his name. Not answering, he veered toward the direction that William Bonney had fled. He reckoned it was light enough to track the criminal.

CHAPTER EIGHTY-TWO

WETZEL IMMEDIATELY FOUND SIGN OF BONNEY'S HURRIED DEPARTURE—upturned and disturbed pine needles and duff on the forest floor. The trail led him for approximately a quarter mile through open ponderosa pine woodland, and then ascended a ridge where the disturbance became much easier to follow as it appeared Bonney had run directly uphill at that point.

At the ridge top, Wetzel knelt briefly and carefully surveyed the scene in front of him. The sky opened up from pale gray dawn to a bright blue, cloudless sky. Warm sunlight streamed onto the forest floor through the pine tree canopy. Wetzel lay the pistol down and pushed his Stetson back on his head with his thumb. Moments passed. He saw no movement or anything out of the ordinary in the woodland scene before him. The disturbed sign indicated that Bonney had followed the ridge east as it paralleled the larger Whiskey Creek below it to the south.

Wetzel worried that Bonney had a rifle, and he had only handguns. There was nothing he could do about it other than being aware that ambush from a distance was a real possibility. His gaze swept the country ahead of him to ascertain movement or anything out of the ordinary. Seeing nothing, he retrieved the pistol and stood. A wave of dizziness and nausea flooded through him momentarily, but then subsided. His head ached, his left arm was useless, his right side hurt uncontrollably and was bleeding again, but he somehow willed himself to continue.

The sign continued along the ridge on its ascent toward the head of Whiskey Creek. Wetzel breathed heavily as he strode along, the sign now somewhat more difficult to follow. Then abruptly, Bonney had dropped off the ridge into the adjacent smaller canyon to the north. Wetzel reckoned this drainage led back to the Silver Cell Mine and eventually the highway.

Wetzel made the decision to climb the next adjacent ridge and get above the obvious trail down the smaller canyon taken by Bonney. He reasoned that if Bonney decided to climb out of the canyon he had chosen to descend, it would most likely be this second ridge away from Whiskey Creek and law enforcement. He had a difficult time climbing the ridge but made it, out of breath, weak and trembling. Leaning against a tree he peered down into the canyon below hoping to see the retreating form of William Bonney, but he did not.

Wetzel started down the ridgeline, stopping often to listen and observe. Continuing for several hundred yards, he again leaned against a tree and waited. Suddenly, a covey of quail erupted from the quiet scene below. He pinpointed the location in his mind—a large alligator juniper tree and a copse of oak trees from where the quail had flown.

Moving carefully, Wetzel descended the ridge on the far side to eliminate the possibility of being highlighted and proceeded toward the suspected ambush site. After several minutes, he dropped to his knees and peered over. Fifty yards distant, Bonney knelt behind the alligator juniper tree, his rifle aimed up the canyon in the direction where he expected pursuers.

Too far away for an accurate pistol shot, Wetzel maneuvered carefully another twenty feet along the far side of the ridge. With the pistol in the ready position, he moved slowly over the lower end of the ridge toward a tall mountain mahogany shrub thirty yards behind Bonney. Sweat trickled down his neck and darkened his shirt front and under his arms. Ever so carefully he moved as his eyes bored into Bonney's black-shirted back.

The shrub was almost within reach as Wetzel's booted foot turned on a rock that he had not seen. Bonney turned sharply, but his rifle caught in the tree limb he had used for support.

Wetzel knelt, pistol out in front, one-handed. "Drop it, Bonney!"

Bonney hesitated, and then swung the rifle around. Wetzel fired and missed as Bonney brought the rifle to his shoulder. He fired the second and third rounds, knocking the fugitive down. Wetzel stood and advanced as he fired again and again. Out of ammunition, he flung the pistol away and drew his .357 revolver ready to fire again.

He kicked the rifle away and stood over Bonney covering him with the revolver. Blood from the man's neck wound pulsated out onto the forest floor, several crimson wounds to his chest blossomed as Wetzel stood over him.

Bonney's dazed eyes showed disbelief that he had been bested and was dying. His lips curled back into a sneer. "I'll … kill … *you—*"

Wetzel felt another wave of dizziness and nausea. "Reckon not, Bonney." He swallowed hard, and then fired a .357 round between the fugitive's eyes. Then he sat down and lost consciousness.

Wetzel awoke briefly; images of his friend Maggie dying in his arms flooded his mind. Darkness enveloped him.

CHAPTER EIGHTY-THREE

Juarez, Mexico, late summer 1974

Pablo Enrique smiled, white teeth displaying the perfect mouth of a powerful man. A handsome man, he thought, and a very rich one. All was going extremely well; his cartel had attained almost total control in Mexico and would soon control much of the southwestern border in the United States, most notably New Mexico.

Enrique was a tall, heavy-set man with gray, thinning hair turning white at the temples and sideburns. A closer look indicated a dark, swarthy complexion with deep-set black eyes that were hardened without feeling or empathy. Large powerful arms and hands extended at his side.

He entered his bedroom, sat down on the bed and removed his expensive shoes and stockings. Standing, he removed his tailored suit jacket, shirt and pants tossing them on the bed. Next he removed his shorts, tucked in his belly and stood admiring his naked image in the mirror. *Damn, what a fine specimen of a man!*

Suddenly he felt the presence of some else in the room; he turned swiftly and saw the man in black sitting in an easy chair on the other side of the room. Terror froze his movements temporarily, but the old confidence returned. "Tomás, *mi'jo*? How is it you visit me unannounced?"

The man in black said nothing.

Enrique observed blood dripping from the chair onto the floor where Tomás sat quietly. He smiled, "Let me get some clothes on and we'll celebrate your return." Then without waiting for a reply, he took a step toward the closet. The man in black retrieved an automatic pistol with a silencer from his lap and pointed it directly at Enrique's chest.

"No. I don't think so." He gestured with the pistol. "Get on the floor, *cabron*."

Enrique's temper flared. "Like hell I will." He pointed a finger and shouted, "You show *me* some respect, you ungrateful—"

The automatic pistol spit a muffled report. Enrique went down with a terrified scream, grasping his left knee. He shouted through clenched teeth, "I'll have you tortured, cut up into little pieces ... my men—"

"*Your men*?" The man in black laughed an ugly laugh. "We're the only two men alive in this compound, *culero*." He raised the pistol once again and fired hitting Enrique in the other knee.

Screaming in pain and the realization he was disabled for life, Enrique's eyes widened in a wild fear he had never experienced before in his life. He had seen it in the eyes of others as they were tortured or about to be murdered, and he had laughed at them. Now he was on the receiving end of terror from a man who most men, including him, feared greatly.

He swallowed hard; he begged for his life, pleaded for mercy.

The man in black stood unsteadily, laid the pistol on the dresser next to him. "Why did you order my brother's death and then lie to me?" he said calmly.

Enrique saw blood dripping from Tomás's pant legs, and that he appeared to be seriously wounded. Renewed hope flowed through his veins. "The *bruja* poisoned him, Tomás. I had *nothing* to do with it."

The man in black moved quickly; a knife flashed in his hand, first to the right then left. Straightening with a groan, he stood over the cartel's chieftain and watched blood flow freely from severed femoral arteries.

Enrique screamed as he clutched at his legs to stem the flow of blood, but to no avail. Blood pooled on the expensive carpet. After a few minutes the screams lessened to a moan. Enrique uttered a strained whisper. "I curse … the day … I took you … and your brother in. Goddamn you to hell."

Tomás looked down on him in contempt. "All of us have to answer for our sins one day, *cabron*. But you—you will see what hell's like *today*."

And then he was gone as quickly as he had appeared, leaving a trail of blood behind as he strode lithely from the hacienda.

CHAPTER EIGHTY-FOUR

Fall, 1974

Wetzel wrapped the soft cotton lead rope for his pack burros around the rubber-covered saddle horn, stretched in the saddle, and spurred his horse to pick up the pace. It was a beautiful fall day in the Gila Wilderness—blue skies with a few thin clouds drifting lazily by overhead, nice cool temperature, a perfect day to be outside doing what he loved best. He had camped at Prior Cabin in Woodland Park the previous night and was leaving the wilderness after completing a ten day tour of duty. He peered back briefly to see how the burros were doing. The lead burro Rosita looked up at him as she batted her long eye lashes. Chochi, trotting along behind her, stubbornly refused to look up at his master.

He spoke to the gelding bay horse he rode. "Come on, and pick it up, boy. Can't you see I'm ready for some chocolate and a beer?" Thinking about what he had said, he chuckled. "Wel-l-l, I reckon not necessarily in that order, and maybe not at the same time."

He rode along at a quick trot, and soon saw Gila Center below in the distance. The Forest Service administrative site with its Visitor Center, housing, helitack base, and barn were always a welcome sign beckoning to him at this point in the trail.

Within thirty minutes, he had descended to the West Fork of the Gila River, followed it along through the rocks and rabbit brush, and rode up to the corrals at the Forest Service barn. He tied a slip knot with the lead rope for the mules on the saddle horn and dismounted to open the gate. It was late afternoon. He led the horse and burros inside the corral and closed the gate behind them. *Yessir, a perfect day, ending well.*

A soft voice called out to him, "You look plumb tuckered out, ole man. You need help unloading them burros?"

Wetzel whirled around and saw Lacey Whippit sitting on the top rail of the corral across from him. She smiled broadly at him as he stood there with his mouth open. She wore a faded denim jacket over a blue work shirt, faded blue work jeans, and her old riding boots. She jumped down, brushing off the seat of her pants, the pony tail swinging behind her.

He smiled back at her. *Maybe it is a perfect day at that.*

Wetzel dropped the reins and stepped toward her. "I can always use help, Lacey."

"Aw'ight then."

They held each other close in a tight hug. Neither one wanted the other to break the spell of that moment. Wetzel had not spoken to her at length since the violence at Whiskey Creek. Finally, they broke the embrace. With a lump in his throat, he unsaddled his horse as Lacey worked at the diamond hitch on the pack of one of the burros.

They unpacked the burros and stored the gear in the tack room. After watching the horse and burros roll in the corral dust, Wetzel removed his chaps and spurs, placed them on his saddle in the tack room, and with Lacey's hand in his, they walked out to the front of the barn and sat down on the concrete loading dock. The golden sun had dropped nearly to the horizon in the west with just enough hazy clouds for a beautiful sunset.

She spoke first. "Jack, I want to thank you for all that you done for me. I … I would have died that night if you and Mac hadn't come to help. And … Mr. Reagan … he gave his life for *me.* And that feller in black …" She swallowed hard.

Wetzel put his arm around her and hugged her close. "Mr. Reagan found new meaning in his life when he began working for you, Lacey."

She looked up into his eyes. "And you? Have you healed from your wounds?"

"Oh, yeah. Just took a month of hard work outside."

"I stopped by the Heart Bar Game Ranch to check on Mac." She laughed heartily. "He said he was fit as a fiddle and still mad at you for tracking Bonney without him."

"Thank God, he and Steve Hunt followed my tracks and found me unconscious."

A Forest Service truck turned off the road from the Visitor Center and headed toward the barn. Wetzel looked at Lacey. "You want to take a little walk with me?"

She smiled at him and hopped off the loading dock.

"Come on." He led the way up the road from the barn, waving at members of the fire crew as they drove past. Lacey followed him up the road and past the Visitor Center to a small parking area above the Middle Fork of the Gila River, just down from the housing area. He took a small path down to the river with her following. He turned and smiled at her. "It's just a little farther. Are you up to it?"

"I reckon so, Jack Wetzel. We've come this far, ain't we?"

Not answering, he turned and continued on the trail. The water of the Middle Fork coursed along on its way to the confluence of the West Fork and then together they would join the main Gila River a few miles farther down the canyon. Walking through an amazing stand of sunflowers that stood almost as high as Wetzel and extended for at least a quarter mile along the trail, Lacey stopped and peered at the beauty and wildness of the area. Wetzel waited for her where the trail left the sunflowers and skirted down along the river.

They heard a giggle and then a laugh. Shortly, they came upon a couple standing near the river; they were both naked, the steam from the hot springs swirled around their legs. Startled, they turned toward Wetzel and Lacey.

Wetzel grinned. "Carry on, folks."

Moments later, Wetzel abruptly left the trail and headed up the slope of a side canyon to an alcove about 200 yards above. He turned and took Lacey's hand as they ascended together through the rocky, rough terrain. At the alcove, Wetzel espied a flat rock. They sat down next to each other, and he pointed out the petroglyphs and scattered, broken pottery. "Ancient or pre-historic Indian site, Lacey." He extended his arm and pointed toward the high ridge above, "A lot of arrowheads up there. They want us to start catching folks who steal these artifacts."

Lacey asked, "Are these Indians from the same bunch that lived up at the Cliff Dwellings?"

"Yes, they were a part of the Mogollon culture and here only a short time." Wetzel cocked his hat back on his head with his thumb. "Anyhow, I come here often just to think and enjoy the peace and quiet."

"Uh huh."

He looked at her, a puzzled look on his face, "What?"

"And to enjoy the scenery at the hot springs?"

Wetzel laughed. "Wel-l-l, maybeso … maybeso, Lacey."

It was her turn to laugh, and then she lapsed into quietness.

"I sold the mine and my property up on Whisky Creek last week, Jack."

His gaze locked on her dark brown eyes.

She peered down at the Middle Fork for a long time. "For a *lot* of money."

"Good for you. I can't think of anyone more deserving of it."

Her eyes returned to his. She said nothing.

Wetzel broke eye contact and sighed. "What about the sheep, Lacey? And your dogs? Mr. Reagan took a real liking for them."

She swallowed hard. "Yes, he sure did."

"You sell 'em?"

"No, Jack. I didn't have the heart." She stood, reached down, picked up a rock and tossed it downhill as she listened to the river below. "I got me a Mexican feller who knows sheep to tend 'em for me." She turned back looking at Wetzel. "And got me a permit from the Forest Service up on Granny Mountain for them sheep. I reckon you're the Range Con that will be checking up on me?"

Wetzel laughed. "I'll be darned!" He stood next to her. "Hadn't heard that, but I'm tickled for it."

She smiled at him. "Uh huh."

"Where will you live?"

Her face clouded over. "I … I … need to get away for a while, Jack." A tear rolled down her cheek and then another. "It … it's been too much for me; my dad and then my brothers. Mr. Reagan … all gone."

Wetzel took her in his arms and held her close. She cried.

"I know, Lacey. I know."

"I plan to travel … some … well, *a lot*." She looked up at Wetzel, "I have to get away from this … *evil* place. *Anywhere!*"

Wetzel held her tighter. He said nothing.

"Oh, Jack. I have this fortune and … I … just don't give a tinker's damn about it or living anymore."

"You have your whole life ahead of you, Lacey. You're a beautiful, intelligent woman. You'll find your way. I guarantee it." He placed his hands gently on either side of her face and turned it up toward him. "Go travel; see the world … find yourself again."

"An' them sheep o' mine?"

"I'm going nowhere. I've found my niche and purpose in life. I'll keep an eye on them."

"An' mah dogs?"

He smiled. "And the dogs, too. You bet."

"And mah cat?"

Wetzel grimaced and scratched his nose. "I'm not much of a cat person, Lacey. Why not give him to your sheep herder?"

"That's a great idea." She reached up and kissed him lightly on the lips. "Thank you, Jack Wetzel … for everything."

They sat back on the flat rock and enjoyed the quiet of the wilderness, the company of each other, and watched the last remnants of the golden sunset melt into the horizon. They heard the man below at the hot springs call to the woman. Light began to fade as dusk slowly transitioned into dark.

Finally, Lacey spoke. "Jack?"

Wetzel pulled his Stetson back down on his head and placed his arm over her shoulders. He said nothing, waiting for her to finish.

"Jack, will you be here … when …" As the last of the evening light faded, she saw his hazel eyes soften as a slow smile spread over his tanned face.

"I reckon I'll always be here for *you*, Lacey Whippit. You can count on me."

A LOOK AT: RED SKY AT MORNING

This action-packed story about an Old West group of lawmen, the Arizona Rangers, is set in the Arizona Territory of 1906-09. Murderers have fled to Mexico; miners have revolted in Cananea, Mexico. American citizens have been murdered and threatened. Ruthless, brutal smugglers are running guns across the border into Mexico to sell to the Yaqui Indians, and they will stop at nothing-- Young Joaquin Campbell has become an experienced Ranger. Elliott, his old friend and mentor, has resigned from the Rangers only to be called back repeatedly as his deadly skills as a gunman and his leadership ablilty is sorely needed.

OUT NOW

ABOUT THE AUTHOR

John McLaughlin retired after a thirty year career in law enforcement with the U.S. Forest Service, National Park Service, and the Bureau of Land Management. His career occurred primarily in the Southwest where he became an experienced Law Enforcement Ranger, Firearms Instructor, Wildland Firefighter, Farrier, and Animal Packer.

McLaughlin and his wife of forty-one years share time living in Peoria, Arizona, and their property located south of Silver City, New Mexico. Winner of the Western Writers of America's Spur Award, McLaughlin has a long standing love of books of all genres. However, he takes a special interest in fictional and non-fictional accounts of the Old West.